His
Pretend
Amish Bride

Center Point
Large Print

Also by Rachel J. Good and available from
Center Point Large Print:

His Unexpected Amish Twins

**This Large Print Book carries the
Seal of Approval of N.A.V.H.**

His Pretend Amish Bride

UNEXPECTED AMISH BLESSINGS

Rachel J. Good

CENTER POINT LARGE PRINT
THORNDIKE, MAINE

This Center Point Large Print edition
is published in the year 2021 by arrangement with
Kensington Publishing Corp.

The text of this Large Print edition is unabridged.
In other aspects, this book may vary
from the original edition.
Printed in the United States of America
on permanent paper.
Set in 16-point Times New Roman type.

ISBN: 978-1-64358-944-2

The Library of Congress has cataloged this record
under Library of Congress Control Number: 2021932382

Chapter One

As she did every morning, Priscilla Ebersol finished mopping the kitchen floor, but today she hurried through her Saturday morning chores, because she and Matthew planned to have a picnic at the lake. The crunch of buggy wheels in the driveway stopped her. Matthew hadn't come so early, had he? She was still wearing her black work apron and a kerchief rather than her prayer *kapp*. She'd have to run up and change her dress too.

She peeked out the window. *Not Matthew. The bishop.* Why had Bishop Troyer come calling?

Priscilla hurried to the door to greet him. "*Gude mariye*, Laban. I'm afraid Mamm and Daed aren't here. They left for Centerville to get groceries a short while ago."

The bishop stood on the doorstep a moment. "I would have preferred to have them here, of course. But this can't wait. I'm sure you know why I'm here."

Actually, she didn't. But she couldn't leave him standing on the doorstep. "Please come in." Priscilla opened the door wider so he could enter.

Brushing past her, he headed into the living room and plopped down in the rocker. When she followed him into the room, he asked, "Are any of your brothers or sisters around?"

"The girls went to clean Dawdi's house this morning. Zeke is organizing the basement, and Asher is helping."

"Perhaps you could ask Zeke to keep Asher downstairs until I'm gone. That would be best, don't you think?"

"Of course." Asher's behavior could be unpredictable. They didn't always know what would set him off. Noises, smells, and touches often did, but sometimes his meltdowns seemed random.

Priscilla knocked on the basement door. Zeke had hooked it to prevent Asher from wandering off. Her brother clomped up the stairs and unlatched the door. "*Jah*?"

"Bishop Troyer's here. Could you keep Asher in the basement until Laban leaves?"

"That won't be a problem. Emma knocked two puzzle boxes off the shelf before she left. They each have a thousand pieces, and Asher is sorting them into the correct boxes. Good thing one is fall colors and the other is of a green field with purple flowers."

"That's a perfect job for him." Asher loved painstaking, repetitive work.

"I know." Zeke grinned. "I'm getting a lot done while he's doing a job that would make me nuts." Then he raised an eyebrow. "What does the bishop want?"

6

"I have no idea, but I'd better not keep him waiting." While Zeke rehooked the basement door, Priscilla scurried back to the living room and sat across from the bishop.

Laban stared at her, his gaze sober and sad, as if she'd done something sinful. She tried to think of anything that might merit such a look. Nothing came to mind. Yet a heavy ball of guilt formed inside, and she lowered her eyes.

"It always pains me," the bishop said, "when I have to speak with members about their . . . um, failings. Especially in a case where, up until now, you've been a teacher the children can look up to."

Children? Had she done something wrong at school? Priscilla loved working as an assistant at the special needs school under Ada Rupp. Ada was mentoring Priscilla so she could take over as head teacher next year. Had she made a major mistake? If so, why hadn't Ada mentioned it?

"I've already spoken to Matthew about this, and he's very sorry and ashamed."

Matthew? Now Priscilla was thoroughly confused. She couldn't imagine Matthew doing something that would require a visit from the bishop. And what did it have to do with her?

"My greatest concern," Laban said, "is the influence your behavior will have on the children. When you took the teaching job, you agreed to

7

be an example they could follow. It grieves me to know that's in question."

With each word the bishop spoke, Priscilla struggled more to figure out what he meant. Her thoughts were as jumbled as the puzzle pieces Asher was sorting. What had she done that the bishop considered grave enough to come here to discipline her?

His shaggy brows pinched together, Bishop Troyer leaned so far forward the tips of the rocker touched the floor. His glasses magnified his piercing gaze, which penetrated deep into her soul. Priscilla shrank back, her mouth dry, and a frisson of fear snaked through her stomach.

Swallowing hard, as if it hurt him to speak, the bishop said, "After Deacon Raber caught you and Matthew in the, um, compromising position last night, Matthew at least had the grace to face the disapproval and apologize. But you fled. Of course, that would be one's natural reaction, but you need to confess."

Priscilla pinched her lips shut to hold back the words that longed to burst from her lips. *But . . . but . . . I wasn't out with Matthew last night.*

She couldn't contradict the bishop. Yet this had to be a mistake.

If it was true . . . Priscilla's chest constricted until she ached to breathe. Matthew wouldn't have been with someone else. She had to talk to him, straighten out this mix-up.

With nervous fingers, she pleated the fabric of her apron, her throat too tight to speak. She'd been taught never to talk back to her elders, and she certainly couldn't accuse the deacon of making an error. Keeping her head bowed, she listened quietly to the bishop's lecture on staying away from all appearances of evil.

"I still need to discuss this with the school board." For a brief second, compassion warred with sternness in his eyes. Sternness won. "The school board will meet with you, but I'm sure you understand why we can't keep you on as a teacher."

But I didn't do anything wrong, she wanted to say. Instead, she clamped her mouth shut to trap the words.

The bishop rose. "If you haven't already confessed to your parents, I expect you to do so. Matthew has promised it won't ever happen again. He'll kneel and confess before the church. I trust you'll do the same."

Confess in front of the church? What did the bishop think she and Matthew had done? Her thoughts whirling, Priscilla pushed on the arms of the chair to stand and let the bishop out, but he laid a hand on her shoulder to keep her in place.

"You don't need to see me out. Stay there and continue your confession to God." He strode from the room.

Priscilla sat, stunned and confused. The vague

sound of the front door shutting echoed down the hall. The sharp noise reverberated inside her head as one mental door after another slammed shut, cutting off rational thought. *Matthew. Teaching. Confession.* None of the bishop's words made sense.

What did he think she'd done? And what had he meant about Matthew?

Gabriel Kauffman opened the doors of his milking barn to turn his camels out into the pasture. He stood in the center of the rural road, watching for cars and buggies as the camels clomped across the street to one of his fields.

A buggy horse flew around a curve in the road, heading straight toward him and the last two baby camels.

"Stop," Gabriel shouted, waving his arms and jumping up and down to attract attention.

The man holding the reins was leaning forward, urging his horse to gallop at breakneck speed. He hadn't seen Gabe.

Gabe yelled louder, gesturing wildly.

The driver glanced up, and his mouth opened in a wide O. He yanked on the reins. Dragged the horse to the right.

Gabe threw himself in front of the last camel baby. He'd take the impact. Try to save his newborn camel.

At the last second, the buggy swerved. Almost

tipped onto two wheels. With one final wrench on the reins, the man whipped into the store driveway. Gravel sprayed from the wheels, pelting Gabe.

Behind him, the tiny camel let out high-pitched squeaks. Poor little thing must have been hit by flying gravel. Heart pounding, Gabe whirled to check on her as the buggy tore up his long driveway. Then it came to an abrupt and shuddering halt.

Gabe herded the baby into the field and closed the gate behind her. Arms crossed, he turned. He expected *Englisch* cars to speed on these back roads, but most buggy drivers plodded along. This one had acted like a late-night, buggy-racing teen. Gabe winced. That comparison made him ache inside.

The man circled in the driveway and headed toward Gabe at a sedate pace. With a sheepish look on his face, the driver pulled up next to Gabe.

"I'm so sorry. I didn't mean to scare you. I was in a hurry and didn't expect to find anyone on the road."

"I see," Gabe said, but he wasn't quite sure why any Amish man would travel at that pace. It had to be hard on the horse. And it had been equally hard on Gabe. His pulse still drummed in his temples, his chest ached from the rapid staccato of his heart, and he struggled to erase horrific pictures from his mind.

The man glanced toward the field, rubbed his eyes, and looked again. "Camels? I thought that's what I saw. I've never seen camels here before."

"That's because I just bought the farm. I needed more farmland for my animals, so I moved to the Lancaster area."

"Why camels? Why not cows or goats?" The man shook his head. "I'd love to stay and ask more questions, but I'm in a hurry."

"You surely were." Gabe hoped his words didn't sound overly critical.

"I apologize again." Thrusting out his hand, the man said, "Welcome to the neighborhood. I'm Matthew King."

"Pleased to meet you, Matthew. I'm Gabriel Kauffman." He shook hands. "I won't keep you, but stop back any time."

"I'll do that." Matthew settled his straw hat more securely on his head and flicked the reins.

Gabe waited until Matthew had galloped out of sight before walking along the shoulder of the road to the building that housed his store.

His eight-year-old nephew, Timothy, gave him a gap-toothed smile. "I don't need help."

Gabe ruffled Timothy's hair as he passed. "I know. I'm headed into the office. I trust you to handle the business out here."

So far, few local people were aware he'd opened the store, but many of his out-of-state regulars headed here on weekends. They all swore by the benefits of camel's milk and were willing to make the long drive and pay the high prices.

Gabe sank into his wooden desk chair and took several deep breaths. He was still a bit shaky after the near-accident. Pulling out the account book, he forced himself to record yesterday's sales. Concentrating on a mundane task should help. But visions of another accident haunted him.

He'd thought moving here would erase the past. Instead, another out-of-control buggy flashed through his mind. Gabe buried his head in his hands. Would he ever be free of that nightmare?

When Matthew's horse galloped into the driveway a short while after Bishop Troyer had left, Priscilla hurried to the door and flung it open. Now she'd find out what the bishop had meant.

Matthew tied his horse and hurried up the sidewalk to the house, glancing over his shoulder several times. His face and shoulders were set into such tense lines, Priscilla's stomach roiled. The worries she'd tried to push from her mind flooded over her.

"Are you all right?" she asked.

"It's been a rough morning. First the bishop confronted me. Then I nearly collided with a camel."

Surely she'd misheard him. "A camel?"

"*Jah*, some man just bought that large farm for

13

sale in Bird-in-Hand. He's raising camels."

"A camel farm?" Priscilla practically shrieked. "Are you serious?" She tried to calm herself, but if Matthew was right, this might be the answer to her prayers.

"Do you know if he'll be selling camel's milk?"

Matthew stared at her like she was crazy. "Who'd want that?"

"Lots of people." Not wanting to face his skeptical look, she kept her real answer to herself. She wanted to buy some.

"Look, we can talk about that later." He waved a hand dismissively. "I need to tell you something before the bishop gets here."

"You're too late. He's already been and gone." And Priscilla wanted an explanation for the bishop's lecture. She hoped Matthew could clear up her niggling doubts.

"Laban said he had some errands to run. I thought I'd beat him here." Matthew's face drained of color. "Wh-what did you tell him?"

His pallor and shaky voice set off alarm bells in Priscilla's mind. Something was wrong. Very, very wrong.

"What could I tell him?" she asked. "I had no idea what he was talking about. I just listened to his lecture about sin."

Matthew blew out a long, slow breath. "Oh, good. That was perfect." Fear flashed across his face. "You didn't deny it was you?"

14

"I didn't deny or confirm anything. But I want to know what's going on."

A dull red crept up Matthew's face, and he lowered his head. "Pris, I'm really sorry. I owe you an apology. I, um, did something terrible."

The small windmill blades churning in Priscilla's stomach whirled faster, scraping and scratching her insides. She longed to flee. She didn't want to hear words that might tear her world apart.

"I don't want you to think I didn't love you. I did."

Did? That meant he loved her in the past, but no longer?

"I don't know how to explain this, but I—I, well, I met Mara Bontrager in the apple orchard one day. She came out to give me some instructions from her *daed*. She stayed to talk to me. I, um, thought she was . . ." His voice trailed off.

Priscilla didn't want to hear any more. She could sense where this was going. His boss's daughter, a pretty, petite blonde, was a bit of a flirt. But would she flirt with a man who was courting someone else? Evidently, she had.

"It started out innocent," Matthew insisted. "She'd come and sit with me while I ate lunch." He hung his head. "Soon we started sharing lunches she'd fixed. I didn't mean for it to pro-gress."

And all this time, he'd still been courting her? Priscilla balled her hands into fists.

"One day she asked if I'd meet her in the orchard after dark." He swallowed hard. "I shouldn't have gone. But I did."

Those whirling blades scraped Priscilla's insides raw. She wanted to hold up a hand, beg Matthew to stop. It took all her willpower to choke back a cry of anguish.

"We met again last night and . . ."

Priscilla averted her gaze from his scrunched-up face, the guilt in his eyes. *Don't finish. Please don't say any more.*

"We got a little carried away." Matthew extended his hands as if begging for forgiveness. "I'm sorry, so sorry. I didn't mean to hurt you."

But he had. How could she deal with this betrayal? Did she still want to court him?

"When Leroy saw us, we'd been kissing—"

Kissing? She and Matthew had never kissed. Not yet.

And Matthew and Mara had done more than kiss. At least according to the bishop. Priscilla squeezed her eyes shut, wishing she could block out the image of Mara in Matthew's arms. Her insides felt as if he'd twisted her heart in his bare hands, squeezing out all the joy and love, leaving her drained and depleted.

Priscilla couldn't meet his eyes, so she concentrated on Matthew's shirtfront, his Adam's apple bobbing up and down. All she wanted him to do was finish and leave.

When he spoke again, his voice was thick and uncertain. "We, um, did a little more than kiss. That's when Leroy Raber spied us."

Priscilla willed herself to sit still. She forced her hands into a serene position in her lap. Her insides might be in shreds, but she'd keep her outer composure.

"I, um, shielded Mara until she could turn and run. Leroy assumed it was you."

An understandable mistake. She and Mara were about the same size, and Leroy would expect Priscilla and Matthew to be together.

"You didn't correct him?" Her words came out shaky and desperate.

Matthew pursed his lips and stared at the floor. "You know how strict her *daed* is. I didn't want her to get in trouble."

But what about my reputation? We're the ones who are courting. We've even been talking about marriage.

"Anyway," Matthew continued, "I came over to ask you a favor. Would you be willing to—"

Forgive you? It wouldn't be easy, but she'd get down on her knees tonight and pray for the right attitude, for God to give her His heart, His love, His mercy, His forgiveness. And for Him to heal her hurt.

Matthew hesitated. "I know this is a lot to ask,

17

but could you let everyone think it was you in the orchard?"

She'd been expecting him to ask for forgiveness and beg to stay together. Instead, she sat there stunned. "You're asking me to lie?" Not only lie, but cover up his wrongdoing? With another woman?

"Not lie exactly," Matthew said. "Just not contradict Leroy."

He expected her to stay silent as gossips repeated the falsehood? Not to defend herself when parents objected to her teaching their children? Or when the school board decided she wasn't a fit teacher? Allowing people to believe an untruth was lying by omission, so he was asking her to lie for him.

"You have such a good reputation, I'm sure the rumors will die down quickly." Matthew held out imploring hands. "If people knew the truth, Mara's reputation would be ruined."

"I see," Priscilla said stiffly. But she didn't. Not at all.

Matthew was willing to smear her reputation to save Mara's. And he expected Priscilla to protect a cheater. Mara wasn't the only one to blame. Matthew had willingly participated in the betrayal.

She squeezed her eyes shut to ease their stinging. And prayed no tears would fall.

"I'm sorry." Matthew reached out and touched her arm.

His fingers burned her flesh. Her eyes flew open, and she jerked her arm away. Did he think they could go back to their old relationship?

"Will you forgive me?"

"It's what God wants us to do." Priscilla managed to push the words past her tear-clogged throat. But her heart protested. She'd wrestle with this later when she was alone in her room.

Matthew heaved a loud sigh. "I knew you'd understand." He rose. "Oh, Bishop Troyer recommended we stay away from each other for a while to reduce the temptation."

The only temptation Priscilla fought was to throw one of the couch pillows at him. "I don't think the bishop was referring to me." She hoped the sarcastic edge to her voice would stab his conscience.

His flushed face revealed her barb had reached its target. "I suggested we could break up."

So you'll be free to court Mara? A worm of bitterness wriggled through her heart.

When she didn't answer, he shuffled his feet. "I thought maybe you could tell everyone you broke up with me."

Matthew was offering to let her save face after he'd destroyed her hopes, dreams, and reputation? She pivoted, keeping her back to him. "Consider it done." Then she forced herself to walk from the room slowly and demurely.

Matthew followed her into the hallway. Until

the front door closed behind him, Priscilla maintained her facade of politeness. Then she leaned her forehead against the door, and her calmness cracked into a million pieces.

Chapter Two

"Priscilla, are you all right?" Zeke asked anxiously, peeking out from behind the basement door. "I thought I heard crying."

She kept her tear-streaked face turned away from her brother and said brokenly, "I'll be fine." *Maybe someday.* "I just broke up with Matthew."

"*Ach*, no wonder you're upset. I'm sorry."

So am I. "It was for the best." Everything that happened was God's will, and He promised all would turn out for the good. But right now, clouds of gloom blocked even the smallest rays of sunshine.

"It will get better," her brother promised. "But if you broke up with him, why are *you* crying?"

Swiping at her face, Priscilla turned to face him. "Ending a relationship is difficult."

"*Jah*, that's so." Zeke nodded as sagely as if he'd been through it himself.

At twelve, he hadn't, of course. But his grown-up manner made Priscilla smile despite her tears.

She needed to do something to get her mind off things. Doing chores wouldn't prove enough of a distraction. Camels. Matthew had mentioned a camel farm. She seized on the idea.

"Zeke, I'm going out for a while. Tell Mamm

and Daed I'll be back later to finish my chores."

His eyes widened. She'd never run out of the house before, leaving her work undone. But she'd also never felt so blindsided.

After changing into a clean dress and her black half apron and donning her *kapp*, Priscilla fled to the barn. Hitching her horse to the buggy, usually a mindless task, took all her concentration.

Once she climbed in, she sat for a moment to still the whirling thoughts. Then she clucked to her horse and started off. As Butterscotch trotted down the backcountry roads, the wind blowing past stung Priscilla's aching eyes.

When she turned onto the road where the camel farm was located, she slowed. In a distant field, large brownish blobs wandered the fields. As she drew closer, the blobs appeared more like humped cows.

Priscilla managed a watery half smile. She'd found the camels. Now she prayed they had a store where they sold camel's milk.

A small wooden sign by the side of the road said *Kauffman's Organic Farm*. With a tug on the reins, she steered into the steep gravel driveway. A large metal building stood at the top of the hill. On the door, a hand-printed sign listed the hours.

Priscilla scanned it. *Saturdays: 9 a.m. to 4 p.m.* Good. It was open.

She pulled past the building to park her buggy.

As she got out to tie up her horse, the metal door banged open.

A petite woman struggled out, her hands filled with two gigantic insulated bags. She set them down and went inside for two more. Then she clicked open the tailgate of an expensive SUV with dark-tinted windows.

Were those bags filled with camel's milk? If so, maybe this woman in her embroidered jacket with an elegant scarf wound around her neck had bought out the store. The woman slammed her trunk shut as a small boy emerged from the house next door carrying a small stack of bills.

"I have some change," he called, waving some bills in the air.

"Excellent," she said, heading toward the passenger door. "I'll be right in. I just need a few insulated bags." She waited until he'd gone inside, then she walked over to the side of the building where large cooler chests sat, stacked one on top of the other. Each chest had a name printed neatly in black marker on the front.

Curiosity kept Priscilla standing there, semi-hidden behind the buggy.

Grunting, the woman lifted one of the heavy chests and lugged it to her SUV. The chest said *Graber.* An Amish name—but the woman definitely wasn't Amish. She transferred two more chests. *Allgyer* and *Hess.* Maybe she was an *Englisch* driver who delivered orders to the Amish and Mennonites.

She didn't look like any driver Priscilla had ever seen. Her expensive leather shoes, her silky blonde hair swishing around her shoulders, and her haughty air spelled money. Lots of it.

Before Priscilla could be caught gawking, the woman entered the store again. Priscilla stepped from behind the carriage and crossed the parking lot. She reached for the knob, but the door opened abruptly, almost hitting her.

The petite woman rushed out, calling over her shoulder, "I forgot my insulated bags. I'll be right back."

She breezed past, letting the door slam. Priscilla opened it and walked into a wide, spacious warehouse. Shelves full of facial products and lotions lined each wall. A few shelves farther down held raw honey, natural peanut butter, and jars of vitamins.

Across the room, the young boy sat at a desk, with a money box and stacks of invoices close at hand. As in many Amish businesses, the children often ran the stores.

She didn't see any refrigerators. "Do you sell any camel's milk?"

"Yes, we do." The boy stood and headed toward her. "Did you want a certain size?"

"What sizes do you have?"

"From pints to gallons."

"Where would I find them?"

The woman entered the building and swept past Priscilla. She pushed open heavy hanging plastic behind them, and freezing air rushed over Priscilla's back. The boy motioned for Priscilla to follow the woman into a huge refrigerated room lined with shelves filled with glass jars and bottles.

Arctic temperatures chilled Priscilla's nose and hands, and she shivered. Now she understood why the woman wore a coat and scarf. If she made another trip here, she'd dress properly.

Beside her, the woman slid gallon jugs of milk into her insulated tote bags. The bottles clinked as she lifted the bags. "I'm ready to check out," she said as she flung open the door, pushed aside the plastic, and exited the refrigerated room.

Priscilla had to get out of the cold. She'd grab the smallest container of camel's milk they had. She hoped Asher would try it. She wouldn't buy a large bottle, in case he refused to drink it.

A handsome man entered through another door at the far end of the refrigerated space. "Are you finding everything you need?"

"I'm looking for camel's milk." Priscilla's teeth chattered.

"You're standing by the gallons. If you want a smaller size, they're down here."

"A-a p-pint, p-please."

"You're shivering." He lifted a pint from the

nearest shelf. "Why don't you come in here and warm up?" He led her through the far door and into a small office.

Blessed heat enveloped her as she stepped through the plastic. She stood over a small kerosene heater and rubbed her hands together.

"I can tell you're a first-timer. Our regulars all wear coats. If you want to go back in to look around, feel free to borrow my jacket and gloves." He pointed to a nearby peg.

"*Danke*, but I just wanted a sample today. I'm not sure if I can convince my brother to try it. Can you tell me how much this is?"

"That size is fifteen dollars."

Fifteen dollars? For one pint? She'd read camel's milk was costly, but she hadn't expected it to be this expensive.

Heat rushed to her cheeks. Not only had she not been prepared for the price, but in her hurry to get out of the house and away from thoughts of Matthew, she'd forgotten to bring money.

"I'm so sorry. I don't have my wallet." Her face and neck burning, she turned toward the freezer door and lifted the plastic sheeting. "I'll just put this back." It seemed everywhere she went today, she faced shame.

"No need to do that." His deep voice stopped her. "Could you wait here? I have a question for you." His dazzling smile made her blink. "But first, I should help that lady with her bags. My

26

nephew's a little young to do all the heavy lifting."

He pointed out of the office door to where the lady in the embroidered coat was digging through her designer purse. Priscilla stood in the office doorway as he hurried across the room.

She should return the milk and leave. That would be the wisest course of action—both because she didn't have the money and because she didn't need to get friendly with a man who intrigued her.

To prove how right she was, he turned his winning smile on the lady, who returned it with a flirtatious look. Why would anyone want to be in a relationship with a man who could easily be tempted?

"Are you the one I talked to on the phone?" the *Englischer* purred, batting her long eyelashes.

"Probably. I usually do answer the phone. Gabriel Kauffman, at your service."

His deep voice reverberated in Priscilla's chest, but she hardened herself against the pull. Although his back was now to her, from Gabriel's smooth answer, Priscilla suspected he was charmed.

"I'm Fleurette Moreau." The woman extended a dainty hand with highly polished, long, clawlike nails. A predator.

"Pleased to meet you," Gabriel said, holding her hand a beat too long. Although, to be fair, he did attempt to pull away before she let go.

27

The young boy gave Fleurette a total, and she opened her wallet. Priscilla frowned as the woman handed over three hundred-dollar bills and received two twenties in change. How could that be all she owed for those six gallons of camel's milk plus all the other things she'd loaded into her car? Especially when the pint Priscilla held cost so much? Maybe Fleurette had paid for the rest earlier. The boy had gone to get change, after all.

After the woman paid, Gabriel said, "Let me get these bags for you."

In a sickeningly sweet voice, she replied, "Thank you *sooo* much, but I'll take them myself."

Ignoring her, he bent to take the carrier handles. "They're much too heavy."

Gabriel's solicitous tone sickened Priscilla. Was he only being polite, or had he fallen for Fleurette's charm?

"I said *no*." Fleurette's sharp tone sliced through the air. When he straightened, she laid a hand on his arm. "I don't want to bother anyone."

"It's no trouble at all." Gabriel leaned down again. "I'm happy to help."

"No, no!" Her voice grew shrill. "I can do it myself."

Before he could reach the handles, she swooped in to block him and grabbed the bags. She could hardly lift them, and Gabriel stared at her, a puzzled frown drawing his brows together.

Fleurette's actions made Priscilla curious. She

evidently wasn't used to lifting heavy loads. Why didn't the woman want assistance when the insulated carriers dragged her down? She struggled to the door with the bottles clanking.

Gabriel rushed to open the heavy metal door and stood staring after her. A sharp pang shot through Priscilla. Did all men make fools of themselves around beautiful women? If Matthew were here alone, would he have followed that woman to the door? How many times had he been interested in other women? Was Mara the only one?

How odd! Gabe wasn't sure what to make of this *Englischer* with her fancy clothes and Jersey accent—at least, he was pretty sure he'd identified it correctly, because he had many regular customers from Jersey and Philly. Or he had before he moved to Lancaster.

Usually women who dressed like Fleurette expected assistance. They never carried their own purchases. And she certainly didn't look as if she was used to toting heavy bags.

He would have opened her car trunk if she hadn't turned and glared at him. She set the bags beside the passenger door, clicked her key fob to unlock the car, and then stood with her arms crossed, tapping her foot, until he let the shop door swing shut. Before it did, he glimpsed her license plate. He'd been right about New Jersey.

Shaking his head, he turned to face the pretty

29

Amish woman who'd forgotten her wallet. He had no idea why hearing her plight had made him determined to give her that bottle of milk for free. God seemed to have laid it on his heart.

He walked across the room to where she stood, looking as if she wanted to flee. He suspected she might not accept a gift, so he intended to make it seem as if she were doing him a favor.

As he got closer, her eyes, filled with sorrow, grew bleak. He'd been through enough rough times to understand her pain. And he wanted to comfort her. But she was a stranger. That was one thing he could remedy right now.

"I didn't introduce myself earlier. I'm Gabriel Kauffman. Welcome to my camel farm."

"You're the owner?" She sounded surprised.

A lot of people were when they discovered he was twenty-four and ran such a successful business. He had no idea how this move to Lancaster would affect his income, but he'd needed more land. Even more importantly, he'd had to get away.

She stared at him with a quizzical look, and he realized he'd never answered her question. "Yes, this is my camel farm."

"I'm so glad you moved to this area."

If everyone in Lancaster was this enthusiastic, he'd do a terrific business. "That makes me happy."

"I've been reading about the benefits of camel's milk. I never thought I'd find a camel farm in this area." Although her eyes still held sadness, excitement bubbled in her words.

"You didn't come in only out of curiosity?" He had a lot of people who stopped by just to look at the camels and see what he had in the store. She must have sought him out, so maybe she'd become a regular customer.

"Well, I'm curious, but I've read so much about the health benefits. I was hoping it would help my brother Asher. He's autistic."

"I have some great stories about successes we've had with autistic children. I'd be happy to tell you about them sometime."

"I'd love to hear them."

Her wide, generous smile sent a jolt through him, but he steeled himself against it. Women were off-limits for him. He'd never take a chance with hurting another woman. Never.

He responded with a cautious half smile. Best to keep this businesslike, especially when he found her interest in camel's milk so intriguing. *Sure, Gabe, and you didn't happen to notice how attractive she is.*

He'd gotten far off track here. He forced himself back to the conversation. "One day when you have time, stop by and I'll share the stories." *Real smart, inviting her back again so you can spend more time with her.*

"I have a lot of chores today, but I'll plan to come back. Maybe next weekend?"

"That would be fine." Though his answer was clipped, his heart was singing.

"If you'd rather I not—?"

He sighed inwardly. He hadn't meant to make her feel unwelcome. "No, I'd be happy to have you anytime." *Ach*, that sounded overly friendly. What was it about this woman that tied him in knots? And he didn't even know her name yet.

Trying again, he said, "I always love to talk about camel's milk with people who are interested. As I'm sure you can guess, not many people know much about it. So, when I find someone who's actually researched it . . ."

She laughed. "I know what you mean. Not many people share my interests. I'm always reading about ways to help special children. That's why I convinced one of my friends to open a horse therapy business."

Now Gabe was even more intrigued. Her eyes shone with passion. For the topic, of course. He jerked his mind back to the conversation. "I'd like to hear about that too." What was wrong with him? He should be avoiding her, yet here he was encouraging her to spend even more time with him.

"Really?" She lowered her eyes as if he'd embarrassed her.

"I'm always fascinated to learn new ways to help people. That's the main reason I started a camel farm." And to assuage his guilt.

"I see." She didn't sound convinced, and she'd gone from animated to hesitant, as if she distrusted his answer.

"Back to the milk," he said, pointing to the pint in her hand. "I planned to give away one free sample to anyone willing to introduce my products to people in their communities." Actually, he'd only just come up with the idea, but it might be a good way to get the word out. "If you find it works for your brother, would you be willing to tell others about it?"

"Of course. I teach in a special needs school, so I'm sure some of the parents will be interested. But I'd be willing to do that even if I paid for the milk."

Her generosity touched Gabe. "That's really kind of you."

Her brows drew together. "Kind? Shouldn't we share anything we know that will help others?"

"Of course." Gabe had been in business long enough to know most people were only out for themselves. Perhaps if his life had followed a different path, he would have stayed locked into his selfishness despite being raised to care about others and put community and family needs above his own.

Priscilla couldn't believe Gabriel would give away an expensive container of milk to a complete stranger. He had asked her to advertise

33

for him in exchange, but she still didn't feel right about not paying. "I can get money and come back to pay for this."

Gabriel shook his head. "*Neh*, I'm serious about the free sample. Haven't you ever gotten a free sample in the grocery store?"

"Of course. Actually, my friend Hope Graber offered a free horse therapy lesson for each student when she opened her business, and many of them signed up for sessions."

"I hope giving away free products will work for my farm too. With someone as nice as you telling people about my products, I'm sure it'll help."

At his compliment, Priscilla drew back a bit, warning herself against his flattery. Earlier, she'd wondered if he tried to charm women, and now she was convinced of it. Yet, she struggled with an attraction to him.

It's only because he's interested in camel's milk and horse therapy. Matthew had always looked bored when she shared information about helping special children.

But she wouldn't be talking to Matthew. Not anymore. The truth hit her so hard, her lips trembled. She turned away to regain her composure.

"Are you all right?" Gabriel moved closer, and her stomach clenched.

No, she might never recover. And the last thing she needed was to be attracted to anyone else. Ever.

Gabriel stared at her with sympathetic eyes, waiting for an answer.

She needed to give him some explanation. "I—I had some bad news right before I came here."

"I'm sorry. I hope you didn't lose someone . . ." He winced as his voice trailed off.

She had, actually. But not in the way he meant. Priscilla only shook her head.

He blew out a breath as if relieved. "I didn't mean to pry."

Beneath the kindness and caring in his tone, Priscilla detected a deep sadness. She almost asked him the same question he'd asked her. Was he all right? But she stopped herself.

They both stood there uneasily, Priscilla with her gaze fixed on the ground, and Gabriel studying her. She wanted to go but didn't trust herself to speak. Not when she was all choked up about Matthew's betrayal.

A wave of dizziness swept over her. She hadn't eaten much breakfast, because she'd been busy planning the picnic. And then she'd had two shocks with the bishop's visit and Matthew's request.

Now she was hungry and shaky. Or was some of it from Gabriel's nearness?

"I should get back to work," he said. "It was nice meeting you, um—"

"Pr-Priscilla Ebersol."

Gabriel held out his hand, and she reached out

to shake it. When their palms met, the warmth shocked her, and the strength of his fingers curving around hers in a gentle embrace brought memories of Matthew flooding back. He'd held Mara's hand and kissed her. An ache started deep inside and grew until a small sigh hissed from between her teeth. She tried to hold it back but was powerless to stop it.

Like a sharp knife blade to the heart, the memory of that morning pierced her soul. She sucked in a sharp breath and blinked back the tears that threatened to fall.

Without letting go of her hand, Gabriel stepped closer and took her elbow to support her. "Is something wrong?"

She shivered at his touch. That added to her other churning emotions set her head whirling. "I-I . . ." She'd intended to say she'd be fine, but she struggled to get the words out.

"Timothy, can you slide that chair over here?" Gabriel called as he continued to support her.

Maybe if he'd let go, she'd be fine, but the brush of his sleeve against her arm, the laundry-fresh scent of his shirt, the heat flowing from his skin everywhere it touched hers . . . She willed him to let go, but she wanted to stay like this forever.

What was wrong with her?

For the past four years, she'd thought about no one but Matthew, and now in only a few hours, she found herself attracted to someone else. No— it was only shock and loneliness.

The young boy she'd talked to earlier scooted a chair across the floor in their direction, and Gabriel lowered her into it. "Feel free to stay there until you're feeling better."

"I'm fine. Just a little light-headed. I didn't eat a meal before I came." And she'd recover faster if he'd stop hovering.

He kept one hand on her shoulder as if to steady her. "We can take care of that." He motioned with his head to the office. "Tim, get one of the sandwiches from my lunch cooler and some water."

"*Neh, neh.*" Priscilla struggled to get up.

But Gabriel's hand held her firmly in place. "You're not going anywhere until I'm sure you've recovered."

Then she'd be stuck here for a long, long time, because Priscilla wasn't sure she'd ever recover from Matthew's betrayal.

Chapter Three

As much as she appreciated Gabriel's thoughtfulness, he misunderstood the reason for her wooziness. But the only way to correct his mistake was to tell the truth. Priscilla wasn't ready to share that with anyone, let alone a stranger.

"What's taking so long?" Gabe fretted while he waited for Tim to bring the sandwich.

"You don't need to feed me," she protested, trying to rise. "I don't want to take your lunch."

His hand remained firmly fixed on her shoulder. "I always make extra. And I'm not about to have a customer faint in my store. That wouldn't be good for business."

After Tim brought the sandwich, Gabe hovered over her while she ate, making her self-conscious about the size of the bites she took. She tried to nibble daintily, but her stomach growled for her to eat faster.

"Would you like some camel's milk too?" His eyes twinkled. "I hear it's very healing."

Priscilla smiled but then forced herself to stare down at her lap as she lifted the last piece of homemade bread to her lips. Gabe's sparkling brown eyes were mesmerizing.

What was wrong with her today? She never noticed men's eyes or features. She'd always concentrated all her attention on Matthew. And their relationship had ended only a short while ago. It was much too soon to think about anyone else. After what Matthew had done, she wanted nothing to do with men.

All the humiliation and hurt flooded back, and she tried to suppress an involuntary whimper. But it slipped out.

"Are you choking?" Gabe leaned over her and thumped her back.

Her face fiery, she stuttered, "*N-Neh*, it—it's not that." How could she have made such a fool of herself?

She should have stayed home and done her chores. Hard work helped in getting over a heartbreak. Instead, she'd dashed out the door and ended up fighting an attraction to a stranger.

Only because she was overwrought. She never would have noticed him otherwise.

Liar, her conscience taunted her.

Well, maybe she might have, but she'd have erased him from her mind with thoughts of Matthew. Now thinking about Matthew brought nothing but shame.

Gabe still hovered over her. "Are you feeling better? Your face has more color."

Priscilla pressed her hands to her cheeks. He considered her flushed face a sign of health? Or was he mocking her?

She peeped up through her lashes to steal a

quick glance at him. Rather than a smirk, his brows were scrunched in concern.

"Was one sandwich enough?" he asked. "I can get you another."

She'd never been coddled in her life. As the oldest daughter, she'd taken care of her younger siblings from the time she'd turned six. Even with Matthew, she'd been the one who tended to his needs. Evidently, he'd become so used to her indulging his every whim, he had no qualms about asking her to cover for his misdeeds.

A gentle hand landed on her shoulder again. "You just winced. Are you in pain?"

Priscilla stifled a cynical laugh. She ached, but not in the way Gabe thought. "I'll be all right." *Eventually. At least I hope so.*

"Are you sure? You're welcome to stay as long as you need to."

"I should get going." She had chores to do, and as much as she wanted camel's milk, common sense warned her to avoid Gabe. If she'd thought about it ahead of time, she would have expected the store owner to be a wrinkled old man. Instead, this camel farmer was drop-dead handsome. And he did unexpected things to her pulse. Only one word flashed through her mind despite his thoughtfulness and caring eyes: *Danger.*

Gabe wanted to reach out to help Priscilla to her feet but kept his distance. He stayed alert in case he needed to catch her if she collapsed. She still appeared fragile, but with the way her jaw was set, he suspected she wouldn't welcome his assistance.

She also seemed to be sending out distinct *don't-touch-me* signals. They warned him not to interfere.

The shop door banged open, startling them both. Priscilla, who'd been partway out of the chair, dropped back down as if she'd been shoved. He'd been correct about her weakness.

A short, stocky *Englisch* woman with close-cropped gray hair strode into the room. "I'm supposed to pick up orders for Graber and Allgyer. Are they ready yet?"

Gabe had asked Tim to pack those two hours ago. Had his nephew been too busy with customers? He should have been keeping a better eye on the business.

Tim emerged from the freezer and waved toward the door. "They're right outside there with the other pickups. They should be on top."

"No, they're not."

"Let me check, Hazel." Gabe strode to the door, and Tim followed at his heels.

"I put them there." Tim pointed to a small tower of coolers. "Someone must have gotten them already. I stacked them up in order of pickup times." He led the way to the front of the

41

pile, where names printed in black magic marker identified each one.

"That's where I found them last time," Hazel said. She waved a hand toward the pile. "As you can see, they're not there."

"But I put them on top."

"Are you sure?" Gabe asked him, trying to be gentle and not accusing. "Maybe you forgot them?"

Tears formed in Tim's eyes, and he blinked several times. "No, I didn't. Another cooler's missing too. I don't remember who it's for, but I filled eight. Now we only have five."

"The other one was for Hess."

At the soft voice behind them, Gabe whirled around. Priscilla stood in the doorway, a bit unsteady on her feet. He wished she'd stayed in the chair until she'd recovered completely.

Or maybe he only wanted her to stay because he had a strange desire to get to know her better. Meeting an Amish woman who'd researched camel's milk and animal therapy, one who also worked with special children, was a rarity. It would be good to have someone to talk to about his passion.

He shook his head. *No, not a woman.* He forced his mind back to the conversation.

Tim was gaping at Priscilla. "How did you know that?"

"Because I saw them when I pulled in."

So, Tim had taken care of the orders. Gabe dragged his gaze away from Priscilla to mouth *I'm sorry* to his nephew. He should have trusted him.

"And just before I entered the store," Priscilla added, "a woman loaded them into her car."

"What?" Tim practically shrieked.

Gabe had been about to ask the same question. "Who?" But there'd only been one other customer when Priscilla had been in the store. "The *Englischer*?"

When Priscilla nodded, Gabe's stomach knotted. *New Jersey plates.* How would he ever trace her? If only he'd studied the numbers more closely.

Squeezing his eyes shut, Gabe pictured the plate, but no numbers or letters came into focus. He'd only been concentrating on the color and the words *Garden State* at the bottom.

"You okay?" Hazel's raspy voice interrupted his concentration.

"Just trying to remember what her plate said, but I can't."

"I wish I'd looked. I did wonder if she was a driver for the Amish, although she seemed much too fancy."

"It's not your fault." Gabe chuckled inside at the thought of that dressed-up, perfumed woman offering to drive others around in her brand-new SUV.

But he wasn't laughing when he thought of the money they'd lost. This business was operating on a shoestring until he established himself in the Lancaster area.

"I should have said something. I thought it was odd."

Priscilla looked so distressed, he longed to comfort her. "Please don't blame yourself."

Then he turned to Tim. "Can you fix two coolers for Hazel to take?" They'd have to buy more coolers to replace the ones they'd lost.

Tim scurried inside, and Gabe apologized to Hazel. "I'll go help him. I'm sorry to hold you up."

"No worries." Hazel waved a hand. "Not your fault."

Gabe headed for the door but stopped in front of Priscilla. He examined her for a minute. "Are you well enough to drive? If you still feel shaky, I'd be happy to drive you home, if you don't mind waiting until we've repacked the three orders."

"I can drive myself."

Was that regret in her eyes? She lowered them before he could be sure.

"Be careful," he said. "And *danke* for the information on who took the coolers. I have her name, so I'm sure we'll be able to find her." Fleurette Moreau was an unusual name. How many women had that name in New Jersey?

"I hope you do. And *danke* for the sandwich."

"You're very welcome."

What was wrong with him? Hazel stood tapping her foot, waiting, and he couldn't tear himself away from this petite blonde. The exact opposite in every way from—

Gabe refused to allow those thoughts to overwhelm him.

"I'll let you go, then," he told her, but part of him wished she'd stay. "I hope you'll be back."

"I'm sure I will."

Although he shouldn't, Gabe hoped it would be soon.

Nothing could erase the wounds of Matthew's betrayal, but the camel farmer's thoughtfulness had eased some of her distress. He'd been kind to feed her and care for her. Priscilla refused to examine the other feelings he'd stirred in her.

She'd barely entered the house with the camel's milk when her parents arrived home. Mamm and Daed both carried groceries to the kitchen. When Daed headed to the front door, Priscilla followed. She needed to talk to him, but it would be best to catch him while he was alone.

"Daed," Priscilla said, "can I talk to you?"

"Could it wait until I've unloaded the wagon and unhitched the horse?"

Priscilla would rather not wait, but she sighed and joined him at the wagon.

After they'd carted one more load inside, Daed

headed to the barn to park the buggy. Priscilla trailed after him.

"Can I talk to you while you work?" she asked. "I'll help with the horse."

"I was hoping for a bit of peace and quiet." Daed's rueful smile revealed he'd been hoping for a break from Mamm's constant chatter.

"Please? It's important."

Daed led the horse into the stall and turned. "It must be, for you to be so persistent."

"The bishop came by to talk to me this morning while you were gone."

"The bishop?" Daed's hands stilled. "You haven't done anything wrong," he said with certainty, then he added, "Have you?" His eyebrows met in the middle as he turned to study her.

"That's what I want to talk to you about."

A concerned look in his eyes, he waited for her to continue. Priscilla recounted the whole story, including Matthew's visit and request.

When she finished, Daed stroked his beard, as he often did when he was worried or thinking deeply. "Matthew is asking you to take the blame for someone else? How do you feel about that, *dochder*?"

"I'm confused. Christ took the blame for our sins, so perhaps I should follow His example. And I don't want Mara to get in trouble. I know how strict her *daed* is." Although being Christlike toward the person who'd stolen her boyfriend would be one of the hardest things she'd ever been asked to do. "But I worry, by staying silent, I'll be living a lie."

"It is a dilemma. Perhaps you and I should take this question to the bishop."

"But Matthew asked—" Priscilla burst out.

At Daed's sober look, she bit back her protest.

After caring for the horse, Daed shut the stall door. "Bishop Troyer will keep this in confidence, and I believe he should know the truth. If he's missing important facts, how can he make wise decisions?"

Priscilla hung her head. "I hadn't considered his needs."

Daed set a comforting hand on her shoulder. "You had many other things to think about. I'm sure finding out about Matthew was a blow."

Biting her lip, Priscilla nodded. Tears welled in her eyes, but she refused to let them fall.

They headed back to the house together.

When they reached the back porch, Daed stopped. "We need to let your *mamm* know. I think perhaps only the basics, so she can defuse rumors."

Priscilla nodded, although she wished to keep this from Mamm. She loved her mother, but Mamm tended to run away with ideas that often ended up backfiring.

Daed stomped his boots hard on the mat to dislodge the bits of straw and mud that clung to them. Priscilla did the same and then followed him into the kitchen, where Mamm was still unpacking groceries.

"Esther, I'd like you to come into the living room," Daed said. "Priscilla needs to talk to you."

Priscilla's throat closed up. She'd been hoping Daed would tell Mamm.

"In a few minutes, Joseph. The rest of these things need to be put away." Mamm bustled around the kitchen, carrying things to the pantry. "Actually, why doesn't she tell me while we unpack?"

"All of that can wait. This won't take long, and it's important." Daed motioned for her to precede him into the living room.

Her forehead crinkled, Mamm crossed the kitchen and went into the other room. Daed tilted his chin to indicate Priscilla should enter next. He brought up the rear.

When Priscilla walked into the room, her stomach clenched. Mamm was sitting in the rocker where the bishop had been seated that morning. All the confusion and pain from the morning washed over Priscilla. Matthew standing in the doorway, telling her about Mara, asking her—

Blocking out those memories, Priscilla sent Daed a pleading look.

Daed's face was grave. "Something happened with Matthew that shouldn't have."

Mamm gasped and turned narrowed eyes on Priscilla. "You're not—"

She needed to reassure Mamm that her virtue was intact. "Of course not."

Daed cleared his throat, trying to get Mamm's attention. When she looked his way, he began again. "The bishop came calling this morning because—"

"*Ach,*" Mamm interrupted in a semi-hysterical voice. "If the bishop felt the need to discipline you, that's not good. You need to get married right away. We can't have people gossiping about you. And that's the best way to deal with temptation."

Once Mamm got started, she ran on and on like one of those *Englisch* trains, zipping past the crossroads, flattening everything in her way.

Barely pausing for breath, she said, "November is only six weeks away. We could act like we'd—I mean, you'd—always intended to get married during the traditional wedding time. People might question the suddenness, but . . ."

She fanned herself. "All the preparations will put a strain on me, but I'm used to it. Everyone always—"

"Esther." Daed's voice cracked through the air.

Mamm kept fluttering her hands, and her mouth remained open, but her words stopped.

Priscilla wrung her hands in her lap. How would Mamm react to not having a wedding?

She'd been even more excited than Priscilla when Matthew asked to court her. Parents didn't usually get involved in relationships or marriage plans, but Mamm had started preparing for the wedding after Priscilla's first date.

"First of all," Daed said, "Priscilla won't be getting married. At least not now. But definitely not in November. And not to Matthew."

"What?" Mamm's screech brought Zeke pounding to the top of the stairs.

"Is everything all right?" he asked.

"Your *mamm* got a bit upset over some news."

Zeke met Priscilla's eyes. *Matthew?* he mouthed. When she nodded, he shot her a sympathetic look. All of Priscilla's siblings understood how excited Mamm had been about next year's wedding.

"The noise upset Asher."

"We'll try to be quieter up here," Daed promised.

"Oh-oh-oh." Mamm clutched at her heart and sounded as if she were struggling to breathe. "What happened with Matthew?" She sounded close to tears.

"Priscilla broke up with Matthew today. For a very good reason, I might add." Daed kept his tone level and calm.

"No!" Mamm turned to her. *"Let not the sun go down on your wrath.* Apologize. Do what you have to do to make things right."

"I—I can't marry Matthew." Priscilla's words came out strangled. Then she cringed, waiting for the explosion.

Instead, Mamm's face crumpled. "Not getting married?" she moaned. "But—but . . ." She continued spluttering until Daed's stern frown stopped her.

"Priscilla made the right decision under the circumstances. We will speak no more about this."

"But," Mamm wailed, "who will want to court her after hearing what she's done?"

"Our daughter has done nothing wrong. We will make sure Bishop Troyer and Deacon Raber know the truth. She has broken up with Matthew, and that will be the end of the matter." This time, at the firmness of Daed's tone, Mamm went completely silent.

But her question played over and over in Priscilla's mind. If, like Mamm, everyone assumed the worst about her, no decent man would offer to court her. She'd not only lost Matthew; she'd also lost any chance to marry.

Head in his hands, Gabe sat at his desk after Priscilla left. He'd never been so drawn to a woman before, which meant she spelled trouble. How many Amish women had researched camel's milk and worked with special needs children? She'd be the perfect helpmeet, except—

Gabe groaned. He'd made a promise, and he'd never go back on his word.

Tim peeked into the office. "Is something wrong?"

Pasting a smile on his face, Gabe reassured Tim, "I have a lot on my mind right now."

"You're not mad at me about the coolers?" Tim edged back a few steps and hung his head.

"At you? Of course not. It's not your fault."

His nephew blew out a long breath. "*Pheww.* I thought maybe you'd be upset."

"I am upset, but not at you." He didn't want to think about this loss when the business couldn't afford any additional expenses. He could barely keep up with the ones he had. "We'll need to buy new coolers before next weekend's orders. For now, maybe we'll keep them inside beside the doorway so we can keep an eye on them."

Tim puffed up his chest. "And I'll watch for that lady who took 'em."

"Good idea." Gabe also planned to pay close attention to Fleurette if she returned. "I don't think we'll be getting many more walk-in customers today. Why don't we start putting the extra milk into the deep freezer?"

They both put on knitted caps, heavy coats, and thick gloves to transfer the leftover milk into the freezer. Gabe pasted labels on several shelves and dated them. Then he and Tim carted most of their stock from the refrigerator to those shelves.

When they were done, Gabe removed his winter gear, flexed his chilled fingers, and sat down to finish recording the previous week's billing. His thoughts were so consumed by the theft and by Priscilla, he struggled to concentrate on accounting.

He totaled the columns for inventory again and compared them with the totals from Tim's receipts, which equaled the amount of money in the cash box. Gabe had subtracted the stolen coolers and the pint he'd given Priscilla, but something was wrong. Very wrong.

"Tim? Could you come in here for a second?"

His nephew scurried into the office.

"I want you to go over these receipts carefully." One by one he laid them out in the order in which they'd been filled or checked out. Tim verified each of them.

Gabe shook his head. Tim was young and new at this. Maybe he'd mistaken the sizes and undercharged the customers. Gabe gathered up the receipts and slid them into a file folder. He'd do a quick test to be sure Tim understood directions.

"If I ask you to get me a gallon of camel's milk, which one would you choose?" Gabe pointed to the clean, unfilled bottles on the wooden storage shelves across the room.

"That one." With no hesitation, Tim pointed to the correct container.

"For camel's milk, how much would you charge?"

Tim repeated the right price. He ran through the tests without missing an answer. His nephew had not been the problem.

"Did I mix something up?" Tim's face screwed up into anxious lines. "I tried really hard to do everything right."

Gabe reached out and ruffled Tim's hair. "You did it perfectly. I only wanted to be sure I'd trained you properly."

"If I did a good job, why are you frowning?"

"I didn't realize I was." He tried to smooth out his furrowed brow. "I'm confused about why the books aren't balancing. Maybe I miscounted when we stocked the shelves."

After donning his winter gear, Gabe entered the deep freezer to recount the milk they'd shelved as well as the remaining stock on the regular refrigerator shelves. Not counting the losses from the plastic coolers, twelve additional gallons had gone missing.

Chapter Four

"Don't hold the meal for us," Daed said to Mamm. Then he motioned for Priscilla to follow him to the barn.

"But you need to eat something." The distress in Mamm's voice came from more than worrying about them missing a meal. She seemed even more upset than Priscilla about the breakup. "At least let me fix you a sandwich to take with you."

"You don't have to," Priscilla forced herself to say. "I made plenty of sandwiches for—" *For the picnic that never happened.* She winced.

How many picnic lunches had Matthew indulged in with Mara? Had Mara spent time making all of his favorite foods the way Priscilla had done this morning?

Daed patted her shoulder awkwardly.

Mamm stopped heading toward their gas-powered refrigerator and turned, her eyes damp. "*Ach.*"

If Priscilla didn't come up with a distraction, her mother might burst into tears. "I put a pint of camel's milk in there for Asher."

"Camel's milk?" Mamm stared at her. Then she glanced at Daed with a question in her eyes. A question Priscilla could read clearly. *Has our daughter gone crazy?*

At Daed's shrug, Mamm cleared her throat. "I know this has been upsetting for you, but camel's milk?"

The disbelief in her tone made Priscilla want to defend herself. "I went to a camel farm this morning. A man just bought that large property in Bird-in-Hand, and he's raising camels." She stepped around her *mamm* and opened the refrigerator. "It's on the top shelf." She pointed out the small bottle.

"I see," Mamm said faintly. "What do we do with it?"

"I'm hoping Asher will drink it." Her brother was quite fussy about what he put in his mouth. "If he does, I'll get more."

Mamm wrinkled her nose. "I'm not sure this is safe."

"I've read a lot of research on it. It's supposedly good for autism." Priscilla hoped Mamm wouldn't forbid her to experiment.

Her parents were old-fashioned and hesitated to try new things. Yet Priscilla had coaxed them into letting her take Asher to Hope's horse therapy farm. And that had been helping. Also, getting Asher a weighted blanket had calmed him. So had changing his diet.

"We can discuss this later," Daed said.

As she grabbed two of the sandwiches she'd lovingly prepared that morning, a sharp pang sliced through her, and she bit down on her lip.

How could this have happened? Had she done something wrong? Why else would Matthew stray?

"Priscilla?" Daed's voice broke through her gloom. "We should go."

Stepping aside so Mamm could set out lunch for the rest of the family, Priscilla struggled to get her emotions under control before turning around. She handed the sandwiches to Daed and headed for the door. Outside, he offered her one, but she waved it away.

"*Danke*, but I've already eaten." Even if she hadn't, she'd never bite into one of *those* sandwiches.

Daed didn't seem convinced. "You're sure?"

"I'm positive."

They walked in silence toward the barn. When they reached the entrance, Priscilla halted. "I don't think we should do this."

"What?" Daed stopped beside her.

"What if the bishop's wife overhears us?" Betty Troyer rivaled Mamm as one of the biggest gossips in their district. "Besides, Mara is her niece. The bishop might feel obligated to tell her parents."

"That's possible." Daed tugged at his beard. "But perhaps her parents should be warned. I'd certainly appreciate it if someone told me one of my children had been misbehaving."

Although part of her might want to see Mara

punished, Priscilla couldn't deliberately hurt Mara or Matthew. Most of all, she didn't want to make Matthew's *mamm* suffer.

"If they tell Mara's parents, Matthew will lose his job."

"*Jah*, Mel Bontrager is strict. I can't see him keeping Matthew on the job."

Exactly what Matthew had said when he'd asked her to keep his secret. "I can't do that to Matthew's *mamm*." His widowed mother, an invalid, depended on him for support. Priscilla couldn't harm an innocent woman, especially not one she cared for as much as she did Ruth.

"Are you sure you want to keep this a secret, *dochder*?" Daed studied her face. "You'll be the subject of gossip."

"I know, but what do you think God would want me to do?"

"Some people say we should call out sin, but I've found over the years that often it's best to let God deal with the situation. Why don't you pray about it?"

Priscilla nodded. "I will. The bishop did say he expected us to confess. If Matthew does that, he'll have to tell the truth."

It meant waiting more than a week for the next church Sunday, but it would be better for everyone in the community to hear the story from Matthew rather than for Priscilla to be a tattle-tale.

・ ・ ・

On Monday morning, after milking his camels and cows, Gabe went into the store to package up the milk. The sign in the window listed only afternoon and evening hours on weekdays. Mornings by appointment only. Even after he'd lined the shelves with newly filled bottles, he stayed, because he didn't want to miss any random customers.

Being inside his empty, cavernous warehouse added to Gabe's loneliness. Before moving to Bird-in-Hand, he'd owned a smaller farm, a gathering spot for family and friends. They'd drop in at all hours to talk or help. Here, he had his brother's family, but he'd made no friends yet, and the rest of his family still lived in Bucks County. He missed Tim's company during the daytime.

Gabe paced the floor, trying to come up with marketing ideas to attract new customers. *Lord, You led me here, but I don't know how to promote our products. You know how hard it is for me to talk to groups or to strangers. Please show me the way.*

One of his *Englisch* friends from his old hometown had suggested getting a computer and online presence to expand his business, but Gabe didn't want to run afoul of his new bishop. He'd wait until he'd met the church leaders before asking.

When the phone rang an hour later, Gabe was glad he'd stayed in the store. His customer, Henry Defarge, had a thick Philadelphia accent and a brusque manner.

Except Defarge didn't order milk. Instead, he snapped out a sharp, blunt question. "How much to buy you out of the business?"

Shocked, Gabe couldn't come up with a coherent answer. Maybe he'd misheard. "Excuse me?" he finally managed.

"I want to buy the camel farm."

Didn't people usually look over a property they were interested in and spend some time negotiating before making an offer? "I'm sorry, but my business is not for sale."

"Everyone has a price," the man insisted. "What's yours?"

"I'm afraid you're mistaken. I have no intention of selling. Not for any price."

"You will, sooner or later. When you get to that point, call me, and I'll take it off your hands."

"Thank you for your offer." Gabe tried to be polite. "I appreciate you calling." He was pre- paring to hang up the phone when Defarge stopped him.

"Can you supply us with camel's milk once a week?" he barked.

"Of course. How much do you need?"

Gabe sucked back a gasp when Defarge gave him a number. That would take almost all of his weekly supply. But he didn't want to turn away a major customer. "We could do that."

He scratched numbers on a scrap of paper on his desk. In addition to the loyalty discount he gave his regular customers, he should give an extra percentage off for a bulk order.

"You'll give us a good deal, right?" Henry disguised his question as an *if-you-don't, I'll-twist-your arm-until-you-hurt* demand.

A bully, for sure and certain, but this sale would be amazing for Gabe's business. "Your bill would be—" He gulped before quoting the amount he'd figured. The number sounded so high, but he'd lose money if he went much lower.

"I hope that isn't your best price." Henry's words, heavy with sarcasm, hung between them.

Gabe didn't want to lose such a big order, so he lowered his price. And lowered it again at Henry's insistent prodding.

When Gabe protested another cut, the man's semi-sinister laugh turned smarmy. "I know you Amish like to help others. This milk is going to a charity that helps kids with allergies and other health problems. Camel's milk is good for that, isn't it?"

"Yes, it is." If it would help children, Gabe couldn't deny one more price cut. The final number was so low, though, he'd barely break even.

"Let's do the same with your cow's milk."

Defarge's hearty laugh churned Gabe's stomach.

This time Gabe started higher because Defarge would weasel him down. Still, the man again managed to cut Gabe's profit margin to practically nothing. The only thing that prevented Gabe from backing out of the deal was knowing he'd be helping children. Besides, most of his milk might not sell. If it sat in his freezers, he'd have no way to pay bills. Perhaps once he built up a customer base here, he could renegotiate.

A few people stopped by after he opened at noon. Two of the women said Priscilla had sent them. He sold them each a gallon of camel's milk and one of regular milk, so giving Priscilla the free pint had paid off already. An older couple strolled through the store and checked out the refrigerator but left without buying anything.

When the door opened later that afternoon, Gabe had returned to his desk with a stack of bills—both business and personal—to figure out how he'd manage to pay them with the money from Defarge. But Tim didn't race into his office the way he usually did. Gabe hoped nothing was wrong.

"Tim?"

"He's not here yet," a woman answered.

Gabe shot up from his chair. He'd been sitting back here when he had a customer. He hurried out of the office and halted. *Priscilla?*

He ran a hand over his bowl cut, hoping his

hair wasn't too disheveled, and adjusted his suspenders. He was brushing dust and lint off his pants when she turned to face him. Clasping his hands in front of him, Gabe tried to act casual. "Can I help you?"

She smiled, setting his pulse racing. That wasn't good. He needed to get his reactions under control.

"*Jah*, I hope so. My brother drank the milk without complaining, so we'd like to buy more each week."

"In that case, you can get the discount I offer regular customers." Gabe rushed over to the counter, picked up a brochure with a sign-up sheet, and handed it to her.

"*Danke*, I'd appreciate that." She filled out the sheet and added her biweekly order amount.

Priscilla had sent the two customers who had stopped by earlier. Perhaps he should offer her the same discount he'd given the Philly distributor.

"And thank you too," he said.

She lifted her head. "For what?"

"You've sent people to the business."

He tried not to peer at her address on the form. Now he'd know where she lived. Not that he needed that information.

He couldn't help being happy to see she'd be stopping by twice a week for milk. And his joy had nothing to do with increased sales.

Gabe shook his head. He needed to keep his

mind on business, but it proved difficult when she was around.

Priscilla could hardly concentrate on printing information on the form with Gabe standing beside her. She checked Wednesday and Saturday pickups.

"I'm glad my friends stopped by." She'd suggested it to several people, and it pleased her that a few of them had come. Some members of the community had been avoiding her.

Gabe moved a little closer as if checking out her answers. He made her so nervous she worried she'd make mistakes. And was it his nearness or her heavy coat making her so hot?

"I hope they'll like the camel's milk and will return," Gabe said.

"I do too." Priscilla finished writing and handed him the paper. "Have you been busy today?"

Gabe wished he could say yes, but he had to be honest. "There's always plenty to do with milking, bottling, stocking shelves, and doing book work. But if you mean customers, besides your friends, only one couple stopped in."

"I'm sorry. I hope it picks up." She didn't want him to go out of business. And not only because of Asher's milk.

Gabe followed her into the refrigerated room and carried the gallon she selected. "Actually, I did have a large phone order, which will help."

"That's great."

"I guess."

Gabe's lackluster answer made her curious. "You don't sound too happy."

"I suppose I should be grateful, but the man talked me down to a very low price. It's for charity, though, so I shouldn't complain." He held the refrigerator door with his back so she could go into the store.

Being so close to Gabe, Priscilla needed to get her pulse under control. She took several deep breaths while he set the milk container on the counter, but the extra air didn't help.

"At least this time I have money with me," she managed to tease, despite her slightly unsteady breathing.

"Well, I would offer to give them to you free, but after this weekend's thefts—"

"You had more than one?" Priscilla stopped counting out money to stare at him.

Gabe shrugged. "I probably shouldn't have said that. I don't know for sure. It's just that I'm missing payments for twelve gallons of camel's milk."

"*Ach*, I wonder if . . ." Priscilla didn't like to accuse someone without proof. Fleurette had taken the three coolers, but she'd paid for the camel's milk after that.

"What?" Gabe stared at her.

"Fleurette put several refrigerated bags in her

trunk before she took the coolers. Maybe she'd paid for them, though. I wasn't in the store, so I can't say for sure. And Tim did go to get some change."

"It seems I need to find this Fleurette."

Why did thinking about Gabe finding the beautiful *Englischer* give Priscilla such a pang?

After Priscilla left, Gabe waited impatiently for Tim. As soon as his nephew arrived, Gabe asked, "Will you be all right alone here if I run to the library?"

"Sure." Tim glanced around the empty room. "We're not busy."

"*Jah*, that's for certain. I'll be back by milking time."

Tim usually manned the store alone while Gabe milked, so Gabe had no idea why he was worried about it today. Maybe because of the thefts.

"Keep a close watch on anyone who comes in."

"You mean like that lady?"

"And anyone else." Gabe had examined Saturday's receipts carefully, but he'd double-check with his nephew. "Speaking of Fleurette, did she pay you twice?"

Tim's forehead wrinkled. "Why would she do that?"

"Priscilla Ebersol stopped by this afternoon and mentioned you went to get change while Fleurette was here. Priscilla thought Fleurette

66

loaded bags into her car while you were gone."

"I'm sorry. I guess I shouldn't have left the store, but she asked if I had change for hundred-dollar bills."

"You did the right thing. We expect others to be honest and upright. It's a shame we can't trust everyone."

Tim hung his head. "You can take the money from my pay."

With as little as he paid Tim, his nephew would be going without pay for a long time. "*Neh.* I don't blame you for what happened. I'm going to the library to see if I can find Fleurette's address and phone number. I'd like to get her to pay."

He'd pulled her bill and checked her signature. Even though most customers paid in cash, he always had customers sign their receipts. Luckily, Tim had remembered to do that. Her last name was a bit hard to read, though.

He took off for the library. Even with the research librarian's help, he found no listings for Fleurette Moreau. They tried other spellings— Morrow, Morro—with the same result. He had no way to contact her.

The *Englischer* remained on his mind as he returned home and did the milking. He could report the theft to the police, but she was from out of state. And he'd only just opened his business, so he hesitated to do that. For now, he'd just pray and see what happened.

• • •

Going to the camel farm yesterday had been the highlight of Priscilla's week. Seeing Gabe had cheered her up, but it also had been an escape after a trying time. Yesterday, her friend Ada, the school's head teacher, had not said a word about the rumors, and their aide, Martha, was her usual cheerful self. But several parents had looked at Priscilla askance.

And today, when Betty Troyer, the bishop's wife, came to pick up her son, she'd shot glares in Priscilla's direction. Seeing Priscilla surrounded by children may have kept Betty from a confrontation. Today, though, Priscilla had just helped eight-year-old Lizzie into her *mamm*'s buggy and was walking back alone. Betty cornered Priscilla on the playground away from everyone.

A disapproving frown etched into her forehead, Betty said, "I want you to know I'm praying for you and Matthew."

"*Danke.*" Priscilla tried to sound grateful.

Some of the parents who were picking up their children glanced over, and Betty lowered her voice. "I'm sure the school board will be discussing this with you, but teachers are expected to be examples."

Ada's sympathetic look from the schoolhouse doorway helped Priscilla maintain her composure, but her face flushed.

"If I'd been caught in such behavior," Betty said, "I'd be ashamed. Yet you show up to teach as if nothing happened. No remorse. No repentance."

When Priscilla remained silent, Betty's face turned scarlet. She pivoted and stalked off to collect her children, leaving Priscilla shaking with suppressed anger. She'd just been humiliated by a rebuke that rightfully belonged to Mara. What would Betty think if she discovered her niece was the one who'd done these things?

The last parent arrived as Betty drove off with her children. As soon as Ada had helped Will into his mother's buggy, she headed over.

Priscilla remained frozen in place, shell-shocked. Betty's words still swirled through Priscilla's brain. She could lose her job. She'd hoped Matthew's confession would prevent that.

Waiting until next Sunday would be torture. Then everyone would know the truth. But what if Betty pressured the school board to fire Priscilla before that?

Ada reached Priscilla, put an arm around her, and gave her a brief side-hug. "I'm sorry." Ada's eyes shone with pity. "I wish I could have come over sooner, but I didn't want any of the children to hear what Betty was saying."

Priscilla appreciated Ada's support. Her fellow teacher had received tongue-lashings from Betty too, so she understood. Not once today had Ada said anything judgmental. For that, Priscilla was grateful.

Right now, all she wanted to do was get home. Away from the prying eyes. Away from the knowing looks. Away from the disapproving glares.

Ada walked beside Priscilla to the street, and before they parted ways, Ada leaned over and whispered, "We all do things we regret, but once we've asked God for forgiveness, those mistakes should be left in the past."

But I didn't make this mistake. Priscilla's heart burned with the injustice.

"And don't worry," Ada continued, "I'll do everything I can to keep you here at the school-house."

"*Danke,*" Priscilla mumbled as she turned to head in a different direction.

She appreciated Ada's kindness. But how much influence would Ada have with a school board who believed Priscilla had done wrong?

Chapter Five

Priscilla had just fixed her younger siblings an after-school snack when someone knocked at the door. Her heart clenched as tightly as her hand grasped the knife, making her slices jagged and uneven. The chocolatey aroma of the soft, gooey brownies, usually so homey and comforting, choked her.

The last two times she'd answered the door, it had been the bishop, then Matthew.

She handed the knife to her sister Sarah. "Can you finish cutting these?"

Then she dragged her feet heading to the door. Had Betty come to continue her lecture? Or had the church leaders arrived to pressure her to confess? Or did the school board plan to tell her she was unfit for the job? She built up these three scenarios in her mind, but when she opened the door, Hope stood on the porch.

"Hope?" What was her best friend doing here when she usually had horse therapy lessons at this time?

"*Jah*, it's me. I just stopped by to pay on the loan you gave me."

"But don't Chloe and Jabin have lessons now?"

"Usually they do, but Micah and I thought coming over here was more important."

71

"Micah's with you?" Priscilla peered over Hope's shoulder.

"Not this time. I thought you might want to talk."

Priscilla would love to, but she couldn't share the secrets she was hiding. She appreciated Hope acting as if everything were normal. No disapproving glances. No frowns of censure. No condemning looks. No drawing away from a sinner.

Priscilla bit her lip. "I suppose you've heard the rumors."

"I try not to listen to gossip. Or to believe it. Especially not about my friends."

"Matthew and I broke up."

"I'm so sorry." Hope hugged her, then stepped back. "You've been together since you were eighteen. That's a long time."

"I know." Never, during those four years, had she considered anyone else. And now she couldn't. Or wouldn't. Gabe's face popped into her mind. As much as she was drawn to him, she'd made up her mind. Never again would she let anyone else inflict that kind of hurt.

"Priscilla?" Hope's eyes radiated sympathy. "Can you tell me what's going on?"

As badly as she wanted to discuss it, Priscilla couldn't share the truth. "*Neh*. I wish I could, but I can't."

"Are you confessing on Sunday?"

Priscilla shook her head. "Only Matthew needs to confess." *Well, Matthew and Mara.*

Hope's startled eyes made Priscilla realize her mistake.

"Oh, no," Hope cried, "I'm so sorry. I never thought Matthew would—"

"No, no. I don't want you to think Matthew forced me to do something. He didn't. I mean . . ." Now she'd talked herself into an even bigger misunderstanding. "Hope, I can't tell you what happened. Not until after Matthew confesses."

Sarah peeked her head into the living room. "Did you want me to bring you both some brownies?"

The thought of eating anything made Priscilla feel ill. "None for me. Only for Hope."

"You're really not going to have any?" Hope asked after Sarah brought her a plate with a generous piece. "I've never known you to turn down chocolate."

"I can't." Actually, except for the sandwich Gabe had fed her, she hadn't eaten much since Saturday.

Hope finished her brownie, then reached into her pocket, and handed Priscilla a check. "Here's my first payment."

"But this isn't due for months yet." When Priscilla lent Hope the money for her horse therapy farm, she had given her friend generous repayment terms. Hope didn't need to pay her first installment until five months from now.

"I know, but the business is going so well, I wanted to pay you back now."

Hope's broad smile made Priscilla's heart ache. Would she ever know that deep happiness again?

"I'm so glad it's been successful." Priscilla was happy she'd played a small part in helping the horse therapy farm get off the ground. Maybe she could do the same for Gabriel. She didn't know Gabriel well enough to offer him a loan the way she had for Hope, but she could help him get customers. And she'd just thought of the perfect way to do it. She only hoped he'd agree.

The next afternoon Gabe glanced up to see Priscilla framed in the doorway, and his heart skipped a beat. Her smile radiated sunbeams of joy into his heart and into the room.

"I had an idea yesterday while my friend Hope was visiting, and she agreed it would be an awesome opportunity for both of you." Priscilla waltzed across the room to where he was sitting at the counter.

"Well, if it made you this excited, I can't wait to hear it." Gabe stood and offered her his chair.

"I don't have time to sit. I promised Mamm I'd make supper tonight because she's at her quilting circle, but I wanted to tell you so we can get started with the planning."

Whatever her idea might be, Gabe intended to give an enthusiastic yes.

"You know how my school, the horse therapy farm, and your business all serve similar customers? I thought we could have a day at Hope's farm to introduce all the parents at my school and everyone who takes horse therapy to the benefits of camel's milk."

"That's brilliant."

"And I thought you could invite your customers to come too. People who are willing to try camel's milk for health problems would probably be open to horse therapy. And that would help Hope's business."

"Of course. It sounds great. I don't have a lot of customers here yet, but I can send invitations to the ones from Bucks County. It's only about an hour's drive. Some of them come here to pick up milk. If they're interested in horse therapy, perhaps they can schedule lessons for the days they come for milk."

"That's a great idea. Hope would really appreciate that."

Gabe made the mistake of staring into Priscilla's sparkling eyes. Then he couldn't look away despite warning bells sounding an alarm. He needed to curb his enthusiasm and not get too involved.

"I'm so glad you like the idea." Priscilla was practically dancing with excitement. "A big event like this will probably attract the newspapers."

Gabe had to grip the counter to control the urge to sweep her into his arms. He forced himself to concentrate on Priscilla's plan rather than her charm.

Her idea would give him a chance to let the community know he'd opened his business. If it went well, it could give his camel farm a big boost.

He'd focused so hard on dragging his attention away from Priscilla, he almost missed her next question.

"Do you think you could bring a camel along for people to see?"

"I have one mama and baby that used to be in a petting zoo, so they're rather tame."

"Bringing a baby would be *wunderbar*. I'm sure the children will love to see it. I could also invite the other special needs schools and the Community Care Center. They work with children and adults with special needs."

He was so caught up in his enthusiasm for Priscilla's plan, he almost forgot his nervousness in large crowds of strangers. But then she dropped a bombshell.

"Once everyone has gathered, you and Hope could each talk about the benefits of camel's milk and horse therapy. If people knew more about the advantages, they'd be willing to try it."

Gabe tumbled to earth with a thud. *Talk to a*

group? A large crowd? He could barely draw in a breath. *No, never!*

Priscilla stopped talking and stared at him. "What's the matter?"

He forced himself to suck in some air. Then he explained, "I like your ideas, and I think they'd be a great way to market, but . . ."

"But what?" Priscilla didn't want to hear any objections. She and Hope had spent a lot of time coming up with this idea last night. Hope had left the house thrilled. And Priscilla had stayed up most of the night to be sure she hadn't missed any details.

Gabe had a pained expression. "I can't talk to people."

"What?" That didn't make any sense. "You never have any trouble speaking to me. And you seemed fine with that *Englischer.*" Priscilla hadn't seen him interacting with anyone else, but she'd never noticed him having trouble with conversations.

He waved a hand. "I've trained myself to talk to customers, and if I have only one or two, I'm fine. But to talk to a crowd?" Gabe shook his head. "I could never, ever give a speech."

"Giving a speech is no different than talking to one person. Look at one individual in the audience, and speak to that person. Forget everyone else is there."

Gabe's head whipped back and forth like wheat blowing in a violent wind. "I can't. I just can't."

Priscilla couldn't let go of her idea. Not after she'd spent so much time planning—and scheming, if she were honest—to come up with a way to spend more time with Gabe. She enjoyed his company, and she wanted to help him succeed. It hurt to have her hopes dashed.

"I'm sorry," Gabe said. "I wish I could be a part of it."

"You still can. We could set up a booth where you could talk to people one at a time."

"I could probably manage that."

He looked so pained, Priscilla almost wanted to scrap the idea.

Then he brightened. "You know so much about the benefits of camel's milk, and you're used to teaching. Could you deliver the speech?"

Priscilla had intended to stay behind the scenes. She'd have a lot to handle with keeping things running and taking care of her scholars with special needs. Many of them got agitated or upset in crowds and acted out. Doing a speech seemed impossible.

"I don't think so." Right now, the only answer that came to mind was an emphatic no. She'd definitely not have time for that.

Maybe she could figure out a way to help Gabe feel more comfortable about speeches. Perhaps if he rehearsed what he wanted to say?

She'd be happy to listen to him practice. Right now, he looked too overwhelmed to appreciate that suggestion, so she'd give him some time before she offered her thoughts about practicing a speech.

She made a show of glancing at the clock. "I'd better get home to make supper."

"Priscilla, wait." Gabe reached for her hand to stop her from leaving, and sparks shot through her.

"Sorry," Gabe mumbled and let go of her hand.

Had he felt it too? The warmth and imprint of his fingers remained on her skin. Priscilla forced herself to breathe. *In . . . out . . . in . . . out.* Had Matthew ever touched her that way? If he had, she didn't remember it affecting her like this. She struggled to control her pulse.

Then Gabe stared into her eyes, and she was lost. "Please," he begged. "Will you do the speech for me?"

Drawn into those sparkling depths, Priscilla was powerless to resist. What could she say but yes?

Every day for the rest of the week, Henry Defarge called Gabe several times a day. Each call began the same way—with Defarge barking the same question into the phone, "You ready to sell yet?"

The relentless pressure rattled Gabe, but he managed to keep his tone neutral. No sense in offending a large commercial customer. He forced out two words. "Not yet."

Sometimes Defarge listed all the disadvantages of owning a business, which made no sense to Gabe. If the man believed that, why would he want to purchase this one?

On Friday, Defarge became pushier than usual. Gabe clammed up, the way he usually did in arguments. His mind ran around and around in squirrelly circles, and he couldn't find the beginning or the ending to make a full sentence.

Defarge took Gabe's silence as agreement. "So glad you've finally come around," he said. "I think we should do business in person, though. Sign the contracts and all that as soon as possible."

Gabe managed a strangled no, but Defarge talked right over him, outlining his plans for the takeover, the papers Gabe would need, and the arrangements they'd both need to have their lawyers handle.

Taking a deep breath, Gabe tried once again. "No, I don't want to—"

"Oh, right, right. I forgot you Amish aren't big on lawyers and contracts. How do you manage these land purchases, then? The government usually wants the forms in triplicate and all that stuff."

"No," Gabe said. "I—"

"Listen, don't worry about it. I'll talk to my lawyer to find out how to take care of everything.

He's done deals with the Amish, so I'm sure he can figure it out. Once he has the paperwork ready, we can go from there. I need to run, so I'll turn it over to him today."

Before Gabe could stop him, Defarge hung up.

Gabe sat, phone in hand, as drained and squashed as if a team of horses had trampled him. How would he ever get Defarge to understand he didn't plan to sell?

If he called the man back, he'd find himself tripping over words. Trying to get a word in edgewise against Defarge's forceful personality had proved impossible, even if Gabe could manage to form coherent thoughts and sentences. Maybe a letter would work.

Gabe pulled a sheet of paper from the drawer and began his defense. His arguments against the sale flowed from his pen rapidly and easily. He finished writing, signed and dated the letter, and dug out an envelope. Once he found Defarge's New Jersey delivery address in his files, he added it to the front of the envelope. Tomorrow morning he'd run to the post office to send it off.

He hoped he wouldn't miss Priscilla's milk pickup while he was gone. Her visits had become the highlights of his week.

Priscilla planned to run to Gabe's farm first thing in the morning, but Mamm's turn to host the quilting circle occurred only once every three months, and the house needed to be spotless. Priscilla's excitement at seeing Gabe surpassed last Saturday's anticipation for the picnic with Matthew—the picnic that had turned out to be a disaster.

Despite her best efforts to rush through the chores, Priscilla didn't get out the door until almost noon. Not wanting to get dizzy again in Gabe's store, she took a lunch to eat on the way. This time, she also brought her winter coat and gloves.

She pulled past Gabe's building to park at the hitching post, tied up her horse, and headed for the door. A berry red convertible shot up the driveway, spraying gravel under its tires. Priscilla jumped aside to avoid getting hit by the car or the flying stones. The car slowed and glided to a stop in front of the entrance.

A heavyset man with a florid face and hanging jowls emerged from the driver's side. "Sorry, little lady. I didn't see you there."

Priscilla opened her mouth to respond, but he interrupted her. "Tell Gabe I'll be right in. I need to collect all the paperwork."

With a shake of her head, Priscilla entered the store. Gabe's smile when he spotted her brightened her day.

She headed toward the counter. "A man outside told me to let you know he'll be in soon with some paperwork."

"Paperwork?" Gabe scrunched his brows. "Not sure what that's about. I hope I didn't make any mistakes in the forms I had to file for the business."

"I have no idea. He didn't say." Priscilla was close enough now to appreciate the sparkle in Gabe's eyes. And once her eyes met his, she had no willpower to look away.

Behind her, the door banged open. "Oops, hope I'm not interrupting anything."

Reluctantly, Priscilla turned to face the man who'd driven the sports car. She should grab her milk and leave, allowing the men to talk business. But she wanted to discuss the event at Hope's farm with Gabe, so she stepped back when the man approached.

"Well, my lawyer went over all the documents last night, and he says this should take care of everything." He stuck out a beefy hand. "Sorry. Should have introduced myself first. Henry Defarge. We spoke on the phone."

Gabe's face paled, and Priscilla instinctively moved nearer.

Defarge slapped a stack of papers on the counter in front of Gabe. "I'm so glad you finally decided to sell the business."

"Sell?" Priscilla said faintly. Gabe had only opened the business a short while ago. Why would he be selling it already? "You're not selling, are you?"

Gabe's mouth moved as if he were struggling to find words, but no sound came out.

"Oops, looks like I put my foot in it," Defarge said. "You didn't have time to tell the little lady yet?"

"No." The word exploded from Gabe's lips, startling Priscilla as well as Defarge, who took a step back.

Defarge glanced over his shoulder at Priscilla. "Well, ma'am, I didn't mean to break the news this way."

Priscilla ignored him and focused on Gabe. "You can't sell the business. You just opened it." She regretted barging into his personal matters when he stared at her miserably and shook his head.

Defarge pressed his belly against the counter and whipped a pen from his pocket. "Here's the initial agreement. Now, this price is only good if everything I listed checks out."

Gabe stared at him, then down at the papers. Finally, he lifted his gaze to Priscilla in a mute plea. What did he want from her? Not agreement, because she could never give that.

"Wait, Gabe," she begged. "Before you sign, let's talk about it. Please?"

Defarge huffed and stepped back. "Gabe, I'll give you five minutes to explain it to her, but I need to get these papers executed so I can get on the road."

"Can we go into your office?" Priscilla asked Gabe. She tried to keep the desperation from her voice. If she'd known he was in financial trouble, she would have offered to help sooner. She'd loaned Hope about a third of her savings. Would the rest be enough to cover Gabe's costs and save the camel farm?

He nodded and motioned for her to precede him. As soon as they got inside and shut the door, Priscilla burst out, "You can't sell the farm. If you need money"—she lowered her voice—"I'd be happy to lend you some."

Gabe shook his head.

"Please? I don't want to see you lose the farm."

Holding up a hand, Gabe swallowed. "You know I told you I can't do speeches?" When she nodded, he continued, "I also have trouble talking when people pressure me or when they argue."

Priscilla had no idea where he was going with this. It seemed unrelated to the sale of the camel farm, but she kept quiet and allowed him to speak.

"Defarge has been hammering me all week to let him buy the business. My brain starts whirling, and I can't find the words to answer. I said no, but he misunderstood."

"Deliberately?" she asked.

Gabe laughed. "You're probably right. I've been so busy struggling to speak that I didn't pay attention to the bullying. I sure did feel it, though."

"So, you don't need money?"

The tenderness in Gabe's eyes set her pulses tingling. "*Danke* for the offer, but I can pay my bills."

"I'm so glad to know that. I was hoping you'd be around here for a long time." Heat rushed to her cheeks. She hadn't meant that the way it sounded. Or had she?

Gabe could hardly believe her generosity. She'd offered to give him—someone she'd just met— money to finance his business. And not only that, she'd revealed how much she cared about his future. She wanted him to stick around the area.

"I can't believe you'd offer money to a stranger," he said.

"You're not a stranger," she retorted. Her already pink cheeks darkened to scarlet. "I mean, we're friends, aren't we?"

"Of course." And Gabe pushed aside the desire to be more than friends. "But even friends aren't always so generous."

"I helped Hope with—" Priscilla clapped a hand over her mouth. "I'm sorry. I didn't mean to say that. It sounded like I was bragging."

"You go around giving money to your friends?" Gabe couldn't believe it. What was she, an heiress?

"No, only Hope. So far. She was in a bad situation soon after her horse therapy farm opened.

But she's already started paying me back."

"You're rich?"

Priscilla laughed. "I helped another friend with a jam-making business, training a few of her employees and doing some canning. She paid very well. I saved all of it, so if you do need a loan, don't hesitate to ask."

Gabe shook his head. She was a wonder. Not only was she beautiful, but she was knowledgeable about camel's milk and special children, she cared about others, and she was generous and kind. Guarding his heart when he was around her was proving more and more difficult.

"You two done yet?" Defarge called.

With Priscilla beside him, Gabe stepped out of the office with more confidence. Beside him, Priscilla spoke. "Thank you for your offer, but Gabe will be declining it. He plans to hand this business down to his children."

Gabe turned startled eyes in her direction. They hadn't discussed that, but as soon as Priscilla said it, he felt its truth in every bone and sinew in his body. He wanted this business to be a legacy for his sons and daughters.

If only he could have Priscilla beside him in that as well as this. A sharp pang shot through him. That could never be. He believed in honoring his vows.

Defarge's face darkened, and he swept Priscilla

with a scathing glance. Gabe stepped in front of her for protection.

Defarge peered around him to shake a finger at Priscilla. "You're making a mistake interfering with men's business, young lady." He turned to Gabe. "I thought Amish men didn't let their wives boss them around."

With Priscilla nearby, Gabe gained enough courage to say, "Amish men are the heads of their households, but they do consider their wives' feelings." Not that Priscilla was his wife, but saying that one sentence had taken a lot of strength, and he couldn't handle getting into a detailed explanation.

"You're going to regret this," Defarge warned as he gathered his papers, pivoted on his heel, and slammed out the door.

Priscilla giggled nervously. "He's pretty upset. I hope he doesn't cause trouble for you."

So do I. But Gabe didn't want to alarm Priscilla. He changed the subject. "Did you come to pick up your milk? We set it aside this morning." Actually, he'd let Tim do all the other orders, but he'd personally prepared Priscilla's.

Her grateful smile more than paid him back for that small effort.

Gabe accompanied her to the cooler and carried her gallon containers for her. "I'd like to give these to you for your help with Defarge."

"Absolutely not." Priscilla pulled out her wallet, and her lips turned up into a teasing grin. "I don't want to be the cause of you selling the business."

He laughed. "Well, there is that. But, seriously, if you hadn't come in when you did, I might have caved and given Defarge the whole business."

"No, you wouldn't."

Gabe loved the confidence in her voice and her belief in him. If he could take some of that assurance into his conversations, he could move mountains. All he needed was the faith of a mustard seed. Priscilla's presence would help too.

When Gabe refused her money, Priscilla marched over to Tim and handed him her cash. Tim looked toward him, and Gabe started to shake his head, but Priscilla intervened.

"You can either put my money in the cash box, Tim, or I'll leave it on the counter."

Although Gabe wasn't good at disagreeing with people, he had strong feelings about this. "I'd rather you didn't pay."

"But you did tell Defarge that you listened to women."

How could he argue with Priscilla when her sassy grin set his pulse on fire?

After a quick apologetic glance at Gabe, Tim took her money. Triumphant, Priscilla strode to the door.

Gabe carried her bags to the buggy and put them inside for her. "Negotiating with you is tough. I need to keep you around to fend off pushy people like Defarge." *Right, Gabe, spending more time together would be a real smart idea.*

"I'm happy to help anytime."

"I appreciate it." *More than you'll ever know.* Priscilla might believe he could have handled Defarge, but Gabe was well aware of his limitations.

After she'd left, he sat at his office desk while Tim took over the store. In his mind, Gabe went over the encounter with Defarge, mainly to reminisce about Priscilla's part in it. But Gabe had gotten a creepy feeling around the *Englischer.* And something definitely seemed fishy about the man and his offer.

In addition to Defarge's insistence on signing a contract immediately, one thing still puzzled Gabe. He'd had only a fleeting glance at the papers Defarge had set on the counter. The price the man intended to offer was higher than what Gabe had paid for the property and his livestock. Surely, Defarge had checked real estate prices in the area. Why would he pay such a large amount?

Unless he planned to find flaws to knock down the price, the way he'd bargained for the milk. He did say the price depended on everything checking out.

With how persistent Defarge had been with the phone calls and paperwork, Gabe worried the man would never give up. If he was determined to take over this business, there was no telling what he'd attempt. He'd been pretty upset with Priscilla. Gabe only hoped Defarge wouldn't hurt her if he decided to get revenge.

As usual, being around Gabe lifted Priscilla's spirits. She rejoiced that she'd been able to assist him in getting rid of Defarge. His smile of gratitude had quickened her heart. And when he said he'd need to keep her around, she worried he'd hear it hammering.

Stop it, she scolded herself. She found herself adding meaning to Gabe's every word and gesture. He'd been relieved to get rid of the annoying businessman. That was all it was, nothing more.

She'd gotten so caught up in the drama, she'd forgotten to talk to Gabe about practicing a speech. She'd have to make time to go back and discuss it. Of course, it could wait until next Wednesday when she went to pick up her next milk order. After some of her comments today—like that she wanted him to stay around here for a long time—she'd be better off avoiding him for a while, so he didn't get the wrong idea.

Or maybe it wasn't the wrong idea. As much as she tried to steel herself against her attraction to him, she struggled to tamp down her feelings. She'd be foolish to get involved in another relationship, even if Gabe showed interest. For all she knew, he could have a girlfriend. She had no way to find out. The last thing she wanted was to be a Mara to another woman.

Gabe seemed too upright and honest to do that, but then, so had Matthew.

Chapter Six

Priscilla woke with a stomachache the next morning. *Church Sunday.* Could she plead illness and stay home? How could she face all the stares, the shock, even the sympathy after Matthew confessed?

She dragged herself downstairs to help fix breakfast. "Mamm, I don't feel well."

Before her mother could respond, Daed, who was passing through the kitchen, patted her shoulder. "It won't be easy, but you'll get through it. Take some time to pray."

"I think you and Matthew should announce your engagement," Mamm said. "That way this fuss will blow over quickly."

"No." Priscilla panicked. What if Mamm suggested that to Matthew? "We broke up."

"Like I said before, if you apologize to him, I'm sure you can work everything out."

Maybe it had been a mistake not to tell Mamm the truth. It had kept her mother from gossiping about the situation all week, but Mamm would be shocked today when Matthew mentioned Mara's name during his confession.

Although she didn't usually argue with her parents, Priscilla couldn't let her mother's comment pass unchallenged. "I didn't do anything wrong. Matthew—"

Her mother whirled around from the stove and placed one hand on her hip. The other held a wooden spoon pointed at Priscilla's heart. "Priscilla Mae Ebersol, stop right there. Are you saying you've never sinned?"

"No, that's not what I meant."

"It certainly sounded that way."

Priscilla tried again. "Matthew, well, he . . ." It was much too painful to put this into words.

Mamm jiggled the spoon in the same motion as her head shaking. "No child of mine will ever try to blame someone else for their mistakes. It takes two to"—she pinched her lips together for a second—"do whatever you two did. You will NOT place the guilt on Matthew."

Her eyes squeezed shut, Priscilla tried to block out the picture of Matthew with Mara. "But, Mamm, you don't understand."

"Whenever something happens between two people—things like this or even an argument—you are both at fault."

Not this time. Or was Mamm right? Had she done something to drive Matthew away? Had she neglected him when she'd thrown herself into helping train people for the jam business? Still, he should have talked any problems over with her. They could have worked it out. He'd never given her a chance. Or if he preferred to date Mara, he should have first broken off his other relationship.

Mamm's voice softened. "I'm sure you're

ashamed of what happened, but accusing Matthew—" She stopped suddenly and studied Priscilla's face. "He didn't force you, did he?"

"No, but it wasn't—" Before Priscilla could say *me,* her mother held up a hand.

"Not another word. Your father was right about praying. You need to spend some time on your knees before we leave for the service. I hope you plan to confess as well."

"Mamm . . ."

"Priscilla, I mean it. I don't want to hear Matthew's name again until you've taken responsibility for your part in the problem."

Today Mamm would hear the story from Matthew's lips. Perhaps then she'd understand the truth.

Gabe had always enjoyed Sunday services at home, where he'd been surrounded by friends. Now he'd have to overcome his shyness to make new ones here. If only Priscilla lived in his district. It would help to see a familiar face in the crowd. Gabe tried not to dwell on his other reasons for wishing to see her.

Tim tapped on the farmhouse door a short while after Gabe had finished the milking. As usual, his brother Saul had arrived early. Gabe should have expected that.

"I'm almost ready," he told Tim. "Tell your *daed* I'll be right out."

He combed his still-damp hair and jammed on his hat. Then, with a quick prayer for courage, he headed out to Saul's carriage.

"*Danke* for taking me," he said to his brother as he squeezed into the back seat with his three nephews. His sister-in-law sat up front next to Saul, holding their six-month-old daughter.

"No problem." Saul clucked to the horse, and the buggy started with a jerk. "It's nice to have you nearby. It's hard living so far from family."

Gabe's nephews chattered the whole way to the Lapps' house, keeping Gabe from fretting about making conversation with strangers. He was grateful he wouldn't have to enter a stranger's house alone. Knowing he'd be going in with his brother took some of the edge off his nervousness.

Even after they'd walked into the Lapps' house, Gabe's lively nephews kept him busy, and he managed to smile and greet each person he met. He had no trouble talking one-on-one with people. He'd had plenty of practice with that in the store.

But when a small group of men surrounded him, he became overwhelmed. He stared at his shoes and tried to separate out the different voices that merged in his ears. Several people were asking questions at once.

Saul managed to sort them out for Gabe by repeating them one at a time. When Gabe answered the first question, Saul moved on to the next. When people filed in for the service, Gabe's constricted breathing loosened, and he followed his brother to the benches in the men's section.

Tim sat beside his *daed*, but the two smaller boys sat on either side of Gabe. Tim was old enough to listen to the sermon, but Saul pulled two tiny animals from his pocket and passed one to each boy. Gabe smiled. They appeared to be the same carved wooden animals his *mamm* had used when he and Saul were young.

Would his nephews fight over them the way Gabe had once done with Saul? Gabe still remembered his *mamm*'s fierce frown. That day, she'd taken the animals away for the rest of the long, drawn-out sermons—sermons that now seemed interesting and helpful. As a child, though, Gabe had wriggled and jiggled despite his mother's warning hand signals. The next Sunday, Saul surrendered his favorite animal, and Gabe had been triumphant. Until he realized he'd prefer Saul's cow to the horse he now held.

If the service hadn't already started, Gabe would have leaned over and apologized to his brother for the past and for being so bratty. Maybe he'd do it after church. Now, though, he intended to concentrate on the sermons. He was glad he did, because the messages touched his heart.

After the service, it didn't take long to turn the

church benches into tables for the meal while the women set out food in the back of the room.

"Let's eat." Saul ushered Gabe toward the line of men waiting to fill their plates. "Once we have our food, I'll introduce you to some members of the youth group."

Youth group? At twenty-four and as a business owner, Gabe considered he'd outgrown the singings. He'd stopped going when—

Saul nudged him. "You go first."

Gabe shook off his gloom. Picking up his utensils, he inched along behind the man in front of him and heaped his plate with peanut butter spread on bread, smear cheese, pretzels, red beets, and pickles.

Then he waited for his brother to get a glass of lemonade and accompany him to a table. Saul headed for a table filled with twenty-something guys.

"This is my brother Gabe. He just moved here from Bucks County," Saul announced.

The man closest to them turned to Gabe and asked, "You're the one who bought Eldon Frey's farm?"

"*Jah*, I did." Gabe set down his plate.

"I'm Levi Allgyer. We live on the other side of town. Nice to meet you."

"*Gut* to meet you too." Gabe settled on the bench beside Saul and nodded to the others at the table.

The boy beside him stuck out a hand. "I'm Gideon Hartzler. You have camels, right?"

Gabe shook his hand. "We do. And cows."

"My *daed* has a stand at the GreenValley Farmer's Market. If you have small bottles of milk for sale, I'm sure he'd be happy to carry them."

"*Danke.* That would be great. I'll talk to him about it."

Gideon bit into a pickle and squinched up his face, but then he chewed with relish. When he finished, he said, "We sell barbecued chicken and offer some drinks to customers. I don't know how popular camel's milk would be, but it can't hurt to give it a try. We can take some cow's milk too. That'll sell well."

Gabe hadn't expected to talk business at lunch, but soon questions about camels were flying at him from all directions. He was fine answering one person's question, but as soon as he became the center of attention, he stiffened.

Sensing his distress, his brother spoke up. "Maybe we could give Gabe a little time to eat first. Then he can answer questions."

"Sure." Several of the others tucked into their food or talked quietly among themselves.

"Hey, Gabe," one of the young men farther down the table called, "the singing's here tonight. We gather for games at four thirty. You're welcome to join us."

Gabe finished chewing and swallowed his bite

as well as the lump in his throat. *"Danke."* He tried to make his answer sound noncommittal. If anyone put him on the spot, though, it would be hard to refuse.

When Priscilla entered the Eshes' house for the church service, Hope was waiting inside the door. She grabbed Priscilla's hand and drew her to one side, away from the crowd.

"How are you?" she whispered.

"Sick." The word didn't even begin to describe the nausea flowing over her in waves.

"You're trembling." Hope squeezed Priscilla's hand. "I would be too. Will you be going up front to confess?"

When Priscilla shook her head, Hope's eyebrows rose. "You're not?"

"I can't," Priscilla said miserably. If only she could tell Hope the truth. But with people milling all around them, she wouldn't take a chance of someone overhearing. "You'll see why after Matthew confesses."

"Let's sit together."

"Jah, that will help." But it wouldn't calm her roiling stomach or ease her shame when Matthew told everyone about spending time with Mara. Priscilla pressed a knuckle against her lips to hold back a cry of pain.

Hope's eyes filled with distress. *"Ach,* Priscilla, I wish I could do more."

No one could heal this but God. "You're doing plenty." Hope had rescued Priscilla from the gossiping groups who kept glancing over at her.

"I wanted to send you a card and some flowers, but I wasn't sure if your breakup was temporary. I thought maybe the bishop had suggested staying apart for a while."

Friends from the youth group—her buddy bunch—usually sent cards and gifts to couples who had broken up. No one had sent her anything, so everyone must be assuming she and Matthew planned to get back together.

Priscilla tried to whisper, but her words came out fiercely. "Matthew and I will not be getting back together. Not ever."

Hope's eyes widened, and she took a step back. "That sounds final. Are you sure?"

"Very sure."

"I'm so sorry." With a sympathetic glance, Hope said, "We should go into the kitchen." She studied Priscilla. "If you're ready?"

Was anyone ever ready to face censure? After a quick prayer, Priscilla pasted on a neutral expression. "All right."

Facing the rumors flying around when she didn't deserve the disapproval would be hard enough, but Priscilla dreaded the meal after church. Once everyone knew the truth, she'd have to endure their pity. That would be even worse.

Several women glanced at her askance when she entered, but most greeted her in the usual manner and then resumed their conversations. A few stopped whispering together when she passed, and Priscilla wondered if they'd been chatting about her. Matthew's confession would provoke greater gossip.

So far, Priscilla hadn't spotted Mara in the crowd. Maybe she'd stayed home, the way Priscilla had longed to this morning. That might make this a little easier. Hearing Matthew's confession would be hard enough, but seeing the woman who—

Across the room, Betty stared at her, and Priscilla shriveled inside. She couldn't bear another lecture. Especially not in front of so many people. Priscilla pressed herself against the wall on the opposite side of the kitchen and sucked in a breath.

Hope turned to her in concern. "What's wrong?"

Priscilla hissed out air between her teeth as Betty threaded her way through the crowd, heading in their direction.

Hope followed Priscilla's gaze. "Oh no."

She motioned for Priscilla to shift around and deftly inserted both of them into a gaggle of girls discussing a mission trip to help with flooding in the Midwest. From the corner of her eye, Priscilla tracked Betty's progress across the room.

"I wish I could go," Hope said, "but I don't see how I could possibly take time off from my horse therapy business." She nudged Priscilla to get her attention. "Would you want to go in the summer?"

Everyone turned toward Priscilla. A few of the stares seemed critical, but most of the group seemed to be more interested in her answer than in judging her. Betty halted but kept an eye on the group.

"Me?" Priscilla, her mouth dry, struggled to come up with a coherent answer. "I-I've always wanted to go. Do you think they'll still need help after school's out?"

"I'm not sure," Miriam said. "Some groups are helping areas that flooded almost two years ago, so it's possible."

As if making up her mind to confront Priscilla, Betty advanced toward them. Hope must have noticed too, because she pinched her lips into a tight line. Unaware of Betty's approach or Priscilla's mounting distress, the others chimed in with their plans.

Just before she reached the group, Betty stopped and pinned Priscilla with a piercing look. A look that made her want to shrink back against the wall. Seeing Priscilla visibly shaken, the girls ceased talking and glanced over to see what had upset her.

Taking that as an invitation to join them, Betty

nodded at the girls. "I wanted a moment to speak to Priscilla alone."

The words dropped into the silence like a heavy boulder into a lake. Unease rippled out from the splash, and several girls backed away. Betty's steady stare dispersed the rest of them. All except Hope.

She gave Priscilla's hand a quick squeeze before letting go to smooth the front of her apron. Then she faced Betty. "Whatever you need to say to Priscilla, you can say in front of me."

Betty hesitated. "I'm not sure that's appropriate."

"Hope is my friend, and I'd like her to stay."

With a heavy sigh, Betty said, "I understand you don't plan to kneel in front of the church today. You should be up there confessing."

Priscilla would be, if she had something to confess.

Hope beamed at Betty. "That's kind of you to care so much about Priscilla, and it's good advice."

Startled, Betty took a step back, and her eyebrows arched. "It's what God would have us do when we sin."

"So, if Priscilla hasn't chosen to do it today, I'm sure she has a good reason." Hope's sweet smile stayed in place.

"I suppose," Betty mumbled. "I'll be praying," she said to Priscilla before heading off.

"*Danke*," Priscilla whispered once Betty was out of earshot.

"Of course," Hope responded. "I only spoke the truth."

As she crossed the room, Betty looked over her shoulder at the two of them. This time, her concerned frown appeared more motherly than judgmental. Was it because she truly cared? Or was she putting on a pious act in front of the other members?

Inwardly, Priscilla berated herself. Her judgment of Betty was harsh. She had no way to assess whether or not Betty's actions were genuine.

Right now, she had little time to think about that, because the service was about to start.

With Hope, Priscilla filed into a bench on the women's side of the room. As they sang from the *Ausbund*, each line seemed to drag more than the one before, and every verse of their second hymn, "Das Loblied," slowed in Priscilla's mouth, making the syllables stretch long and interminably.

The seconds crawled by until Priscilla wanted to beg for mercy. She refused to check the men's side of the room, because she might fall apart if she glimpsed Matthew. She only prayed he had come today and intended to confess. Although she dreaded the pity she'd face, at least she'd leave church with her reputation intact.

Matthew must have worked everything out with Mara's *daed*, because he still had his job. If he'd lost his position, Priscilla's *mamm* would have heard and spread the news. Unless Matthew's admission would be a shock to Mel today. Maybe Matthew counted on the community to pressure Mara's *daed* to forgive him. But would Mel allow Mara near Matthew after he heard the news?

At least I prevented him from firing Matthew in a fit of temper. This way, Mel would be forced to take his time and make a measured, well-reasoned decision because the whole church would be scrutinizing his actions. And despite the disapproval Priscilla had faced, she was glad she'd protected Matthew's *mamm*. And soon, very soon, everyone would learn the truth.

Her stomach tied in knots, Priscilla clasped her hands in her lap to keep from wringing them when Matthew stood and moved to the center of the church. She stared down at her white church apron to avoid seeing the people gawking at her.

Briefly glancing up through her eyelashes, Priscilla teared up at the picture of Matthew on his knees. Humbling himself before God. Once that would have set her heart fluttering. Now it only caused her stomach to sink with dread. Hearing him tell everyone he'd been with Mara would rip her apart inside. She already imagined the gasps.

His head bowed, and his words barely audible,

Matthew mumbled, "I've done something I am ashamed to admit. I . . . got carried away and kissed and touched, um, places I shouldn't have. I have begged God's forgiveness, and I ask you all to pray for me."

Matthew's words buzzed in Priscilla's head. Wait, he hadn't mentioned Mara. He hadn't said . . .

Most heads craned in Priscilla's direction. They all assumed Matthew had been with her. Instead of clearing her, his confession made her appear guilty. Everyone must be wondering why she hadn't knelt and admitted her wrongs.

In addition to cheating on her with Mara, Matthew had once again—this time in front of the whole community—betrayed her. He'd implicated her when she was innocent. If she contradicted him, she'd look like she was pointing fingers to deflect the blame.

Chapter Seven

After the service, Priscilla fixed her gaze on the floor as she exited. Her bowed head might make her appear guilty or ashamed, but it prevented her from seeing anyone's condemnation. If only she could find a place to hide so she didn't have to face the prying eyes.

"I'm so sorry," Hope whispered as they made their way to the kitchen after church.

Her eyes filled with reproach, Mamm stared at Priscilla as they both helped to prepare the meal. Her mother also kept to herself and avoided her usual chattering. Mamm's attitude tore at the fragile barrier Priscilla had erected to hide her feelings, and she fought back tears. If her own mother didn't believe in her innocence, why would anyone else?

Rather than carrying serving dishes out to the food tables, Priscilla made lemonade and filled empty platters in a far corner of the kitchen, keeping her back to the hustle and bustle around her.

"Priscilla?" A soft voice startled her.

Matthew's *mamm* had rolled her wheelchair behind Priscilla. She had been so intent on blocking everyone out, she hadn't noticed Ruth's approach.

"I'd like to talk to you privately. Would you be able to stop by on Tuesday after work?"

"Of course." Ruth probably intended to lecture her too. Unless Matthew had told his *mamm* about Mara. If he had, why would she want to talk to his ex-girlfriend? If he hadn't, should Priscilla tell her the truth? Knowing Ruth, she'd likely insist Matthew tell the congregation about Mara.

Ruth stayed beside Priscilla, helping with the kitchen chores but also serving as a buffer between Priscilla and the rest of the women. Did Ruth do that on purpose or accidentally? Either way, Priscilla was grateful. Unlike her son, she remained supportive and loyal.

The whole while they'd been courting, Priscilla had assumed Matthew loved her, but every time he had the opportunity to proclaim her innocence, he hadn't cared enough to clear her name. Mara's needs had come first for him. That cut as deeply as his cheating.

Gabe hoped to slip out without committing to attending the youth meeting, but Levi stopped him as they exited the house.

"Hope we'll see you tonight," he said.

Saul came up behind them, carrying his youngest son, who'd fallen asleep. "Gabe will be there. I'm sure he'll enjoy getting to know all of you."

"Great." Levi gave a brief wave. "See you tonight, then." He hurried over to help an elderly woman into her son's carriage.

Gabe sighed to himself. His brother had trapped him into going.

"Could you get in the back," Saul asked, "and hold Jayden?"

"*Neh.*" His sister-in-law slipped past him with the baby. "I'll get in the back. Gabe will need more room to hold Jayden."

After they'd all settled in, Gabe turned to his brother. "I wish you hadn't done that."

Saul wrinkled his brow. "Done what?"

"Said I'd go to the singing."

His brother flicked the reins to start the horse. "You'll have a good time. They're a friendly bunch."

Besides being uncomfortable in groups of strangers, which Saul certainly knew, Gabe had another excuse for not going. "If I go to the singings, people may think I'm looking for someone to court. I can't do that. You know my situation back in Bucks County."

"It's time you let go of that. How long has it been? Five years now?"

More like seven. "You don't understand." Gabe had made a promise. A promise he intended to keep.

For a while, they rode in silence, and Gabe gazed down at his sleeping nephew. Jayden's weight in Gabe's arms and the damp patch on his sleeve where his nephew's head lay brought back Priscilla's words. She'd stirred a longing in his soul to have a family. He wanted to pass down the business to his children. But that might be an impossible dream.

That yearning stayed with him as he milked the cows and camels later that afternoon. Saul had sent Tim over to help, so he tended to some of the cows while Gabe milked the camels. Camels grew used to one milker and usually only gave milk to the person they'd bonded with. Even then, it was hard work for only a tiny yield. People always questioned why camel's milk was so expensive, but unlike cows, who readily produced milk, camels gave very little.

Despite Tim's help, Gabe didn't finish until almost five thirty, and he still had to clean up. By the time he arrived, he'd missed the volleyball game and the food. Everyone sat at the tables— boys on one side, girls on the other—singing a hymn.

If he'd been late like this in his home district, he'd have received a letter of reprimand. Would he get in trouble here? Most likely not for the first time. Maybe if he explained his situation to the parents who oversaw the attendance, they'd understand why he'd rather not join the group.

Although most of the girls, except for a few shy ones, smiled at him, Gabe gave only fleeting smiles in return. Granted, they were just being friendly, but he didn't want anyone to think he was interested. After he'd acknowledged everyone with a nod or smile, he kept his eyes fixed on the songbook even though he knew the words.

When they took a break for a snack, some girls made beelines for their boyfriends, but several clustered around Gabe.

They introduced themselves and giggled as he struggled to respond. Once again, they fired questions at him, making him nervous and mute.

"Are you the one with the camels?" "Where did you come from?" "Are camels hard to care for?" "What made you choose camels?" "Do you like it here?"

Remembering Saul's assistance earlier, Gabe tried to concentrate on one question at a time, but his cheeks burned as he stuttered out his first answer.

"Wait," one girl said. "Maybe we should give him some time to think between questions."

He shot her a relieved smile, and she beamed at him. He hoped he hadn't given her the wrong impression.

"Why did you choose camels?" she asked.

Keeping his eyes fixed on the floor, Gabe went into a rambling explanation of his reasons and made a hash of trying to list the benefits of camel's milk. If only Priscilla were here, she'd be able to explain all this better than he could. He wasn't sure if any of what he was saying made sense, but maybe if he kept talking, he wouldn't have to answer any more questions.

He sighed with relief when everyone headed back to the tables to resume singing. As he rushed toward the spot where he'd been sitting, he passed two girls whispering together.

"I wonder if he has a girlfriend," one said.

She looked up to see Gabe beside her, and scarlet crept up her neck and into her cheeks. He longed to settle their speculation by telling them he was unavailable. Instead, he walked by as if he hadn't heard.

But the question raised a longing in Gabe that stayed with him throughout the singing and on his lonely ride home. A longing for a relationship, to be close to someone, to have a home and family.

Although he shouldn't be thinking about any girls, Gabe had evaluated all of them tonight by one ideal—Priscilla. And no matter how nice these girls seemed, none of them even came close to her.

On Tuesday, Mamm picked Priscilla up after school to take her to Ruth's. After helping Asher into the back seat of the buggy with her other brothers and sisters, Priscilla took the front seat beside Mamm. Her mother planned to take Asher for his horse therapy at Hope's farm, so she'd drop Priscilla off and pick her up in a little over an hour.

Although Priscilla usually loved visiting Ruth, all day long she'd dreaded this visit. Since Sunday, she'd struggled with forgiving Matthew. Each time she recalled his confession, she had to pray about her anger.

He'd still be at work today, so she wouldn't run into him. And she had no idea what she'd say to him when she eventually faced him. But sometime soon they had to talk.

When Mamm pulled the buggy into Ruth's driveway, Priscilla steeled herself. This was the first time she'd been at Matthew's house since . . .

All the happy memories of spending time here with him and his *mamm* were swept away in a tsunami of pain.

Closing her eyes and taking a deep breath, Priscilla forced herself to open the buggy door.

Before she exited, Mamm laid a hand on her arm. "Please make peace with Matthew."

Priscilla had been trying, spending time on her knees and begging God to fill her with forgiveness.

"Remember what I said about apologizing. One person has to make the first move. Why not be the first to say you're sorry?"

"Mamm!" Priscilla's cry, low and desperate, came from deep inside her wounded soul.

"I know it isn't easy, especially if you feel you were wronged."

Priscilla turned her head away so Mamm

wouldn't see how much her words hurt. They had to find a way to let Mamm know what happened without starting a chain of gossip.

"Matthew is at work," Priscilla said through gritted teeth. "I'm visiting Ruth."

"If the chance arises, I hope you'll take it," Mamm said as Priscilla stepped from the buggy.

She waved goodbye to her family and waited while Mamm turned Butterscotch around and headed down the driveway. Then, after praying for courage, Priscilla knocked on the front door.

"Come in," Ruth called out.

Like she'd done so many times before, Priscilla turned the knob and entered. Only this time everything had shifted, and nothing would ever be the same.

Ruth waited for her in the kitchen. "Would you like some tea?"

Sipping a hot drink might soothe Priscilla's nerves. "*Danke*, that sounds good."

Ruth had everything set out, and Priscilla lifted the steaming kettle from the stove to pour water into the cups. Then she sat in her usual spot near Ruth.

They both remained silent as they stirred in sugar and took their first sips.

Then Ruth set her cup in the saucer with a small clink. "I'm glad you came. I don't know who else I can talk to about Matthew. I'm worried. He's been so secretive lately."

Despite the tea she'd just swallowed, Priscilla's mouth went dry. Yes, Matthew had definitely been keeping secrets. From everyone.

"When I found out the two of you were no longer courting, it broke my heart."

It had broken Priscilla's as well.

"Matthew said you were the one who ended the relationship." Ruth sounded close to tears. "I didn't ask you here to change your mind, but I thought you might know what's been going on with him."

Priscilla choked on her tea and took a while to regain her composure.

"I love my son, but he dislikes rules. I never worried when he was with you. Now I'm not so sure."

She'd be even more concerned if she knew the whole truth. Learning he'd been sneaking around behind her back had been painful for Priscilla, but the fact that he'd lied to the whole church revealed he hadn't come clean before God. And hiding what he was doing from his *mamm* and Mara's *daed* made it even worse.

Ruth studied her. "One thing confused me about his confession. Why did he do it alone?"

Priscilla took a sip of tea. How did she answer that?

Ruth didn't give her a chance. "I know you, Priscilla. You'd be the first to confess if you'd done something wrong. You didn't join him, so there must be a good reason for your silence."

Jah, a very good reason, but not one she could share with Ruth. Priscilla's hand trembled a little as she lowered the cup into the saucer and racked her brains for an answer.

"Please look at me, Priscilla," Ruth commanded. After she'd probed Priscilla with her gaze, she nodded. "I thought so."

Priscilla hoped her eyes hadn't revealed any secrets.

Ruth took her hands. "It used to be we could talk about anything, you and I."

"I know." Priscilla lowered her eyes.

"Answer me one question: Were you with Matthew that night?"

Ruth somehow had guessed the truth. Tears rushed to Priscilla's eyes, and she blinked to hold them back. Even Mamm hadn't had this much faith in Priscilla's integrity. All the love Priscilla harbored for Ruth washed over her, overwhelming her, so she couldn't speak.

All it would take was one shake of her head, but Priscilla couldn't bring herself to confirm Ruth's fears. Finally, she choked out, "I don't feel right telling you. Please ask Matthew."

"That won't work." Ruth let go of Priscilla's hands and clenched the arms of her wheelchair.

The hurt underlying Ruth's words made Priscilla ache. "I'm sorry."

"You're like the daughter I never had." Ruth's

voice trembled. "Can you at least explain?"

"Please don't ask me to do that." Besides, Priscilla had no explanation. She had no idea why Matthew had strayed. Sometimes she blamed herself, but she kept coming back to one point: Matthew should have discussed it with her if he had a problem with her. They could have worked things out.

"I asked you here because Matthew refuses to answer me. I have one more question." She paused and looked right into Priscilla's eyes. "Have you been meeting Matthew secretly in the evenings since the bishop suggested you spend time apart?"

Although she didn't want to and as much as it pained her, Priscilla could answer that. "*Neh*, I've not seen Matthew at all."

Ruth lowered her head and traced a swollen, arthritic finger around the rim of her empty teacup. "I was afraid of that. I hoped it was you, prayed it was you, but you'd never have kept him out so late."

Each word was a stab to Priscilla's bloodied heart. How many nights was Matthew out? The thought of Matthew with Mara—

She refused to allow herself to visualize it. How did Mara's father not realize what his daughter was doing?

"Is he with someone else?" Although she phrased it as a question, Ruth's tone indicated certainty. Before Priscilla could respond, Ruth held up a hand. "Never mind. I can see the answer in your eyes."

Priscilla couldn't stop the spurt of hot tears that flooded her eyes.

"Do you still love him?" Ruth's gentle probing opened the wound Priscilla had been trying to conceal.

Priscilla had to be honest. "I don't know." And she truly didn't. A different face intruded on her thoughts. Gabe. Had she ever truly loved Matthew if someone else could distract her that easily?

To give herself time to compose her emotions, Priscilla took the teacups to the kitchen sink and washed them. By the time she returned to the table, Ruth had her eyes closed. Her lips moved as if in prayer.

Priscilla hesitated, reluctant to interrupt. But Mamm would be here soon, and she didn't want to leave without saying goodbye.

Then Ruth lifted her head, her eyes shining. "Everything is in God's hands. All we need to do is trust."

Priscilla nodded. That was true. God had everything under control. She could trust His leading.

She'd been dating Matthew since they both turned eighteen. In all that time, she'd never really prayed about their decision to court. It had just seemed right at the time. What if she'd prayed about God's will? Would she have saved herself this heartbreak?

She wanted to ask Ruth that question. Matthew's *mamm* had always proved to be a wise counselor.

As if Ruth had read her thoughts, she reached for Priscilla's hand and squeezed it. "I'm sure you have many regrets, but the most important thing right now is to ask God what He wants you to learn."

Ruth's advice would keep Priscilla from focusing on the past and instead turn her attention to how she needed to live in the present. "I'd better go outside. Mamm should be here soon."

"I'm glad you came." The quaver in Ruth's voice revealed the depth of her feelings.

Priscilla leaned down and hugged her. "*Danke* for everything." Then, her eyes misty, she left the house.

To her surprise, her family's buggy stood in the driveway, and Butterscotch was tied to a post. But where was Mamm? She hadn't come to the door.

As Priscilla hurried toward the buggy, Mamm's voice floated from behind the house. Turning, Priscilla followed the driveway around to the barn. When she spotted Matthew, her steps faltered.

He was home from work early. And what was Mamm doing out here with him? Priscilla had a good suspicion.

"I hope you'll forgive my daughter," she was saying as Priscilla came up behind her. "I know you two can work things out."

Matthew shifted uncomfortably from foot to foot. "I don't think—" His eyes widened when he spied Priscilla. He glanced around like a trapped rabbit searching for escape.

"I know Priscilla misses you."

At those words, Matthew searched her face. Did he think she'd sent Mamm to plead her case? To try to get them back together?

"Mamm?" Priscilla hadn't intended her tone to be that sharp. But she had to stop her mother from bargaining for a boyfriend.

"*Ach*, Priscilla, you frightened me. Why were you sneaking around like that?"

Priscilla ignored the question. "What are you doing?"

Mamm's sheepish smile revealed her guilt. "I was just telling Matthew how much we've missed him."

Matthew glanced at Priscilla, and his gaze skittered away.

"I know he did something he shouldn't have, but he confessed. You need to forgive him," Mamm wheedled.

Bile rose in Priscilla's throat. *Jah*, he'd confessed. But he hadn't told the truth.

The daggers she shot in Matthew's direction hit their mark. He squirmed and ran a finger around

121

the back of his collar. At least he had the grace to look ashamed.

"We should go." Priscilla took Mamm's arm and steered her toward the buggy.

"But I want to invite Matthew to supper tomorrow night."

"Matthew has other plans." Priscilla kept her voice low.

Mamm dragged her to a stop, and a gleam lit her eyes. "With you?"

"*Neh*, not with me." Definitely not with her. Not ever again.

Daed was waiting for them when they arrived home. "I wondered where everyone was. The boys should be out here to help with the milking."

"I'm sorry we're late." Mamm scurried into the kitchen to start supper.

"Just a minute," Daed said to Priscilla. "You look upset. What's going on?"

"If I hadn't interrupted her, I'm afraid Mamm might have tried to convince Matthew to marry me."

"*Ach*, I'm sorry. I'll set her straight."

Priscilla clutched her hands together. "You're going to tell her about Matthew?"

Smoothing down his beard, Daed looked troubled. "I don't think that'll be necessary." He beckoned for Priscilla to follow him into the kitchen.

She moved to help Mamm while Daed sat at the

table. He cleared his throat, and Mamm looked over at him.

"Esther, Priscilla has broken up with Matthew. I don't believe he's the best choice for our daughter."

"They've been dating for years, and you never objected." Mamm dabbed at her eyes with the edge of her apron.

"I've changed my mind, and so has Priscilla. Please don't try to get them back together."

"But—but . . ."

Daed rarely gave orders. He preferred to discuss decisions with Mamm or the family, if it concerned them. So one stern gaze proved to be enough to silence her.

But talking to Ruth and running into Matthew had stirred up a hornets' nest of emotions. And Priscilla endured the sting of each one.

Chapter Eight

Priscilla grumbled to herself the next morning as she sat in a long line of traffic waiting for the crew working on the road to turn the *Stop* sign to *Slow*. She'd done an errand for Mamm and had gotten a bit behind. Now she'd be late for school. Priscilla prided herself on being early, so this would ruin her perfect record. One more glitch on this gray, rainy morning.

The cars ahead of her moved through the roadblock, but the worker flipped the sign as she approached. Now she'd have to be patient while another long line of cars passed before she could get through. By the time she pulled her buggy into the parking lot, all the scholars had entered the schoolhouse, and Ada had shut the door.

She raced across the parking lot and into the building, arriving in the schoolroom chilly and drenched. "Sorry I'm late," she puffed out between gasps. "I didn't walk this morning because . . . I had to run an errand for Mamm . . . before school, and Main Street is . . . under construction."

"Oh, Priscilla, I'm so glad you're here. We won't have time to talk right now, but can you stay after school? We have something we need to discuss."

"Of course."

From Ada's pursed lips and sorrowful eyes, Priscilla guessed Betty had complained about her lateness. From time to time, her friend's gaze, filled with pity, flicked toward her, but they had no time to chat. With the thunderstorm outside, the scholars had indoor recess and lunch at their desks.

As the clock inched its way toward the end of the day, Priscilla could barely concentrate. Finally, at three o'clock, she, Ada, and Martha helped the students gather their lunch boxes and made sure the walkers donned reflective safety vests. Priscilla had been on edge all afternoon and couldn't wait for dismissal.

As usual, toward the end of the day, the scholars grew restless. Two of them had meltdowns. Martha managed her brother Lukas's screaming fit, and Priscilla distracted Will with a toy wind-mill while Ada put away the supplies he'd been using.

When Betty drove into the parking lot to pick up Lukas and Martha, Ada sent Priscilla into the coatroom to check for several last-minute lost items. "Take your time," she whispered.

Priscilla appreciated Ada's thoughtfulness when Betty's strident tones echoed through the schoolroom.

"Did she not show up at all today?" Betty demanded.

"You mean Priscilla?" Ada's calm, measured tones contrasted with Betty's fretful ones. "Yes, she arrived. Road construction on Main Street held her up this morning."

Betty sounded disbelieving. "She walks to school."

"She didn't today," Ada explained.

"And now she's left early before all the scholars?"

"*Neh*, of course not. She's busy hunting for lost items."

"If you made sure they went in the proper cubbies, that wouldn't be a problem." Betty's tart response made her displeasure obvious.

"I appreciate the advice," Ada said calmly.

Priscilla stayed hidden until Betty had gone. Then she came out holding the missing items.

Ada flashed her a rueful smile. "Perfect timing."

"I planned it," Priscilla admitted.

"I don't blame you. I do wish you'd been here early this morning, though. You picked a bad day to be late."

"Why? What happened?"

As she often did, Will's *mamm* pulled into the schoolyard twenty minutes after dismissal.

"Let's get Will ready to go, and then we can talk." Ada led Will over to his mother, then she and Priscilla both waved them off.

When Ada returned, her face was grave, but

she made an effort to smile. "Let me tell you the good news first. We got approval for the field trip to Hope's farm, and the regular schoolhouse will join us. I haven't told the scholars yet, but we'll need some parents to go with us. I don't know how some of our scholars will be around the camel."

"Camels," Priscilla corrected. "Gabe's bringing a mother and baby."

"That'll be fun for all the children."

Priscilla hoped so, but even more, she prayed it would help both of her friends get more business.

Ada's smiled slipped. "Now for the not-so-good news." She hesitated and didn't meet Priscilla's eyes. "John Beiler stopped by this morning to speak with you. He waited around until almost time for school to start."

Ach, John was on the school board. He might assume she always arrived late.

"I did tell him this was the only time you'd ever been late, but I'm not sure he believed me." Ada took a deep breath. "He came to tell you the school board will meet on Saturday at one. They want you to attend."

"Saturday afternoon?" They usually met once a month in the evening. They must consider this an emergency. Choking back her worry, Priscilla asked, "Did he say what it was about?"

Ada shook her head. "A sudden meeting like

this? I imagine it's about you and Matthew, don't you?"

"I figured that. I meant do you think they'll . . ."

"I don't know." Ada looked troubled. "I did tell him you're doing a wonderful job with the scholars. I wish I could be there with you."

"I wish you could too." Priscilla didn't look forward to facing the school board members alone.

"I know this won't be a problem," Ada told her, "but John stressed several times that you shouldn't be late."

Priscilla sighed. Now in addition to being in trouble over Matthew, she'd probably be called to account for being tardy.

Would they take away her teaching position? She loved working with these children, and she'd dreamed of taking over as head teacher next fall. All because of Matthew, her hopes might come crashing down.

Gabe paced near the door. The clock hands had passed three, and Tim should be here soon, but Gabe wasn't watching for his nephew.

Priscilla had signed up for Wednesday pickups. Gabe had already set aside her order. Now he could barely wait until she arrived, because he had some good news she'd appreciate. How long would it take for her to get here after school? He hoped she'd come right away rather than waiting until later in the evening.

A fancy SUV with tinted windows pulled up outside the shop. Jersey plates, but not Henry Defarge, who drove a red Lexus convertible. But could this be another person from the company threatening him?

The SUV door clicked open, and Gabe's eyes widened as Fleurette stepped from the driver's side. He should have recognized her vehicle, but he'd been so busy puzzling over her behavior and checking out her license plate the last time she'd been here that he hadn't noticed its appearance.

If Priscilla was right, Fleurette had put the coolers into her trunk. No wonder she'd insisted on carrying her own bags and stood waiting until he went back into the store to load her purchases. She hadn't wanted him to see all the stolen goods she'd stashed in her car. Had she also taken the additional missing gallons of milk?

He should confront her about the theft, but as usual, when it came to confrontations or presentations, he clammed up. After all, how did you accuse someone of stealing without any proof?

He pushed open the door as she neared. Gathering his courage, he determined he'd say something. He just didn't know what yet. He only hoped when the time came, he could push understandable words out in the right order.

"Remember me?" Fleurette strode to the door, an expensive leather folder clutched tightly in her arms.

"*Jah*, um, yes," he mumbled. Now was not the time to be tongue-tied. He needed to ask questions, demand answers.

Before he could open his mouth, she breezed through the door he held open. "You don't sound too pleased, but maybe when I tell you why I'm here, you'll change your mind." She headed straight for the desk Tim used for tallying up sales.

Gabe fought the urge to rush ahead of her and clear away the receipt books, business brochures, and unopened mail. For some reason, he'd rather not have her prying eyes on any of it.

She frowned at the plain wooden straight chair. "Do you have any other seats?"

He could offer her one of the large plastic buckets they used for storing milk. He pinched his lips together to hold back a snicker at the thought of Fleurette in her linen pants and silk blouse sitting on the bucket. Although it wasn't too much worse than the dust-covered chair.

Taking pity on her, he ducked into his office and pushed out the old rolling office chair he'd gotten at a benefit auction for two dollars. He'd duct-taped the rip in the leather seat. It might not be beautiful, but it would be more comfortable than the wooden chair. And it was clean.

"Take your pick," he said as he scooted the chair closer to her.

She eyed both chairs, and her nose wrinkled. "Never mind. I'll stand. This won't take long."

The door banged open, and Tim rushed in. "Sorry I'm late."

"It's all right. We don't have any customers yet," Gabe assured him.

"But . . ." Tim looked at Fleurette.

Gabe motioned to the two chairs. "We were just getting ready to talk."

Tim's gaze flicked back and forth between them. "What do you want me to do, then?"

"The orders for today's pickups are on my desk. You can pack those coolers." Gabe glanced at Fleurette for a reaction, but other than tapping a toe impatiently and appearing bored, she exhibited no guilt. "And the shipment of vitamins that came yesterday can be shelved."

Tim nodded and headed for the office. Gabe returned his attention to Fleurette. "You had something to show me?"

"My husband is tired of buying small quantities of milk." She set her calfskin folder on the desk and opened it.

Gabe didn't recall selling to anyone named Moreau. "Your husband?"

"Henry Defarge." Her abrupt manner indicated that she'd rather not discuss him.

Defarge, the businessman from New Jersey

131

who had tried to buy the business last week, the one who bought a huge order every week, but only paid a pittance? And his wife had stolen camel's milk? She must assume he didn't suspect her because he'd never pursued her for payment or even mentioned it since she came in the door. Either that or she was brazen.

"Instead of small shipments each week, we'd prefer to buy the business."

Gabe struggled to find words. He'd been through this with Defarge and preferred to avoid an argument. "I did discuss this with your husband."

"I know." She shot him a seductive smile. "But you'll find I'm much more persuasive than my husband."

Gabe hoped she didn't mean that the way it sounded.

"Here's what we're proposing." Fleurette ran a finger with a bloodred nail down the first paper in her folder. "We won't go any higher than the price my husband planned to offer, but you'll find we can be flexible on some of the other negotiations."

"Negotiations?" Gabe echoed faintly. Hadn't he made it clear he didn't plan to sell?

"You're interested in how I plan to sweeten the deal?" She moved closer.

At the predatory look in her eyes, Gabe scrambled backward, but bumped into the wooden chair behind him. Pinned in place, he tried to ward off her embrace.

"I'm happy to add certain unwritten considerations into the deal." She snaked her arms around his neck and pressed closer, trying to draw his head down to meet her pursed lips.

"I-I'm not interested," he managed to stammer, struggling to free himself without hurting her.

The store door opened behind him, and Gabe swiveled his head. *Priscilla?*

She stood framed in the doorway for a few seconds, one hand on the doorknob, her eyes wide with shock. Then she turned, and the door slammed.

"No!" Gabe kicked at the wooden chair behind him, pushed Fleurette away, and raced to the door.

By the time he reached the parking lot, Priscilla's buggy was rattling down the driveway in a flurry of gravel.

"Priscilla, wait!"

Back ramrod straight, she ignored his calls. He pounded after her, but he was no match for her horse's speed.

Fleurette sidled up beside him and set a hand on his arm. "Don't worry. Wives get over their little snits. Most men have a little extracurricular activity on the side."

"We don't. Amish men believe in being faithful to their spouses."

She waggled her eyebrows as if she didn't believe him. "How quaint."

"Nothing quaint about it. It's God's will." He'd never been so vocal in an argument before, but Fleurette had just destroyed the best relationship he'd had in his life. The thought of never seeing Priscilla again devastated him. Even worse, she'd think he was a cheat.

Guilt washed over Gabe as he realized the truth. He'd been falling for Priscilla all along. But he had no business thinking of her that way, not when he couldn't date or marry.

Priscilla couldn't get away fast enough. She was driving recklessly, but she couldn't let Gabe catch up to the buggy. He might mistake the moisture in her eyes for tears.

After Matthew, she'd vowed never to let another man close enough to hurt her. And she'd intended to keep that vow. Somehow Gabe had wormed his way past her defenses and into her heart.

She hadn't meant for that to happen, but now that it had, she had to face the truth. Men couldn't be trusted.

After spending time with Gabe, she'd been convinced he was different. Finding out he could be tempted—and, even worse, by an *Englischer*—was a blow. She'd wondered about him the first day she'd come here after he'd been so solicitous toward that woman Fleurette. Since then she'd started to trust him and to believe he was honorable. How could she have been so wrong?

After she reached the end of the driveway, Priscilla slowed her horse. "I'm sorry, Butterscotch," she whispered. Her horse shouldn't pay for her pain.

Lord, please show me what to do, she pleaded. Only God could help her with her runaway feelings. She let Butterscotch mosey along as she poured out her sadness in prayer.

When she was done, she felt lighter. She released Matthew and Gabe from her expectations. What they chose to do was between them and God. Her responsibility was to love them as a Christian sister. Except her feelings for Gabe were definitely not sisterly.

Maybe this was God's way of warning her she shouldn't get involved with Gabe. Or maybe . . . His face flashed through her mind. He'd looked desperate. Had she made a mistake?

Now that God had freed her mind of old distress, a clearer picture came into view. Gabe's arms hadn't been around the *Englischer.* In fact, he might have been wriggling away. Had she jumped to conclusions because of Matthew?

The only way to find out was to go back to the store. After checking both ways, Priscilla turned Butterscotch at the next crossroads. She clucked to encourage the horse to gallop. If she'd misjudged Gabe, she owed him an apology.

After tying Butterscotch to the railing, she hurried toward the store. This time she eased the door open a crack. Gabe stood behind a wooden chair that he'd placed between him and the *Englischer.*

With his white-knuckled hands clenched on the top rail of the chair and his tense jaw, he appeared ready to fend off an attacking lion. He hadn't picked up the chair and pointed the legs in the woman's direction . . . *yet.* But he sure looked like he longed to do so.

Startling people often threw them off balance. Priscilla shoved the door so hard, it flew open and crashed into the wall. The woman jumped. Gabe did too, but he went backward, away from the *Englischer.*

The woman exhaled a shaky breath. "You scared us."

That had been Priscilla's intention. But when the *Englischer,* still clutching her hands to her heart, pivoted, Priscilla was shocked. *Fleurette Moreau? The thief?*

A cunning smile crossed Fleurette's face before she turned to Gabe. "See, I said your wife would forgive you. Didn't take her long, did it? But with you being such a hunk, I can understand it."

His wife? Priscilla shot Gabe a *what-is-she-talking-about?* look that he met with pleading eyes and a slight flick of his head, as if indicating he wanted her to stand beside him.

Fleurette sneered as Priscilla moved next to him. "Standing by your man? Even though you don't know what he was up to while you were gone?"

"I didn't do anything." Gabe glanced at Priscilla as if begging her to believe him.

"I know," she said with conviction.

The gratitude in Gabe's eyes warmed her all the way to her toes.

With a huff, Fleurette picked up an open folder on the desk. "If you two are done making googly eyes at each other, maybe we can get down to business."

Priscilla faced her. "You came to pay for the camel's milk?"

"What are you talking about? What milk?"

"The camel's milk you stole the last time you were here." Priscilla glanced at Gabe to check for confirmation.

Although he stayed silent, his nod encouraged her to continue questioning the *Englischer.*

"Don't be ridiculous." Fleurette flicked her hand, dismissing Priscilla. "I only took a few samples to advertise the business. It brought you in a huge order."

Priscilla wasn't about to let her cheat Gabe. "It was more than a few samples. You carted off multiple gallons, along with three large coolers."

"I hope you aren't accusing me of stealing. You have no proof. Those coolers sitting outside could have been taken by anyone passing by." Fleurette's eyes narrowed. "If you repeat those lies, I'll sue you for character defamation."

Pent-up anger toward liars raced through Priscilla. Matthew had done wrong and then framed her. She'd been silent in the face of his lies, but she wouldn't allow this woman to get away with hers. "I watched you do it."

Despite her makeup, Fleurette paled. Then she blustered, "You certainly did not. No one was outside."

They'd just caught her in a lie. "So you are admitting it?" Priscilla pressed the point. "I was tying up my horse when you came out of the store and loaded multiple bags. You might not have noticed me on the far side of the buggy, but I definitely saw you." She didn't tell Fleurette that she'd been secretly staring at her fancy embroidered coat and wondering why she'd dressed like that in warm weather.

"I paid for those bags. Ask the boy." She called to Tim, who had come out of the freezer with a cooler. "I paid you for the milk, didn't I?"

Tim studied her for a moment before nodding.

"See?" she said triumphantly, turning to Priscilla.

Gabe stood there, shifting uncomfortably as his gaze bounced back and forth between them, two deep furrows on either side of his nose. Did he want her to stop questioning the customer?

But Priscilla had one more question, which she directed at Tim. "Did this lady pay you twice? Once before you got change and once after?"

"*Neh*, only one time."

Fleurette sniffed. "You told your son to lie."

"He's not—"

Gabe cut her off with a discreet wave of his hand. He looked so distressed, Priscilla kept silent.

Tossing her head, Fleurette shrugged. "No need to get all het up over a little milk when all this will be mine soon." She indicated the store and the fields beyond the window.

Priscilla gasped. "What?" She turned to Gabe.

For the first time, he spoke up. "*Neh*, I'm not selling." The finality of his words reassured Priscilla.

"You might change your mind if you're sued."

If only Priscilla could wipe that gloating smile off Fleurette's face. Instinctively, she moved closer to Gabe, wishing she could ward off the blow she sensed coming.

Chapter Nine

At the word sue, Gabe's mouth went dry. Fleurette sounded so sure of herself.

"My niece has been hospitalized due to a severe reaction to your milk. A lab analyzed the rest of the gallon and found it contained mainly cow's milk. Liesel is severely allergic to cow's milk."

No, please, God, don't let it be true. Gabe never filled the cow's milk and camel's milk bottles at the same time. They weren't even kept in the same area, but what if Tim had made an error? The thought of a little girl being in the hospital because of something he did . . .

Gabe could hardly breathe. If she was sick because of his milk, he'd take responsibility, but how could he afford more hospital bills? The ones he was already handling had been draining him.

"That's not true," Priscilla burst out.

Fleurette bristled. "Are you calling me a liar?" Whipping her cell phone from her purse, she thrust it toward Priscilla. "I have the hospital listed in favorites. Go ahead and call."

Priscilla backed up a few steps as Fleurette shoved the phone near her face. Gabe stepped over to stand between them. He might be tongue-tied when it came to sparring with people, but he wouldn't let Fleurette bully Priscilla.

The *Englischer* pounced on him instead. "I can tell by the guilty look on your face—it's the truth. Your wife may not know what you've done, but you do."

After stepping around him to face Fleurette, Priscilla stood her ground. "I didn't mean your niece wasn't in the hospital. I meant Gabe would never dilute his camel's milk."

Gabe winced, and Priscilla picked up on it. She turned questioning eyes in his direction. "You didn't, did you?"

"Not on purpose."

Priscilla planted her hands on her hips. "Accidentally? That's impossible. The cow's milk is through that door." She pointed to the nearest freezer door. "The camel's milk is on the very end of the shelves behind that door." She waved to the far door, where Tim was exiting with another cooler. "They aren't even close together, right?" she demanded of him.

"True, but what if Tim mixed up the cow's milk and the camel's milk?"

His nephew almost dropped the container he held. "I'd never do that."

Gabe regretted his words. "I didn't think you did. I was just giving an example."

Priscilla interrupted. "Even if someone had mixed them up, they'd only pour one kind into the bottle before sealing it."

Brilliant. He'd been so busy trying to figure out how it could have happened, he'd missed the most important point. "You're right. The containers would have contained all cow's milk. It would never have been mixed with camel's milk."

"Unless someone else tampered with it," Priscilla challenged Fleurette. "You should call the police," she said to him.

"You're bluffing." Fleurette's lips widened in a self-confident smile. "Henry told me Amish people never go to the cops." Her voice held a slight quaver.

So that explained why she'd had no fear of stealing from him.

"Normally we don't need to," Priscilla said.

With her hands on her hips and her eyes flashing, Priscilla made Gabe's heart race. Unlike him, she didn't trip over her words or get tongue-tied in an argument. And not only was she a skilled debater, she was defending him.

The tense lines on Fleurette's face relaxed a little, but Priscilla hadn't finished.

"We usually don't have any problems that we can't handle ourselves, but we do call the police when we need them."

"You don't have any reason to call." The shakiness in Fleurette's voice quickly hardened into slickness. "Besides, you have no proof. You have no security cameras inside or out."

"And you have no proof Gabe mixed the milk," Priscilla answered.

"We had it tested." The *Englischer*'s gloating smile made it clear she'd won.

"But if the container was open, the mixing could have happened anywhere." Priscilla picked up the leather folder and handed it to Fleurette. "I believe this belongs to you. And just so you know, the local police know we tell the truth, so they'll take my word as proof."

Fleurette snatched the folder and frowned at Gabe. "You need to get better control of your wife. I thought Amish wives were supposed to be docile and subservient."

For the first time since the feud began, Gabe managed a comeback. "I don't know where you got that idea." Or the idea that Priscilla was his wife. Her husband had said almost the same thing.

Surely her husband had told her Priscilla had turned down the offer to buy the business. Or maybe not. Perhaps he didn't want to admit he'd been outfoxed by an Amish woman.

Fleurette stalked across the room to the exit. "You haven't heard the last from me." She stormed out the door, letting it slam.

Gabe exhaled a long, slow sigh. His relief over Fleurette's departure was short-lived. Her parting words had sounded like a threat. How far would she go to take over his business?

If it hadn't been for Priscilla's snappy answers, he'd probably be paying another massive hospital bill right now. But he did worry about that little girl.

"I hope that story about her niece being in the hospital is fake."

"It probably is." Priscilla's statement, so sure and certain, reassured Gabe. "She wouldn't harm her own relative."

He hoped not. "*Danke* for standing up for me. I told you my tongue gets all tangled up when someone attacks me. I'll have to keep you around as my wife." He tried to say it teasingly, but some of his wistfulness oozed into the words.

He hoped Priscilla didn't pick up on his true feelings. He couldn't court her. No sense wishing for something that could never be.

His wife? All the air in Priscilla's chest escaped in a rush. The fluttering from earlier returned full force, and she couldn't draw in another breath.

Her jealousy at seeing him in Fleurette's embrace had made it clear how much she cared. Despite her decision not to trust a man, any man, she'd given away her heart. Was Gabe indicating he felt the same way?

"I definitely need to have you around for protection whenever Fleurette or her husband shows up." This time, Gabe's joking tone, accompanied by a laugh, made his intentions clear.

144

At least she hadn't revealed her interest in him. She tried to match his laugh, but hers came out rather hollow. "I guess the two of them don't know as much about the Amish as they think they do."

"That's for sure." Gabe rubbed a hand along his unshaven jaw. "If they did, they'd realize I'm not married."

Gabe's movement brought Priscilla's attention to his strong, masculine jawline. Although it proved he was unmarried, that didn't mean he wasn't courting someone. She bit her lip to keep herself from blurting out that question. Not that she needed to know. He'd made it clear his mention of her as his wife had been a joke.

"Anyway, I couldn't have done it without you."

His words soothed a little of the wound caused by his joke. "You didn't seem to need my help," she said.

"*Jah*, I did. If you didn't believe me when I told you about my speech problems, now you've seen how I fumble for answers."

"You did fine. I'm worried I talked too much."

Gabe shook his head. "Definitely not. You said just the right things."

That reminded Priscilla of why she'd come in the first place. "With all that went on with Fleurette, I almost forgot. You might need to prepare a talk for the event at Hope's horse farm."

"I was counting on you. Won't you be there?"

Priscilla's eyes stung. "I want to, but I may not be able to."

At Gabe's caring *Why?* Priscilla decided to spill the whole story. It wouldn't matter if she damaged her reputation with Gabe. He'd made it obvious just now that he wasn't interested in her. And he didn't know Matthew, so she wasn't harming his reputation or jeopardizing his job.

"You remember the first time I came into the store? I told you'd I'd had a shock?" Priscilla asked him.

How could he forget? He'd been drawn to her immediately, but when she'd collapsed trembling into the chair, his heart went out to her. He'd fretted about her after she left and hoped she'd made it home safely.

"Well," she continued, "I'd just found out"— she glanced at the floor and bit her lip—"my, um, boyfriend . . ."

The word stabbed into him. He should have expected anyone as lovely and kind as her to be in a relationship. Besides, he had no right to think about her that way.

". . . I guess now he's my ex-boyfriend . . ."

Though it shouldn't have affected him this way, Gabe's spirit danced with happiness. Not at her loss, but at his gain.

". . . Anyway, Matthew had just told me he'd been cheating on me."

"What?" Gabe's voice shook with anger. Any man lucky enough to court her should have realized her true worth. Why would he even look at another woman? "You're better off without him. He didn't deserve you."

Priscilla's eyes shot wide open.

He shouldn't have been so forceful. Gabe softened his tone. "I'm sorry. No wonder you were shaken up when you got here."

She winced and lowered her eyes. "I just rushed out of the house without eating and came here to distract myself."

That explained why she'd nearly fainted. "It must have been a shock."

Priscilla glanced up at him through her lashes, causing a deluge to sweep through him. "I'm sorry for causing so much trouble that day."

"I was happy to help." If he'd known why she'd arrived in such a state, he would have offered more than a sandwich.

"I appreciated it." A sweet, generous smile lit her face.

Her expression seemed to invite him to come closer. Gabe clutched his suspenders to keep his hands to himself.

Forcing his mind back to the conversation, he puzzled over how a breakup with her boyfriend—ex-boyfriend!—connected to the speech at Hope's. They'd gotten off track here, and he needed to get the conversation back to neutral ground.

"So, about Hope's?" he prompted, praying for a distraction.

"I'll get to that, but first I have more to explain." Priscilla traced small circles on the cement floor with the toe of her shoe. "Matthew confessed in church last Sunday."

She'd have to forgive him, but Gabe hoped they hadn't gotten back together.

"But he didn't mention who he, um, kissed and—" Priscilla's cheeks flushed crimson. "Everyone assumed it was me. They want me to confess, but I can't."

"Of course not. You didn't do anything wrong. That's easy enough to clear up. Just tell everyone the truth."

Priscilla shook her head. "Matthew's seeing his boss's daughter in secret. Her father's strict, so he's afraid she'll get in trouble. He asked me not to tell."

"I can't believe he asked you to lie for him." She'd sacrifice her reputation for a cheater and a louse?

"I couldn't either." Priscilla swallowed hard and appeared to be blinking back tears. "But if her *daed* finds out, Matthew will lose his job, and he supports his widowed *mamm*. I can't do that to her."

Gabe shook his head. She still cared about his *mamm* and wanted to protect her. Yet that heel couldn't even clear Priscilla's name. He'd

148

love to confront the coward. "But it isn't fair to you!"

Priscilla brushed off his comment. "That's not the issue. Today I learned the school board is meeting Saturday to decide if I can keep my job. They don't believe I'm a good role model."

"So instead of this Matthew losing his job, you're sacrificing yours? A job you love? A job you're good at? For a lie?" Anger vibrated through every word.

"I hadn't thought of it like that."

"You should."

"I debated about telling the school board the truth. Now that I've waited this long, though, I'm afraid they might not believe me. They might think I'm making it up to keep my job. And I can't tell them who Matthew was with."

"You still need to try. Think about the scholars you teach. You'll also be hurting them." Priscilla might not defend herself, but maybe she'd consider the children. At least Gabe hoped she would.

"I'll think about it," she said.

But she didn't sound at all certain. Knowing Priscilla, she probably didn't realize how valuable she was to the scholars. Just in the short while he'd known her, he could tell she cared about the children in the school, and she'd spent time researching ways to help them.

While she'd recounted her story, his hands had

knotted into fists. She'd roused his instincts to protect her the same way she'd defended him today. He'd love to give this Matthew a piece of his mind. But he had no idea how to find him. And what if he managed to confront Matthew and couldn't say a word?

The gray cloud hanging over Priscilla dissipated after sharing the story with Gabe. He'd championed her the way Matthew should have. She tempered her excitement by reminding herself of Gabe's reaction after he'd made the wife comment.

Despite killing her fantasies with practical—or realistic—interpretations of Gabe's words, Priscilla couldn't control a small thrill at his anger on her behalf. She had to be careful not to read too much into his response, though. After all, he'd demonstrated his kindness and caring while she was still a stranger.

Priscilla basked in the sunshine and gentle breezes on the way home, and she hummed under her breath while she fixed supper. Only Mamm's odd glances quieted her.

When everyone had gathered at the table and bowed their heads for the silent prayer, Priscilla asked for God's wisdom about what to tell the school board. She also added an extra *danke* to God for Gabe's friendship.

She lifted her head and met Mamm's eyes. The

concern radiating from her mother's look wiped the smile from Priscilla's face. And it brought thoughts of Matthew crashing back.

"I'm worried about you." Instead of passing the platter of ham, Mamm held it while she studied Priscilla's face. "You don't seem at all bothered about your reputation. Not confessing in church. Not apologizing to Matthew. If I were you, I'd be hanging my head in shame."

"Esther," Daed warned, "we talked about this yesterday."

"But what about her future?" Mamm wailed. "No one will ever want to marry her."

"You don't know that." Daed silenced her with sternness.

"Actually, a man told me today he'd like me to be his wife." The second she said it, Priscilla regretted it.

Mamm leaned forward eagerly. "Who was it?"

If only she could erase her words. "He was only joking."

"Maybe he wasn't. He couldn't be from our district, though. Nobody would say that, especially after—"

"Enough!" Daed thundered.

Pinching her lips shut, Mamm subsided. Daed sent Priscilla a sympathetic glance. Her siblings all concentrated on their plates, and no one said a word. Asher, who had shrunk back at Daed's loud tone, sat rocking back and forth in his chair.

Normally, he would have had a meltdown, but since his therapy at Hope's and drinking camel's milk, his nervous reactions to upsetting things had been confined to stims like hand-flapping, rocking, or flicking his hat brim.

"I'm sorry, Asher," Daed said in a quiet voice. "I shouldn't have yelled like that." He directed an apologetic look to everyone at the table, including Mamm.

Priscilla wished she'd held her tongue. Most of this was her fault. Keeping the truth about Matthew from Mamm had caused a major misunderstanding. One that they'd find hard to correct later.

The saltiness of the ham prickled her tongue, and the baked potato crumbled into dry and mealy flakes. Priscilla ate mechanically, chewing and swallowing each bite. She had to clean her plate, but she wished she could set her fork down and skip eating the rest of the food. All her earlier happiness slipped away.

They'd almost finished their supper when Mamm sucked in a sharp breath. "Camel's milk," she said suddenly.

All eyes turned toward her, but she pinned Priscilla with a pointed gaze. "Is the man who asked to marry you from the camel farm?"

"He didn't ask to marry me." Although Priscilla wished he had.

"You said he did."

"I told you he meant it as a joke."

Mamm's eyes narrowed. "Why would anyone tease about something like that?"

"He said it because an *Englisch* customer thought I was his wife."

"What gave her that impression?" The suspicion in Mamm's tone made Priscilla's supper curdle in her stomach.

"I assume because we're both Amish."

"And he's a married man?"

"No, he's single." Priscilla could guess where this was headed. "The woman obviously doesn't know much about the Amish to make that mistake."

"I see," Mamm said, but it was clear she saw much more than what Priscilla had told her.

Two of Priscilla's sisters cleared the table, while she helped Mamm serve dessert. Priscilla cut a thin sliver of shoofly pie for herself because she'd have trouble choking it down.

After they settled back at the table, Mamm wouldn't let the subject drop. "It sounds like this woman had a reason to make such a mistake. Why did you tell us he asked to marry you?"

"I didn't say he asked to marry me." Priscilla wished she'd never started this. Mamm would never let it drop. "After the *Englischer* left, he teased that he wished he could keep me around as his wife." To forestall her mother's questions, she added, "He's rather shy, and the woman was being pushy. I stood up for him. That's all it was."

"But he said he wanted you as his wife?"

"Just as a joke." How many times would she have to repeat it before Mamm listened? And accepted the truth? "He appreciated my helping him out of an awkward situation. He only meant he wanted me to deal with her if she came back. It was all in fun."

Mamm's raised eyebrows made it clear she didn't see it the same way. "Is this man one of the workers or—?"

"No, he's the owner."

As if the air had been released from a balloon, Mamm slumped in her chair. "Oh, so he's an older man."

Priscilla had made the same mistake, but she didn't correct Mamm's comment as she scraped up the last sticky bits of molasses and pie crumbs.

Mamm was nibbling at her lower lip and seemed lost in thought.

Before she could ask any more questions, Priscilla hopped up from her chair, grabbed several plates, and hurried to the sink. "It's my turn for dishes tonight." She turned to her youngest sister. "Are you ready to dry?"

That ended the conversation. But Priscilla worried about the calculating gleam that had appeared in Mamm's eyes earlier. That glint had died once she'd discovered Gabe was the owner and believed him to be an older man. Had she been hoping the camel farmer might be someone Priscilla could marry? If so, her thoughts weren't far from Priscilla's fantasies.

Chapter Ten

Gabe fumed about Matthew over the next two days. If only he had a way to help Priscilla. He had no idea how to contact the man, and he worried Priscilla might not stick up for herself. He did the only thing he could do—pray.

Every time Priscilla came to mind, Gabe sent up another plea to God. And because she remained in his thoughts most of the time, many, many prayers floated heavenward.

The phone rang just before closing on Friday, and a woman asked for the owner. After his experiences with Defarge and Fleurette, Gabe considered not revealing his identity. But it wouldn't be honest to lie.

"I'm the owner," he said. "Gabe Kauffman."

"Wonderful. I'm Alyssa McDonald with the *Central Pennsylvania Star.* We do print, online, and TV news for the area. I understand you own a camel farm. I'd like to learn more because I'm sure readers and viewers of our lifestyle section would be fascinated."

Air wheezed in and out of Gabe's lungs in the same erratic pattern as the woman's rapid-fire words. He needed to answer her.

Alyssa breezed on without pausing for breath. "Would you be available for an interview one day next week? What about Monday? The story would get you a lot of press."

Gabe clenched the phone in his hand and tried not to hyperventilate. How could he say no? Being featured in the news could help grow his business, but what if he couldn't answer any of her questions? He still hadn't managed to croak out a reply.

"Either ten a.m. or four p.m. would work well for me." Alyssa made it sound like he had no option but to cooperate.

He needed to respond. If he took an afternoon appointment, Priscilla might be able to attend. Having her here would help.

"Four." The word exploded into the receiver. *Ach*, he'd made a fool of himself.

"Wonderful. I'm excited about this opportunity. I'll be bringing Jake Davis along. He's a great shot. Maybe you've seen some of his work."

Shot? Guns? Gabe's mind raced. But she'd said *work?* Ach, *no! She must mean photos.* Most reporters in the area understood the Amish belief about not taking photographs. But what if she or Jake was new? He didn't want her showing up with a cameraman expecting to get pictures of him.

"Four on Monday, then. I appreciate your willingness to do this."

"No." *Ach*, that sounded like he was turning down the interview. "I mean no photos."

"None?" she practically shrieked into the phone. "People will want to see the camels."

He'd done it again. "Camel photos? Oh. I meant—I meant people."

A trill of laughter drifted over the phone line. "Right. Yes, yes, I'm aware the Amish don't want to be photographed. I planned to have our cameraperson shoot some footage of the farm and inside the store and barn. No one needs to be in any of the shots."

"I see." He could have kept quiet.

"I did hope, though, to see camel milking and take some pictures of you from behind, if you'd be all right with that."

Gabe didn't particularly want his picture, even of his back, splashed across the papers. The last time someone had snapped his picture for the newspaper . . .

Roiling started in Gabe's gut and crawled up toward his mouth. Acid burned in his chest. That picture had been from behind too.

"Are you there?" Alyssa's question startled him.

Gabe's mind had traveled miles away and back in time. "*J-jah*, um, yes." Not entirely true. Although he remained aware of the phone biting into his palm as he squeezed it too tightly, most of him remained stuck in the past.

"Great. See you at four on Monday. If anything comes up between now and then, just give me a ring on my cell." She rattled off numbers so fast Gabe could barely discern them, let alone jot them down.

By the time it dawned on him he should pick up a pen, she'd already said goodbye and hung up. Gabe sat there, dead phone in hand, fighting to drag himself back from the edge, before the past closed over him like quicksand.

Then he began sinking. Down, down, down into the depths. Thrashing and flailing only made you go under faster. Soon muck would close over his head, and he'd drown. He needed a life-line.

Lord, help me.

Priscilla's face drifted into his awareness. Her sweetness. Her calmness. Her caring.

Inch by inch, he pulled himself free. He replayed her last visit. Her logic in figuring out the milk dilemma, her bravery in confronting Fleurette, her fierceness in defending him.

The way her smile set off sparks. The way her eyes lit a blaze. But for now, her magnetic pull dragged him back into the room. Back into normality.

Tomorrow he'd see her again because she had a milk pickup scheduled. Focusing on that, he released the regrets of the past.

Being around Priscilla always lifted his spirits, and he could ask her about coming on Monday to help with the newspaper reporter. For now, though, he pushed the upcoming interview from his mind. After all Priscilla had done for him, he wished he could do something for her.

He had to find a way to help her keep her job. Someone needed to make Matthew tell the truth.

Lord, if I can do anything at all, please show me how.

Priscilla tossed and turned most of the night, waking well before dawn on Saturday morning. Gabe's words still haunted her. He'd claimed the scholars needed her. If they did, should that be her first loyalty? Or should she keep Matthew's secret and protect his job and his *mamm*?

Daed came into the kitchen as Priscilla finished drying the breakfast dishes. "*Dochder*, we need to talk when you're done there."

Priscilla had a good idea of what they needed to discuss.

Her sister finished washing the last pot. "I'll leave you alone then." After sending a sympathetic look in Priscilla's direction, Sarah slipped from the kitchen. She must assume Daed planned to lecture Priscilla.

Priscilla sat near Daed at the table and endured another pitying glance.

He planted his elbows on the table. "I'm afraid we made a mistake not telling your mother the truth. I don't feel right keeping things from her.

160

And I'm also worried about her response to you."

"Don't worry about me." Priscilla had gotten used to Mamm's criticism. She tried not to let it bother her.

"Still, I don't like to see her making wrong assumptions about you." He cleared his throat. "Any man would be honored to marry you. And I'm not just saying that because you're my daughter."

"Could we wait until after the school board meeting?" Priscilla closed her eyes and rubbed her forehead. She couldn't handle a barrage of questions. Mamm was sure to want every last detail. Right now, she needed every ounce of her energy to get through the meeting.

"Of course. I'll be praying that all goes well. I'd also like you to pray about whether or not God wants you to reveal Matthew's secret."

"I don't know if they'll believe me. Not after all this time."

"They may not, but I can back up your story. It would be better for them to hear it from Matthew, though."

"Well, that's not going to happen, because he didn't even tell the truth when he confessed." Saying those words brought back his betrayal.

Dad must have noticed her jitteriness. "Why don't you weed the garden this morning? Keeping busy can help to take your mind off the situation."

Priscilla rose from the table. *"Danke."*

If only she could go to Gabe's and collect the Saturday milk delivery. Unfortunately, Mamm had taken the buggy to do some errands, so visiting Gabe would have to wait until later that afternoon.

Priscilla took Daed's suggestion, hoping it would distract her, but kneeling beside rows of plants, doing a mindless job that occupied only her hands, not her brain, did little to keep her mind from straying. Most of the time it went directly to the worst-case scenario.

Soon after Gabe entered the store that morning, a middle-aged Amish woman tapped at the door.

"Is it all right to come in? I see your hours are nine to four today, but the sign in the window still says *Closed.*"

Gabe held the door open and waved her into the store even though it wasn't nine yet. "My nephew usually takes care of the sign, but I'll do it now." As soon as she was inside, he flipped the sign to *Open* and then held the door for Tim, who scooted through a minute later.

"How come you changed the sign? I'm not late, am I?"

Placing a finger over his lips, Gabe motioned with his head to where the lady stood examining the shelves.

"Oh, I see," Tim whispered.

His voice low, Gabe said, "The camel's milk is in the refrigerator. Why don't you fill the bottles while I help the customer?"

Tim scuffed a toe. "You don't trust me?"

"What?" Gabe had no idea what he meant.

"I let that Fleur-lady steal. Now I can't help with customers?"

Still keeping one eye on the woman who appeared to be idly browsing the shelves, Gabe knelt and set his hands on Tim's shoulders. "I trust you completely. And you can take care of the customers the rest of the day without my help. I just—"

The woman turned and looked as if she wanted to ask a question.

"May I help you with something?" Gabe rose and headed toward her, while Tim scampered through the metal door into the refrigerator.

"I hope so," she said. "Do you know if the owner will be in today?"

"He definitely will." Gabe held out a hand. "Pleased to meet you. I'm the owner."

Instead of shaking his hand, she stood there staring at him. "I saw the sign outside. You're Gabriel Kauffman?"

"I am."

"My daughter didn't mention how old you were, and I certainly didn't expect you to be this—this, um, young." Flustered, she gazed at his outstretched hand. "I'm sorry. I'm Esther

Ebersol." She pumped his hand enthusiastically. "I'm glad to meet you."

Daughter and *Ebersol* rang a bell. Wasn't Priscilla's last name Ebersol? That was a common last name in Amish country, but he could trace a faint resemblance in the plump, lined face in front of him.

"You look like her—or rather, she looks like you."

Esther patted the small graying wings of hair that peeked out from beneath her *kapp*. "Why, *danke*, that's so kind of you." She examined Gabe. "You look too young to be married yet." She glanced at his unshaven chin. "I mean, I can see you're not married."

A clue the *Englischer* had missed. "I'm twenty-four, if that's what you're wondering."

"Twenty-four? A perfect age. I mean for a business owner."

From the moment Esther walked through the door, Gabe had sensed she'd come for something other than camel's milk, but this conversation certainly seemed to be taking a bizarre turn. Discovering she was Priscilla's *mamm* made it even stranger.

"Was there something I can help you with?" Perhaps that would remind her of what she'd come for.

"You own this whole farm"—she waved at the fields outside the window—"yourself?"

Gabe nodded, then added, "Well, the bank owns some of it, of course, but I aim to pay off that bill as quickly as possible."

Esther beamed at him. "*Gut, gut.* It's nice to have so much land to divide among your children." She paused. "Although I guess you don't have any."

Gabe rubbed his beardless chin to remind her of his single status. "Not yet," he said drily.

She tittered. "Well, of course not. But you do want children, don't you?"

"Certainly. Doesn't every man?" Well, maybe not some *Englischers*, but he'd never met an Amishman who didn't want a big family.

"So, will you be starting a family soon?"

"Not until I'm married."

"I expected that. I just meant—"

"Am I engaged? No, I'm not." And not likely to be any time soon.

This almost sounded like a job interview for a husband. Had Esther's purpose in coming here been matchmaking? Had Priscilla asked her to find out more about him? Or had Esther cooked this up on her own? In that case, Priscilla might be mortified to discover what her *mamm* was doing.

"It's hard to believe you're not courting anyone."

Had he indicated that? He didn't remember her asking about his dating status. Perhaps it was just as well she hadn't, because even he had no idea how to answer that question.

165

But if Esther intended to set him up with Priscilla, he needed to let her know that was impossible. "With just opening this business, I need to spend long hours here. I don't really have time to court."

"You could use some help."

He certainly could, but at the moment, he couldn't afford to pay anyone other than his nephew.

"My daughter loves reading about camel's milk. She talks our ears off about it. I'm sure she'd be willing to work here in the evenings. Maybe you know her? Priscilla? Priscilla Ebersol?"

"Of course I do. She does know a lot about camel's milk."

Now that he'd discouraged her matchmaking, she'd turned to job-hunting? He'd love to have Priscilla working here. She'd been an amazing ally last night with Fleurette.

"I'm afraid I don't have a budget for hiring employees yet, but I'll keep her in mind for when I do." Actually, he kept her in mind more often than that. But it wasn't something he'd share with her mother.

"Priscilla loves finding out more about camel's milk and things like that. I'm sure if you asked her, she'd volunteer her time. Besides, she has her evenings free now that she and Matthew King have broken up." Esther sighed, as if she regretted that.

"She's better off without him," Gabe snapped, then wished he could shove the words back into his mouth.

Her mouth hanging open, Esther stared at him. "You know about Matthew?"

"You mean about Priscilla dating him? Or about what happened in the apple orchard?"

Esther gasped. "Priscilla told you about that?"

She'd also warned him that only her *daed* and Matthew knew the whole truth, so Gabe guarded his answer. "*Jah*, she did."

"But you still called her *your wife?* She said you did it in front of a customer."

Knowing Priscilla had shared that comment with her family made Gabe happy. But the hopeful note in Esther's voice alerted Gabe to a possible trap. A trap he needed to avoid. "We were only joking."

"Oh." Esther's face fell. "I suppose with her past, no man will consider marrying her."

"What do you mean?" Gabe couldn't keep the indignation from his voice. "Any man would be privileged to marry someone as wonderful as your daughter." Even me. If I were free to marry.

Beaming, Esther gushed, "You're as wonderful as Priscilla said."

She'd praised him to her family? He'd love to know what she'd told them.

"The real reason I came," Esther confided, "is to invite you to supper tonight."

Supper? Tonight? With Priscilla? His first instinct was to jump for joy and accept the invitation, but his brain urged him to proceed with caution. Priscilla's *mamm* seemed to be trying to hook a husband for her daughter. A role he could never fill.

As if guessing the reason for his hesitation, Esther said, "My husband is fascinated by the benefits of camel's milk, and I'm sure you'd like to meet Asher to see how your milk has helped him."

Gabe would definitely like that. Spending more time around Priscilla would be a plus. And he could find out how her interview with the school board went. Besides, what did he have to look forward to but a long, lonely evening?

"*Danke* for the invitation." He kept his tone neutral. "As far as I know, I'm free tonight." Should he say he needed to check his calendar?

"*Wunderbar.* We eat at six, but feel free to come sooner."

"By the time I'm done milking, it'll be close to six."

"We'll see you then." Esther headed toward the exit, then turned. "*Ach*, wait. Do you need our address?"

"*Neh*, I have it on the application for the milk." If he were honest, he still remembered it. Gabe hoped the flush creeping up his neck didn't give him away.

Just before Esther pushed open the door, Gabe asked, "Do you know the name of the orchard where Matthew works?"

Esther halted and faced him with wary eyes. "You're not planning to ask him about what he and Priscilla—"

"Of course not." But what could he say to alleviate her fears? "A Matthew King had a near-accident with one of my camels a week or so ago. I just wondered if it might be the same one."

She stood there uncertainly for a moment—then gave him the name.

"*Danke.* I'll check it out. With King being such a common name, I doubt it's the same person, but I do need to talk to him."

This Matthew King might not be the one who almost collided with Gabe's baby camel, but it definitely was the Matthew King Gabe wanted to see.

Chapter Eleven

After Priscilla's *mamm* left, Gabe paced back and forth. The thought of confronting Matthew King left him cold inside. Would he be able to get a word out, form coherent sentences, get his point across?

Gabe couldn't let that hold him back. Priscilla didn't deserve to lose her job because of Matthew's deception. Even if Gabe messed up his words, made no sense, or looked like a fool, he needed to at least try.

"Tim, can you come out here a second?"

"Be right there. I'm almost done with the cow's milk."

While he waited, Gabe should unpack some stock, fill orders, and balance books, but instead he walked from one end of the store to the other, rehearsing what he might say. As he ran each point through his mind, his mouth formed the words, and they flowed smoothly. But that was no guarantee they'd come out that way once he and Matthew stood face-to-face.

When Tim emerged a short while later, he gazed at Gabe with curiosity. "Are you all right?"

"Fine." At least he was right at this moment, as long as he didn't dwell on Matthew. "Listen, I need to run an errand. It might take some time.

You'll be able to handle everything, right?"

"*Jah*." Tim's chest under his small suspenders puffed out. "I'll watch out for robbers."

Maybe Gabe shouldn't go. The cow's milk still needed to be bottled. And what if Fleurette or Defarge returned? Or if they both came together? Would they pressure Tim? What if one of them distracted his nephew while the other one stole? But Priscilla's needs were more important than possible financial losses.

Gathering his courage, Gabe left Tim in charge of the store and drove his buggy to the orchard. He slowed his horse as he went past. Teams of men and a scattering of women had spread out among the rows of apple trees, some on ladders, others picking low-hanging fruit. A few Mennonite teens stayed close together and worked swiftly, stripping apples from branches and dropping them into bags strapped to their waists. One Amish girl hurried to a nearby wagon and emptied her bag into a huge bin, then rushed to another tree.

Gabe scanned the fields for straw hats. An Amish worker carrying a ladder approached a tree close to where Gabe had pulled over. The man leaned the ladder against the tree and climbed rapidly. His face looked familiar. The same Matthew King who'd almost run over Gabe's camel.

Whispering a quick prayer for the right words

to say, Gabe urged his horse off the road and tied him to a post. Then he hopped the split-rail fence and approached the foot of the ladder. Matthew's fluid movements were impressive. He grabbed three apples in each hand and dropped them into his pouch.

Gabe disliked interrupting Matthew's rhythm, but his concern for Priscilla increased his bravery. After taking a deep breath, he forced himself to call up to the man almost hidden among the branches, "Matthew? Matthew King?"

Matthew stopped mid-pull. "*Jah?*"

"I'd like to talk to you."

"Did Mel send you with instructions?"

"No, I'm here to talk about Priscilla."

The ladder shook and, with jerky movements, Matthew returned to picking. "I can't talk during work hours."

"We can talk while you pick," Gabe pointed out.

Matthew glanced around nervously. "I can't afford to lose my job."

"I can understand that." Gabe couldn't keep a touch of sarcasm from his voice. "Priscilla doesn't want to lose her job either."

His face pale, Matthew demanded, "Who are you?"

"A person who cares about Priscilla."

"How long have you known her?" Matthew's rapid-fire question sounded like a challenge, and the tilt of his eyebrows revealed his suspicion.

Interesting. Matthew seems jealous. Is he wondering if Priscilla was cheating on him?

"I'm not sure that's your business," Gabe retorted. "I'm not here to talk about my relationship with Priscilla."

In reality, *friendship* would be more accurate, or even acquaintance. But *relationship* might keep Matthew wondering. Usually Gabe preferred not to upset people, but after what Matthew had done to Priscilla, he deserved to squirm.

"I'm concerned about Priscilla's future." Matthew might not have long to talk, and Gabe needed to make his point. He hadn't anticipated Matthew viewing him as a rival. But maybe that would work to his advantage.

Matthew's eyes narrowed. "Her future? Exactly what kind of a relationship do you two have?"

For a man who'd just cheated on and jilted his girlfriend, Matthew certainly acted as if he still had a right to supervise what Priscilla did. Or was he the kind who liked to keep several girls dangling?

Ignoring Matthew's question, Gabe went straight to the point. "Priscilla meets with the school board today at John Beiler's house. You not only smeared her reputation, but now you're making her lose her job so you can save yours."

Matthew dismissed Gabe's concerns with a snort. "Everyone thinks highly of her. She won't lose her job."

"Oh, really? What do you think the school board will say about her supposed wrongdoing? That she'll be a good role model for children?"

"You don't know what happened. Priscilla would never tell—"

Gabe cut him off. "About Mara?"

His voice shaking, Matthew demanded, "What do you want?"

"I want Priscilla to keep her job, but she's being called before the school board today."

For the first time, Matthew looked regretful. "I didn't mean for her to lose her job. She loves working at the school."

"And I'm sure she's a great teacher."

"Yes, she is. She's very good with children."

Gabe crossed his arms. "So, what do you intend to do about it?"

"I don't know." He looked around to see if others were in earshot. "I have to work."

"You don't get a midday break to eat?"

"Well, I do, but I already have plans."

"You can cancel them. Doing the right thing is more important than any arrangements you might have with Mara."

Matthew blanched, and his hand faltered. "How do you know we have plans?"

"Just guessing, but you proved me right."

"All right," Matthew agreed in a sullen tone, "I'll do it."

"I'm glad to see you have a conscience."

"I—I have to wait for Mara. She'll be upset at the change of plans."

"I can stay here and tell her," Gabe volunteered.

"No, no. I need to tell her myself."

"I'm sure you won't mind if I stick around to be sure you get off safely."

"They don't like us leaving the orchard during breaks."

So Matthew hadn't been planning to go. Gabe needed to increase the pressure. "Maybe I should mention your evening activities to your boss."

"You don't know what you're talking about."

"Don't I? Maybe I'll tell him what happens in these fields at night. If I owned this place, I'd want to know. I might hire someone to patrol for prowlers."

"We're not prowlers." Then realizing what he'd admitted, Matthew backtracked. "I mean, we've never had prowlers in the orchard after dark."

"You know that for a fact?" Gabe pressed his point. "I'm sure your boss will want to be certain."

Matthew tried for a nonchalant look, but the effect was spoiled by the fear in his eyes.

Gabe didn't trust Matthew. He returned to his buggy and pulled alongside the fence so his driver's window faced the spot where Matthew was working. He planned to stay in plain sight to be sure Matthew followed through.

Matthew still worked rapidly, but his previously smooth movements had turned jerky. Every once

175

in a while, he glanced over his shoulder to see if Gabe had gone.

Gabe returned his looks with a steady stare he hoped made his message clear. *I don't trust you to do the right thing, so I'm not leaving.*

A short while later, a pretty blonde tripped through the trees with a wicker basket in hand, trying to appear casual, but her destination was obvious. That must be Mara.

Now Gabe would see if Matthew kept his promise.

"Are you ready to eat?" she cooed.

"I can't, Mara. I have to run an errand during my lunch break."

"But I brought the picnic basket and everything."

"I'm really sorry." He turned to glare at Gabe.

"But you promised we could go to the creek today." Mara's whining grated on Gabe's ears.

"I know, but something's come up. We can go tomorrow."

Mara tossed her head. "I might have other plans. In fact, I'm sure plenty of people would be happy to share this lunch with me today."

A sick look crossed Matthew's face. "*Neh*, Mara, don't—"

"If you don't have time for me, I'll find someone who does." She flounced off.

Matthew stared after her, anguish twisting his features.

Gabe couldn't help feeling sorry for him. But

176

this fool had cheated on Priscilla with a shallow flirt like Mara. What had he been thinking?

Matthew glowered at Gabe as he climbed down, then he stomped toward the barn. He swiveled his head as he walked, scanning the orchard. Probably trying to see if Mara had made good on her threat.

Gabe untied his horse and headed for the driveway leading to the barn. He waited nearby until Matthew's buggy rumbled down the wide, gravel-lined path. After Matthew turned onto the street, Gabe followed at a distance to be sure he headed to the school board meeting.

Not until Matthew pulled into a house with several buggies parked by the barn did Gabe head back to the shop. He only prayed it was the right house and that Matthew hadn't tricked him. Gabe had done what he could to save Priscilla's job and reputation.

One thing surprised him, though. In his worry over Priscilla, he hadn't stumbled over his words. Maybe the key to getting over nervousness was to let concern for someone else override his fears.

A twinge of guilt nagged at Gabe for using blackmail. But he had to protect Priscilla. He tried to tell himself that helping her was his way of repaying her for defending him, but the truth of the matter was he cared about her. Was it right to have these feelings for someone when you couldn't act on them?

Priscilla arrived ahead of time and sat in her buggy, one hand on the reins, the other pleating her apron fabric into tiny bunches. The whole way here, she'd argued with herself about whether or not to tell the school board about Mara. Gabe's advice ran through her head. *Jah*, she would. Then an image of Ruth intruded. *Neh*, she shouldn't.

Ach! If she didn't stop this, she'd be late. That was the last thing she needed. John Beiler already had concerns about her tardiness.

Climbing out of her buggy, Priscilla tied up Butterscotch with shaking hands. Smoothing down her dress and apron, she paused for a brief prayer.

Lord, please help me to say the right thing. I don't want to do anything to harm Ruth, but if it is Your will for me to keep teaching, please take charge of the meeting and my mouth.

Swallowing hard, she mounted the steps to the porch. Her future was at stake. She tapped at the door. Before she could compose herself, John's wife answered, a sleepy baby in her arms.

"I was just headed upstairs to put Ellie down for a nap." With a sympathetic smile, Naomi waved toward her left. "The other couples are in the living room."

All eyes turned toward Priscilla when she reached the entryway, and her steps slowed. How could she face their accusations? She couldn't talk back to the school board. She'd prepared remarks to rebut the charges. But with everyone's concerned looks focused on her, her throat constricted. She'd be lucky if she could manage a nod or head shake. Now she understood Gabe being tongue-tied.

John Beiler glanced at the clock hanging on the wall and nodded, a look of approval in his eyes. She'd arrived five minutes early. One hurdle crossed. How would she manage the others?

Floyd Chupp motioned her to a chair facing him. "Have a seat. I'm sure you know why we called you here today."

Someone knocked at the door. John Beiler stood. "Naomi's upstairs with the baby. Excuse me while I see who it is."

John's voice drifted into the living room. "Matthew?"

Her Matthew? No, not hers anymore. What was Matthew doing here? Priscilla craned her neck to peek out the door, but John's body blocked her view.

"I have something I need to tell the school board."

Priscilla would know that voice anywhere. Definitely Matthew.

"We're in another meeting right now," John said in a kind voice, "but you're welcome to come back another time."

"*Neh*," Matthew insisted. "It needs to be now.

179

It's about Priscilla. You can't make a fair judgment without knowing this."

Did he plan to tell the truth? Priscilla's eyes watered. If he did, he might save her job. *Please, Lord, help him to be truthful.*

"I don't know." John glanced over his shoulder at the others, a question in his eyes.

"Let's hear what he has to say," Floyd said.

John opened the door and led Matthew into the room. He waved to the rocker next to Priscilla. Then he took his seat on the empty couch cushion beside Floyd and Mary Chupp. James and Martha Raber sat on chairs at the other end. Lined up like that, they appeared to be a row of judges, ready to condemn the guilty.

They all sat there silent until Naomi hurried down the stairs and perched on the arm of the couch beside her husband. His eyes turned tender as he smiled at her. "Is the baby asleep?"

She nodded, and a secret look passed between them.

Priscilla's heart ached at their love for each other. Would she ever experience that? Joking with Gabe about being his wife had made her feel warm and fluttery inside, but did she have any hope of a relationship? After Matthew, she was afraid to trust anyone. And with her reputation in tatters . . .

The school board members turned their attention to Matthew.

His Adam's apple bobbed up and down as he cleared his throat. "The deacon—your brother"—Matthew nodded in James's direction without meeting his eyes—"believed he saw Priscilla that night, but it wasn't her. The girl I was with looks a little like Priscilla."

"Who was it?" John asked.

Matthew hung his head. Staring down at his clenched hands, he refused to answer.

"Matthew?" Floyd prompted.

Lifting his head, Matthew met the question with defiance in his eyes. "I won't smear another girl's reputation."

He'd suddenly developed a conscience and a spine? At least when it came to protecting Mara. Too bad his chivalry hadn't kicked in earlier. Still, Priscilla was grateful he'd come of his own accord to defend her.

"Yet when you confessed, you let everyone assume Priscilla was guilty and unrepentant?" The reproach in Floyd's tone had to sting.

Priscilla hoped the sharp rebuke would make Matthew think twice about concealing the truth. Or, to be more accurate, lying.

He could have destroyed her career, her life, her future. Even with his confession today, the rest of the community remained unaware of her innocence. Would Matthew straighten that out too? He had to know nobody from their district would date her.

Priscilla smiled. She might not need to worry about that. Perhaps in time, Gabe . . .

John leaned forward, his attention on Priscilla. "Why didn't you speak up instead of letting us believe a lie?"

Under his searching gaze, she *rutsched* in her chair. If she said because Matthew had asked her to, she'd be blaming him for her decision. Lowering her gaze, she answered, "I didn't want Matthew to lose his job. I was worried about Ruth."

"It's good to care about others, but if we don't have the facts, we can't make the right decisions."

"That's what Daed told me." She should have listened to his advice and spoken to the bishop. He'd also suggested she pray about it, which she hadn't done—except for her desperate prayers today.

The three couples turned to one another and seemed to be conferring silently. Then John nodded and turned back to Matthew and Priscilla.

"Naomi," John said, "could you show Matthew to the door?" He faced in Priscilla's direction again. "Matthew, you may go. Thank you for coming. Priscilla, perhaps you could sit in the kitchen while we confer. We can have root beer and cookies after we come to our decision."

The second John dismissed him, Matthew shot out of his chair and hurried to the door.

Priscilla should head to the kitchen, but she

needed to talk to Matthew first. "Matthew, wait!" She rushed after him.

Rather than stopping, he hopped off the porch and headed to his buggy. "I don't have time. I need to get back to work."

"I just wanted to thank you for coming and telling the truth." He'd only done what was right, but for him to take off work to make sure she could keep her teaching job had been a sacrifice.

Matthew climbed into his buggy. "Don't thank me. Thank your boyfriend."

What? Priscilla stared at him. Whatever was he talking about?

He started out of the driveway, but before he drove past her, he pulled to a stop beside her and leaned out of the driver's window. "You know, I wondered why you took my news about Mara so calmly. You just sat there with your hands in your lap. I don't feel so awful about cheating on you now that I know you were doing the same thing."

"Huh?" Before Priscilla could ask what he meant, Matthew's horse galloped down the driveway and out into the street. She stood staring after him, puzzled and uneasy. Had someone started more rumors?

Chapter Twelve

All afternoon, Gabe worried about Priscilla's meeting. Had it gone well? Did Matthew clear her? What had the school board decided?

He paced up and back so many times, Tim asked, "Is anything wrong?"

"I don't know. I'm just concerned about something."

Appearing grown-up and serious, Tim said, "Mamm says worrying isn't trusting God."

That hit Gabe hard. How many times had his parents stressed the same saying? He hadn't followed their advice. Instead, he'd been trying to control the situation. He needed to let go and let God handle it.

I'm sorry for not resting in Your will, Lord. Please help me to trust and believe everything will work out for good.

He ruffled his nephew's hair as he walked past. "Thanks, Tim. I'll be in the office working on the books." He'd try to get through his usual Saturday jobs and stop dwelling on situations that were out of his control. He'd place Priscilla in God's hands.

Yet, he couldn't stop images of her from flooding his mind as he totaled up numbers. Her kindness. Her gentle voice. Her generous smile. Her fierceness in defending him.

And tonight, he'd have supper with her family. He had some concerns about Priscilla's matchmaking *mamm*. As much as he wished he could court her daughter, he had other obligations that prevented him from following those desires. He needed to leave all of that to God too.

He stopped in the doorway to the office and turned. "Oh, I need to go to someone's house for supper tonight. Would you be able to help me with the milking so I can get done earlier?"

"Sure," Tim agreed readily, even though he'd have to do his own chores, including more milking, when he went home.

The nice thing about his nephew being so young is that he didn't ask why. His brother and sister-in-law would have peppered him with questions. Questions about him and Priscilla. Questions for which he had no answers.

Priscilla walked through the front door, rejoicing after the school board meeting. They'd lectured her about not telling the bishop—or them—the truth, but in the end, they'd decided in her favor. So now, she not only had her job, but she had a chance to teach next year as well. If they chose her.

She'd stayed for a while to visit with Naomi and play with her other children. Then realizing the time and that her parents might be wondering if she was all right, Priscilla headed home, a joyful song on her lips.

By the time she unhitched the horse and walked into the kitchen, Daed was heading out to do the milking.

"How did it go, *dochder*?"

She met his caring smile with a broad grin. "I still have my job, and perhaps I can be the schoolteacher next year after Ada marries."

"*Wunderbar.*" The worry lines on Daed's eyes melted into an expression of pride and joy.

"What?" Mamm practically screeched. "They don't choose teachers yet. Besides, you can't take the teaching job for next year. What about your wedding?"

My wedding? Priscilla stopped dead and her smile faltered. Did Mamm still believe she and Matthew would marry?

"Esther?" Daed's quelling frown stopped Mamm's protest. "We've already talked about this."

Mamm's only answer was to pinch her lips together. After she huffed out a sigh, she shrugged a little too casually. "Even if Priscilla doesn't make things right with Matthew, she might meet someone else."

Daed pulled on his lower lip. "I suppose so, but we'll let God deal with that. Meanwhile, we should be rejoicing with our daughter."

Flashing a fleeting semi-smile, Mamm turned to Priscilla. "I'm glad they let you keep your job." But the insincerity in her voice made it clear she'd prefer if her daughter didn't get asked to teach next year.

Daed opened the back door. "I can't wait to hear all about the board meeting after I'm done with the milking." He'd made it partway out when Mamm stopped him.

"Try to be quick about it, because we'll be having a supper guest tonight." She had a strange, rather mysterious, smile on her face.

"Really?" Daed's eyebrows rose.

From the triumphant look on her mother's face, the guest was somehow connected to their conversation.

"Wh-who is it?" Priscilla asked.

"It'll be a surprise." Mamm studied her. "Maybe you should clean up some before you help with supper. You're a bit *strubbly*."

Priscilla took a step back. If Mamm had slapped her, she couldn't have been any more surprised. *Since when does my appearance at a meal matter?* Unless . . .

Had Mamm invited Matthew? A horrible burning sensation began in Priscilla's stomach and traveled up through her chest. *Please, God, no.* But when would Mamm have had time to invite him? He'd been at work all day—at least Priscilla assumed he had—except when he came to the school board meeting. Her mother had gone out to run errands early this morning. Had she talked to Matthew then?

Why had he agreed? With a sinking feeling, Priscilla recalled Matthew's comments about a boyfriend. Had Mamm tried to make him jealous?

Gabe appreciated Tim's help as he rushed through the milking. As soon as they finished, he hurried inside to freshen up. The closer it got to six, the more nervous he became. Why had he agreed to do this? Meeting Priscilla's family, having supper with them, might give them the impression he wanted to court their daughter.

He should have declined. He had a standing invitation to eat evening meals at Saul's house. He tried not to impose too often, but he could have told Esther he planned to eat with them this evening.

Gabe fumbled with his shirt buttons. No doubt about it, he had cold feet. As much as he wanted to see Priscilla and hear about the afternoon, it troubled him that Esther might turn this into a bigger deal than simple friendship. Gabe couldn't deny his growing feelings for Priscilla, and tonight would do little to curb those desires.

He'd made a major mistake in suggesting she should pretend to be his wife. Not only did it give Priscilla and her *mamm* ideas, it also preoccupied his thoughts. Pictures of them as a happy couple flitted through his mind all day long. He needed to avoid such temptation.

After brushing his hair several times until it shone, he donned his straw hat and headed for the barn. Despite his hesitation about her *mamm*'s expectations, he couldn't wait to see Priscilla. He only hoped Matthew had done the right thing.

Gabe stopped at the store to pick up Priscilla's milk order. He'd been so *ferhoodled* when Esther stopped by that morning, he hadn't thought to give her the order. And he'd been hoping Priscilla might drop by to get it after her meeting. The fact that she didn't worried him. Had the meeting lasted too long? Or had she been too upset? He hoped not, but he'd soon know the outcome.

When he pulled in the Ebersols' driveway, a boy a few years older than Tim came rushing out of the house.

"Oh, *gut*, you're here. Mamm was afraid you might not come." He directed Gabe to the barn and helped him unhitch the horse. "Nobody knows who's coming for supper. Mamm wanted it to be a surprise."

"Not even Priscilla?"

"You know my sister?"

Gabe smiled. "We've met. She comes to the camel farm to get milk for Asher."

"Are you from the camel farm?" The boy studied him.

"*Jah*, *I* am. I'm Gabe Kauffman." He held out a hand.

The boy shook his hand. "I'm Zeke. Your milk is helping Asher, but . . ." He snapped his mouth shut.

"But?" Gabe prompted.

Zeke fixed his gaze on the ground and scuffed his toe. "I shouldn't of said anything."

"If something's wrong with the milk, I need to know. I wouldn't want to harm anyone." Not like he'd done in the past. And not like he may have done—even inadvertently—to Fleurette's niece.

"*Ach*, no, it's not your milk that's the problem. I—well, I shouldn't have said anything."

"About what?"

Zeke kept his head lowered, and Gabe could hardly hear Zeke's mumbled words. "It's just that my sister broke up with her boyfriend, and Mamm's upset. She wants Priscilla to marry him."

"After what happened?" Gabe's hands had knotted into fists at the word *boyfriend,* and he struggled to control his rising anger. He'd gotten the same impression about Esther's matchmaking intentions when she visited his store.

His eyes wide, Zeke lifted his head to stare at Gabe. "You know what happened? But Priscilla hasn't told anyone. Except maybe Daed."

Protecting Matthew's job was one thing. Priscilla cared about his mother's welfare. But not to confide in her family—why was she concealing Matthew's wrongdoing from her own family?

Zeke was staring at him as if waiting to hear why his sister had confided in a stranger. Yet Gabe had no explanation to give. Why had Priscilla confided in him rather than in her family? Perhaps because he was a stranger? He didn't know Matthew, so she didn't have to worry about hurting Matthew's reputation.

That made Gabe sad. Priscilla had gone to great lengths to keep Matthew's infidelity a secret. She must still be in love with him.

Priscilla was adding butter and milk to the potatoes when the kitchen door opened behind her.

"He's here," Zeke announced.

She stiffened, and her stomach clenched. How could she sit across the table from Matthew all evening? It would be torture. Even thinking about it made her sick. She wouldn't be able to choke down a bite of food.

Keeping her back to him, Priscilla pretended to be intent on her work. She pounded the masher up and down in the bowl, sloshing milk up over the sides.

Her mother returned from setting a bowl of applesauce on the table. "I'm so glad you're here." With a *mind-your-manners* glare at Priscilla, she added, "And I know my *dochder* is too."

No, your dochder *is not.* Priscilla wished her mother would stay out of her love life.

"*Danke* for inviting me," a man's voice said.

Priscilla's nerveless fingers dropped the masher into the bowl. Milk splashed out, spattering her hands and the countertop. She hardly noticed.

That deep bass voice wasn't Matthew's. This voice strummed a chord deep within her. But it was impossible. *He* couldn't be here.

She whirled. What was Gabe doing in their kitchen?

"*Gut'n owed*, Esther. *Gut'n owed*, Priscilla."

Gabe's friendly smile set her pulse racing, and her stomach flipped from churning to quivering. She still wouldn't be able to eat, but this time for a good reason.

Questions raced through her mind. How did Mamm know Gabe? He'd called her Esther, so they'd met. But when?

Last night, Mamm had assumed the camel farmer was old. Her errands this morning. Had she gone to Gabe's store? What if Mamm had told him Priscilla had repeated his comment about marrying her?

Her cheeks burned. What must he think?

Gabe held up the gallons of milk. "Did you want these in the refrigerator?"

"*Ach*, I'm so sorry. I completely forgot to pick those up." Priscilla rushed over for them.

"You had enough on your mind today."

192

Mamm's eyebrows rose. "You know about that too?"

Now her mother would think they were much closer than mere acquaintances.

"Um, Priscilla mentioned it in passing." Despite the redness inching up his neck, Gabe managed to sound casual.

Unfortunately, he had no idea how good Mamm was at ferreting out information. She'd soon cross-examine him about their whole conversation. Priscilla needed to divert Mamm's attention.

"The potatoes are getting cold." Reluctantly, she turned her back on Gabe to finish mashing them and wipe up the mess.

"*Ach*, we can't be serving you cold food. Come in, come in." Mamm led the way into the dining room.

Priscilla breathed out a soft sigh. She'd averted the first snag, but with Mamm, there'd be plenty more. Smoothing down her apron, Priscilla picked up the bowl and carried it into the dining room in time to overhear Mamm questioning Gabe about how they met.

Gabe glanced across the room at Priscilla as Mamm pointed out a place for him directly across from where Priscilla usually sat. "Your *dochder* came in to buy milk for her brother. Asher, isn't it?"

"*Jah*. If she only bought milk, how do you know so much about her?"

193

"Well, I . . ." He silently signaled to Priscilla for help.

She had no idea how to respond, so she was grateful when Daed entered the room.

"Esther, why don't you let our guest sit down and have a bite to eat before you start questioning him?" The twinkle in Daed's eyes took some of the sting from his words.

He turned to Gabe and extended a hand. "Welcome, young man. I'm Joseph Ebersol. And you are?"

"Gabriel Kauffman." He shook hands with her *daed*. "Nice to meet you."

"Likewise. Why don't you have a seat?"

Mamm rounded the table, sidled up next to Daed, and bent close to his ear. Her attempt at whispering carried across the room. "He's the camel farmer who said he wanted to marry Priscilla."

Priscilla wished she could melt into the floor and disappear. Why had she ever told Mamm about Gabe's joke? Now she'd put him in an impossible situation. Her mother would never let a potential suitor go.

Poor Gabe! And poor her. Mamm would bombard them both with questions, comments, and directives. Before Gabe knew what was happening, Mamm would force him into announcing their engagement.

Daed frowned. "Esther, I don't think this is a

194

good idea." His quiet response could barely be heard.

Mamm only beamed. "I'm sure everything will work out fine."

Priscilla tried to determine if Gabe had caught the undercurrents. If so, he might be feeling as if he were on the menu instead of meatloaf.

She needed to make sure he understood none of this setup was her doing. She only hoped he'd believe her. And would still want to be friends.

Her sisters rushed into the room, and Priscilla went to get Asher. She and Zeke tried to prepare him for company by explaining they had a visitor named Gabe and telling Asher where he'd be sitting. Mamm had put Gabe at the opposite end of the table, but Asher still rocked back and forth in his chair.

Following the prayer, Mamm went straight to work gathering information. "So, Gabriel," she said as she passed him the bowl of mashed potatoes, "How did you get into camel farming?"

Gabe cringed. He hated being asked this question. If he answered honestly, it would be to make as much money as possible. That always made him sound greedy. Especially when he never explained why he needed the income so desperately.

He pulled out his second-best reason, and one that had grown increasingly important. "I like helping people, and camel's milk is good for so many problems. People use it for diabetes and autism. It's anti-inflammatory, so it can help people who have immune problems or milk allergies."

"You sound just like Priscilla. She gave us a speech about that when we were deciding whether or not to let Asher drink the sample she bought."

Gabe smiled. The sample he had given her. She'd been so upset she'd forgotten her wallet that day. If God hadn't nudged him to give her the milk, she might never have turned into a customer and then a friend. And, if he were honest, something more than a friend. Although he stopped himself from defining just what that meant.

Joseph paused while raising a forkful of peas to his lips. "Priscilla brought home some articles from the library. They said camel's milk calmed some autistic children."

"*Jah*, one study said autism disappeared completely for two children and a few adults."

Priscilla beamed at him from across the table. "I read that. The library printed me a copy."

"I wish that study had been bigger and better documented, but researchers are conducting studies now that may give us more information."

Priscilla appeared as excited as he was about

that. "The librarian requested other articles for me. I asked her to watch for those studies as they come out."

How was it possible that a beautiful woman like Priscilla was interested in camel's milk? If only he were free to ask to court her. They had so much in common. He needed to keep his attention on the conversation, not on Priscilla.

"A few other studies have indicated it helps with autism. What have you seen with Asher?" Gabe directed his question to Joseph.

"He's already sleeping better, aren't you, *sohn*?" Joseph leaned forward to attract Asher's attention.

"He's much quieter," Zeke added, "and he looks us in the eyes more."

Priscilla smiled at Zeke and then Asher before turning back to Gabe. "I did warn everyone that it could take two weeks or so to see results. But it's been helping. Right, Asher?"

Her brother gave a slight nod.

Then Esther broke in. "So, Gabriel, why don't you tell us all about your life before you came here and why you chose Lancaster?"

Gabe gulped. He certainly couldn't reveal everything. "I grew up in Bucks County, and most of my family still lives there. Except for my brother Saul. He met a girl from this area when he went on a mission trip to a flooded area years ago."

"That's why you moved here?" Clearly, Esther didn't want to hear his brother's story.

"Yes. When the farm next to Saul's went up for sale, he suggested I buy it so I'd have more room to expand." And to get him away from the constant reminders of the past. But Gabe had discovered fleeing didn't erase the memories.

"You're going to buy more camels?" Esther appeared delighted at his plans.

Gabe squirmed under her scrutiny.

Joseph gestured toward Gabe's almost-full plate. "Why don't we let the young man eat his supper? He's barely taken a bite."

With a sigh, Esther concentrated on her own food. She waited until Priscilla and her sisters were clearing the plates and bringing in dessert before resuming her inquisition. "Do you have anyone special back home, Gabe?"

How do I answer that?

Forks clattered against a stack of dessert plates. Her cheeks pink, Priscilla stared at him, her eyes begging him to forgive her mother's nosiness. At the same time, though, she seemed to be eagerly awaiting his answer.

"Esther," Joseph warned.

"I waited until he'd finished his meal."

"I don't think—" Joseph began.

But Gabe interrupted him. The delay had given him time to come up with a response. "To answer your question, of course I have someone special back home." Priscilla's tiny gasp made him sorry he'd chosen this retort, but he kept going. "Plenty of *someones,* actually."

Esther's eyebrows shot up almost to her graying hairline.

Gabe continued, "I have my *mamm, daed,* three brothers, two sisters, my aunts and uncles, sixteen cousins . . ."

Joseph chuckled. "Well done, Gabe." He laid a hand over his wife's. "I think that's our guest's way of telling us we've done enough questioning for one night."

Priscilla's *daed* had removed the heat, allowing Gabe to relax. During the whole meal, he'd been on guard against giving away secrets and against revealing his growing attraction to Priscilla. He hoped he'd succeeded.

Chapter Thirteen

Priscilla's heartbeat had gone from racing to stutter-stopping after Gabe's first answer to Mamm's question. Thinking he had a special someone had sent shock waves through her. Although she appreciated his humorous way of avoiding Mamm's prying, she now had no idea if he had anyone special.

The way Gabe's fingers had clenched his fork whenever Mamm lobbed another personal question his way made Priscilla long to deflect her mother's attention. Other than spilling something, which could easily be cleaned up, she could come up with nothing to stop Mamm. Trying to pull her mother away from her favorite pastime was more difficult than dragging a reluctant donkey toward a plow.

At Daed's suggestion they leave their guest alone, Gabe's tense shoulders and the tight lines around his mouth relaxed. He must expect he'd eat the rest of his meal in peace. Unfortunately, he didn't know her *mamm.*

Mamm hadn't reached the really embarrassing questions yet. Any minute now, she'd start with *So, Gabe, what are your intentions? I understand you asked my daughter to marry you.*

At the moment, Mamm was chewing a bite

as she glanced back and forth between the two of them. Priscilla's hand shook slightly as she lifted her milk glass to her lips. What did Gabe think of her after he discovered she'd told her family about his teasing? Would he assume she'd attached a deeper meaning to his casual words?

As soon as she was done chewing, Mamm turned to Priscilla. "I told Gabe you'd be happy to help in the store."

Priscilla choked on her milk. *What?* Spluttering, she tried to set her glass down without sloshing milk across the tabletop.

Mamm swiveled her head in Gabe's direction. "Priscilla's also good with milking, if you need extra help."

"*Danke.*" Gabe tugged at the back of his collar. "One thing about camels, though, is they only let certain people milk them. So far, they've only bonded with me."

"That must be hard," Daed said.

"It can be," Gabe agreed. "I haven't found anyone else they trust yet."

The clatter of her sisters clearing the dessert plates drowned out the conversation for a few moments, and Gabe leaned back in his chair with a contented smile. When it had quieted, he turned to Mamm. "The meal was delicious."

"I'm glad you liked it. Why don't we go into the living room for some coffee?"

"Actually"—Gabe turned desperate eyes in Priscilla's direction—"I was hoping to talk to your *dochder* for a few minutes."

Priscilla's heart leaped. Gabe wanted to be alone with her?

Mamm stood. "It's a lovely night. Why don't you take a walk?"

Priscilla pressed her lips together to hold back a sigh. Between Mamm's nosiness and her eagerness to get them together, she'd probably scare Gabe off.

A walk would be perfect. Gabe couldn't wait to get outside and away from the uncomfortable questions. Being under Esther's intent, searching gaze had made him sweat. Having coffee would allow her to put him on the spot again.

He'd answered her questions as truthfully as he could without giving too much away, but doing so meant continually being on guard. Quite unlike the restful peace he experienced in Priscilla's presence.

Esther stood and waved her hands to shoo them out the door. "Sarah can take your turn drying dishes tonight," she told Priscilla.

Priscilla seemed as keen as he was to head outside. Did she want to spend time with him? Or was she just glad to escape her mother's scrutiny?

Not that he blamed her. He too would be relieved to get outside.

"*Danke* for having me," he told her parents. If he said his goodbyes now, maybe he could leave after talking to Priscilla and avoid more of Esther's curiosity.

As soon as he'd bid everyone good night, Priscilla hurried him out the door and far enough from the house that no one could eavesdrop on their conversation. She kept glancing over her shoulder as if expecting someone to follow them.

When they were alone, she faced him. "I'm so sorry about Mamm. I hope you don't think"— she lowered her eyelashes so he couldn't read her expression—"I, well, asked her to do that." Her cheeks pinkened, making her even more attractive.

Now it was Gabe's turn to avert his eyes. To avoid temptation.

"I only told my family about your bride comment as a joke. I didn't expect Mamm to take it seriously." She hesitated. "No, that's not the whole truth. I sort of bragged about it because Mamm made a comment that hurt." Shuffling her toe in the dirt, Priscilla hung her head.

Gabe's heart went out to her. "What did she say?" Based on Esther's remarks in the store, he had his suspicions.

"It's not important." Priscilla flicked her hand as if to brush off the slight.

"It is to me," he said softly.

Priscilla's eyes opened wide, and she stared at him.

He hoped she hadn't misinterpreted his meaning. "I don't want to see you hurt. I don't like to see anyone get hurt." He'd seen enough pain already. If he could relieve someone's suffering, he'd do his best.

Gabe waited silently for her answer.

Looking off into the distance, she winced. "Mamm only said if I didn't marry Matthew, I'd never get married."

"Matthew? Why would she want you to marry him?"

"She doesn't know what happened. Daed and I worried about her telling other people."

After tonight, Gabe certainly understood why. "She thinks Matthew was with you?"

Still not meeting his eyes, Priscilla nodded.

"That's so unfair," Gabe burst out. "Why should your reputation suffer? I hope he didn't make you lose your job today. I forgot to ask at supper."

Priscilla laughed. "I don't know when you'd have gotten a chance. Besides, it's probably better you didn't. Mamm would have wondered how you knew and quizzed you about that too."

Gabe tried not to grimace. "At least you know she cares about you."

"True. Although I do wish she didn't always keep such a close watch. Not that I want to do anything wrong, it's only that—"

"I understand." But Gabe wanted to steer the conversation back around to Matthew. Had he done the right thing? "So how did the school board meeting go?"

"You're not going to believe this, but Matthew showed up."

Gabe struggled to act surprised. "Did he tell the truth?"

"Kind of." Priscilla pursed her lips. "He told the school board he wasn't with me, but he didn't say who he was with. Actually, that might be for the best. Then he can keep his job, and"—she brightened—"I got to keep mine. I'm hoping they'll ask me to be the teacher next year because Ada's getting married."

"That's wonderful!" Gabe grabbed his suspenders and held on to keep himself from sweeping her into his arms. What was wrong with him? He'd never been this attracted to any woman. Not even—he blocked that thought before it took him down a dark path.

"It was a miracle." Priscilla flashed him a brilliant smile.

"It certainly was." He definitely agreed. Even if this miracle had some human help, Gabe had been led by God. And only God could have encouraged Matthew's truth-telling.

"So, you said you had something to ask me?"

In his excitement over Priscilla's victory, Gabe had forgotten why they'd come out here. "Want to walk a little?" Moving would keep him from dwelling on his nervousness.

Originally, he'd considered asking Priscilla for help, but now he worried about imposing. And what might her *mamm* think?

Dusk had fallen, blurring the edges of the landscape as they strolled along the country lane. Gabe remained silent for several minutes.

Priscilla debated internally. Should she question him? Or was that too much like Mamm? In the end, she chose to wait. He'd answered enough questions for one night. And he'd told her he got tongue-tied sometimes. Maybe patience would allow him to gather his thoughts.

When he finally spoke, he surprised her. "A reporter from the *Central Pennsylvania Star* called today, and they want to do a lifestyle article about camel farming."

"Oh, Gabe, that's so exciting. The *Star* is the biggest newspaper in this area. It will help get the word out about your business."

"Yes, but what if my words get tangled and I mess up the interview?"

"Maybe you could practice ahead of time. You did fine tonight telling my family about the benefits of camel's milk."

"But one person questioned me at a time."

Only one person. Mamm. Pushing away her embarrassment, Priscilla concentrated on Gabe and his concerns. "Won't it be just one reporter?"

"I guess so. But she'll be bringing a photographer, and who knows if anyone else will be there. Even speaking to her on the phone, I made a fool of myself."

Priscilla suspected he'd done fine. "You made an appointment, right? That's the main thing."

"Monday at four." Gabe stopped walking and turned to her, his eyes pleading. "I thought if you came, it might help. You know so much about camel's milk, you could fill in any dead spots in the conversation. That is—if you're willing."

She stopped herself from blurting out she'd be delighted, and instead said, "I could come right after school to be there when they arrive."

"That would be *wunderbar.*"

Priscilla had planned to make a joke about pretending to be his wife, but at his appreciative look, her breath caught in her throat.

Gabe broke their gaze. He needed to watch himself. No point inviting trouble. He drew in several breaths to calm the thumping in his chest. "Maybe we should head back." Could she hear that hint of nervousness?

Pinpricks of stars emerged from the shadowy sky overhead. If they were courting, he'd make excuses to keep her out here to admire the moon. Soon it would hang full and orange against the black backdrop of the heavens.

He jammed his hands into his pockets to prevent himself from reaching out to hold hers.

He'd never felt this drawn to anyone before. Walking beside her without speaking didn't make him tense and uncomfortable. Instead he relaxed into the quietness and enjoyed the peace.

"It's so beautiful at night," Priscilla whispered. "I wish we could keep walking."

"Me too," Gabe admitted, "but I promised my sister-in-law I'd go along to her brother's church tomorrow."

At the word *church,* Priscilla's face scrunched up. "I'm glad tomorrow's an off-Sunday for us."

Gabe wished he hadn't mentioned church. "I'm sorry. It has to be hard for you to face all the judgment." He'd been subjected to that himself, but he'd never been totally innocent. Not like Priscilla.

"It is." She sighed. "What the school board learned in confidence, they won't share with others. Most people will never know what truly happened."

"Matthew owes the community a full explanation."

A rueful smile tilted one corner of Priscilla's mouth. "That's as unlikely as a cow laying an egg."

"You never know." Maybe Gabe could find a way to prod Matthew. He'd have to come up with an idea.

"You look like you're far away. What were you thinking about?"

Her question startled him. "Umm . . ." He didn't want to lie to her, but he also didn't want to tell her what he was plotting. "I wish we could find a way to make Matthew confess."

"Threatening to reveal his secret might work, but he'd lose his job." She shook her head. "I'll ignore the rumors. Soon something else will come along to distract the gossips."

"True." But the parents in her church might discourage their sons from dating Priscilla. Although that made him sad for her sake, he had to admit part of him rejoiced. He disliked thinking of her marrying.

Gabe shook his head. That was unfair of him. A woman as lovely and sweet as Priscilla deserved to be married and have children.

"You're doing it again," Priscilla pointed out.

"Doing what?"

"You're lost in thought."

"When you're alone as much as I am, you get used to thinking rather than speaking. Or you start yammering to camels."

Lucky camels. Priscilla wished she could take their place. "I'd love to hear what you say to them."

"You'd be bored. I talk about the business—problems, plans, pricing . . . Not to mention all the uninteresting details of my day."

"I'd find it fascinating."

Gabe studied her. "You really would, wouldn't you?"

"Of course." And not only because she found Gabe compelling. She genuinely wanted to learn more about running a camel farm. "Maybe you should give me information before the reporter shows up. Then I can do a better job of answering questions."

A blind twitched in the window of the darkened house. Mamm must be keeping an eye on them.

"My mother," she said with a slight nod toward the window. "I guess that's a signal for me to come inside."

"I'll let you go, then. But I'll see you on Monday. Thank you so much for agreeing."

"I'm happy to do it." Priscilla practically skipped back to the house. Not only would she get to see him two days this week to pick up the milk, but she'd get to spend Monday afternoon with him.

When she was out of his earshot, she hummed a happy tune. A tune that died on her lips when she opened the front door to find Mamm waiting. Priscilla sobered and wiped the smile from her face.

"Well, *dochder*, what did you talk about?"

"Not much."

Priscilla's response didn't sit well with Mamm, who frowned and planted her hands on her hips.

210

Her disapproving silence indicated she intended to get answers.

Sighing inwardly, Priscilla gave her some of the details of their conversation. "He wanted to know how the school board meeting went."

"He knew about that?" Her tone put Priscilla on the defensive.

"I mentioned it while I was picking up milk."

"Doesn't seem like that would be something that would come up in casual conversation."

"I had to explain why I might not be able to help with the event at Hope's farm." To forestall more questions, she volunteered, "I've been helping Hope and Gabe plan a school trip to the farm so people could learn about camel's milk and horse therapy."

"I see."

Priscilla slipped past Mamm and headed for the stairs, but the inquisition wasn't over.

"Gabriel said he had something to ask you. What was it?"

Telling Mamm about the newspaper would prolong the conversation. And she might be impressed, making her even more certain Gabe was the right choice for a husband. Before the magic of being around Gabe wore off, Priscilla longed to go to bed and keep him in her dreams.

But she had to be respectful of Mamm. "He asked me to help him on Monday." Priscilla squirmed at the misdirection.

"He took my suggestion already?" Mamm beamed. "Why couldn't he have asked you that in here?"

"You do know he's shy, right?" Now, she'd compounded her falsehood. Lies resembled snowballs, the way they kept growing.

"He didn't seem to be."

"Well, you did ask him a lot of questions."

"Priscilla Ebersol, are you implying I'm nosy?"

"Mamm, I never said that." Priscilla had thought it, though. *Forgive me, Lord, for judging.* When she got frustrated, she needed to remember Mamm had her children's best interests at heart. Even when she was meddling.

Chapter Fourteen

Gabe rushed through his milking on Monday morning, his hands unsteady. Priscilla had promised to come early for the interview, but if she ran late, he'd be alone with the reporter. This interview could make or break his store's success. He took a few deep breaths and tried to block the images flooding his mind—all the possible disasters.

As soon as he sterilized the equipment and washed up, he hurried over to bottle the milk and clean the store. In case they took interior pictures, he wanted everything spotless.

He'd asked Tim not to come in after school today. That way, the paper wouldn't inadvertently snap any pictures of his nephew. He also didn't want any distractions during the interview. Struggling to answer questions while hiding his attraction to Priscilla would provide enough distraction.

By midafternoon, he'd straightened all the refrigerated shelves, filed all the bills and papers, swept and mopped the floors. He stopped for a brief lunch and then went back to dusting and organizing the store shelves. Keeping his hands and mind busy helped to alleviate some of his nervousness.

A loud knock on the door startled him. The reporter was here already? Priscilla wouldn't arrive for twenty more minutes. He whirled around. A man in a blue uniform stood outside the door. The sign said *Open,* so why hadn't he come in?

As Gabe rushed to the door, the man pushed on the door and stepped inside. Gabe stopped. The gold letters on the man's blue baseball cap spelled out *FDA.*

"Good afternoon. I'm Darnell Jackson from the FDA." The man held out his badge, but Gabe was too confused to check it closely.

The FDA? That didn't make sense. He'd been inspected when he opened, and routine inspections occurred every two years. He'd had no trouble with the FDA in Bucks County. His farm had passed every time.

Mr. Jackson unclipped a form from his clipboard. *Notice of Inspection.*

Gabe struggled to find words. "But—but I just had an inspection." At least he'd cleaned the whole place today. They wouldn't find any violations.

Mr. Jackson's serious gaze sent fear spiraling into Gabe's stomach. The inspector shook his head. "I'm afraid we've had several reports about the quality and authenticity of your products."

"What?"

"Because many people buy camel's milk for

infants and children who can't tolerate cow's milk, mislabeling products can be dangerous or even deadly."

Gabe's mouth dried out. He'd never do that. An image of the fancy *Englischer* flashed through his mind. *Fleurette.* Had she reported him?

The inspector continued, "We've verified that a six-year-old girl was treated for anaphylactic shock, due to a severe milk allergy."

"What—?"

"Anaphylaxis narrows airways and cuts off the breath. If people don't get medication right away, it can be life-threatening."

Gabe hadn't been asking for a definition of anaphylactic shock. He'd read enough about milk allergies to know the symptoms. He just struggled to put his questions into full sentences. If only Priscilla were here. She'd know what to say and ask. Right now, all Gabe cared about was being sure he didn't commit a blunder. A wrong answer might put his business in jeopardy.

A frown marred Mr. Jackson's forehead. "Luckily, the little girl was in the doctor's office at the time because her aunt had an appointment for a flu shot. Otherwise, she would have died."

If she had, would I be charged with murder?

"Her family is vigilant about her diet." The inspector tapped his pen against a line on the clipboard. "The only new food they'd introduced was camel's milk. From your store."

Gabe should apologize, but if he did, the inspector might think he was admitting his guilt. Yet, if his milk had caused her health issues, he should take responsibility.

Mr. Jackson gave Gabe no time to respond. Flipping through the sheaf of papers, he folded a thick pile backward over the clip. "According to the report, the little girl's not allergic to camel's milk. They had her tested before they bought large quantities."

That makes sense.

The inspector swept on, reading from notes in front of him. "Her aunt also had the foresight to keep the small container of milk the child was drinking. A lab in the Philly area tested what was left." He looked up, and his eyes bored into Gabe's. "The only place they bought camel's milk was from you."

"I didn't—"

Holding up a hand, Mr. Jackson rustled through more pages. "If you're going to claim you didn't sell them the milk, I'm afraid they bought it at only one place." He produced a receipt. "This is yours, isn't it?"

Gabe couldn't lie. "*Jah*, I mean yes."

"For further proof"—Mr. Jackson lifted the sheet to reveal the next page—"Henry Defarge, one of your large commercial customers, let us test the few bottles he had left."

"But he's—" Gabe swallowed hard. He wanted

to explain Henry was Fleurette's husband. *Would Mr. Jackson think that was suspicious?*

After flicking through several pages, the inspector reached a sheet filled with statistics. "Here are the results." He turned the clipboard to face Gabe. "Every one of those samples contained a percentage of cow's milk. Some were only one-quarter camel's milk."

"That's not—" Gabe choked on the word *possible.*

He and Tim might have accidentally mixed up one bottle if they'd run out of milk during bottling and later finished filling the bottle with the wrong milk. But they took precautions against that by bottling each kind in a separate place, and Gabe often capped partially filled bottles of camel's milk and billed people less.

"We issued a recall for all your camel's milk sold within the last two weeks. You should have gotten a notice."

No, he hadn't. Tim usually collected the mail from the box at the end of the lane on his way up to work. Had his nephew lost or dropped the letter?

"Because milk allergies can cause death, I'm afraid we'll have to close your business until we complete the inspection and ensure you're in compliance with all regulations."

Gabe's thoughts raced. All these coincidences. How likely was it that the little girl just happened to be in the doctor's office when she drank the milk? And that Fleurette immediately sent the milk for testing? Or that her husband provided the other samples? If Gabe pointed that out and accused Fleurette of a setup, the inspector might assume Gabe was covering up his guilt.

Mr. Jackson unclipped a sign from under the stack of papers, walked over, and taped it to the door.

Gabe stood there stunned. The FDA had just closed the store. He had no idea for how long.

What was he going to do? If he couldn't sell his milk, he'd lose his business.

Priscilla fidgeted with impatience as parents picked up their children after school. Every minute was time she could be spending with Gabe. She hoped the reporter didn't come early.

Ada studied her. "What's wrong? It's not like you to be so jumpy."

"I'm a bit nervous. I promised to help Gabe Kauffman at the camel farm with a newspaper interview."

"Really?" The curiosity in Ada's voice made Priscilla wish she'd kept the news to herself.

"*Jah*, he's shy, and I've read a lot about camel's milk, so he asked if I'd be there to answer some of the questions."

Ada's *hmm* sounded like she suspected a budding relationship. As much as Priscilla wished it were real, Gabe had made it clear his only interest was friendship. Well, except for the way their eyes met. Although, if she were honest, she might be reading more into those looks than Gabe intended.

"You look all starry-eyed." Ada's words snapped Priscilla from her daydream.

Priscilla shook her head. "*Neh*, I'm only . . ." *Only what? Falling for him?*

Betty Troyer's buggy rattled into the parking lot, ending those uncomfortable thoughts and distracting Ada.

Martha scurried toward Lukas, who was examining a dead leaf. "Time to go," she said and walked him to the buggy.

Betty's sideways glance at Priscilla seemed to be a little less judgmental. Her brother was on the school board. Perhaps he'd told her Priscilla wasn't guilty. If so, would she spread that rumor the way she passed around negative ones? Somehow Priscilla doubted it. Still, if Betty reduced her animosity even a fraction, it would make their encounters a little less unpleasant.

Even Ada noticed. "Is Betty softening toward you?"

"I wondered that." Priscilla debated about telling Ada the truth. Now that Matthew had told the school board, perhaps she could confide in a few friends. She didn't have to mention the other girl's name, although it might cause speculation.

Sooner or later someone was sure to come to the correct conclusion.

Before she could decide, Ada laid a hand on her arm. "Now that Betty's gone, you can go. I can handle these three students."

Priscilla shook her head. "I don't feel right leaving you here alone."

"I'll be fine. It bothers me to see you so nervous." She gave Priscilla a gentle push toward the road. "Get moving. You don't want to be late."

"Are you sure?" As much as Priscilla longed to hurry to the camel farm, she disliked skipping out on her job.

"I'm positive. Go on." With a shooing motion, Ada made it clear she expected Priscilla to scurry off.

"*Danke.*" Priscilla tried not to appear too eager, but excitement over seeing Gabe quickened her steps.

The minute she reached home, she hitched up the horse. Mamm stopped her as she headed down the driveway.

"How late will you be working? Will you be home for supper?"

Priscilla longed to get moving, but if she didn't answer Mamm's questions, her mother might hold her here with a long-winded conversation. Priscilla didn't know how long an interview might take, but to be on the safe side, she said,

"I'm sure I won't be back by suppertime."

"I thought not." Mamm handed her a wrapped sandwich. "I'm so glad Gabe asked you to work. Do you think—?"

"Mamm, I need to get there before four. I don't want to be late the first day."

"*Ach*, that would never do. Go on. Go on." Her mother waved toward the street. "What are you waiting for?"

Smiling to herself at Mamm's question, Priscilla headed off. She only nibbled at her sandwich, because nervous anticipation had tied her stomach in knots. Once she'd finished the sandwich, Butterscotch's usual plodding soon started her *rutsching* on the buggy seat. Her horse seemed to be slogging through the thick blackstrap molasses Mamm used for shoofly pie.

Priscilla didn't want to urge the horse into a trot, because if she arrived too early, Gabe would know she'd rushed there right from school, making her appear overeager. Especially not after Mamm's supper invitation and questions on Saturday night.

When Priscilla finally pulled into the parking lot, she spied a sign taped to the window. *Closed Until Further Notice.*

Gabe must have posted the sign to keep the shop quiet during his interview. That might make him less anxious.

She tied up her horse and approached the door. *Wait.* That sign had been placed on the door by the FDA. What was going on?

Through the glass, Gabe and a man were talking, and Gabe's face was tight with tension.

Ach, the reporter had arrived already. Ignoring the closed sign, Priscilla yanked open the door. She had to rescue Gabe.

"Priscilla?" Gabe sounded startled and less than welcoming. "I, um . . . This is Mr. Jackson. He's . . ."

She smiled at the reporter and held out a hand. "Hello, I'm Priscilla . . ." Her words trailed off at Gabe's frown. Had he changed his mind about having her here at the interview? She'd just barged in, assuming he wanted her to help. But his expression revealed his embarrassment. Was he uncomfortable around the reporter? Or had she caused his uneasiness?

Gabe shifted from one foot to the other. As much as he'd wished for Priscilla to appear, he now wished she weren't here to witness his humiliation. He also needed to let her know what was happening, but he couldn't tell her in front of the inspector.

"Mr. Jackson's, uh, here because, well . . ." Gabe's words tangled in his head. Explaining the whole situation was much too complicated.

"Your wife?" Mr. Jackson asked.

Priscilla met his eyes. Gabe wanted to beg her to say yes, but he couldn't ask her to lie.

Without waiting for either of them to reply, the inspector turned to Priscilla. "As I've been telling your husband here, we're closing down the business temporarily while we do an inspection. We've had a young girl almost die because the camel's milk had been mixed with cow's milk."

"Fleurette actually hurt her own niece?" Priscilla burst out.

Mr. Jackson looked startled, then he smoothed his features into a professional mask. "We do not disclose the names of victims."

"She's not a victim. Well, the little girl is, but Fleurette doctored that milk."

"Ma'am, I'm afraid that's not the only proof. We tested many other samples of your milk."

Despite the gravity of the conversation, Gabe repeated the words *your milk* to himself, picturing them as real. He'd gladly share the ownership of this business with Priscilla. Pulling his mind from that thought and all it implied—the two of them working together as a couple—Gabe concentrated on Priscilla's reaction.

She pinched her lips shut and stared at the inspector in dismay. "You found more cow's milk mixed with camel's milk? How many bottles did Fleurette tamper with?"

"You're quite mistaken. The other bottles came

from one of your large commercial customers."

"That can't be right." With a question in her eyes, she turned toward Gabe.

Henry Defarge, he mouthed.

"Her husband?" Priscilla faced the inspector. "The commercial business wouldn't happen to be owned by Henry Defarge by any chance?"

Mr. Jackson's eyes narrowed. "So you're already aware of the problem?"

"We certainly are." Priscilla's tart tone revealed her annoyance. "Henry Defarge and Fleurette Moreau want to buy the camel farm. They're working together to force Gabe out of business."

Shaking his head, Mr. Jackson tapped on his clipboard. "Many people, when they're confronted with an inspection, try to shift the blame or come up with wild conspiracy theories."

"What Henry and Fleurette are doing *is* a conspiracy. You do know they're married?"

The way the inspector's eyebrows shot up, he hadn't known, but he recovered quickly. "They have addresses in different states. She's in Philadelphia, and he's in New Jersey."

Having Priscilla here had taken some of the heat off Gabe, giving him time to think. When he lived in Bucks County, he'd traveled from Philly to New Jersey to deliver milk to some customers. "It's only across the river." Some people had businesses in one state and lived in another.

Priscilla's smile of approval set his heart

thumping. He forced himself to look away.

She jumped in to add, "They may have different last names and live in different places, but they're in this together. They threatened Gabe after he refused to sell his business to them."

"I'll note your concerns in my final report, but I'm afraid we have to continue our process." His skeptical look indicated he didn't believe her.

"How long will it take?" Gabe managed to ask.

"This will be a bit more involved than the usual five days or so, and the milk analysis may hold things up." When Priscilla started to protest, he held up a finger. "We have a child who almost died. We can't risk any other deaths."

"I'm sorry." The heavy weight of hurting a child rested on Gabe. He hoped and prayed it hadn't been his mistake. Even if it hadn't, his milk had been used, so he was still involved.

"I am too," Priscilla said. "We both feel terrible about the little girl, but it's not Gabe's fault."

The inspector shot her a disbelieving look. "We'll see."

But Gabe's heart overflowed with gratitude that Priscilla believed in him.

A large van with the newspaper logo drove past the door and into the parking lot.

Ach, no. The reporters had arrived.

Priscilla had to stop them from finding out about the inspection. They'd publish this false

225

accusation rather than the real story. If that happened, Gabe's reputation would be damaged. Few people would trust him, even if the true story came out later.

Priscilla rushed out the door and stood blocking the sign. When the reporters approached, she held out her hand. "I'm Priscilla Ebersol. Gabe is tied up and asked me to speak to you."

"Alyssa McDonald." The redhead pumped her hand vigorously. "This is Jake Davis, our cameraperson. Can we go in?"

Priscilla shifted uncomfortably. "Not right now, but the camels are out in the fields," she said to Jake. "You could take pictures of them."

"Yeah, I'll get some shots." Jake walked over to the fence. "Okay if I jump this and go into the field?" he called.

"Camels can be bad-tempered," Priscilla warned. "Don't get too close."

"Don't worry," Jake said as he hopped over the wooden barrier. "I'll keep my distance. I've heard camels can be ornery. And they spit when they're upset, so I'm using a zoom lens." He patted his camera.

"You mind if I tape you?" Alyssa asked.

"Umm . . ." Priscilla hesitated. Would her parents object?

"I won't publish it or share it with anyone. It's only for me. I like to be sure I've quoted people correctly."

"I guess so." After all, Alyssa would only be taping what Priscilla had already said.

"Thanks." Alyssa patted the small spiral notebook in her hand. "I've taken shorthand, so I'll get most of it on here."

Priscilla nodded, suddenly shy. Knowing her every word would be recorded made her nervous about giving the correct answers.

"So how long has Gabe been in business?"

The first question and already Priscilla was stumped. He'd mentioned being here a few weeks. Or had he said a few months? "He only opened here recently, but he came from Bucks County, where he had a camel farm, so he's been doing it awhile."

"Do you know what year he first opened?"

"I, umm, you'll have to ask him."

"Any idea when he'll be free?"

Priscilla shook her head.

Alyssa turned to study the field. "Those baby camels are adorable."

"Yes, they are. The camels on the hill there are females." Priscilla pointed to a group of mothers and babies.

Maybe she could keep Alyssa occupied with talking about the camels. She took a step closer to show her the male but stopped. She couldn't move around. If she did, Alyssa might see the sign.

Stepping back against the door, she gestured to

227

the right. "See the male over there, doing a dance to attract the females?"

Alyssa laughed. "That's universal. All males like to show off."

Not Gabe. Priscilla almost said that aloud. And neither did her *daed* or most of the other men she knew. Except maybe Matthew.

"I suppose some do," she said to Alyssa, "but it's not the Amish way."

"You're supposed to be humble, aren't you?" Alyssa turned to face Priscilla.

"*Jah*, we are. God does not want us to put ourselves above others."

"Must be nice." Alyssa sighed. "Sometimes I get sick of the rat race and all the politics at work. Everyone trying to one-up everyone else. People talking behind your back, tearing you down."

"The Amish aren't perfect. We have gossips too." *And people trying to tear you down.* Priscilla had been through plenty of that.

"Really? I got the impression the Amish were perfect."

Priscilla smiled. "We're no different than anyone else. We make mistakes, we sin. We ask God and others for forgiveness."

"I'd love to do a piece on your lifestyle sometime." Alyssa wrote something in her notebook. "Right now, though, I need to get back to the camel farm. So, how many camels does Gabe own?"

228

Not another question Priscilla couldn't answer. This interview was going poorly. She had to be honest. "I don't know. You'll have to ask him." She needed to get the interview onto a topic she could talk about. "If you want to know anything about the benefits of camel's milk, I can tell you about that."

"I did read some before I came, but I'd be happy to hear more."

"Well, I teach at the special needs school, so I—"

"Wait," Alyssa said, interrupting her. "You have special needs schools in the Amish community?"

"Of course."

After jotting a quick note on a different page, Alyssa looked up. "This is so fascinating. I'm new to the area, so I look forward to finding out more about that. Would you be willing to talk to me about it?"

"Of course." Priscilla continued, "Anyway, I'm always looking into ways to help the scholars and my brother, who's autistic. My friend Hope has a horse therapy farm, and—"

Alyssa's eyes lit up. "Amish hippotherapy?"

When Priscilla nodded, Alyssa flipped to the previous page. "What's her name and address, if you know it?"

Priscilla provided the information and went on to her explanation of discovering camel's milk. "I'd read some studies on camel's milk and autism. I wished I could find some to try it. Then my—my, um, friend—"

Could she still consider him her friend after his betrayal?

"—he mentioned passing the camel farm, and I came right over. My brother's been using the milk, and it's calmed him."

"That's great!"

The enthusiasm oozing into Alyssa's answer warmed Priscilla. The reporter really seemed to care.

"Once I met Gabe, we discovered we both had an interest in helping children, so I organized an event with him at Hope's therapy farm to help those with special needs."

Pages ruffled. "When is it?" Alyssa waited with her pen poised.

She'd write about the event? Getting newspaper coverage would help both Gabe and Hope. Priscilla told her the date.

Gesturing toward the pasture, where Jake was still snapping pictures, Alyssa said, "Why don't we walk over there while we talk?"

Alyssa would think it odd for Priscilla to refuse. But she couldn't move. What excuse could she give to keep standing in front of the door?

Chapter Fifteen

"I need to milk now," Gabe said to the inspector. They wouldn't interfere with that, would they?

"Figured that." Mr. Jackson headed for the door. "I plan to watch the whole procedure from start to finish to see how the milk could end up mixed together."

Although having someone watching made Gabe nervous, at least Mr. Jackson would see the impossibility of combining the two kinds of milk.

"I don't want you to do anything differently now that I'm here. Our purpose isn't to put you out of business, but to help you fix the problems we identify."

"I appreciate that." Gabe motioned toward the exit. "I'm always glad to hear suggestions for improvement."

When they reached the door, Priscilla stood blocking the way. As Gabe opened the door, she kept her back plastered to it. He couldn't believe it. She'd been hiding the sign from the reporters.

"Are you Gabe?" A lively redhead bounced toward him. "I'm Alyssa McDonald. Pleased to meet you." She held out her hand.

Gabe shook it, but worried about Priscilla being caught between the door and the building. She snaked her way out and held the door open so the sign didn't show.

"Why don't I lock up for you?" Priscilla grabbed the edge of the door so it didn't close.

"*Danke*." Gabe breathed out the word in relief. "That would be a help."

He turned to Alyssa. "I'm going down to the barn to milk if you'd like to come."

Alyssa beamed. "Awesome. I've enjoyed talking to Priscilla, but it'll be good to get your answers. I'll just go call Jake. He's been taking pictures of your camels. I hope that's all right. He'll want to see the milking too."

"Of course." If this woman stayed talkative, it would make Gabe's interview much easier. He only hoped she didn't ask questions he couldn't answer.

To Gabe's relief, Priscilla held the shop door open until he'd escorted the reporters and inspector partway down the driveway. When everyone was far enough away that the sign wasn't visible, she closed the store and hurried to join them. What a thoughtful thing to do!

She caught up with them as they crossed the street to the milking barn. Gabe showed them around quickly, making sure to stress his sanitation and procedures for the inspector.

Jake still snapped pictures. Although Priscilla had never been in his milking barn, she pointed out things to Alyssa. Growing up around cows and reading about camels gave her enough knowledge.

Gabe shot her a grateful glance. "Camels get very jittery around strangers," he told the others. Not that he blamed camels for being uncomfortable with people they didn't know. Gabe was too.

Priscilla picked up where he left off. "If anything changes in their routine, camels don't give much milk. They give only a small amount of milk as it is, which is why camel's milk is so expensive."

"How much does it cost?"

"A pint is fifteen dollars."

Alyssa's eyebrows arched way up. "Wow. Just for a pint?"

"That's right." Priscilla gestured to the exit. "That's why we all need to stand way back. If we're outside there"—she indicated the chest-high wooden fencing—"we can still see inside."

"Gotcha." Alyssa turned a toothy smile toward Mr. Jackson as they backed outside the small barn. "I see you're from the FDA. You here for an inspection?"

Gabe sucked in a breath and waited for Mr. Jackson's answer. Whatever he said would be published in her story.

Tight-lipped, Mr. Jackson only nodded, and Gabe exhaled slowly. Maybe he'd keep this closure a secret from the reporter.

Alyssa leaned toward him. "How's it going so far?"

"We do not discuss ongoing investigations with the public, and especially not with the newspapers." Mr. Jackson's frigid expression warned her not to ask him questions. "You can search the database to find our final decisions."

"Investigation?" Alyssa's eyes lit up with curiosity. "Not a regular inspection then?"

"I said," he answered stiffly, "we never discuss anything. Please don't jump to conclusions about my word choice."

His coldness didn't deter Alyssa, who moved closer to Priscilla. "Can you tell me what's going on? Inspection? Investigation?"

Gabe needed to round up the camels, but he didn't want to miss Priscilla's answer.

She met the reporter's questions with a friendly smile. "Why don't I tell you more about camel's milk, since that's what the article is about?"

With a silent exhale, Gabe left, confident Priscilla could handle the reporter. He had no idea why Priscilla helped him this way, but he appreciated it.

Her sweet voice floated after him. "Did you know camel's milk is good for IBS, autoimmune problems, and diabetes?"

"Really?" Alyssa's question held a touch of disbelief. "Why don't more people know about it, then?"

"I've wondered that too."

Gabe rushed to round up the camels, but when he reached the road, he slowed. A vision of Matthew racing around that curve haunted him. He looked both ways before urging the mother camels to cross the street with the babies.

Thoughts of Matthew brought up his irritation. Gabe had determined to get Matthew to clear Priscilla's name, even if it meant he'd lose her. He had no right to keep her back from a happy home and family. No matter how wrenching it would be to see her with someone else.

The minute Gabe was out of earshot, Alyssa pinned Priscilla with a searching gaze. "Everyone's so evasive. This whole FDA thing makes me wonder what's really going on?"

"You know," Priscilla said to Jake, "the camels coming across the road are cute. They'd make good pictures."

"Thanks." Jake spun around and readied his camera.

"You're not going to tell me anything, are you?" Alyssa looked crestfallen.

Priscilla ignored Alyssa's remark and suggested, "Why don't you watch the camels too?" She prayed the milking would distract the reporter. If they could get her out of here without seeing the sign on the door, she might write a great article about Gabe's farm.

Her heart skipped a beat as Gabe stood in the center of the road, waiting for the smallest camels to cross. He looked as if he'd protect them with his life. His tenderness made her misty eyed. If only she'd courted someone like Gabe. She could have trusted him never to betray her.

Alyssa leaned over and whispered in her ear, "Are you all right?"

Priscilla had to guard her reactions around this eagle-eyed reporter. "Aren't the babies the cutest things? I can't help being touched when I see them. They remind me of God's love."

"Huh?" Alyssa looked puzzled. "What do camels have to do with God?"

Now it was Priscilla's turn to be surprised. "God created them. Isn't it amazing how God made so many different animals and people? We're all unique, and God created each one of us special."

"If you say so." Alyssa rolled her eyes. "So, you think God's responsible for this mop of unruly red hair? I've always blamed my parents."

"Of course He is. But we shouldn't pay much attention to what's on the outside. God looks on the heart, and we should too."

Alyssa made a face. "I'm not sure my inside looks much better than my outside."

"That makes sense. We're all sinners. That's why we need God's forgiveness."

"Don't tell me you're a sinner." Alyssa gestured

toward Priscilla's Plain clothing. "You dress all prim and proper. Anyone can tell you're a goody-goody just by looking at you."

Priscilla shook her head. "Once again, that's looking on the outside. People can dress like this but do wrong things." Like Matthew, for example.

And you for judging him, her conscience chided.

She needed to be honest. "Even if I try hard to live right, I'm human and make mistakes. None of us can be perfect."

"Don't I know it." Alyssa sighed. "I have a long way to go."

"But no matter how hard we try, we still sin. That's why we need to ask for God's forgiveness."

"You have no idea some of the things I've done. God could never forgive me."

"All sin is alike in God's eyes. And God can forgive everything. That's why Jesus came. He took the punishment we each deserve for our sin on Himself."

"I remember some of that from Sunday School as a little girl, but I haven't been to church in years."

Alyssa remained silent as Gabe brought in the camels. She watched him closely and took a few notes.

Priscilla longed to continue the conversation, but Gabe needed the barn quiet during the milking. Once the milking ended, she'd make time to finish talking to Alyssa. Priscilla positioned everyone outside the stall a safe distance away.

Jake leaned over the wooden railing to take pictures, but Gabe was sitting on the opposite side of the camel. "This is going to be difficult."

She had a better view. A view she hated to give up. Gabe's business came first, though. "Switch places with me," she whispered.

Sighing inwardly, she moved to the farthest place so Alyssa and Mr. Jackson could see better. Never again would she have such a good excuse to stare at Gabe as he worked.

As he settled himself onto his stool for milking, Gabe wished he'd planned this better. When he'd picked four o'clock for the interview, he'd been so nervous, his only thought had been to have Priscilla present. He hadn't factored in milking time. Now he had to milk in front of three strangers, including one who was noting his every action for violations and two who were recording everything for the public.

Taking a few deep breaths, he tried to calm himself. The camels always gave less milk when he was tense.

He cleaned the first camel's udder carefully, conscious that Mr. Jackson would be watching his every move.

Alyssa scribbled furiously in her notebook while he went through each step.

Usually he enjoyed the milking, spending time with each camel, sensing its mood, and coaxing it to give as much milk as possible. Today, he operated by rote. Milk production would be much lower than usual, but it didn't matter, because he couldn't sell it anyway. Mr. Jackson had warned Gabe that all the milk he collected over the next few days might need to be discarded.

Gabe wished he could give it to Priscilla or donate it to children at her school, but he suspected Mr. Jackson wouldn't allow that. Not until he proved he sold only pure camel's milk.

He prayed as he worked. *Lord, help us find a way to reveal the truth about Fleurette and Henry.*

Leaving his burdens with the Lord, Gabe relaxed. Everything happened for a reason. He might not understand why this was happening, but God had a plan. Gabe just had to trust.

Milking took longer than normal, and the minute he was done, Alyssa bombarded him with questions. How many camels did he have? How long had he been in business? Why did he choose camels? Why had he moved to Lancaster?

With Priscilla standing nearby for support, Gabe managed to respond to each one, although he kept his answers brief. He needed to take care of the cows. She wouldn't want to watch that, but how could he get them to their vehicle without seeing the sign?

Priscilla must have read his mind. "Should I take the milk up to the store refrigerator while you finish answering questions down here?"

"The bottles won't be too heavy for you, will they?"

She laughed. "I'll be fine."

Alyssa stared at Priscilla admiringly. "I love seeing strong women."

Although Gabe would have preferred to keep Priscilla here, he fished the keys from his pocket and handed them to her. He'd tested each batch under Mr. Jackson's watchful eyes before combining them. He had storage tanks here, but today's milk barely filled two large containers.

When she reached for the keys, he whispered, "You remember which side the camel's milk goes on?"

She nodded. He hoped she wouldn't make a mistake. Mr. Jackson would trail along with her. He needed to observe each step of the process. Once again, Gabe had to remind himself to trust God.

Priscilla lifted the covered containers and started off slowly and carefully. Jake looked as if he planned to follow her, so she pointed out a cute group of baby camels. That might keep him busy for a while.

Her nerves on edge, she headed across the street and up the hill. Any mistake she made would reflect poorly on Gabe. Having the inspector on her heels the whole way added to her stress.

When they reached the store, she set down the containers to unlock the door, hoping that wasn't a problem. Would he mark Gabe down for that?

She propped the door open with one of the coolers. If Jake or Alyssa came up, they couldn't read the notice. Only the blank back of the page would be visible.

She'd just finished setting the containers in the correct side of the refrigerator when a deep voice called out, "Anyone in here?" Priscilla rushed out to find Jake traipsing around the store.

"Okay if I take a few shots in here?"

Priscilla waved toward the shelves. "I'm sure Gabe'd be fine with that. I can also show you around the refrigerators, if you'd like."

"Great. Let me do these first."

Mr. Jackson watched both of them through narrowed eyes as Priscilla took Jake into the refrigerated room for pictures. Maybe this didn't meet the inspector's safety standards, but Gabe kept this room open to the public.

"Looks super neat and organized," Jake remarked. "Doesn't it?" He directed that question to Mr. Jackson.

Mmm was the inspector's noncommittal reply.

Couldn't he at least give Gabe credit for

orderly shelves? Even if Mr. Jackson didn't admit it, he ought to write it in his report. The precise arrangements impressed Priscilla. She prayed Mr. Jackson felt the same way. Gabe must have straightened everything for the newspaper photos, but that worked out to be God's perfect timing. The refrigerated room couldn't have been in any better shape than it was right now. Definitely one blessing.

A little while later, Alyssa popped her head into the doorway. "There you all are. Gabe answered a lot of questions." One hand on the doorknob, she asked, "Want me to shut this? It's getting breezier."

"No!" Priscilla practically shrieked. She raced over and pressed her hand against the door. "Let's keep it open for Gabe."

Alyssa cocked her head at Priscilla's lame excuse. "Gabe has to milk the cows. He won't be back for a while."

Priscilla struggled to come up with a better reason.

Mr. Jackson saved her. "I'm heading down to watch the milking. We should lock up the building while we're gone." He spoke to Priscilla, but tilted his head toward the exit, conveying that the others should leave too.

"But I haven't seen the store." Alyssa strode over to Jake. "How're the pics coming?"

"I'm almost done."

Mr. Jackson stood by the door, rapping his knuckles against the doorjamb in a *hurry-up* rhythm.

Alyssa wrinkled her nose and huffed. "If I don't look now, I'm not sure when I'll have time to come back."

The knuckle-tapping sped up.

"Oh, all right." Dragging her feet, Alyssa headed for the exit.

Once again Priscilla planted her back against the door, this time to hold it open.

Jake snapped a few more pictures before following Alyssa. "You'll be okay, Lys. I got plenty of shots. I'll give you copies of anything you missed."

"Thanks, Jake." She sailed out the door.

All three of them turned to wait for Priscilla.

"Why don't you go on ahead? Gabe's probably started the milking by now. I'll just close up here."

Mr. Jackson's gaze locked on Priscilla. The slight negative flick of his head indicated he didn't want her out of his sight, but she had no intention of closing the door until Alyssa and Jake were gone.

The standoff could have taken all night, but Alyssa started down the hill. "I have a few questions to ask Gabe before we leave."

Jake caught up with her. As soon as they were out of sight, Priscilla shut and locked the door, and Mr. Jackson race-walked down the hill.

Priscilla wanted to talk to Alyssa about God, but as soon as she and Mr. Jackson reached Alyssa, the reporter turned her attention to the inspector.

"You seem determined to scrutinize every detail of this business."

"It's my job."

A suspicious look in her eyes, Alyssa studied him. "Seems like a lot more than ordinary supervision."

With a shrug, Mr. Jackson shouldered past her and continued his rapid descent.

The reporter stared after him. Priscilla moved up to walk beside her, hoping for an opening to resume their previous conversation.

To her surprise, Alyssa brought up the subject. "I guess you people believe everything in the Bible is true."

"We do. It's God's Word."

Alyssa shook her head. "I'm not sure I buy that, but I do admire you for sticking to your beliefs. It can't be easy to live so differently than the rest of the world."

"We believe God wants us to be separate and not get involved with worldly things."

"I could never live without electricity." Alyssa ran a hand through her hair. "Yikes! I can't even imagine what I'd look like without my hair dryer."

Priscilla smiled. "If you were Amish, you'd pull

it back into a bob, and nobody would notice."

"A bob? I thought you kept your hair long."

"That's what we call our hairstyle. *Englischers* call it a bun."

"So you have a bun under that white thingy?"

With a nod, Priscilla tried to turn the conversation back to God. She touched the *kapp* on her head. "This is a prayer covering. It reminds us to always be in prayer."

"I'd hate to think about that all day long. I'd probably not do half the things I usually do."

"Wouldn't that be good?"

Alyssa laughed. "Yeah, probably." Then she sobered, and her thoughtful look changed to sadness. "You really believe God can forgive *anything?*"

"God's Word promises He will."

"God's Word?"

"The Bible," Priscilla clarified. "It tells us all about God's love and forgiveness."

They'd reached the milking barn. Alyssa put on a businesslike expression and lifted her notebook and pen as if she were ready to take notes. "I have a few questions for Gabe."

Priscilla regretted the abrupt end to their conversation.

Just before they entered the barn, Alyssa turned. "My grandpa gave me a Bible for graduation. He's not around anymore, but maybe I should try reading it."

"That's a great idea." Priscilla hoped Alyssa would follow up.

After Jake and Alyssa entered the barn, Priscilla hesitated outside and bowed her head. *Please, Lord, touch Alyssa's heart and draw her toward You.*

Maybe some good might come from Gabe's problems after all.

Chapter Sixteen

Gabe waited until the inspector reached the barn to begin the milking. That way he could see it from start to finish. Gabe hoped observing it once would be enough.

As soon as Mr. Jackson entered the barn, Gabe began moving the cows to the milking parlor, cleaning their udders, and hooking up the machinery.

Alyssa burst through the door, startling Gabe and the first cow. She skidded to a halt and pressed one hand over her mouth. "Oops! So sorry! I didn't realize you'd started. Are cows as skittish as camels?"

If they were, this one would have stopped producing milk already. "*Neh,* they aren't as bothered by people, and they don't seem to mind who milks them."

"You use machines?" Alyssa's horrified expression almost made Gabe laugh. "I thought you Amish didn't believe in electricity." She sounded almost sad that she'd discovered the Amish weren't perfect.

"Actually, I don't. I use an air compressor to power my equipment."

"Oh." Somehow, she made that seem worse.

"When we have a lot of cows to milk, we

could be here all day if we did it by hand. Amish commercial farms use machines like this too." Gabe had nothing against hard work—he did plenty of it—but if he wanted to make a living, he had little choice.

"Okay, then. Would you have time to answer a few questions?"

Gabe preferred to keep his mind on his work, especially when Mr. Jackson was examining his techniques. But if Alyssa wrote a good story, it could bring in customers. Provided, of course, that the inspector cleared him of wrongdoing.

Although he was late on the milking, he obliged her. "I can do it once I have all these cows hooked up." Ordinarily, he'd do all this without thinking, keeping his hands busy while his mind wandered elsewhere. But conscious of Mr. Jackson, today he paid close attention to every small detail.

After he'd finished, Priscilla caught his eye. She made a show of handing him the keys in front of Mr. Jackson. Then she gave Gabe a reassuring glance before slipping out. He assumed that meant she intended to stand in front of the door. How could he ever repay her for all she'd done?

He spent a few minutes answering the rest of Alyssa's queries. With a huge smile, she headed for the door. "Thanks for the interview," she said. "Jake took so many photos, we can do a full spread in the Sunday news."

Sunday? That would give him only a week to

clear up this FDA mess. How likely was it that Mr. Jackson could compile all the information and get the test results in that time?

Gabe prayed while he milked the rest of the cows. Under Mr. Jackson's stone-faced stare, Gabe tested and stored the batches of milk. The inspector gave no indication of whether or not he approved of Gabe's actions.

"I'll bottle the cow's milk tomorrow," Gabe told him, "but I still need to take care of the camel's milk tonight."

Mr. Jackson's curt nod made it clear he wasn't too pleased, but Gabe wanted to follow his usual routine. That way the inspector could see the care he took during bottling—and how unlikely it'd be to have a milk mix-up.

Priscilla would have gone home by now. Gabe wished he'd been able to thank her. She'd done so much to help him, not only during the interview but in protecting his reputation. But he regretted that the time he'd anticipated spending with her had turned into a nightmare.

To his surprise, however, her buggy was still parked in the lot, and she stood by the door, blocking the sign.

"You didn't need to stay all this time," he said, then regretted it when her cheeks pinkened.

Flustered, she stammered, "I, well, I wanted to be sure no one saw . . ." She waved a hand vaguely in the air. "Alyssa and Jake stayed to talk to me. They, um, just left a few minutes ago."

He tried to correct his mistake. "*Danke.* I didn't mean to sound critical. It's just that I didn't want to keep you so long."

"I'm happy to help."

"I really appreciate everything you did."

Her cheeks changed from pink to red. "It was nothing."

It certainly hadn't been nothing. She'd saved his reputation. But he couldn't say that in front of the inspector, who'd just caught up with him.

"*Danke,*" he repeated, unsure of how to express all that was in his heart.

Then he made the mistake of looking into her eyes, and he couldn't break his gaze. A magnetic pull drew him into their sparkling green depths. Behind him, Mr. Jackson cleared his throat, and Gabe jumped.

"I don't have all night." The inspector strode to the door.

With an apologetic smile at Priscilla, Gabe hurried over to unlock the door. Priscilla followed them in.

Gabe stopped her as she headed into the refrigerated room. "Take my jacket if you plan to stay."

She shook her head. "You need it."

"I'm used to the cold. You're not." He retrieved his jacket, and Priscilla let him help her into it while Mr. Jackson *tsked* impatiently.

She stood off to one side so the inspector had

a better view of Gabe as he bottled the milk. After he finished, Mr. Jackson collected most of the milk Gabe had shelved that morning, as well as some of the frozen milk. He took a bottle or two from each shelf, writing the dates on the containers with a black marker.

"You're not taking any cow's milk?" Gabe asked as the inspector ignored that part of the freezer and refrigerated room.

"I'll take a few random samples to test, but cow's milk is less expensive. I don't expect you'd be pouring camel's milk into those bottles."

Of course he wouldn't. Nor would he do the reverse. Rather than protesting, though, Gabe assisted Mr. Jackson as he loaded bottle after bottle into insulated coolers and placed them in his trunk.

After the inspector drove down the driveway, Gabe exhaled a long breath. Then he turned to Priscilla. "*Danke* for staying. Let me drive you home. I don't want to think of you on the roads alone."

A puzzled frown wrinkled her brow. "I drive by myself all the time."

"But it's dark." Darkness brought back awful memories. Buggies blended into the blackness. And teen drivers grew more careless at night. He certainly had proof.

When she seemed about to refuse, he said, "I don't want anything to happen to you."

"You're kind to offer, but Mamm will need the buggy tomorrow morning."

"Can I at least follow you home?"

"You don't have to do that." Despite her protest, a small smile bloomed on her face.

He could tell she wouldn't mind. "I don't have to. I want to be sure you get home safely." Maybe he could protect her the way he'd failed to protect Anna.

Priscilla enjoyed the opportunity to watch him as he hurried across the street and up the hill to his house near the barns. She wrapped her arms around herself, recalling Gabe's arms brushing hers again, the way they had when he'd enfolded her in his jacket. Her imagination wandered until buggy wheels crunching on gravel dissolved her daydreams.

Gabe pulled in beside her and leaned over to talk to her through the passenger window. "I can't thank you enough for everything you've done. I just realized you missed supper because of me. I hope your family isn't upset."

Neh, Mamm's probably rejoicing that we're spending extra time together. But Priscilla didn't want to remind Gabe of her mother's matchmaking, so she tried to reassure him. "I had no idea how long the interview would take, so I told Mamm I wouldn't be home for supper. She made me a sandwich to take along."

"A sandwich isn't much of a meal. Would you let me take you to Yoder's Buffet?"

Go out to supper with him? Did he mean as a date? Yoder's was a popular spot. What if someone saw them? It might start new rumors.

She shrugged. What difference did it make? No respectable man in their district would take her out knowing her reputation.

Disappointment flared in Gabe's eyes. He must have misunderstood. She hadn't been shrugging off his invitation.

"I'd be happy to go with you." In trying to correct her mistake, she came across too enthusiastic.

Gabe's smile—pleasant, rather than chilly—comforted her. He seemed to have taken her response as friendly, not overeager. "Let's go, then."

He didn't offer to take her in his buggy, which was just as well. If Mamm found out about this meal, she'd have them married off by November. The only thing that might stop her was needing more time to plan all the details. But she'd insist on next November, for sure and certain.

"I can lead the way," Gabe offered.

He'd only moved here recently, and she'd been driving these country roads for years. Most likely he didn't know the shortcuts. But because of the tension lines on his face, Priscilla bit back a protest and waited for him to pull ahead.

As she'd suspected, he drove the long way

around. By the time they arrived, the parking lot contained only cars, no buggies. The Amish had gone home to bed. Only tourists ate this late at night. Priscilla relaxed. No one would be around to see them and misinterpret Gabe's intent.

Priscilla's *Englisch* friends thought nothing of going out with a man one time, then moving on to the next. They called it "casual dating," but that ran contrary to the Amish way. From the first time Priscilla accepted Matthew's invitation to drive her home from a singing, she'd considered him in the light of a future husband. That meant blocking out any interest in other men.

She tried to tell herself that her attraction to Gabe had hit her so hard because of the rebound effect. All the feelings she'd once concentrated on Matthew had nowhere to go. Gabe had been the first man she'd seen that day, and he'd been so kind and supportive, she'd turned those emotions in his direction, resulting in a crush. But no matter how often she tried to explain them away or ignore them, her feelings for Gabe grew stronger the more time she spent around him.

Between Gabe's teasing about being his wife and Mamm's matchmaking, Priscilla's daydreams strayed more and more toward romance. Yet her instincts warned her not to trust another man. Not so soon after Matthew's betrayal.

She'd grown up with Matthew, spent lots of time with him, and had been sure of his character.

How very wrong she'd been. What did she know about Gabe beyond the few times she'd seen him at work? How could you judge a man's heart? How could you believe in him and trust him?

As soon as they arrived at the restaurant, Gabe realized his mistake. He should never have asked Priscilla to come to a restaurant. With her *mamm*'s matchmaking and his "pretend-wife" teasing, which had been more serious than he'd like to admit, he might end up entangled in an uncomfortable situation.

At the time, he'd only been concerned that she'd missed a meal because of him. But now it hit him that she might consider this a date.

He swallowed hard. Part of him wished it could be, but he had no right to think of her that way. And he didn't trust himself not to ruin Priscilla's life. After all, he'd destroyed Anna's.

Shaking off his gloom, he opened the door for Priscilla and followed her inside. While the waitress led the way to a booth near the buffet, Gabe could pick out the tourists, who nudged each other and stared. The locals paid no attention.

Once they'd been seated and had given their drink orders, Priscilla leaned toward the waitress and whispered, "Separate checks, please."

No way would Gabe allow her to pay. "*Neh*, bring me the bill."

As the waitress glanced from one to the other, obviously curious, Gabe shook his head. "It's my fault you missed your supper. The least I can do is pay."

Priscilla's brow wrinkled. "I don't want you to buy my food."

"I insist." Gabe turned to the waitress. "One check."

"If you're sure?" She checked with Priscilla.

"I'm sure," Gabe said firmly.

The waitress smiled a bit uncertainly. "I see. Will you be having the buffet?"

"I am." He gestured to the menu. "Please order whatever you want," he told Priscilla.

"The buffet for me," she said, handing her menu to the server.

The minute the girl left, Priscilla stood. She must be hungry. Gabe was glad he'd suggested going out to eat.

"Let's get our food," Priscilla suggested, "and then we can talk about the bill. I didn't want to argue in front of the waitress."

"Nothing more to discuss. You can either accept the meal or I'll pay you for the hours you worked this evening." Gabe stopped. "Actually, I should do both."

Priscilla put her hands on her hips. "You'll do no such thing."

She appeared so attractive with the slight flush to her cheeks and an indignant expression on her face, Gabe's pulse beat out an unsteady rhythm. He forced himself to look away. He had to be careful.

To lighten the mood, he tried joking as they walked to the nearest food bar, "Your *mamm* might get the wrong idea if I don't pay you."

Beside him, Priscilla froze. "I'm so sorry."

"For what?" He turned, and she ducked her head.

"For Mamm. I don't want you to think—"

"You're not responsible for your mother's actions."

Priscilla refused to meet his gaze. "It's just that . . ."

"Listen," Gabe said as gently as he could, "your *mamm* has your best interests at heart. I can't fault her for that. I'm sure you didn't have anything to do with her plans." Although he couldn't help wishing she had.

Gabe! Stop it! He needed to keep his mind away from fantasies. Especially those that involved Priscilla.

"Excuse me," a woman said behind him.

"Sorry," Gabe muttered to the line of people waiting behind them. "We'd better get our food. We can talk about this at the table."

They filled their plates from the various food bars and settled into the booth. Then they both bowed their heads to pray.

When he opened his eyes and met her shining

green ones, he gulped. To distract himself, he picked up his fork and knife to cut into the meat on his plate. "I can't wait to try their broasted chicken." His comment made no sense when he was slicing off a bite of roast beef, but it was the first thing that popped into his head.

"Have you tried it at Amos's Place?"

"Not yet. Running the farm doesn't give me much time to eat out."

"I can understand that."

Gabe chewed slowly, trying to come up with a neutral subject to discuss. He should have purchased a take-out meal for her to avoid this awkwardness.

Priscilla leaned toward him. "What are you going to do about the FDA? We need to find a way to show them this was Fleurette's and Henry's plot."

"But how? You did try to say that to the inspector, but he warned us not to pass off the blame."

"You're not. You didn't do anything wrong."

Priscilla's fiery defense warmed him deep inside. She believed in him, championed him. No one had ever done that before.

"I still feel guilty, though, about the little girl in the hospital," Gabe admitted.

"That's not your fault. I can't believe anyone would deliberately harm a child."

"Neither can I." Back when Fleurette had first

told them about her niece, Priscilla had convinced him the story was fake. Now that it had been proven, it bothered Gabe that his milk could have caused a child's death.

He swished a piece of beef around in the puddle of gravy. "If they hadn't been in the doctor's office, my milk might have been responsible for murder." Gabe winced.

"A doctor's office?"

"That's right. You weren't there when the inspector told me what happened." He recounted all the details.

Priscilla sucked in a breath. "Who takes milk to the doctor's office? I've seen people take juice or water, but milk spoils."

Gabe hadn't thought about that, but it made sense. "But how can we prove it was a setup?"

"Fleurette didn't leave the papers about buying the business, did she?"

"*Neh*, and neither did Defarge." Usually you left the offer with the seller to look over the terms. That was odd.

"So it's only your word against his. We also have no proof of the threats." She sighed.

Gabe loved that she'd used the word *we*. She not only put herself on his side, but she also sounded as if she planned to help him.

Chapter Seventeen

Gabe's tender smile sent joy swirling through Priscilla. If only she'd met him first, rather than Matthew. She clenched her hands together in her lap. How different her life would be! Of course, that depended on if he'd been interested in her.

She needed to get her mind away from those thoughts and concentrate on the FDA problem. "God knows what's needed. For now, the best solution is for us to pray."

"*Jah*, I've been doing that. And trusting God has a purpose."

"Of course He does." He also had a reason for everything that had happened with Matthew, although she had no idea what God wanted her to learn. The main good that had come out of the breakup was discovering Matthew's unfaithfulness before they married.

"Are you all right? You looked so sad and faraway. I didn't mean to burden you with my problems."

"That's not it at all." Priscilla nibbled at her lower lip. Should she confess what had been on her mind? Not wanting Gabe to believe he'd upset her by confiding about his business woes, Priscilla decided to be honest. "I'm sorry. My thoughts were on Matthew."

Gabe's mouth tightened. "I see."

No, he didn't. "Not in a good way," she explained. "When you mentioned God's purpose, I wondered what reason God had for the breakup. I'm grateful I discovered the truth before Matthew and I married." Priscilla grimaced. "Being tied to someone for life, knowing I could never trust him, would have been unbearable."

"I can certainly see the good in that. God kept you from a lifetime of unhappiness."

"True." She didn't point out that she might have exchanged it for a lifetime of loneliness.

The hostess led a couple past them, and Priscilla bit back a gasp. Engrossed in talking, Matthew's neighbor Marty Miller and his girlfriend Olivia didn't look their way. Priscilla scrunched down in the booth, trying to hide from view. Being petite helped, but she couldn't make herself small enough to be unnoticeable.

A worried look in his eyes, Gabe stared at her. "Are you all right?"

Priscilla held up a finger as the two headed to a table in the opposite corner of the room. After they were seated, she angled herself to keep her back to them.

"I'm sorry," she said to Gabe. "Two people from my church are here."

"You don't want them to see us together?" His understanding look reassured her he wouldn't take offense if she agreed.

"Everyone believes Matthew and I did something wrong." She squeezed her eyes shut, but she couldn't erase the picture of Matthew and Mara in the orchard. "If they see me with a strange man . . ."

"I'm so sorry. I didn't mean to make things worse for you."

"It's not your fault." Priscilla should never have agreed to come here. What had she been thinking? Her face blazed. She hadn't been thinking; she'd been concentrating on the sensation of Gabe's arms around her, wrapping her in his jacket. And on spending more time alone with Gabe.

Shaking off the memory, she pulled herself back to the restaurant. "Marty lives next door to Matthew," she said flatly.

The two men had never been particularly close. Being rather quiet and self-contained, maybe Marty would keep tonight's encounter to himself.

"I don't want to be responsible for blackening your name even more. We can leave if you'd like."

Priscilla peeked over her shoulder. Right now, the couple seemed to be absorbed in their conversation and oblivious to others around them. Standing up to leave might draw more attention to them, and they still had food on their plates. "Let's finish our meal."

But Marty's presence left Priscilla too edgy to

relax and enjoy being with Gabe. She lifted bites to her lips, chewed, and swallowed, but the food had turned dry and tasteless.

"Would you like dessert?" Gabe asked.

Normally, she looked forward to the pies and ice cream. Tonight, though, she had little appetite. "I'll pass."

"But the desserts are the best part." He glanced over at Marty. "They only ordered dessert, so they won't be here long."

"Maybe we should go." Priscilla disliked making Gabe miss out on the treats, but she was desperate to get out of here.

Their waitress passed, and Gabe signaled for her and asked for the check. After the waitress returned with it, Gabe stood and angled himself to shield her from the other couple's sight. He stood so near she almost brushed his chest as she slipped out of the booth. Her breath whooshed out in a quiet hiss, and she prayed Gabe would think she was worried about being spotted.

Once they left the restaurant, she might be able to draw some air into her constricted lungs. Right now, though, being around Gabe—and worrying about Marty and Olivia—had taken her breath away.

Gabe tried to concentrate on blocking Priscilla from view. But the warmth of her body so close to his, the light floral scent of her hair, the . . .

Stop it, Gabe. Remember Anna.

He hoped Priscilla couldn't hear the rapid drumming of his heart as he hustled her toward the cashier. "Why don't you go outside?" he suggested as he got in line to pay. As much as he wished to keep her near, he needed to protect her reputation.

Priscilla looked as if she wanted to protest, but she heeded his advice. "I'll pay you later," she said before scurrying toward the door.

"Priscilla?" a woman's voice said behind him. "I thought that was you."

"O-Olivia." Her face pale, Priscilla gave the girl a wan smile.

Trying to act as if he didn't know Priscilla, Gabe paid for their meal, but he struggled to keep his eyes off her. He wished he had some way to intervene.

"Marty's in line back there." Olivia pointed to a spot behind Gabe. "And who are you here with?"

Priscilla's gaze flew to Gabe's. She seemed to be begging him for help. But what could he say to avoid rumors?

Priscilla beat him to it. "This is, um, my boss, Gabriel Kauffman. I help out at his camel farm sometimes."

Olivia raised an eyebrow. "Really? A camel farm? Do you milk the camels?" She stared at

264

Priscilla with wide eyes before turning toward Gabe.

He smiled at her. "*Neh*, I have to do that. Camels prefer only one milker. But Priscilla is a big help in the store. I couldn't run the business without her."

"Where's the camel farm? We'll have to check it out."

As Gabe gave her directions, Marty joined them.

"Did you know there's a camel farm in the area?" Olivia asked him.

"I heard about it from a neighbor. You must be Gabriel?" Marty extended a hand. "I'm Marty Miller."

"Nice to meet you." Gabe wondered if the neighbor was Matthew. Regardless, Gabe wanted to do something to clear Priscilla's name.

These two didn't seem like the gossipy type, but if they mentioned this meeting to their friends, rumors might spread. And Marty was studying him with a question in his eyes.

"Priscilla works for Gabe at the camel farm," Olivia said.

"Really? I thought you taught at the same school as Ada," he said to Priscilla.

"I do. I help out at the store some evenings. Mamm suggested it because she knows I'm interested in camel's milk for children with special needs."

"And I was grateful to find someone knowl-edgeable about camel's milk to work in the store. We had some unexpected business this evening, and Priscilla was kind enough to skip her supper to take care of things. I didn't feel that was fair, so I decided to buy her a meal. She didn't want to come, but I insisted." He hoped his prattling didn't sound like a lame excuse.

"I see," Marty said, but he didn't sound convinced.

"I don't want to lose my best worker," Gabe said. "It's a blessing to know I can trust her to handle things while I do the milking." He hoped that sounded like they didn't work closely together.

Priscilla gave Gabe a formal nod. *"Danke* for the meal. I'd better get out to my buggy. Mamm will be wondering what's taking me so long to get home tonight." She smiled at Olivia and Marty. "Nice to see you."

Smart idea, Priscilla. Stressing that they were going home in separate buggies made it clear this hadn't been a date.

After they said their goodbyes, Priscilla headed toward the door. "I'll see you at work tomorrow," she said as she left.

Tomorrow? Had she said that for Olivia and Marty's benefit? Gabe was positive Priscilla wouldn't lie to save her reputation. But she didn't have a milk pickup until Wednesday. She'd probably been so flustered that she confused what day she usually came in. He almost opened his mouth to point that out when it dawned on him: He wouldn't be able to give her—or anyone else—milk during the FDA inspection.

Priscilla escaped to her buggy, hoping she hadn't given away her interest in Gabe. Otherwise, the others might wonder if she were more than an employee.

Gabe had impressed her tonight. Despite what he said about not being able to answer questions under pressure, his responses had come across as polished. And he had definitely sounded believable. Perhaps because he wasn't emotionally involved. Unlike her. She needed to get these feelings under control.

Priscilla urged Butterscotch into a trot. Mamm might be concerned about how late she'd stayed tonight.

But when Priscilla got home, her parents had already gone to bed. With a prayer of gratitude, she tiptoed up to bed. Soon after her head sank onto the pillow, she drifted off into dreams of being in Gabe's arms.

Normally, she woke before dawn, but the next morning, Mamm had to call her twice. Reluctantly, she left the comfort of Gabe's embrace. The chill of the hardwood floor on her feet snapped her back to real life. With a sigh, she dressed and pulled her hair into a bob. Then she headed downstairs to help with the morning chores.

"You're late this morning, *dochder*," Mamm said when she entered the kitchen. "If you can't get up the next day, maybe you shouldn't work at the camel farm on weeknights."

Priscilla didn't want her parents to forbid her to go. "It won't normally be as late as last night." Should she explain about the restaurant?

Besides, staying out past her usual bedtime hadn't caused Priscilla's struggle to rise this morning. Wanting to spend more time in dreamland had been the issue.

Daed stomped into the kitchen carrying milk pails. Zeke and Asher followed. Asher cradled the egg basket as if it were a newborn baby. Usually one of Priscilla's sisters gathered the eggs and fed the chickens.

Zeke beamed as Asher set the basket on the table. "Asher did everything by himself this morning with no help."

"That's wonderful." Priscilla grinned at both of them. Since he'd started drinking the camel's milk, Asher had been much more cooperative.

What would happen if they ran out and couldn't get more? That would be a problem for other families, not just hers.

Please, Lord, help Gabe's situation to get cleared up quickly.

• • •

The phone machine was beeping when Gabe entered the store the next morning. The inspector, who'd arrived early enough to oversee the milking and bottling, followed Gabe inside.

Gabe ignored the noise as he transferred the bottled milk to the shelves.

"You know you can't sell those. We don't want anyone to drink them."

"I understand." What else could he do with them, though? He doubted he'd be allowed to give them away. Not if the inspector considered them unfit for human consumption.

"Could one of my neighbors who owns a goat farm use them for soap?" He'd be glad to help out Katie Kurtz and her new husband, Elam.

The inspector frowned. "I'll check with my supervisors. If they agree, the products will need to be clearly labeled for people with cow's milk allergies."

"I'm sure Katie will be extra careful." Gabe went over to bottle the camel's milk he'd brought up earlier.

Mr. Jackson's brows scrunched together. "Aren't you going to check that confounded machine?"

"Machine?" Gabe stared at him. He poured all his milk by hand up here.

"The answering machine." The inspector's cutting tone revealed his impatience and tiredness. He probably wasn't used to rolling out of bed this early or staying out so late at night. Most of his inspections could be done during regular business hours.

"Oh, that." Gabe continued bottling milk. "It'll keep until I'm done."

If the call had been an emergency, the caller would have contacted one of the nearby *Englischers* to give him a message right away. If a business customer called, Gabe never responded, except during business hours. The message on his machine made that clear.

Mr. Jackson huffed.

Englischers, who walked around with phones in their hands, probably expected immediate replies to their calls. That was one of the problems with technology. Everyone wanted instant gratification. *Englischers* often sat around restaurant tables not talking to one another while they each typed furiously on their own phones. What kind of a family life or friendship was that?

Gabe finished and opened the door that led into his office. He headed for the blinking light and beep. Making sure he had pen and paper handy in case he needed to take down contact information, he pushed the button.

Henry Defarge's voice blared into the room. "I understand your milk's been recalled. I'm canceling my standing order, and I expect to be paid back for every bottle I purchased by the end of the week."

Every bottle? Gabe sank onto the desk chair and lowered his head into his hands. Where would he come up with that kind of money? Did Defarge plan to bankrupt him?

His head already bowed, Gabe sent a petition heavenward. *Lord, what do You want me to do?*

The right thing to do would be to return the money. After all, the milk had been recalled. Defarge couldn't use it either. And what about the poor children who depended on that milk? Could Defarge afford to buy more for them?

While Mr. Jackson conducted his other examinations, Gabe sat at the desk with his ledgers open, trying to figure out how to repay every penny. If he cleaned out his personal and business accounts, he might be able to return the full sum, but it would mean not paying his other creditors. That wouldn't be right or fair.

By lunchtime, Gabe was so sick he couldn't eat. He'd passed the point of worrying about his own financial situation. All he cared about now was doing right by all the people he owed. Whatever he did, someone would lose.

The phone rang beside him, but he ignored it. The caller hung up when the answering machine clicked on. *Good.* After all, what could he tell people? That his milk had been recalled, his store was closed, the FDA was inspecting him, and he might be going out of business?

An hour later, the phone rang again. Gabe

271

decided he couldn't be a coward. He excused himself and left Mr. Jackson jotting down customer names and contact information. Would the inspector ask them to provide samples or warn them of the recall?

Gabe hurried into the office and picked up the phone on the sixth ring. He tried to infuse his *hello* with cheer. But he didn't quite succeed.

"I tried calling earlier, but you didn't answer," a woman said.

The queasiness in Gabe's stomach increased to full-blown nausea. *Fleurette Moreau.*

What did she want? Should he confront her?

Chapter Eighteen

Gabe's thoughts whirled, along with his stomach. How could he accuse her of what he suspected? As usual, the words muddled together, and he remained silent.

"Are you there?" Fleurette demanded.

"Yes," Gabe managed.

"I just want to give you a heads-up. My sister intends to sue. She went to a lawyer today, and he assured her she has a good case."

"But—but . . ." Shouldn't she be suing Fleurette?

"Listen. If I were you, I'd hire a good lawyer." Her tinkling laugh prickled like a bug crawling over his skin. "Oh, wait, you Amish don't believe in bringing lawsuits, do you?"

Gabe almost said they did just to stop her snickering. But he couldn't lie. He'd never initiate a lawsuit. Although it sounded as if he might have no choice about participating in one.

"Bet you wish you'd taken our offer, don't you?"

"No." That was the only word he'd gotten out, but it exploded from his lips.

"Well, you soon might wish you had. The lawsuit will smear your name and take everything you have. No one will want to do business with you after that."

Fleurette might be right about *Englischers*, but Gabe hoped the Amish would stand by him and believe in his innocence.

What if they doubted him? The way they'd done with Priscilla?

"Maybe you'll change your mind about selling later this week. Henry might—I'm not making any promises, mind you—just might come in with a lower offer."

Gabe shook his head. He'd never sell to Defarge or his wife.

"Remember, my offer still stands. No matter what Henry decides. I'm sure you can find a way to slip away from your wife and meet me somewhere."

This time, Gabe blasted his *NO!* into the receiver.

"*Ouch!* You didn't have to break my eardrums. Is your wife around? Is that why you're so forceful?"

Gabe's throat constricted, and he choked. All that came out was a low, furious growl.

"Okay, okay. I'll try to call at a more convenient time when you're alone."

Desperate to make himself clear, Gabe spat out each word. Fury, like he'd had toward Matthew, focused his mind on the message. "I. Am. Alone. The answer is NO!"

"Fine. We can discuss other terms for the sale."

"No."

"I hate to point this out, but you don't have any strong bargaining chips. Without your reputation and assets, you're coming from a place of weakness. You'll pretty much have to accept any offer."

That's what this had been about all along. They wanted to buy his business, and they'd set him up. But how could he prove it?

Priscilla planned to head for the camel farm right after school, but Mamm waylaid her.

"Gabriel asked you to come in again today?" Mamm frowned. "I hope he's not taking advantage of you volunteering."

"He's not." Priscilla forced herself to stay still. "Actually, he didn't suggest I come tonight, but I know he needs help." Or at least moral support. She had no idea if the inspector would still be there, but she could at least find out what had happened today.

"You're not pushing yourself on him, are you?"

"*Neh*, Mamm. He appreciates my help. He doesn't like to talk on the phone and things like that, so I handle it for him."

Her mother shot her a sideways glance. "He had no trouble talking when he was here for supper."

Priscilla pressed her lips together so she didn't point out that Gabe had actually done little talking. Then, taking a deep breath for patience, she said, "I promise I won't be gone long tonight. I wanted to finish up something that started yesterday."

"You'll be home for supper?"

"I'm not sure."

"The family belongs together at mealtimes. You missed last night's supper. I want you to tell Gabriel that from now on you need to be here when we eat."

"I will, Mamm." Priscilla didn't anticipate staying late most evenings. Even this afternoon, she only intended to stop in to see if everything had gone well. She'd probably be home early to surprise Mamm.

Finally, her mother let her leave. The closer Priscilla got to the camel farm, the more her spirits soared. Just knowing she'd soon be seeing Gabe made her smile.

The empty parking lot meant Mr. Jackson had gone. With the inspector gone, she was sure she'd find the business open. But her mood plummeted when she faced the FDA sign still taped to the door.

She turned the knob, but the door was locked. Gabe didn't start milking until later. Was he inside or at his house? She wouldn't feel right going to his house. She peered through the glass. The store appeared empty.

She knocked but held out little hope of an answer. Nothing to do but head home.

• • •

Rapping on the door startled Gabe from his discouragement. He had no desire to see or talk to anyone. Besides, the sign on the door made it clear his business was closed. And with the way things looked now, that closure could be permanent.

Mr. Jackson had left, but what if he'd forgotten something? Planting his elbows on the desk, Gabe leaned forward, hoping to glimpse the person outside without being seen.

He had a fleeting glimpse of the back of a prayer *kapp. Priscilla?* What was she doing here? Last night, she'd said she'd see him today.

He leaped from his chair and dashed across the store floor to catch her before she drove away. When the door banged open, she whirled, her hands pressed to her heart.

"*Ach*, Gabe, you scared me."

"I'm sorry. I didn't mean to." In his haste to catch her, he hadn't considered how his bursting through the door might affect her.

Her eyes, wide and vulnerable, met his, and once again, Gabe was drowning in a sea of green. The heat rising in him set his whole body aflame.

Alarm bells clanged. *Danger, danger.* He was straying into forbidden territory. Abruptly, he broke their gaze.

"Is something wrong?"

Her soft, caring voice only stoked the fire.

He had to get his mind on other things. *Now.*

Taking a deep breath, he said, "A lot has happened since last night. Want to come in?"

He held the door open, but as she brushed past him, he regretted it. Inviting her into the empty shop had been a mistake. A huge mistake.

But it was too late.

They shouldn't go into his office. Being in a small, enclosed space together would be too much of a temptation. Gabe struggled to get his racing thoughts and pulse under control.

He headed for the chair Tim used when he wrote receipts. "I'll sit on this and bring out my desk chair for you. It's more comfortable." He carried the wooden chair to the center of the cavernous warehouse. With all that space around them, it might cool his ardor.

"I can take this one." Priscilla headed for that chair.

He gripped the wooden back so hard it cut off the blood supply in his hands. "*Neh*, I'll get you the other chair. Please wait."

Priscilla shuffled from one foot to the other as if uncertain.

"Please?" he repeated. Then he hurried into the office and rolled his desk chair near the wooden one, but a safe distance apart. "Here," he said, glad she'd remained standing. He didn't want to fight over a chair.

He'd situated both chairs so they'd be visible

if anyone peeked through the door glass. Most likely nobody would arrive, but it would prevent him from making any missteps. It might also force him to focus on business rather than on Priscilla.

After she'd taken her seat, he lowered himself onto the chair facing her. Concentrating on his hands, clenched in his lap, Gabe told her about Defarge's call.

"That's so unfair." Priscilla sat on the edge of the chair and appeared ready to jump up and confront Defarge.

Gabe smiled, imagining the man walking through the door to face Priscilla's indignation.

"We have to do something. We can't let them destroy your business."

"I'm not sure I can pay him what he's asking and still keep the business running." He didn't want to admit the request might bankrupt him.

"You shouldn't have to pay him anything. You sold him pure camel's milk. His wife caused the recall. You're innocent."

"You and I both know that, but who will believe us?"

"They shouldn't be allowed to get away with these lies."

Gabe sighed. "But a court would side with him. They'd say I sold mislabeled products."

"A court?" Priscilla leaned so far forward the back wheels of the chair lifted off the floor.

Gabe worried she might tip over. And she'd land in his arms. Was it right to hope that happened? That he'd have to hold her, help her get her balance. Her softness pressing against his chest . . .

He slammed down a heavy metal barrier in his mind to block that picture. He shook his head to dislodge any remaining desires.

What had they been talking about? *Oh, right. Courts.*

"What do the courts have to do with it? Did he threaten to sue you?" Priscilla demanded.

"*Neh*, but I had another phone call this afternoon." His stomach churned as nausea swept over him. "From Fleurette."

"What did she want?" The indignation in Priscilla's expression reminded him of how he'd been drawn to her in the restaurant last night.

"She claimed she only called to warn me her sister plans to sue. But it came across more as a threat."

Trembling with anger, Priscilla gripped the chair arms. "Fleurette's sister should be suing her."

"*Jah*, she should, but she's coming after me. They're trying to put me out of business. She said Defarge might make an offer for the business. I'm sure they'll say they're trying to help me out."

The unfairness of the situation paralyzed Priscilla. What could they do against such powerful enemies? God had promised to protect them. She whispered a prayer for Gabe.

"There has to be something we can do to prove they're lying." She had no idea what, though.

Gabe's discouraged expression made her long to reach out, but he'd placed their chairs too far apart to touch. Had he done that on purpose? She had to admit that had been wise.

When she'd been wrapped up in his story about Henry and Fleurette, she'd been too upset to pay attention to the other signals her body sent. Now she became acutely aware of his presence.

She always had trouble breathing when she was around him. And her chest ached from the rapid fluttering against her ribs. Lowering her gaze, she set her hands in her lap, willing them to stay motionless.

All these feelings for Gabe confused her. She'd ridden beside Matthew many times in his courting buggy. Why hadn't she experienced this jumble of emotions, this desire for closeness, this tug on her heart?

Gabe balled his hands into fists and then unclenched his fingers one by one and stretched them several times as if releasing tension. She could only imagine his anxiety. He could lose the business.

"Even though I suspect Defarge is trying to ruin my business so he can buy it cheaply"—Gabe tapped his fingertips on his knee, a sure sign he was nervous—"I do feel I owe him his money back."

"What?" Priscilla practically screeched.

"They recalled the milk, and he lost out. He couldn't sell it. Even worse, he's been supplying that children's charity. He must have purchased more milk to make up for his losses."

"*Ach*, the poor children. I hope they didn't go without."

"Me too. If I don't pay Defarge back, what if he runs out of money to help the little ones?"

"I see what you mean."

"It'll be tight, but I'll get that money together. It may be the last thing I do before I lose this business."

"You're not going to lose this business," Priscilla said fiercely. She had no idea what she was going to do, but she'd do something. She'd never let Gabe's camel farm go under.

The doorknob rattled, and they both turned to stare. If she and Gabe had thought the day couldn't possibly get any worse, they were wrong.

Chapter Nineteen

Auburn hair and a wide smile showed between the sign and the window edge. *Alyssa.*

The door opened, and Alyssa stuck her head in. "Hey, I hope it's okay for me to pop in for a few minutes. I saw the two of you in here talking."

Priscilla hoped her wan smile didn't match Gabe's sickly one, but she feared it did. The reporter was the last person either of them wanted to see.

Everything Priscilla had done yesterday to hide the FDA sign and protect Gabe's reputation had been for naught. Her heart sank. Perhaps this was God's way of showing her she'd been guilty of a cover-up. Hadn't she accused Matthew of letting people believe something other than the truth? Now she had to face the same failing in her own life.

"Is something wrong? You both look so glum. Any connection to this?" Alyssa pointed behind her to the sign. "What's going on?"

Priscilla and Gabe exchanged looks. From the worry in his eyes, he was hoping she'd answer. But just like Gabe, Priscilla remained speechless.

Alyssa's gaze bounced back and forth between

them. "All righty, then. Let's start with something else first. I had a few more questions for Gabe, and I could have called for the follow-up, but I hoped I'd catch you here." She fastened her gaze on Priscilla.

"Me?" she squeaked. Tension had tightened Priscilla's vocal cords.

"Yes, you." Alyssa flashed Priscilla a brilliant smile. "I had something I wanted to tell you."

Priscilla had been too caught up in Gabe's concerns to pay much attention to the reporter. Now, though, Priscilla couldn't help marveling. The strain lines had disappeared from Alyssa's face, and she had a glow about her. She'd had some good news. A promotion, perhaps? *But why tell me?*

Beaming, Alyssa announced, "Thanks to you, I dusted off the Bible my grandpa gave me as a graduation present. Last night, I started reading the book of John. I'd forgotten a lot of that stuff about God's love and forgiveness."

Priscilla rejoiced. Alyssa certainly had gotten good news—the Good News of the Gospel. Priscilla could take no credit for this; it was all God's doing. He'd touched the reporter's life.

Priscilla thanked Him she'd been given the opportunity to play a small part in God's plan. The Bible would do more to draw Alyssa to Him than any words Priscilla could say.

"If you ever want to talk about what you're

reading," Priscilla said, "I'm always available. I love discussing the Bible."

"Thanks. I do have some parts I'm not sure I understand, but right now, I'm on work time, so I need to do my job." Alyssa glanced behind her and nodded toward the sign. "What's going on with the FDA? This looks serious. I can't run the lifestyle piece if the business is closed."

She directed a pointed look in Gabe's direction, and he shrugged. "It's a long story."

Priscilla sent him an encouraging smile. He'd answered one question without much hesitation. Maybe if Alyssa asked him slowly and allowed time for Gabe to think, he'd be able to respond.

"Oh, good." Alyssa plopped down on the low counter where Tim wrote the receipts. "I love stories of any kind."

But Gabe had clammed up. He sent Priscilla a pleading glance.

"Why don't you tell her what we suspect?" Priscilla suggested.

"Suspect?" Alyssa brightened. "This is sounding better and better." She tucked her legs up and wrapped her arms around them.

Gabe turned to Priscilla. "She needs to know about why the sign's there."

Priscilla shot him an *are-you-going-to-tell-her* look, but he only shook his head.

"The FDA received a complaint that Gabe's milk had been mislabeled."

"And?" When Priscilla didn't answer right away, Alyssa went on. "I may not be an investigative reporter, but even I know the FDA doesn't shut down a business for that. They send you a notice. Give you some time to fix things. Unless you repeatedly ignore the warnings or something bad happens. Even then, they'd recall the product."

"Something bad did happen," Gabe said flatly, but when Alyssa pressed him on it, he gestured toward Priscilla.

She was glad he'd responded to another question. Maybe over time, he'd get more comfortable. Meanwhile, he'd asked her to assist with yesterday's interview, so she'd help out now, but try to get him involved.

Priscilla explained about Fleurette's niece and her allergies. She also told Alyssa about Defarge wanting to buy the business. "The inspection is based on false charges. We're hoping this mess will soon be cleared up."

Although, considering what Gabe had told her a short while ago, that might not happen. If they forced him out of business, the results of the inspection might not matter.

Alyssa frowned. "You're saying this woman, Fleurette, gave her niece cow's milk even though she knew the little girl was allergic? Who would do that?" Alyssa held up her hand. "Wait a minute. Don't answer that. I've seen enough news to know parents and relatives often do terrible things."

"I find it hard to believe." Priscilla never had time to read the newspaper, which was just as well. The only time she saw TV was when she was shopping in some of the larger stores. Then she walked past as quickly as possible.

"I agree the attack happening in a doctor's office is suspicious." Alyssa tapped a finger against her lip. "That definitely sounds planned."

"I thought that too," Gabe said.

"And her husband's in on it?"

"He's the one who wants to buy the business. We haven't told you what happened today." Priscilla recounted what Gabe had told her.

Several times he interjected comments, and Priscilla left longer pauses after Alyssa asked a question to allow Gabe to gather his thoughts. Alyssa seemed skilled at drawing him out. It was her job to interview people, and she was good at it. Gradually, he relaxed and added more to the conversation.

"You did tell this to the FDA inspector, didn't you?"

Gabe sighed. "I tried, but he made it seem like I was trying to pass the blame."

"Hmm." Alyssa nibbled a fingernail for a moment, a faraway look in her eyes. "What if I asked one of the investigative reporters to look into this?"

• • •

Gabe didn't say it aloud, but having someone investigate would be a dream come true.

"Would you?" Priscilla's delighted expression touched him. She seemed to genuinely care about his business and him.

"Why don't you give me all the information you have on these two, and I'll see what I can do." Alyssa hopped off the counter.

"*Danke.*" Gabe stood and led the way to his office.

With all three of them in there, the room seemed overcrowded. Alyssa's position at the front of the desk forced Priscilla close to him. His arm nearly brushed hers as he bent to retrieve Defarge's file from the desk drawer. Her sweet scent drifted to him, enticing him to move nearer.

Ignoring the magnetic pull, Gabe extracted the correct folder. He set it on the desk and opened it, angling the file folder so the buyer's records remained private. He shouldn't give away a customer's personal information. As a business owner, people entrusted him to keep their accounts safe.

"I don't feel right giving out his address." Discouraged, Gabe closed the file folder. No matter how much he wanted the truth to come out, he couldn't do something dishonest.

Alyssa pulled her phone from her pocket. "Henry Defarge," she muttered as she thumbed some keys. "New Jersey business records search. Got it. I'm going to guess he calls his business after himself." She glanced up at Gabe, a question in her eyes.

He didn't nod, but his eyes must have given him away.

"Thought so," she said. "Does 'Defarge Enterprises, Incorporated' sound right?"

Again, Gabe didn't respond. Alyssa studied him closely.

"All righty, then. I have it," she crowed. She tapped a few buttons and scrolled down. "Here it is. President, Henry Defarge. Vice President, Fleurette Moreau."

Her head still bent over her phone, Alyssa jotted information in her notebook. She glanced up once. "Is this the right address and phone number?" She rattled it off.

She'd gotten it correct. Gabe had spent hours searching for Fleurette's information. Alyssa had discovered Henry's in a few minutes.

"Okay, that takes care of the business address, but I really want their home address. He has a website, so ICANN might have that data, unless he masked it."

"Huh?" Gabe had no idea what she was talking about.

"He had to register for a domain name. People often do that long before they start their businesses so they use their home addresses.

Many people never change that data." Alyssa nibbled on her lower lip as she tapped away with her thumbs. "Aha, he used a Philadelphia address. I'm going to guess that's his home address and phone."

Gabe stared at her. He caught Priscilla's eye, and she shrugged. Whatever Alyssa was doing, it seemed to be working. She'd collected the information in record time.

"Excuse me," she said as she slid past Gabe to the worktable behind him. Then she pushed a button on his answering machine and repeated a string of numbers. "I'm guessing Fleurette was the last person to call?"

Answering that wouldn't be giving away personal information, would it? "She was," he said finally.

"Thought so." Alyssa wrote the numbers in her notebook. "I'm hoping this is her cell phone. The 445 area code has only been around for a short while."

"How do you know all this?" Priscilla sounded amazed.

Alyssa laughed. "I have to track people down for interviews. You get to know the tricks." She pulled business cards from a small container in her pocket and handed one to each of them. "If you think of anything more I should know, or if either of them calls or stops by, let me know."

Gabe set the card on his desk, but Priscilla slid hers into her pocket.

"We will." Then she pointed to Alyssa's notebook. "Can I see that?"

"Sure." Alyssa tipped the pages in Priscilla's direction.

Priscilla glanced over the page, and her lips moved as if she were memorizing some of the information. Gabe's stomach clenched. She wasn't planning to contact or visit them, was she?

So far, the couple's threats had only been verbal, but both of them had been ruthless. Anyone who'd risk her niece's life wouldn't hesitate to harm a stranger. He'd never let Priscilla put herself in danger.

Priscilla skimmed the notebook page for the information she wanted. Defarge's business address. She read over it several times to commit it to memory.

When she lifted her head, Gabe's eyes held a warning. Warmth flooded her at his protectiveness. He must think she planned to meet with Defarge. She smiled to reassure him she appreciated his thoughtfulness. Priscilla only wished deeper feelings lay behind his concern.

"I'd better be going." Alyssa scurried out the office door.

"I should too," Priscilla said. She wanted to get home for supper to keep Mamm from worrying.

And she needed to flee her wayward thoughts about Gabe. She followed on Alyssa's heels.

Alyssa stopped so suddenly Priscilla almost ran into her. "I forgot. I came to ask Gabe two questions."

Priscilla waited while Alyssa poked her head into Gabe's office and asked her questions about camels. To Priscilla's delight, Gabe answered both of them without needing her help. The next time they talked, she'd point that out to him. He'd gained some confidence.

Alyssa turned to go, then spun around. "Oh, I'm going to put your profile on hold. I want to wait until the FDA investigation is over and Defarge has been exposed." She sighed. "It'll mean scrambling to finish a different lifestyle story for this weekend, but I want to put your business in a good light."

At Gabe's deep *thank you,* shivers ran through Priscilla. Why did he affect her this way?

Wrapped up in her reaction to Gabe, Priscilla could barely speak. She managed her own *thank you* and a quick goodbye before getting into her buggy.

The whole way home, she rejoiced. She could hardly believe how God had answered their prayers today. Priscilla had no idea what Alyssa could do to prove Defarge's wrongdoing. But just the fact the reporter intended to look into the situation gave her hope.

• • •

Gabe sat in his office after everyone had left. He should be milking, but instead he ran over the whole conversation in his mind. He replayed every detail of Alyssa's fact-finding mission and marveled at how rapidly she'd discovered all the information she needed. He sent up a prayer of thanksgiving that God had brought her into their lives.

Their? He'd automatically included Priscilla as part of his business life. She also seemed to be edging into his personal life. Something he needed to guard against.

He pushed back his chair. Maybe milking could erase these longings. Why had God allowed this temptation? Perhaps like Job in the Bible, he needed to strengthen his faith and trust the Lord.

No matter what he did, though, memories of Priscilla haunted him. Bringing his camels across the street, he pictured her coming down the hill after Alyssa. Sitting on the stool in the barn, he sensed her standing as she had last night, looking over his shoulder, her gaze warm and intense. Carrying the milk buckets to the refrigerator, he saw her taking the milk up the hill and hiding the sign from the reporter.

Everywhere he turned, she'd left her sweet presence behind. *Dear Lord, please keep me from temptation.*

After he'd finished milking the cows, he cleaned

up. He'd promised to eat supper at his brother's house tonight to keep him informed about the FDA inspection. Part of Gabe wanted to skip the meal and reminisce about Priscilla's smile, her gentle words, her caring touch on his arm.

He shook himself. He'd prayed to eliminate those distractions. Being with family would keep him from dwelling on Priscilla. He and Saul could talk business, and his sister-in-law and nephews always provided lively conversation.

He crossed the road and walked past his barns toward his brother's farm. He peeked in at his camels and cows. If only he could adopt their calm, cud-chewing attitude. Lately, he'd been so frazzled.

In one way, Priscilla proved to be a calming influence, but in another, she stirred too many yearnings. Longings for the impossible.

Gabe clutched his suspenders. Priscilla again. He couldn't even concentrate on the peacefulness of his farm animals without Priscilla's face, her voice, her memory intruding. Except he couldn't truly call it an intrusion. Every second he spent with her, every minute he dreamed of her was precious.

Forcing himself into a brisker pace, he headed up the driveway to Saul's house. His sister-in-law, Mary, greeted him at the door.

"*Kumm esse*," she said, ushering him to the kitchen table. "Everything is ready."

Gabe squeezed onto a bench between his two youngest nephews and across from Tim. He could help the little ones if they needed it. Mary sat in her usual place beside Saul, with the baby on her lap.

As soon as the silent prayer ended, Saul pinned Gabe with a probing glance. "I noticed a certain girl seems to visit the store pretty often." Saul waggled his eyebrows.

Tim piped up. "Her name's Priscilla."

"Priscilla, huh?" Saul shot Gabe a questioning glance.

"It's not what you're thinking," Gabe protested, but his fiery face gave him away.

"She's really nice." Tim dug into his mashed potatoes.

"She is?" Saul's smile widened. "I'm glad you think so, but I'm more interested in your *onkel*'s opinion. So, Gabe, is she nice?"

Gabe kept his attention on the slice of roast beef he was cutting and ignored his brother's digs.

"Saul," Mary chided, "stop teasing Gabe and let him eat his food. When he's ready to tell us about his girl, he will."

Even Mary, who seemed to be on his side, believed he was involved with Priscilla. If only they knew how far from the truth that was. Or was it? A one-sided crush was not a relationship. And he shouldn't even have let his feelings go that far.

"Sorry." Saul sounded far from apologetic. "It's just that Gideon Hartzler mentioned you avoid all the girls at the singings. I'm glad to see you're considering dating again. I worried you'd never get over Anna."

Get over Anna? He could never do that. Never.

Chapter Twenty

Priscilla made it home in time to help Mamm with the last of the supper preparations, but the situation with Gabe distracted her so much, she struggled to keep her mind on the work. She backed up and collided with Mamm.

"Priscilla!" Mamm shrieked.

Boiling water sloshed over the sides of the pot Mamm was carrying to drain at the sink. Luckily, it missed her hands as it cascaded onto the floor.

She stepped around the puddle. "What's the matter with you tonight? It's not like you to be so *ferhoodled*."

"I'm sorry. I'll clean that up." Priscilla hurried to the broom closet and got the mop.

Her sisters avoided the spot as she mopped. The linoleum remained slightly damp and slippery. To thoroughly dry the area, Priscilla knelt on the floor and rubbed it with a rag.

Daed entered the kitchen. "Is everything all right in here? I thought I heard a scream."

Mamm lifted the pot from the sink and poured the drained green beans into a serving bowl. "We had a minor accident, but nobody's hurt."

"Priscilla, are you cleaning or praying?" Daed asked, his tone teasing.

Actually, she'd been doing both. She'd stopped

in mid-swipe to pray for Gabe and Alyssa. After one last wipe with the rag, she stood. "I ran into Mamm, and some of the water spilled."

Daed studied her closely. "Are you all right?"

Her *daed* had always been perceptive. His concerned gaze made her long to spill Gabe's story, but she couldn't. Not in front of Mamm.

"Could we go for a walk tonight after supper?" she asked.

From the time she was small, that had been their secret code, meaning Priscilla wanted to ask for his advice privately. They'd taken many walks during her growing-up years, but now that she'd reached her early twenties, those private father-daughter talks had dwindled. Telling Daed about Matthew had been the only confiding she'd done in recent years.

A slight nod was the only acknowledgment he gave, but Priscilla's spirit grew lighter. She needed Daed's help to complete the next part of her plan.

Once they sat down at the table, Priscilla rushed through the meal, eager to talk to him, but she needed to sit and wait until everyone else finished. Under the table, she pleated small creases into her apron to release some of her impatience.

Finally, after negotiating with her youngest sister to take her turn at dishwashing, Priscilla stepped outside with Daed. She waited until they were far enough from the house to avoid being overheard. Then she poured out Gabe's story.

Daed listened without commenting until she reached her request.

"I'd like to send a check to Defarge to cover what Gabe owes." Priscilla stopped walking. "Would you go with me to the bank tomorrow to get a cashier's check?"

Her father frowned. "That's a large amount to pay on behalf of someone you barely know."

Barely know? It seemed as if she'd known Gabe forever. But Daed wouldn't accept that as a reason.

"Mostly I'm concerned about the children who aren't getting the milk. Gabe doesn't have enough money to pay that debt. I'd be helping him too. I don't want to think of him going out of business or the children going hungry."

"I understand your concern. But how do you know this Defarge will use the money for the children?"

They resumed their walk. The thought of Defarge taking the money bothered Priscilla. She didn't want to assist him in his takeover of Gabe's business.

She stopped suddenly.

Daed had moved a few paces beyond her, and he turned. "Is anything wrong?"

"*Neh*, everything's right, thanks to you. I can send the money directly to the charity."

Her *daed*'s secretive smile revealed he'd

already come up with that solution, but he'd given her time to figure it out for herself.

"*Danke*, Daed. That's a great idea."

He laughed. "You're the one who said it."

"But you're the one who thought of it first."

Priscilla wasn't sure how she could convince Gabe to let her pay the charity, but she couldn't wait to tell him he didn't have to pay Defarge. Now all she had to do was find out the name of the charity.

Supper grew more uncomfortable as Saul ignored Mary's advice to turn the conversation to different topics. His brother kept pressing for more information about Priscilla. Gabe side-stepped the questions as best he could, but Saul didn't make it easy.

Finally, Gabe managed to change the conversation to his FDA problem. He related all the events, leaving Priscilla out of it. Almost everything that happened, they'd done together, so Gabe often halted partway through a sentence to reword it. Although he never uttered her name, Priscilla remained on his mind the whole time.

"When can I come back to work?" Tim asked.

"I'm not sure how long this will take. I hope it'll be over soon." Gabe turned to his brother. "I've heard inspections may take about five days, but I don't know how long it'll be until they analyze the milk."

"That should come back fine. I wonder if there's a way to get the inspector to look at this couple you mentioned. If they're trying to put you out of business, the FDA should be aware of it."

"I tried telling the inspector, but he dismissed it as an excuse. I hope the reporter can find out something to help."

"Was that the red-haired *Englischer* who was there the other night? What night was that?" He turned to his wife. "Monday? The night a girl in a buggy—Priscilla?—followed you out of here, and you didn't return until late."

"Saul," Mary warned.

"What? Can't I even find out who my younger brother's spending so much time with?"

"It's not your business." Mary lifted a tiny spoonful of mashed potatoes to the baby's lips. Half of it ended up on her tiny chin. Mary scraped it off and tried again.

It made such a sweet picture. Gabe couldn't help imagining Priscilla with a baby on her lap. She'd be patient too. Teaching in a special needs school, she'd have to be.

He had to keep his mind from straying to fantasies. If she had children, it meant she'd married someone other than him.

"And where did you disappear to on Saturday night? You stayed out late then too."

"Have you been spying on me?" Gabe added a

teasing note to his tone, but his brother's prying bothered him.

"I can't help seeing your carriage drive past. And when I see the same Amish girl day after day, it makes me wonder."

"She's helping out some in the store." Priscilla had been much more than an employee, and Gabe regretted the half truth. But he was reluctant to correct it.

"You can afford paid help already?" With a laugh, Saul added, "In that case, maybe I should have Tim ask for a raise."

"Her *mamm* suggested she volunteer. She knows a lot about camel's milk because she studied its benefits for her scholars with special needs."

"She's a teacher, then?"

"Assistant, I think." Gabe vaguely remembered her mentioning the head teacher, but he'd been too shocked to find a woman knowledgeable about camel's milk to register other details.

"And she appreciates camel's milk?" Saul laughed. "Doubt you'll discover many girls with that interest. Better snap her up."

"Saul," Mary chided, "let Gabe handle his own love life." She smiled at Gabe. "Although if you are interested in her, she sounds ideal."

Gabe agreed with her. Priscilla was ideal. Perfect for him in so many ways. But no matter how attracted he was to Priscilla, he could never let things progress beyond friendship.

• • •

The next day after school, Priscilla headed home, trying to come up with an excuse for visiting Gabe so she could share Daed's suggestion. Mamm would never believe Gabe had asked her to work three nights in a row.

But Mamm surprised Priscilla as she sat at the table eating a leftover piece of rhubarb crunch.

"What are you doing here snacking?" Mamm demanded. "Shouldn't you be at the camel farm picking up Asher's milk?"

"I forgot it was Wednesday."

"You'd better get moving so you don't get caught in rush hour traffic."

Priscilla swallowed the last bite and took her plate to the sink. Mamm had given her an excuse to leave. But how would she explain coming home with no milk?

Perhaps she could convince Gabe to sell her some if Mr. Jackson wasn't around.

Humming, Priscilla set off for the camel farm. She sighed when she pulled past the inspector's car to tie up her horse. She'd hoped he'd be gone.

This time Gabe hadn't locked the door. Most likely because of Mr. Jackson.

"Priscilla?" Gabe's eyes lit up when she came through the door. "What are you doing here today? Not that I'm not glad to see you. I am. Very glad. I mean . . ." His face reddened.

She'd caught him off guard. Now she needed

303

to put him at ease. Would reminding him of the interview the previous day help? She decided to try. "You did a great job of answering some of those questions yesterday afternoon." She didn't want to mention Alyssa's name in case Mr. Jackson was listening.

She wasn't sure he'd appreciate them discussing the investigation with a reporter from the largest newspaper in the area. But she hadn't come here to discuss Alyssa.

"I need to talk to you about something," she said quietly and glanced over her shoulder at the doors to the refrigerated room. *Is he in there?* she mouthed.

"*Neh*, he's down at the barns examining the equipment, but I don't know how long he'll be gone."

"Then I'll tell you quickly. I talked to my *daed* about Defarge, and he had a good idea. What about sending the money directly to the charity rather than repaying Henry?"

"Your *daed*'s a wise man. I'd feel much better doing that. But how do we find out the name of the charity?"

"If you'll let me use your phone, I could call Alyssa."

Gabe swallowed hard. "I should probably do that."

Priscilla stood near him as he dialed. She bunched her apron fabric in her hands to keep from reaching out and placing a comforting hand on his arm. But she couldn't help admiring the way his muscles rippled under his shirt as he lifted the phone to his ear.

"Hi, Alyssa. This is Gabe Kauffman." He stayed silent for a minute. "*Jah*, I mean, yes. From the camel farm."

Again, he listened. "No, we don't have any news. We, um, well, that is, Priscilla's here."

Alyssa's laughter came across the phone line. "You called to tell me Priscilla's there?"

"No, no. She has a question. I mean, we both do."

Priscilla was near enough to catch some of Alyssa's words. She pieced together the rest. Alyssa had been planning to call her about something, but that part ended up garbled.

With a relieved look, Gabe handed over the receiver. "Alyssa wants to talk to you."

As Priscilla took the phone, Gabe whispered, "I'll wait outside for Mr. Jackson. Once I see him headed this way, I'll bang the door open."

"Good idea," she said softly before speaking into the phone. "Hello, Alyssa. Gabe said you wanted to talk to me."

"I certainly do."

Did she have good news? Priscilla pressed the receiver close to her ear. She didn't want to miss a word of this.

"Two investigative reporters from the paper are

following up some leads. I think we may be able to expose their scheme."

"That's wonderful. I can't thank you enough." Priscilla could hardly believe it. If Alyssa cleared Gabe's name, it would end the FDA inspection and the lawsuit.

"That's the least I can do for the person who brought me back to God. It's a debt I can never repay. Last night, I finished the book of John, then I prayed for God's forgiveness."

"I'm so glad." Priscilla's soul bubbled over with joy.

"Me too." Alyssa giggled. "Everyone in the newsroom wants to know what happened to me and why I'm so different. I've had plenty of chances to share the Good News today. One of my coworkers plans to go to church with me this weekend."

Priscilla had never thought her few simple words would make such an impact. She bowed her head. *Danke, Lord.* Only He could have worked this miracle.

"Okay," Alyssa said, "I'd love to talk about this all day, but I'm at work. I need to give the newspaper my attention. Was there something I can help you with?"

Priscilla explained about the charity. "Could you find out the name? Since we don't trust Defarge, we'd rather pay the money directly to the charity."

"Makes sense," Alyssa said. "I'll get on it. Either I or one of the other reporters may include that information in an article, so I can use work time to check it out."

Priscilla thanked her. Once she had that name, she'd take care of Gabe's debt. But right now, she was glad she'd warned him not to pay back Defarge.

As much as she wished she had an excuse to stay, she needed to go. Except for one problem. If she didn't take milk home, Mamm would be upset. And she'd wonder exactly what her *dochder* had been doing.

Gabe stood outside the door, and Priscilla opened it. "Is the inspector coming?"

"Not yet."

"Would it be possible for me to buy some camel's milk for my brother?"

He shook his head. "Mr. Jackson warned me against selling anything while my milk's been recalled."

"Mamm will question why I came here and returned without milk." Priscilla dreaded facing her mother's probing questions.

"Your brother's not allergic to cow's milk, is he?" Gabe asked with a twinkle in his eye.

Priscilla admired his ability to turn the awful situation into a joke. She laughed. "He's been drinking it for years."

"Well, an *Englischer* robbed my store not too

long ago, so if more milk disappears when I'm not looking, I won't be surprised."

"Some people don't feel right not paying for it."

"Well, they have no choice right now. Besides, they've earned it for the hours they put in helping me in the business."

Priscilla clamped down on her lip before she replied that it wasn't business, it was pleasure.

"Anyone who's robbing me better hurry before Mr. Jackson returns and before I turn around to face the parking lot."

Still, Priscilla hesitated. She didn't feel right doing this, but she could always pay later—after Gabe's inspection results revealed the milk had been pure. Scurrying into the refrigerated room, Priscilla took two gallons from the back of the row.

The outside door banged open.

"So, Mr. Jackson," Gabe's voice, unnaturally loud, penetrated through the refrigerated doors. "Do you need anything more from me?"

Priscilla couldn't make out the inspector's low, gravelly answer, but they seemed to be getting closer. She lifted the bottles, trying not to clank them as she slid them into place behind the others. She hoped the thick metal doors muffled any noise.

She shivered. Partially from nerves, but mainly because she'd come in without a coat. Maybe she could slip into Gabe's office without being seen.

When she pushed the handle down, it clanked, and the door creaked as she opened it. So much for sneaking into the office undetected.

Her conscience warned that slinking around meant she was guilty. "Stealing" Gabe's milk was wrong. God had exposed her dishonesty.

"Someone's been in the refrigerated room." Mr. Jackson's ringing tones carried.

"It's only Priscilla."

"Does she go in there regularly? I haven't seen her around here during the day."

"She, um, teaches school."

Priscilla stepped out of the office and faced them. "I'm sorry." The guilt she struggled with probably showed on her face. "I wanted to take two gallons of camel's milk home."

The inspector shook his head. "The milk's been recalled."

"I'm not afraid of that. First of all, I know Gabe didn't mix that milk. And second, Asher isn't allergic to cow's milk. But we really need the milk to help with his autism. I don't want him to have a setback."

"You have a son?"

A son? For a moment, Priscilla stared at him in confusion. Then it dawned on her. He believed she and Gabe were married. They needed to clear that up.

Before she could answer, Gabe said, "Priscilla and I, well, we're not married."

Mr. Jackson's mouth dropped open. "I thought you Amish were straitlaced and didn't do things like that."

His face scarlet, Gabe tried to correct the misunderstanding. "No, I didn't mean, um . . ."

"Never mind." Mr. Jackson waved his hand. "It's not my business."

"But—"

Ignoring Gabe's attempt to explain, the inspector plowed on. "I've finished my work for today. I'll be back tomorrow." He strode to the door. "I suppose I can't stop you and your wife from using your own milk."

"She's not my—"

"Right. I can't stop you and your partner, lover, significant other, or whatever-she-is from drinking your own recalled products." He tapped the clipboard in his hand. "But you can't say you weren't warned."

Priscilla kept her eyes fixed on the inspector as he exited. Of all the titles he'd mentioned, she liked *wife* best. She couldn't meet Gabe's eyes in case he read that truth in them.

Chapter Twenty-One

After some awkwardness—Priscilla avoided his gaze as much as he avoided hers—she ended up taking two gallons of camel's milk home. This time, they made no plans to get together.

He had to admit he'd miss her. He'd gotten used to seeing her every day this week, and he'd love for that to continue. But he had no excuse for asking her to return. He only hoped she'd come on Saturday for her milk. Meanwhile, he'd slog through the rest of the week alone.

Having no business to operate left him at loose ends. Other than milking, he had no major chores to occupy his time. He'd been so busy getting the business up and running, he hadn't had time to miss his friends and family. Now, though, he was lonely.

Staying here in the store reminded Gabe too much of the times he'd spent with Priscilla. That made his isolation even more acute.

His parents always said, "When you feel lonely or depressed, God is nudging you to help others." What could he do? Who needed help? He barely knew anyone here besides his brother's family and Priscilla.

Priscilla. Maybe he could do something to

restore her reputation. She deserved a home and family. But he'd have to sacrifice his daydreams. Daydreams he had no right to indulge. No matter how attracted he was to Priscilla, he could never let things progress.

If he left now, he could catch Matthew before he left the orchard for the day. After extracting a promise from him, Gabe could get back in time for milking. He'd do what he could to secure Priscilla's future.

The last time he'd talked to Matthew, anger had kept his words flowing. Gabe prayed he'd experience that again.

He arrived just before quitting time. Slowing his horse to a walk, Gabe drove along the shoulder of the road, peering past the split-rail fences enclosing the orchard, searching for his target. He didn't spot Matthew anywhere.

Gabe pulled onto a grassy spot near the fence and tied his horse to a post. He climbed the rails, dropped to the other side, and approached an Amish teen.

"Do you know Matthew King?"

The boy continued picking apples. "*Jah.*"

"Where can I find him?"

His hands full, the boy bobbed his head in the direction of the truck where workers were dumping their apples. "The boss's daughter called him over there. She often needs his help."

What kind of help does he give her? Gabe

couldn't help the cynical thought from popping into his head, but his conscience needled him. He hadn't come here to judge.

"*Danke.* I'll check over there."

Gabe headed for the truck, but before he reached it, Matthew emerged from the passenger side, straightening his shirt collar. He glanced from side to side as he jammed his hat back on his head, picked up his apple bag, and hung it around his waist. Whistling, he headed in Gabe's direction with jaunty steps.

The minute he spotted Gabe, he stopped dead. Looking like he wanted to bolt, he clicked his fingers as if he'd forgotten something and turned back toward the truck. No way would Gabe allow him to escape.

Gabe hurried after him and set a hand on his shoulder. Matthew jumped. Then he whirled around and confronted Gabe.

"What are you doing in the orchard? I can report a trespasser, and they'll remove you from the property."

Matthew's slightly shaky words gave Gabe courage. "I think you know why I'm here."

"You have no right to follow me. I have work to do."

"Seems like you'd get more done if you didn't meet Mara during working hours."

"You don't know anything," Matthew blustered, but his face paled.

"The other workers here do. I hear you two spend a lot of time together."

"We do not." Straightening his slightly crooked suspenders, Matthew squared his shoulders and took a step toward Gabe. "Have you been spying?"

I have better things to do with my time. Gabe bit back the retort that sprang to his lips. If he wanted cooperation, he needed to defuse Matthew's anger and suspicion. "*Neh*, I do not believe in spying."

"Then what are you doing here *again?*"

"I want justice." Words jumbled in Gabe's head as he sought to explain what he meant.

"I already did what you asked." Matthew puffed up his chest. "Priscilla kept her job because of me."

He's proud of doing his duty? "You owed Priscilla that and a lot more. I'm here to see that she gets the rest of what she deserves."

Matthew's eyes narrowed. "I cleared her name."

"With three couples who will keep that secret. I want everyone in your district to know the truth."

"The truth?" Matthew's knees jiggled back and forth. He shook his head.

"I heard you explained to the school board without revealing Mara's name."

"How do you know so much about what happened in a private meeting? How close are you and Priscilla? And when did you meet her?"

"I think you asked me those questions before."

"You never answered them."

"And I don't intend to. The only thing I'll say is that Priscilla ended one relationship before starting another."

Matthew's face twisted. "That's hard to believe. Priscilla takes a long time to trust people enough to confide in them."

"Maybe she's so honorable she couldn't confide in friends and had to tell a stranger."

The suspicion simmering in Matthew's eyes proved he disbelieved Gabe's suggestion. But it was true. Priscilla had chosen someone who didn't know Matthew and wouldn't gossip.

"You don't know Priscilla well if you'd say that," Matthew snapped.

Gabe only smiled. "How else would I get the information?"

With a quick shrug, Matthew tried to push past Gabe, who sidestepped to keep him in place.

"I need to get back to work." Matthew moved to go around to Gabe's left, but Gabe blocked him.

"I want you to tell the church Priscilla's innocent," Gabe insisted. "She deserves to be able to date and have a family."

"With you?" Matthew asked through gritted teeth.

Swallowing hard, Gabe repeated the sentence he'd been telling himself ever since he'd decided to come to the orchard. "With whoever God chooses for her."

Matthew snorted. "Sure. Unless"—he studied Gabe—"she turned you down."

Gabe didn't want Matthew probing his personal life. "I thought you had to get back to work."

"I do. But now I'm curious. Priscilla said no, so you're trying to act like the hero to win her heart?"

That comment cut deep into Gabe's conscience. Part of him did want Priscilla to notice him, even though he had no business wishing for that. "You don't know anything about our relationship."

"Sooo . . . you do admit it." Matthew's voice rose in triumph.

"You're doing it again. Misinterpreting what I'm saying."

"And you're not denying it." Matthew juked to one side and almost slipped past.

Gabe countered by cutting off Matthew's escape. "I want you to tell everyone the truth about Priscilla."

"What will you do if I don't?"

Gabe could threaten him the way he had before, and Matthew knew it. His bravado held a hint of fear. But Gabe had recently learned not to point fingers at others. They both believed in a Higher Power. That was enough to make Gabe ashamed of some of the things he'd done recently. It wasn't his place to condemn Matthew. They had both done wrong.

That knowledge kept Gabe's words sympathetic. "You joined the church. I'd think you'd want to make things right. You have more to fear from God than from me."

A sickly look crossed Matthew's face. "Not that it's any of your business, but I already met with the school board and the bishop. I'll be repeating what I said to them in front of the church this Sunday," he mumbled. Then in a sharper tone, he commanded, "Now stop bothering me."

Gabe put on a good face and said, "Good. I'll look forward to hearing about it from Priscilla." He left before Matthew could make a snide remark about Gabe's feelings about her.

As he walked to his buggy, Gabe's shoulders drooped. Although he rejoiced that Priscilla would be exonerated, he struggled with feeling deflated. He'd hoped to champion Priscilla's cause, but his help hadn't been necessary. God had already taken care of the problem.

Priscilla tried not to give in to her disappointment as she drove home from Gabe's. After spending three afternoons in a row with him, she'd miss spending time together. Saturday seemed so far away.

But the inspector's comment about *wife or whatever* mortified her. Did Gabe think she was trying to make people believe they had a relationship? Had she been annoying him by visiting so often? He'd been so stiff after that and refused to even glance at her. She'd been humiliated and unable to face him. She fled as soon as she could.

Maybe she should ask Mamm to get the milk on Saturday. *Neh*, that would be worse. Knowing Mamm, she'd make some comment about marriage.

Her other brothers and sisters had finished their chores by the time Priscilla got home, but Mamm had not.

Sarah gestured to the note on the table. "Mamm went to drop off a casserole. Sarah Esh had another baby yesterday. Mamm wants us to start supper before she gets home. She said there are ingredients for meatloaf."

Priscilla washed up and then chopped celery and onion while Sarah shredded the ends of a loaf of homemade bread. While the meatloaf baked, Priscilla worked on her lesson plans for the next day, but images of Gabe kept intruding.

When it was time to peel the potatoes, she carried her books into the living room. She'd try to do some more when the family gathered around the propane lamp in the living room after supper. Maybe with her parents in the room, her thoughts would be less likely to stray.

The meatloaf was almost done, and the potatoes and peas were bubbling on the stovetop when the front door opened.

"Priscilla?" Mamm's irritated call had an

exasperated edge. When she used that tone, you ignored her at your peril.

"Be right there." Priscilla turned the pots from boiling to simmering. This might take a while.

When she entered the living room, Mamm stood facing her, hands on her hips. "I talked to Marty Miller's mother today at quilting, and she mentioned you ate at Yoder's the other night."

Uh-oh. Had he also told his *mamm* she'd been with Gabe?

"You don't have anything to say?"

"*Jah*, I had supper at Yoder's."

"Yet you didn't mention it? Or who you were with?"

Priscilla gulped. Now Mamm would assume she and Gabe had a relationship. "You were asleep when I got home." The excuse sounded flimsy.

"And how many days since then could you have told me?"

"Two." Priscilla wished she'd been honest. Not telling Mamm had been a mistake. Except Mamm would have turned it into gossip.

"Do you have any idea how not knowing about your date made me feel?"

Upset because you weren't the first to share the gossip? Priscilla kept still. No sense in antagonizing her mother.

"Embarrassed that I didn't even know my own *dochder* is courting." Mamm's voice quavered with hurt.

Priscilla wished she could be honest with Mamm. "I'm not courting. I had to stay late at the store to help Gabe. He felt bad and took me to get a quick bite to eat because I'd missed supper. He was only being kind."

"And you didn't stop to think about what everyone else might think about your behavior? Especially after your recent problem with Matthew."

"Mamm," Priscilla couldn't hold back an anguished cry. She hadn't done anything wrong. But everyone would now be gossiping about her wantonness.

Her mother's disapproving look cut Priscilla to the core, although she had to admit she shared some of the blame for not telling Mamm the whole truth about Matthew. Still, it bothered her that her own mother had never given her the benefit of the doubt, but had immediately assumed Priscilla was to blame.

"You need to consider what others might think, especially now." Mamm's voice softened a little.

Priscilla lifted her chin. "I can't help what other people think."

"The Bible says you should *abstain from all appearance of evil.*"

Sometimes even if you did avoid evil, other people's wrongdoing destroyed your reputation. Unless the school board gossiped or Matthew told the truth, Priscilla had to live with that stain.

• • •

The phone rang soon after the inspector arrived on Thursday morning. Gabe hurried into the office to see who was calling. If Fleurette's or Henry's number showed up, he'd let the answering machine pick up the call, but turn up the sound. That way, the inspector could overhear any pressure or threats.

Instead, a local number flashed across the screen. The digits looked familiar, but Gabe couldn't place them. He picked up.

"Hey, Gabe, it's Alyssa. Any chance you can talk?"

"Um, not now."

"The inspector still there?"

"*Jah*, I mean, yes."

Alyssa's breezy, cheery voice flowed over the line. "Can you call me back when you're free? This is my cell, so ring me anytime."

"All right."

"Any chance Priscilla could be around when we talk?"

"I don't know. I can see. She usually comes in on Saturday morning." He stopped himself from saying *to pick up milk,* in case the inspector happened to be listening.

"Would it be all right if I drop by then to see both of you? I may have some news to share."

It's not like Gabe had any other plans. Having a visit to look forward to—along with spending

321

time with Priscilla, if she could come—would be the highlight of his weekend.

"I'll let Priscilla know you'd like her to be here." *So would I.* And it would give him an excuse to visit her before Saturday.

"Great! See you soon!" Alyssa clicked off the phone.

Gabe sat with the phone in his hand for a few moments, still savoring the connection. One bright, cheery spot in an otherwise rough week had been spending time with Priscilla. This gave him two more opportunities to do that. *Thank you, Alyssa.*

If the inspector left early enough, Gabe could run over to Priscilla's school to avoid her match-making *mamm.* But Mr. Jackson waited until five that afternoon to finish up.

He tapped at the doorjamb and handed over the folders of receipts and sales info Gabe had given him. "Everyone should have been notified, but many of these receipts don't even have names on them. Is everyone in the Amish community aware of the recall?"

"Word of mouth gets around." People who stopped by this week saw the sign, and if anyone had had trouble with the milk over the past few weeks, he'd have heard by now. Someone would have mentioned it to Saul or to Mary, who worked part time at GreenValley Farmer's Market and at Roots Auction. She had friends and relatives there and in the neighboring districts.

And Gideon Hartzler from church had a stand at the market. He'd sold some of Gabe's camel's milk as an experiment. But his address was in the file folder Mr. Jackson held, so he'd received a notice. Gideon would let Gabe know if his customers had any problems.

All the milk Gabe bottled for Gideon and for everyone else, including Fleurette and Henry, had been pure, so even if people didn't hear about the recall, Gabe had no concerns about their safety.

But that gave Gabe an idea. "Have you checked with my regular co-op customers and tested their milk?" If they had any left. He should have thought of that earlier in the week.

The inspector nodded. "Of the people we contacted, most turned over the recalled milk. Samples of those were sent for testing."

After Mr. Jackson left the office, Gabe filed the folders. Then he sat at the desk, his head in his hands. He couldn't ask the co-op members to pay for the recalled milk. How would he be able to afford to return that money as well as Defarge's? If Fleurette sued him, his co-op members and customers would get nothing. Many people were from his district or nearby districts. If he cheated them by not repaying them, facing them would be impossible.

Chapter Twenty-Two

Talking to the inspector had made Gabe late for milking. He'd either have to stop by Priscilla's after supper or wait until tomorrow.

While he milked, Gabe flip-flopped back and forth. If he went this evening, which he wanted to do, he'd reinforce her *mamm*'s wedding plans. But if he waited to see her after school tomorrow, Mr. Jackson might keep him late again. If he waited until then, Priscilla might make other plans.

Right. One day would make that much difference? his conscience taunted, but Gabe's desire to see Priscilla drowned out common sense.

After a hurried cleanup and supper, he hitched up his buggy. Like a magnet, the pull of seeing her again tonight drew him despite his internal warnings. He'd brave her matchmaking *mamm* for a chance to see Priscilla.

When he reached her house and pulled into the driveway, he hesitated. In the glow of the propane lamp, the whole family was gathered around playing a card game. He didn't want to intrude, but he yearned to be a part of that close-knit group.

Gabe's eyes burned. His own parents seemed so far away tonight. He was on his own in a strange town, where he barely knew anyone.

Until now, he hadn't realized how much he missed being a part of the fabric of the community. Here, he could disappear, and nobody would miss him. All the nights with his family and friends came rushing back, swamping him with longing and loneliness.

Filled with nostalgia, he tied up his horse and headed along the walkway to the house. He stopped by the window and debated about turning back. He shouldn't disrupt their game for his own selfish reasons.

Then Priscilla lifted her head, and he sucked a long, slow breath into his aching chest. In the glow of the lamplight, she appeared angelic. As beautiful and desirable outside as she was inside.

A sharp pang pierced Gabe. He'd asked Matthew to restore Priscilla's reputation. Any man who saw her beauty and appreciated her heart would want to marry her. Gabe had no right to even consider it. But that didn't stop the yearning.

He must have moved, drawn her attention, because Priscilla's eyes widened. Her lips formed his name, but she must have said it silently, because no one in the family looked up. Heads remained bent over cards. Only he and Priscilla connected.

Dropping her cards facedown, Priscilla sprang up. Everyone glanced at her in confusion. She gestured toward the window and then the door. Gabe ducked past before they realized he'd been spying on them.

He had no choice now but to head for the front door. The decision had been made.

The door banged open while he was mounting the two steps to the porch. Priscilla stood in the entryway, the light shining behind her and the welcoming smile on her face beckoning him.

Coming here had been a big mistake.

"Gabe?" Although she obviously wondered what he was doing here, the lilt in her voice made it clear she was pleased to see him.

Suddenly, the nervousness that tied his tongue in knots around strangers tangled his reasoning and his words. Only one coherent thought pulsed through his brain. She looked so attractive and appealing he wished he could enfold her in his arms. He clamped his mouth shut before he blurted out his desire.

Priscilla's smile trembled, and her forehead furrowed. "Is everything all right?"

"I, um, *jah, jah,* everything is fine." *Wunderbar*, in fact. Inside his head, his whole being filled with joyous songs of praise.

"Priscilla," her *mamm* called, "invite Gabe in. We can restart the game."

Zeke groaned. "Just when I was winning."

Gabe crashed to earth with a thud. What was the matter with him? Why did he lose his head and all common sense whenever Priscilla was near?

"Would you like to come in?" Priscilla opened the door wider.

Walking through that door would lead to even greater temptation. The more time he spent around Priscilla, the more he wanted to be with her permanently. Gabe struggled to keep his mind on his mission.

"I, um, better not. I only stopped by to, um, ask you something." His traitorous thoughts tossed up many other things he'd love to ask. He almost forgot why he'd come.

Keep to the point, Gabe. Don't get sidetracked.

"Alyssa wants to talk to both of us on Saturday." He rushed the message out quickly to fight off the urge to take her hand and ask her to go for a moonlight walk.

"Saturday?" She appeared almost as dazed as him. "When I come for milk?"

"*Jah.*" So, she planned to come rather than her *mamm.* His spirits soared. "If you tell me what time, I can let Alyssa know."

Esther loomed in the doorway. "Priscilla, why are you keeping Gabe on the porch?" she chided. "Gabe, come in." Esther flashed him a huge smile filled with hopes and dreams for her *dochder*'s future.

He gulped. "I, um, should be going."

"Nonsense. You can join us for a short while. Your milking's done, isn't it?"

"*Jah.*"

"So, you have nothing you have to get back to right away?"

Nothing except my lonely, empty house. "I guess not."

"*Gut, gut.* Then you'll have time for a game of Uno." Esther didn't ask; she bulldozed. "The girls made cracker pudding for our snack. You like that, don't you?"

Of course he did. But he compared answering that question to springing a trap. Gabe was the mouse, and Esther kept placing lures to entice him. Once he took her bait, *bang.* The mousetrap would slam shut, cutting off his escape.

"I, um . . ."

Esther jumped in before he could finish. "Everyone likes cracker pudding. My husband will be glad to see you. And Zeke took a real shine to you last time you were here."

Priscilla's *mamm* cut off every avenue of escape. But she had no idea the most irresistible lure was her beautiful daughter.

Though he was asking for trouble, Gabe accepted Esther's invitation. He stepped over the threshold despite the inner alarms clanging, *Stay away.*

Priscilla could hardly believe Gabe had come to the house. She wanted to hug herself because she'd gotten to spend time with him four days in a row. And now she had an excuse to stay longer on Saturday.

As Mamm led him into the living room, Priscilla hung back. She had to temper her joy before she entered. The last thing she needed was for Mamm—or Gabe—to notice her excitement. But her attempt to calm her racing pulse proved hopeless.

If she stood in the hallway much longer, Mamm would examine her closely. Priscilla wanted to avoid her mother's scrutiny, so even though she hadn't managed to control her reaction to Gabe, she hurried to join her family.

Daed had pulled in another wooden chair from the kitchen. He must have been sure Mamm could coax Gabe to join them. Except Daed had set it right next to Priscilla's place. All the more encouragement for Mamm to continue her marriage campaign.

Her father waved toward the chair. "Welcome, Gabe. Have a seat."

"*Danke.*" Looking uncomfortable, Gabe did as he said.

Priscilla bumped Gabe's elbow as they spread out their cards or took a turn. Each time, Gabe jerked back. Priscilla tucked her arms close to avoid touching him again. But keeping her elbows tight against her body made her movements awkward.

Once they'd started playing, Mamm lobbed

her first question. "How's business, Gabe?"

He stiffened and glanced sideways at Priscilla. She tried to convey a message with her eyes: *Mamm doesn't know.*

Gabe seemed to take her cue. "It's a bit overwhelming at the moment."

"I can imagine," Daed said. "It's always hard getting a business off the ground. I remember when I started my woodworking shop. Getting the word out and bringing in customers took a lot of effort. I imagine it's even harder when you're selling an unusual product like camel's milk."

"That's true," Gabe said. "Most people don't know its benefits."

"You have a lot to do, then. First, you have to let people know why they should drink it. Then you have to get them through the door."

"*Jah,*" Gabe agreed. "It's not easy when—"

Worried Gabe might tell about the inspector, Priscilla interrupted, "It's your turn, Gabe."

"Maybe we should skip the questions and let Gabe concentrate on the game," Daed suggested.

Priscilla sent him a grateful smile. He must have taken over the conversation to prevent Mamm from interrogating Gabe. Now Daed had given a signal not to disturb Gabe while they played. Priscilla appreciated her father's efforts.

One problem solved. But the second, more pressing one sat within elbow-bumping distance, causing a rapid fluttering against her ribs.

"Priscilla?" Daed repeated her name.

Her father's call jolted her back to the room. "Huh?"

"It's your turn."

His concerned expression forced her to pay attention to the game. "Oh, right." She took her turn, twisting and maneuvering to keep from grazing Gabe's strong, tanned forearms.

No matter how hard she tried to ignore his nearness, she remained conscious of his presence and his body heat. Warmth spiraled through her and kept her on edge until the game ended.

Mamm stood. "Why don't we sit in the kitchen for our snack?"

Gabe glanced toward the door as if eager to escape. "I should go."

"Not yet," Mamm insisted. "*Kumm esse.*"

With obvious reluctance, he picked up his chair and carried it to the kitchen while Zeke rolled the propane lamp table into the room. Mamm directed Gabe to sit in the same spot he had when he'd come for dinner, directly across from Priscilla. Although she struggled to keep her eyes off him, he avoided looking in her direction. He stared down at the tabletop as he accepted a plate from her youngest sister. His quiet *danke* could barely be heard.

He ate at the same pace as Daed. He almost seemed to be coordinating his movements with her father's.

Mamm examined Priscilla, and she tore her gaze from Gabe's face, but his hands arrested her attention. She'd noticed them before when he was milking the camels. So strong and steady. Hands of a hard worker. Hands with a gentle touch. Hands she wished to hold.

She shook herself. She had to stop dreaming of Gabe like that. Once in a while, when she met his eyes, she wondered if he returned her feelings. But most of the time, he kept himself aloof.

Tonight, he'd made it clear he had no interest in her by shying away and evading her eyes. Had he sensed her growing attraction to him? Was that why he seemed so uncomfortable and eager to get away?

Gabe had to leave. He had to get out of here before he made a fool of himself. He could barely keep his mind on the game with Priscilla sitting beside him. The emotions cascading through him as her soft skin skimmed against his bare arm had catapulted him into dangerous territory.

Sitting across from her at the kitchen table, he'd managed to focus on his food by mirroring her *daed*'s actions. But even then, he monitored her every movement from the corner of his eye.

Guilt tugged at him for deliberately ignoring her. But if he'd looked up, he'd never be able take his eyes off her. He fought the urge while conversation flowed around him. The dessert melted in his mouth, but he tasted none of it.

When Priscilla rose to clear the table, Gabe relaxed until she reached for his plate. Although she was careful not to touch him, her slender hand came near enough for him to hold. He clasped his hands in his lap and kept his eyes downcast so her parents couldn't read the desire in his eyes.

Relief flooded through him when her *daed* scraped back his chair. "Time for bed."

Gabe wanted to scurry out the door, but he said his goodbyes and *dankes* to each family member, saving Priscilla for last, hoping the others would leave the room.

While two of her sisters did the dishes, Zeke and Asher headed upstairs. Priscilla's *daed* yawned.

"Come on, Esther," he said as Priscilla's *mamm* lingered in the hallway. "Priscilla can walk Gabe to the door."

Esther turned but kept glancing over her shoulder as Priscilla went to the front door and opened it. Just before Gabe stepped onto the porch, her *mamm* turned and stood in her bedroom doorway, eyeing them closely.

"Esther," Priscilla's *daed* said, his quiet tone a warning.

The door shut behind Priscilla's *mamm*, and Gabe blew out a silent breath. He'd been tense enough about being around Priscilla, but having every action scrutinized made him feel as if he were balancing on a rolling log and any minute his feet would fly out from under him. Although being with Priscilla almost guaranteed a fall.

"*Danke* for coming," Priscilla said softly. "I'm sorry Mamm forced you into joining us if you had other things to do."

"I had no other plans." He didn't want her to blame herself for her *mamm*'s actions. "I, well"—he swallowed hard—"miss gathering with my family in the evenings to read or play Dutch Blitz."

Her face filled with sympathy. "That must be hard. I can't imagine living far from my family."

Neither could Gabe, until . . .

"You can visit us any time."

Gabe wasn't so sure that was a wise idea, but it was kind of her to offer. "*Danke.*" He didn't want her to pity him. "I do have my brother's family nearby, and I spend time with them."

"That's good, but you're always welcome here."

Her eyes seemed to convey more than just a friendly invitation, but perhaps that was only wishful thinking. He fished around for something neutral to say. "Well, I'll, um, see you on Saturday."

"What time?"

Oh, right. They hadn't finished that conversation before her *mamm* had invited him to join the game. He should have asked Alyssa when she planned to call. "What would be best for you?

334

I can let Alyssa know." He hoped the reporter's schedule was flexible.

"I can come any time after I've finished my morning chores. About eleven—or later in the afternoon, if that's better."

"Why don't we plan for eleven?" Though he shouldn't, he'd like to spend as much time as possible with her. Evidently, he hadn't learned anything from tonight's experience, or he wouldn't keep exposing himself to more temptation.

Chapter Twenty-Three

They'd been expecting Alyssa's call at eleven. Instead, about five minutes after the hour, she burst through the door, a wide smile on her face. Not her usual toothy grin, but a genuine smile that radiated from deep down inside. She rushed straight to Priscilla and enveloped her in a hug.

"I can't thank you enough," she gushed. "You've made all the difference in my life." Then she laughed. "Well, you started the fire by igniting a spark, but God turned it into a blaze. I'm a different person than I was the last time I was here."

"I'm so glad." Priscilla's spirit thrilled over Alyssa's enthusiasm. Hearing her excitement over the phone couldn't compare to seeing her joyful expression in person.

"Turning my life over to Jesus is the most important decision I've ever made." She flounced across the room. "Okay if I sit here?" she asked Gabe as she prepared to sit on the low counter where Tim wrote receipts.

Before he even nodded, she'd already seated herself. "Do I ever have news for you! Not as good as the news of my spiritual rebirth, but I'm sure you'll be excited to hear this too."

Gabe dragged the chair from the office and

placed it facing Alyssa. He waved Priscilla toward the padded desk chair, and he pulled the wooden one close to hers. Priscilla sat on the edge of her seat, eagerly awaiting Alyssa's news.

"Ready?" Alyssa asked. Without waiting for an answer, she plunged ahead. "Remember I told you I'd asked our investigative reporters to look into Defarge? They found three other owners Defarge and Moreau have forced out of business. The two of them bought the business assets dirt cheap and sold them for a huge profit."

"This is like a game for them, isn't it?" Gabe tried to erase the image of him joining that group of owners.

"Umm, I wouldn't call it that. At least not for the owners." Alyssa lifted a finger in the air. "First, Defarge or Moreau found a buyer and settled on a price. If the owner refused to sell at the price Defarge offered, he and Moreau used fraud and deception to destroy the owners' livelihoods."

"Like they're trying to do to me." Knowing others had also been targeted might be comforting, but how could it help him save his farm?

"Exactly," Alyssa said. "They forced two of the owners into bankruptcy. The other one gave in after they sued. Defarge blackmailed one of the company's workers into giving false testimony in court, and the owner lost."

Priscilla leaned forward, fire in her eyes. "That's so unfair."

"It sure is." Alyssa's expression turned fierce. "And we aim to stop them from doing it again. It looks like they're hounding several businesses right now, including Gabe's. Filing false reports, threatening lawsuits, and blackmailing owners."

"Wait a minute," Priscilla said. "Because they're trying to put Gabe out of business, does that mean Defarge has a buyer for the camel farm?"

Alyssa nodded. "A large cosmetics firm wants the milk for facial products."

"Camel's milk is supposed to soften skin and help clear blemishes," Gabe said. "But why would the company want the trouble of running a small camel farm?"

"They planned to buy several farms and cut out the middleman. But guess who owns the cosmetics company?"

"Fleurette?" Although Priscilla asked it as a question, she seemed sure of the answer.

"Precisely."

"Is there a way to use this information to save Gabe's business?" Priscilla asked.

"We're working on that. They did find a witness in the doctor's office who says the little girl cried and insisted she wasn't allowed to drink milk when Fleurette handed her a thermos. But Fleurette threatened her niece when she refused."

The very idea sickened Gabe. "How could anyone do that to a child?" He and Priscilla had suspected Fleurette of doing just that, but to actually hear she'd coerced her niece made it worse.

"The poor girl." Priscilla's eyes filled with tears.

Her tenderheartedness made Gabe long to reach out and comfort her. Hug her. Clasp her hand.

"We're still looking for other possible witnesses, but that quote will definitely be included in one of the articles."

Gabe dragged his attention away from Priscilla and focused on Alyssa's statement. "You're going to put all this information in the newspaper?" If they did, it might help his business.

"And on TV and radio. The first article will come out on Monday. Then, once the FDA has cleared you, I'm going to do the camel farm piece."

Priscilla bounced a little in her chair. "Wouldn't the thermos be proof that the milk wasn't straight from Gabe's bottle when the little girl drank it? We need to let Mr. Jackson know. Maybe that could help to clear Gabe."

He loved how Priscilla defended him. Having her on his side made him feel supported when everything else seemed to be crashing around him. For a short while, Alyssa's news had distracted him, but Gabe was acutely aware of Priscilla beside him.

Remember your promise, Gabe.

Priscilla sat next to him, so real, so vibrant, so appealing. He fought to keep his mind on that long-ago vow he'd made, determined he'd remain faithful to his promise, no matter how much he struggled with temptation.

This new evidence excited Priscilla. She could barely sit still. Turning to Gabe, she asked, "Did the inspector leave any contact information?" When he nodded, she suggested, "Why don't we call him?"

After she said it, Priscilla worried using *we* might be too presumptuous. She hoped Gabe didn't think she was bossing him around or trying to take over. He had enough trouble with Defarge doing that.

"I need to get going." Alyssa hopped down from the counter. "Lots to do today."

"Thank you for everything," Priscilla said, and Gabe echoed her thanks. Once again, she'd taken the lead. Sometimes she acted as if the business were hers rather than his. No wonder people mistook her for Gabe's wife.

"I'm sorry," she whispered to Gabe.

He wrinkled his brow. "For what?"

"For taking over. Butting in. Telling you what to do. It's your business."

Gabe laughed. "I asked you to do that. I've been concerned I've been making you do all the work."

"I don't mind." The words died in her throat at the look in his eyes.

He swallowed hard and broke their gaze.

"Oh, by the way," Alyssa called over her shoulder as she sailed out the door, "Defarge has no connections to any charity. Absolutely none."

"My milk wasn't going to needy children?"

"No, they were mixing it with cow's milk for Fleurette's facial products, but claiming it was pure camel's milk."

Too bad the inspector wasn't here for that bit of news. They should make him aware of Fleurette's deception. And that brought up another idea.

"Wait a minute. They're mixing milk?" Priscilla couldn't believe it. "If they're doing that, they may have given the FDA those samples. We should let Mr. Jackson know that too."

She dashed to the door as it swung shut behind the reporter. "Alyssa, wait!"

The reporter had her car door open but paused before getting in.

"If Gabe gives you Mr. Jackson's contact information, would you tell the FDA about the milk mixing? They might believe it from you more than from us."

"After all you've done for me, I'd be happy to. Actually, I'll ask one of the investigative reporters to call, because they can answer more of his questions and get a statement from the FDA for the article."

"If you wait right here, I'll get the number." Priscilla dashed back into the store and almost smacked into Gabe, who stood just inside the door.

He held out his hands to steady her, and Priscilla's words came out breathless. "Can I . . . get the inspector's . . . number?"

At first, he appeared flummoxed. Then he finally asked, "For Alyssa?"

His voice, deep and husky, thrummed the strings of her heart. All rational thought fled. She had no answer to his question, because every part of her was tuned to the music her body played to his touch.

Gabe squeezed his eyes shut for a moment, and then he winced. His hands dropped to his sides. "I'm sorry," he said stiffly and backed away.

I'm not sorry, she wanted to say, but she bit her lip to keep her longing to herself.

He spun around. "I'll copy down the number."

The music died as he walked away. When he returned with the numbers jotted on the back of a blank receipt, he held it out with only the tips of his fingers, leaving her plenty of room to take it without brushing against his skin.

Joyful tunes changed to funeral dirges. He had no desire to touch her. Not even accidentally.

Priscilla took the paper and fled outside to give it to Alyssa, hoping she hadn't made a fool of herself. Why did she lose her head like that around Gabe? She had a suspicion but refused to explore it further.

"Here." She held the receipt out to Alyssa. "Thank you for doing this."

"You're welcome." Alyssa slid the number into a clip on her car visor. "I'll be sure they take care of this for you. I want to see you and Gabe keep this business running."

Priscilla pinched back the first response that came to mind. *It's Gabe's business, not mine. And he intends to keep it that way.*

Gabe couldn't believe Priscilla had run into him, and he'd reached out . . . What had he been thinking? Touching her had only increased his longing to take her into his arms.

He closed his eyes to control his desires. It had taken superhuman strength to let go, to turn away. But he'd done it. He'd kept his vow. But had he done it with a pure heart?

God, forgive me.

He'd forced his fingers, fingers that still sensed satiny skin, to close around the cold metal of the pen. He scribbled down the numbers on the only blank paper he could find. This time, though, he fought an internal battle and kept his fingers to himself.

Priscilla rushed out the door, pulling her positive energy with her and leaving the room behind her empty and flat.

She returned, beaming, bringing sunshine into the store and into his life. "Alyssa's taking a friend to church tomorrow. And she's going to have one of the reporters call Mr. Jackson."

"*Danke* for thinking of that. I'm sure if we called, the inspector would consider I'm making an excuse."

"That's what I figured. I want him to take it seriously."

"Now that the newspaper knows Fleurette's diluting her camel's milk, I wonder if the FDA will investigate."

"You can't mislabel products, right?" Priscilla gazed up at him, a question in her eyes.

It took all Gabe's willpower to glance away. "That's why they came after me."

"I guess it would be the same for makeup. If the FDA inspects Fleurette's company, I wonder what will happen."

Gabe hoped it would clear his name. "I suppose they'll make her use pure camel's milk."

"So she'll be even more determined to take over your business."

He hadn't considered that, but it made sense. "You're probably right."

"Unless she gets in trouble for some of the other things she's been doing. I don't wish bad things would happen to others, but in this case, I hope she and Defarge get caught before they destroy any more businesses."

"I agree. I still can't believe what Alyssa discovered. If you hadn't stopped me, I would have paid Defarge back. But he lied about the charity." Gabe resented cutting his prices so low he'd barely made a penny. "I gave him a huge discount because I wanted to help poor children."

Priscilla shook her head. "This whole thing is unfair. I'm so glad neither of us paid him."

"Neither of us?"

Crimson crept up her cheeks, but she didn't respond.

Gabe repeated his question. "Look at me, Priscilla. Why did you say *neither?* That sounded as if you planned to pay him."

"Not him, the charity." She avoided his eyes. "I thought it might help . . ." Her voice trailed off. "I'm sorry."

Sorry? Sorry for being kind? For caring about needy children? For caring about me?

Priscilla had offered him money once before when she thought he might lose his business. What a generous, giving spirit she had!

Yet she stood before him, head bowed, ashamed.

Gabe reached out and lifted her chin with a gentle finger. "Don't ever be sorry for being generous and kind."

He'd meant to comfort her, but he'd made a major miscalculation. He hadn't counted on the flames touching her had kindled. And meeting her eyes . . .

"Gabe?"

His name escaped her lips on a sigh, and he was lost, drowning in sensations he had no right to feel. If he tilted her chin a tiny bit more and bent his head—

No! This was wrong, all wrong.

He yanked his hand away and whirled around, breaking the connection. "I'm the one who needs to say sorry." His words came out harsh. "I didn't mean to—" *To what? To touch her? To draw her closer? To fall in love?*

"I—I should go," Priscilla said in a broken voice that reflected her shattered heart. For a few moments, she'd believed her dreams had come true and Gabe cared about her the way she cared about him. But now, those dreams lay destroyed, scattered into shards.

She needed to get away before she revealed her real feelings. His back, rigid and closed off, remained facing her. At least he couldn't see how he'd hurt her.

With a quick prayer for strength, Priscilla started for the door. If she could keep her composure, she'd head out that door and never come back. At the possibility of never seeing him again every one of those shards pierced her heart. How could she ever walk away and leave him?

And how could she say goodbye without tears?

Dear Lord, please give me the strength.

Gathering all her courage, she stopped with one hand on the doorknob. "I hope this all works out for you."

"Priscilla, wait. I didn't mean—"

Closing her ears to his plea, she yanked open the door and strode into the parking lot. And out of his life.

The finality in Priscilla's voice chilled Gabe. He rushed to the door after her. He'd beg her to stay. But the cold metal of the knob in his burning hand brought back reason.

As much as he wanted Priscilla in his life, he couldn't pursue her. He could offer her nothing more than friendship. And that was unfair. To both of them.

He hadn't meant to get entangled with anyone. Not ever.

Yet he'd led Priscilla on every time they were together. Matthew had betrayed her and broken her heart. Instead of healing her wounds, Gabe had inflicted new ones.

The look in her eyes left no doubt she'd fallen for him, but he had no right to that love. Perhaps she'd only been attracted to him because she'd been hurting.

He'd offered a little kindness when everyone around her had rejected her, condemned her. He may have been the only man who'd even spend time with her.

As soon as Matthew confessed, she'd find plenty of men who'd want to date her. Within a short while, she'd forget him. But could he ever forget her? How could he erase her from his memory when she'd captured his heart?

Chapter Twenty-Four

Priscilla headed for church on Sunday morning with a joyful heart. Alyssa had turned her life over to Jesus, and she'd invited a friend to church. Like ripples spreading outward, Priscilla prayed God's Word would touch one life after another in Alyssa's circle.

The news that the investigative reporters might have found some clues to crimes also gave her hope they'd clear Gabe. Blood rushed to her face at the memory of yesterday. She'd made a fool of herself. At the gentle touch of his fingers on her chin, all her feelings for him had flooded through her. They must have spilled into her eyes, because he'd pulled away. Grown cold and distant.

Even now, remembering the chill in his voice made her shiver. Why had she revealed her real feelings? If she'd kept them hidden, they could have stayed friends. Now she'd even damaged their friendship.

Wrestling her wayward thoughts into submission, Priscilla tried to concentrate on the service rather than on Gabe. She needed to put him out of her mind.

Matthew rose and moved to the center of the room, where he knelt before the congregation.

Priscilla sucked in a sharp breath. What was he

doing? Would he tell everyone about Mara? Or did he need to confess other sins?

Ignoring all the members glancing at her with concern or censure, Priscilla leaned forward to hear every word. Plenty more people would be staring at her after Matthew finished confessing. If he told the truth, that is.

He bowed his head and spoke so softly he could barely be heard. "The last time I confessed, I omitted a detail that I should have included. I was not with Priscilla Ebersol. I wanted to clear her name. Please pray for me."

Pitying eyes swiveled in her direction. Hope, sitting in the row in front of her, half turned and mouthed, *I'm so sorry.*

Beside Priscilla, Mamm swooned, and Priscilla worried her mother might faint. If she'd known Matthew intended to do this, she could have prepared Mamm for the news. There'd be an explosion when they got home.

Daed stared at Mamm from across the room, his expression concerned. Then he turned sympathetic eyes to Priscilla. His lips formed the words, *Stay strong.* She tipped her head up and down slightly to let him know she'd received his message.

Priscilla kept her attention on the ministers, but as soon as church ended, Mamm clutched Priscilla's arm. Rather than heading to the kitchen to help with the meal, Mamm practically dragged Priscilla to a secluded corner of the yard.

"Why didn't you tell me?" Patting a hand against her ample chest, Mamm wheezed out several shallow breaths. "I could have had a heart attack."

"I'm sorry." Priscilla lowered her head. They'd been wrong to keep this from Mamm.

"Why, Priscilla, why?" The anguish in her mother's voice tore at Priscilla's heart. "Why didn't you tell me?"

"I didn't mean to hurt you. It's just that—" How could she explain their reason? She'd only wound Mamm more.

"It's just what?" Mamm begged for an answer.

An answer Priscilla wanted to avoid.

"Tell me."

"Well, Daed and I—"

"Your *daed* knew, but I didn't?"

Priscilla had endured the agony of betrayal, but to see it in her mother's eyes and know she'd been responsible cut Priscilla to the core. "I'm so, so sorry."

But as she'd learned, nothing could repair the damage. Apologizing only stretched a bandage across a gaping wound. All she could do was to ask for Mamm's forgiveness.

When she did, her mother shook her head. "Of course I forgive you. But why?" She spoke quietly, but her words ended in a wail.

"Because, because," Priscilla mumbled, "we

worried you might tell people. I didn't want anyone in the community to know."

Mamm drew in a breath, and a pained expression crossed her face. "Are you saying I'm a gossip?"

How did she answer that without hurting Mamm's feelings? "Maybe not on purpose, but you do like to talk to people. It might have slipped out."

To her surprise, Mamm hung her head. "I do enjoy sharing news—well, gossip, really. It makes me feel . . . I don't know . . . important, I guess. People pay attention to me." Her voice broke. "Trying to get attention. That's *hochmut*."

"Oh, Mamm." Priscilla hadn't realized her mother felt left out or in need of attention.

"I let pride get in the way of good sense sometimes."

More like oftentimes. Priscilla refrained from pointing that out. Mamm was owning up to her problem. This was between her mother and God.

"I wish I'd known about Matthew."

"I'm sor—"

Holding up a hand, her mother interrupted her. "No, I'm the one who needs to apologize. I was so excited—no, proud—that you were getting married. I didn't want anything to spoil that."

Neither had Priscilla. Matthew had destroyed that for her. And for Mamm and Ruth.

Keeping her head bowed, Mamm plucked at

her church apron with work-worn hands. "But not to listen to my own daughter and believe her? That was wrong. So very wrong."

Priscilla bit her lip and blinked her stinging eyes. Mamm's doubting her innocence had cut her deeply.

Tears in her eyes, Mamm lifted her head. "Deep down, I knew you were telling the truth. I was so concerned about our family's—and my—reputation that I ignored what my heart was telling me. Will you forgive me?" She searched Priscilla's face with pleading eyes.

"Of course, Mamm." Priscilla reached out and hugged her.

Mamm returned the embrace with a quick squeeze. Then she glanced around to see if anyone was looking and stepped back. "We should go in to help in the kitchen. Everyone will be wondering where we are."

Priscilla was in no hurry to face the prying eyes and probing questions. Her friends would be wondering who Matthew had cheated with.

Mamm shuffled forward and in a low, sad voice mumbled, "I still need to ask God's forgiveness. And your *daed*'s. He warned me, but I didn't listen." She went only a few steps before halting and turning to face Priscilla. "You tried to tell me, didn't you? That time when you told me you didn't need to confess in front of the church."

"I didn't try hard."

Mamm clapped her hands to her cheeks. "*Ach*, and I tried to get Matthew to come to dinner and . . ."

"It's over now, so don't worry about it. You made Matthew squirm." And though she shouldn't, Priscilla had been glad to see him put on the spot.

"I'm sorry I didn't know it then. I could have given him a piece of my mind."

"Mamm . . ."

"I'm doing it again." Mamm sighed. "Breaking this habit won't be easy."

No, it wouldn't, but it would be wonderful if she did. Then Priscilla could confide in her. So many times while growing up, she had longed to ask for advice, but she'd feared her mother might spill her secrets.

Usually, Gabe enjoyed Sunday evening suppers. Today, though, he'd considered skipping it. But with the swirl of thoughts about Priscilla, he needed a distraction.

As soon as they began eating, he regretted coming.

Saul passed him the platter of cold fried chicken. "So how are things with Priscilla?"

Gabe had come to get away from his thoughts of Priscilla, and two minutes into the meal, he'd been slammed. He pretended to be busy deciding between a wing or a leg, but in reality, his mind raced to come up with a deflection.

"This looks delicious, Mary," he said at last, setting two pieces on his plate.

"*Danke.*" She ducked her head, but not before he caught a glimpse of her shy smile.

"You avoiding my question?" Saul demanded.

"Maybe he doesn't want to talk about his personal life." Mary reached across the table to help Jayden cut his meat.

"I can do that," Gabe volunteered. "He's sitting right beside me." He leaned over to assist his nephew.

Saul ate in silence and waited until Gabe looked up. His brother's gaze locked on him, and Gabe sensed he'd never get away with avoiding the question. Perhaps discussing Alyssa's news might sidetrack Saul.

"The newspaper reporter stopped by yesterday. They've found information about the couple who's trying to take over my business."

His brother's eyes lit up. Saul seemed intrigued. "Tell us about it. We can come back to Priscilla later."

Gabe explained what the reporters had discovered. He dragged out the details in between his nephews' interruptions. He also fielded his brother's questions about Fleurette and the cosmetics company, pausing from time to time to slice meat off the bone for Jayden. Gabe managed to evade any probing about Priscilla until Mary cleared the dinner dishes.

He breathed a silent sigh of relief. Now they only had to get through dessert. Gabe tried to return to Defarge, but Saul interrupted him.

"So why was Priscilla's buggy parked there after the reporter left?" His brother's sly smile showed he didn't intend to give up.

"She didn't stay long." Gabe wished he hadn't sounded so defensive, but the last thing he wanted to think about was the time he and Priscilla had spent together after Alyssa left. He'd dreamed about their encounter last night and woken filled with guilt.

"You sound disappointed."

His human nature had been, but his spiritual side wished Priscilla had left with Alyssa.

"She just let me know that the reporters will contact the FDA. We discussed what might happen if they look into Fleurette."

His brother's *um-hmm* sounded suspicious.

Gabe cut the slice of pie Mary had set in front of Jayden. "Priscilla was also excited because Alyssa asked Jesus into her heart and planned on taking a friend to church today."

Mary's face glowed. "That's *wunderbar.*"

"It is. Priscilla got Alyssa interested in reading the Bible. God did the rest."

"Of course it was the Lord's doing, but it's always amazing when you can make a difference in someone's life." Mary served herself last and sat at the table.

Gabe nodded. *Jah*, it was. He'd encouraged—or should he say blackmailed?—Matthew to tell the school board the truth. Knowing Priscilla had kept her job because of his intervention thrilled him. He'd also wanted to play a part in Priscilla's life today by restoring her reputation. She had church today too. Had Matthew done the right thing?

If so, Priscilla might soon be dating someone else. Gabe rubbed his forehead, then used his hand to shield his eyes while he tried to regain his composure. He had to think about other things.

Jayden slumped against Gabe.

"*Ach*, he's falling asleep," Mary said. "Can you hold him a minute? I'll put Katie in her cradle, then come back to take them up for their naps."

Gabe wrapped his arm around his nephew to keep him from nose-diving into his last few bites of blueberry pie. Mary stood and propped her sleepy baby daughter on one hip.

"I can carry him up for you," Gabe said. He scooped Jayden into his arms and stood. After stepping over the bench, he held out a hand to Jared. "Come on, let's get your brother upstairs to bed."

"Tim can clear the table," Saul said as they headed from the room.

Holding Katie, Mary supervised as Gabe tucked

Jayden into bed and Jared climbed into his. She looked exhausted, so Gabe reached for his niece.

"I can rock Katie until she falls asleep."

Mary's tired *danke* made him glad he'd suggested it. She followed him down the hall to the baby's room and waited while he settled into the rocker. Gabe cuddled Katie close and moved gently back and forth.

"I'll run down and do the dishes." Mary's expression softened as she gazed at her daughter in his arms. "You'll make a good father, Gabe."

She'd meant it as a compliment, but her words stabbed into him. He'd always wanted to be a father. He swallowed the lump in his throat.

"I won't be long." Mary pulled the door shut.

The warmth of a small child in his arms brought a deep yearning for a family of his own. Unbidden, images of Priscilla rose in his mind. In his dreams last night, they'd walked together through fields holding hands. He pictured her holding a baby. She'd be a wonderful mother and wife.

But for someone else. Not him.

Why had God put this desire in his heart? The Bible promised the Lord would give them the desires of their hearts, if they delighted in Him.

But what if my desires are wrong?

Baby Katie's eyes drifted shut, and Gabe hugged her against his chest and continued rocking until her deep, even breathing signaled she'd fallen asleep. Reluctant to set her down, he held her longer. Putting his niece and nephews to bed was as close to being a parent as he'd ever get. He'd take advantage of every moment he could.

But when thoughts of Priscilla as a mother intruded, Gabe stood and carried the baby to her cradle. He knelt beside it and lowered her gently so she wouldn't wake. He kissed her forehead and laid a hand on her head to smooth back her downy hair.

The door opened behind him, and Mary tiptoed into the room. "She's asleep?" she whispered.

Gabe nodded. Mary knelt beside him and smiled down at her sleeping daughter. "She's such a good baby."

"*Jah*, she is," Gabe agreed.

Mary set a hand on his arm. "I hope you don't take offense at Saul's teasing about Priscilla. He isn't trying to annoy you. It's just that he wants you to leave what happened with Anna in the past and move on with your life."

Anna. He could never forget her. Or the promises he'd made. Being reminded of her erected a huge barrier. One that kept him from pursuing his interest in Priscilla. Or in any woman.

He'd never told Saul the whole story. If his brother knew what he'd done, he doubted Saul would give him that advice. No one would.

• • •

When Priscilla and Mamm entered the kitchen, several girls beelined in Priscilla's direction.

Hope reached her first and enveloped her in a hug. "I'm so sorry," she whispered. "Keeping this secret must have been so hard."

Then the other girls surrounded her. Questions flew at Priscilla from all directions. "When did you find out?" "Who's the other girl?" "Do you know?" "Did you break up before it happened?" "Are you all right?"

Priscilla stayed mute and only shook her head. Finally, Hope stepped in front of Priscilla. "It's not fair to ask her all these questions. She chose not to tell anyone about this. We should respect that."

Most of the girls went back to their jobs, filling serving dishes and carrying them out. A few stayed behind to ask for forgiveness.

"We should have known it wasn't you," one of them said, and the others nodded. "Will you forgive us for judging you?"

"Of course." As Priscilla said those words, she released the hurt, the sadness, the deep ache in her soul at the unfairness. God washed away the pain, leaving her spirit light.

Marty Miller's *mamm* walked by with two jars of red beets. Her smile held a trace of pity. "I'm glad you've found someone else."

The girls, who'd been about to leave, circled

around her again. "What? You have another boy-friend? Is that why you and Matthew broke up?"

"No." Priscilla answered both questions with one word.

"Not going to talk about that either?"

Pinching her lips together, Priscilla shook her head. After all, what could she say? She might be attracted to Gabe, but he had no interest in her.

"I could use some help over here," Mamm called, and Priscilla scurried over.

"You looked like you needed some rescuing," her mother said in a quiet voice.

"*Danke.*" Priscilla took the extra knife Mamm handed her and sliced one of the snitz pies.

"I'm sorry, *dochder*, I'm trying to pay more attention to your needs than my own. I've been so self-centered it makes me ashamed."

When women came over to gossip with Mamm, she smiled but kept her attention on cutting. Priscilla could tell how difficult it was for her, but her mother confined most of her comments to the weather, the food, and the sermons. She did pass along some news about two women who were ill and described Sarah Esh's new baby. As she did so, she glowed. Clearly, Mamm loved talking about others, but maybe she could stick to positive and helpful tidbits. Things that encouraged and benefited people.

"You know," Priscilla whispered, "you do have a gift for sharing information."

Mamm beamed. "Maybe it would be easier to do that, because giving up talking to people altogether makes me sad."

Priscilla hid a smile. "I don't think you need to give up talking altogether." That would be an impossible goal for Mamm.

Her mother looked relieved.

"Should I take some of these pies out to the serving table?" Priscilla asked her.

"*Jah*, the men probably need more by now."

Pitying looks followed Priscilla as she crossed the room. Everyone expected her to be devastated. And she was. But not because of Matthew.

His betrayal had hurt terribly at the time. Yet, in the few weeks since it happened, she had moved on without realizing it.

Now, comparing Matthew to Gabe, she wondered what she'd ever seen in Matthew. Gabe was everything Matthew was not—moral, upright, honest, considerate, and other-centered rather than self-centered.

Only one problem stood in the way. Gabe had no interest in her. Sometimes the look in his eyes made her wonder, but whenever he had an opportunity to get close, he shied away.

As she reached the kitchen doorway, Mara, who'd been working in the far corner of the room, glanced up and their gazes met. Priscilla gave her a knowing nod.

Mara's eyes widened. Was she afraid Priscilla

might reveal her relationship with Matthew?

Priscilla had no intention of telling anyone, but Mara didn't know that. She should have guessed from the fact that Priscilla didn't speak out after Matthew's first confession. But Mara would always be tense and uneasy, wondering who might disclose her secret.

As the kitchen door swung shut behind Priscilla, it startled her to discover she held no animosity. Not toward Mara or toward Matthew. Meeting Gabe had erased her bitterness.

Mara and Matthew had to live with the guilt of what they'd done, and they had to conduct their relationship in secret for fear of being discovered. Would Matthew openly court Mara once all the furor over his confession died down? Or would she only be his shadow girlfriend?

In fact, rather than resenting Mara, Priscilla felt sorry for any girl who dated Matthew. He'd proved he lacked strength of character. Mara would always have to wonder if she could trust him.

Priscilla had found another man. One far, far better. One she loved being around. One who would be faithful. One who made her heart sing.

I found the perfect man, but . . . he's not in love with me.

Chapter Twenty-Five

On Monday morning when Gabe opened the door, the phone was ringing. He hurried into the office to answer it before the machine picked up. A local number. Gabe braced himself and picked up the phone.

The man on the other end identified himself as Arjun Patel, a reporter with the *Central Pennsylvania Star.* "I've been looking into Defarge Enterprises. We have a story coming out tomorrow that we'd like to have your comments on before it goes to press."

A swirl of emotions swept through Gabe. Relief, elation, and nervousness. He wished Priscilla were here to come up with the quotes.

After this past weekend, though, he doubted he'd ever see her again. At the time, he'd only been thinking of himself. But as the scene played over in his head since then, he regretted his abruptness, his turning away. She'd been so open and vulnerable he couldn't help wondering how she might have responded if he'd kissed her. He blocked that image before it went further.

"Are you there?" Arjun asked.

"*Jah*—yes." Gabe might be here, but his mind kept wandering elsewhere. To one particular person. He made himself pay attention to this conversation. It might be crucial to his future.

"Usually we email the story so you can check it, but you don't have email, right?"

"Right."

"Okay, interrupt me any time you have a question or comment."

Gabe stayed silent as Arjun read through the whole article. Hope blossomed as the reporter detailed the facts they'd uncovered about Defarge's business activities and about Fleurette Moreau's involvement in the deceptions.

When Arjun finished, Gabe sat there, stunned. "How did you find all that out?" Alyssa had told them some of this on Saturday, but they'd found three people who agreed Fleurette had insisted her niece drink something from a thermos, and right after that, the girl had serious symptoms.

One of the witnesses was the receptionist. She'd been away from her desk when it happened, but she'd heard a child protesting, and she'd opened the office door to see the girl's allergic reaction. While the doctor attended to the child, Fleurette capped the thermos, handed it to the receptionist, and asked her to have it tested.

The reporter ran through some of his research while Gabe marveled at all the sources and angles they'd pursued.

"You've done an amazing job." Gabe still found it hard to believe that the news intended to expose all the wrongdoing and, in the process, clear his business. "You even got a quote from the FDA."

The person at the FDA Arjun had talked to indicated they'd be investigating allegations that a false claim had been filed. If they did, maybe they'd clear his business.

"Any response to the story?" Arjun asked.

"Just thank you. Thank you very much." This would go a long way toward clearing his name.

"One more question: We'd like to do a follow-up story with the businesses Defarge Enterprises targeted. More of a human-interest story. Are you willing to do an interview?"

Without Priscilla? He needed to get used to that. "All right."

"Alyssa will do the interview, if that's okay. She wanted to get more info for her profile piece too."

"That's fine." *Great, in fact.* He had little trouble talking to Alyssa.

"Hang on and I'll transfer you to her desk."

A short while later, Gabe hung up and lowered his head into his hands. He'd set an appointment to talk to Alyssa at four thirty. She'd asked if Priscilla could be there too.

Gabe agreed to ask her, but now that he'd gotten

off the phone, all his earlier doubts crowded in. After what he'd done to her on Saturday, he had no right to ask a favor.

Priscilla checked to be sure her brother and all the other scholars who'd be walking home with their parents put on their reflective vests, while Ada and Martha led the others to the playground to wait for their rides.

Once everyone had their jackets on and had been buckled into the fluorescent yellow vests, Priscilla herded them outside. Asher, who preferred to be alone, headed for a swing, and the others spread out on the playground.

Keeping an eye on two boys kicking a ball and the little girl swinging on one of the wooden swings, Ada moved near Priscilla. "I'm so sorry about Matthew. I wish I'd known," she whispered. "I wanted to tell you that earlier today, but, well, you know."

Priscilla definitely did. Three children had meltdowns first thing that morning. She, Ada, and Martha each handled one. Martha's brother Lukas had been the worst, and he'd been the one to set everyone else off. Other children had watched with fearful expressions as Martha struggled to calm him. Luckily, she did, which made it easier to get the others settled down. But they'd had a rough day.

Martha had apologized several times for her

brother's behavior. "Whenever Mamm's upset, he gets worse," she explained.

"If I can help in any way, please let me know," Ada continued.

"*Danke*." Priscilla wanted to assure Ada she'd be fine and that she was over Matthew. Well, maybe she was fine about that, thanks to Gabe. But he'd brought his own set of problems. Namely, that he didn't return her affection.

She didn't have time to confide in Ada, because two buggies clattered up the driveway. Lizzie's *mamm* emerged and collected her daughter. Will's *mamm* coaxed her reluctant son into the buggy. Soon a flurry of parents arrived, and scholars headed off until only Lukas and Martha remained.

"It's not like Betty to be late," Ada said as they waited.

"I hope nothing's wrong." Ever since Martha's comment about her mother, Priscilla had wondered.

A horse trotted up the driveway. *Good.* Betty had arrived. Instead of motioning for her children to get in the carriage, Betty held up a hand to stop Martha.

She climbed out and headed toward Priscilla. "I'd like to talk to Priscilla alone, please," she said to Ada.

Ada turned to Priscilla with a question in her eyes. That was sweet of Ada to support her, but now that the truth about Matthew had come out, Priscilla was ready to face Betty alone. She nodded to let Ada know she'd be fine.

As soon as Ada had crossed the parking lot to talk to Martha and Lukas, Betty faced Priscilla. "It seems I owe you an apology. I made a mistake. Will you forgive me?"

Betty admitting she'd done something wrong? And asking for forgiveness? Priscilla stood there stunned. Then she recovered. "Of course I forgive you."

"I didn't realize," Betty mumbled.

She never finished her sentence because another buggy rumbled into the parking lot. *Gabe!* Priscilla drew in a quick breath.

Betty turned to see what Priscilla was staring at. "Is that the man you ate with in Yoder's?"

How had Betty heard about that?

Before she could answer, Betty continued, "I hope you haven't jumped into another relationship so soon." She leaned closer as Gabe emerged from his buggy and whispered, "That's the camel farmer. You might want to rethink your choice. I've heard he's under investigation for cheating customers."

Priscilla gasped. Even parents didn't meddle in their children's relationships like that. And what she said about Gabe . . . If anyone rivaled her *mamm* at gossip, Betty took that prize. And unlike Mamm, Betty often added negative opinions and unfair judgments.

Like the one you have toward her?

"I'm sorry, Lord," Priscilla mumbled under her breath. She needed to take the log from her own eye. A little more loudly, she said, "Gabe did not cheat anyone. People who wanted to buy his business tried to make him look bad. You'll read all about it in the newspaper this week." At least she hoped the article would be coming out soon.

Betty appeared taken aback. "Be careful about trusting newspapers. They don't always print the truth."

Normally, Priscilla treated her elders with deference. This time, though, she needed to get her point across. "This news story is completely true. Shady people framed Gabe."

He must have heard his name, because he stopped. As much as she longed to see him, Priscilla hoped he'd stay there until Betty left. She didn't want him exposed to Betty's poison or her curiosity.

Across the playground, Lukas spotted his mother. He threw himself on the ground, kicking, screaming, and flailing. Martha bent over him and talked softly for a few moments before kneeling beside him. She waited patiently until she could slide her arms around his thrashing body. Then she wrapped him close, keeping their backs toward their mother.

"He had a rough day today."

Priscilla had meant her remark as sympathy,

not a jab. But the hurt and irritation on Betty's face showed she'd taken it the wrong way.

"It's not my fault." Betty contradicted her words with a guilty expression.

While Martha soothed Lukas, Betty stalked toward her buggy. She couldn't resist a parting shot. "Remember what I said."

Priscilla had no intention of remembering any of Betty's hurtful remarks. And one thing she knew for sure and certain. She could trust Gabe. He'd never lie to her or to anyone.

Gabe glanced from the sour-faced woman confronting Priscilla to the screaming boy thrashing on the playground. Could he help either one?

He'd stopped his nephews' tantrums. Yet something about this child's meltdown seemed different. With this being a special needs school, the boy might be autistic. He breathed a sigh of relief when one of the teachers or aides bent over him. They'd know what to do.

Turning his attention to Priscilla, he longed to protect her from the woman who seemed to be haranguing her. Would she welcome his interference?

While he weighed that question, the woman spun on her heels and headed for the buggy parked beside his. That made his decision easier. He headed in Priscilla's direction.

"Gabe, what are you doing here?"

That didn't sound like a warm welcome, but he hadn't been expecting one. In fact, he was surprised she even acknowledged him after what he'd done.

"A reporter called me. They'll be running the story about Defarge tomorrow."

"They will? That's *wunderbar*! It should clear your name."

"I hope so." Gabe marveled that she still cared about the outcome for his business, but he'd already noted she had such a generous heart. "They also want to do another piece. Interviews with the businesses Defarge tried to buy—and destroy."

Priscilla's eyes shone. "That will be good publicity."

"*Jah*, it will. Except Alyssa is coming at four thirty for the interview."

"And you wanted me to come?"

"Well, Alyssa asked if you could be there."

If he wasn't mistaken, disappointment clouded her gaze.

"I'd be happy to come."

Had she been hoping he'd needed her? After what he'd done?

Gabe glanced around. "Is your buggy here?" He didn't see a carriage anywhere.

"*Neh*, Ada and I walk to school."

"I can drive you to the store and home if you'd like."

Priscilla hesitated. Was she wondering if his invitation meant more than a simple ride?

"It will be faster that way," he pointed out, forcing his thoughts away from courting.

"I know. I need to tell my family. And my brother needs to get home from school." She held up a hand. "Let me see if Ada will stop by our house. She lives in the opposite direction, but it's not a far walk."

Priscilla hurried over to the teacher standing near the door, who was watching the drama with the boy on the playground. He'd calmed down, and now the older girl was trying to coax him toward the buggy.

After a brief, but animated, conversation, Ada nodded, and Priscilla headed for the swings. Asher slowed to a stop, and she knelt beside him. His face screwed up, and he flicked the brim of his straw hat. Gabe had read enough about autism to recognize stims, repetitive actions children engaged in when they were upset.

Maybe he should let her take Asher home as usual. He'd rather they were a little late than upset a young boy. But Priscilla pointed toward Ada, who waved at Asher. He semi-smiled, and after Priscilla turned to him again, he nodded. She stood and headed toward Gabe.

"Will Asher be all right?" Gabe asked. "We could run him home first."

"He'll be all right." She looked thoughtful. "A

few months ago, a change like this might have caused a meltdown. Since he's been drinking camel's milk, he's been much more flexible."

"I'm so glad it's helping."

As they walked to his buggy, the woman parked beside him glared.

Perhaps she'd been one of his customers who'd bought camel's milk for her son only to have it recalled. If so, he could offer to pay her back. "Is that mother annoyed with me?"

"*Neh*, she's upset with me. That's our bishop's wife, Betty. She lectured me about not dating so soon after Matthew."

Priscilla's tense chuckle made Gabe long to erase any pain Betty had caused. Priscilla didn't deserve to be hurt. Her laugh ended with an indrawn breath. "I don't want you to think I told her we were dating. Betty just jumps to conclusions."

Gabe had been so focused on getting Priscilla to the interview on time he hadn't considered her reputation. "I'm sorry. I should have thought about how this might appear to others."

"Don't worry about it. If not this, Betty would find something else to criticize. I believe she sees that as a bishop's wife's duty."

That surprised Gabe. The bishop's wives he'd come in contact with were caring and humble. "That's too bad."

"It is," Priscilla agreed. "But let's forget Betty."

She turned to him with eagerness. "I'd like to hear about the article."

By the time he finished repeating the news story, they'd pulled into the store parking lot. All the tension he'd expected between them had dissipated, and Priscilla's enthusiasm threatened to lure him in again. Gabe prayed for the strength not to stray past the boundaries of friendship.

When he opened the door, the phone was ringing. "I'd better get that." He rushed to his office and picked up just before the answering machine kicked on.

"Gabriel, Darnell Jackson here. We have the testing results. All thirty-eight bottles from your co-op customers and other buyers in the area checked out as pure camel's milk."

Gabe clutched the receiver harder. *Thank You, Lord!!*

"I'm not authorized to speak about other FDA investigations, but it seems some doubt has been cast on the validity of the original samples we tested. Because we found no violations, an official letter went out today informing you that you may reopen your business."

"Right away?"

Mr. Jackson chuckled. "That would be fine. And, Gabriel, I want to say something, but not in my official capacity." He paused. "I'm really sorry this happened."

"It's not your fault. You were only doing your

375

duty. And thank you for letting me know."

"You're welcome. Good luck with your business."

In a daze, Gabe hung up. He left the office with jaunty steps. Priscilla waited with a question in her eyes, but she'd soon have an answer. He walked past her, removed the sign from the door, and crumpled it.

"Gabe, does that mean you passed the inspection?"

He turned around with a grin but made the mistake of meeting her gaze. Once again, he was drowning. Sinking down, down, down into the depths of her joy-filled eyes.

With all his strength, he forced himself to break the connection before responding, "*Jah*, they tested the co-op milk, and it was all pure. I'm in the clear."

Her breathless *Oh, Gabe* did strange things to his insides, and he fought the urge to glance in her direction. Instead, he prayed for divine intervention.

Alyssa breezed through the door. She must be God's answer to prayer.

Stopping in the doorway, she pointed to the window glass. "Hey, where's the sign?"

Gabe held up the crumpled cardboard.

Her eyes widened. "You took it down?"

He laughed. "Don't worry. I had permission. All the samples they tested were pure, and thanks to you, they're not counting the bottles from Defarge."

"Awesome! Then we can run the lifestyle feature about the camel farm this Sunday."

Priscilla's smile brought sunshine flooding into the room and into Gabe's heart. "You'll be in the news three days this week."

Gabe tamped down the small glow of pride. "That should help the business."

"It will, and the following week we have the fair," she said.

"Fair?" Alyssa looked from one to the other.

With his newfound confidence around Alyssa, Gabe answered first. "Priscilla set up an event at Hope Graber's horse therapy farm. She's inviting other Amish and *Englisch* special needs schools and programs in the area. Hope and I will talk about how our businesses can help children."

"Oh, that's right. Priscilla mentioned it." Alyssa flipped open her notebook. "Let me make sure I have the date and time correct, so I can add it to your Sunday feature. I'm doing a profile on Hope in two weeks, so I'll also include a teaser for that."

This time Gabe let Priscilla answer. She deserved credit for coming up with the idea.

"We're doing it on a Thursday to be sure all the children can go to the farm," Priscilla told Alyssa, "but we're keeping it open into the evening hours for *Englisch* families where both parents work."

"Smart idea." Alyssa wrote down those details, then asked Gabe, "Will you be giving out free samples or coupons for milk? I can mention it in the write-up."

Priscilla's eyes sparkled.

Was she remembering the free sample he gave her? He'd received a terrific return on that investment.

"Coupons. What a great idea!" Priscilla smiled at Alyssa, then turned to him. "You could give those out at the fair."

Gabe beamed at her. "You're right." Trying to sell milk at the fair would be too difficult. He'd have no place to refrigerate it. But a coupon could bring people into the store.

Now that he didn't have to worry about lawsuits, he could invest some money in promotion. God had blessed him with free advertising in the largest newspaper in the area. And Alyssa had mentioned it would be online and on TV. All of this seemed almost too good to be true.

Chapter Twenty-Six

The next morning Priscilla left for school extra early. She warned her brother Asher ahead of time so he could complete his usual routine. As she'd told Gabe yesterday, Asher had been much calmer since he'd been drinking camel's milk regularly. She was grateful she didn't have to face a tantrum.

Her brother flicked at the brim of his hat as they headed toward town rather than to the schoolhouse.

"It's all right," she assured him. "Remember I told you we're stopping at the store first?"

He nodded but didn't look reassured when she pulled into the parking lot of the drugstore. She debated about taking him in with her, but he'd be less stressed if he stayed in the familiar buggy.

"I won't be long. I just need to buy something."

She tied up the horse and rushed into the store. After grabbing several copies of the morning paper, she paid and hurried back to Asher. The fretful frown on his face disappeared when he spotted her.

"Now we're going to school." Priscilla set the papers on the back seat. She'd worried they might be late for school, but they arrived before

Ada, which gave Priscilla time to read through the article twice.

If anyone had been concerned about Gabe's milk, the article made it plain he'd been framed. It also cleared the other businesses. The story indicated an investigation had begun into Defarge Enterprises as well as Fleurette's cosmetics company.

Priscilla could hardly wait until school ended to take a copy of the newspaper to Gabe. Maybe he'd already gotten one, but she wanted to see his reaction to the news. The day seemed to stretch out forever, but Priscilla kept her attention on the scholars until dismissal.

When Betty pulled into the parking lot, Priscilla longed to run over and hand her a copy of the paper to prove Gabe's innocence. Knowing Betty, though, she'd hear about it from someone else soon enough.

After the last scholar had been picked up, Priscilla hustled Asher home. "I'll be right back," she called in to Mamm. "I need to run a quick errand."

She took off before Mamm could ask any questions. As she headed to Gabe's, the smile she'd pulled into a neutral expression all day blossomed. She couldn't stop grinning.

Priscilla pasted a schoolmarm expression on her face before she entered the store, but the minute she saw Gabe, her huge smile broke out again.

She held up the papers. "Did you see this?"

"Not yet." He stared at her as if in a daze as she headed toward him. When he reached for the paper she held out, he grasped the edge far from her fingers.

Maybe she'd been foolish to come here. Gabe's heartfelt *danke* and his eagerness to open the paper lessened her anxiety.

"It's on page three."

Gabe's eyes skimmed the article, and his tense features relaxed. "This is even better than I thought. They added a few new things, and my quote doesn't sound bad."

"It sounds great."

Appreciation flared in his eyes, but he quickly glanced away.

Priscilla wished she'd been less enthusiastic. "I'd better go. I told Mamm I wouldn't be long." She spun around before he could notice the heat creeping into her cheeks.

"Thanks for everything," Gabe said as she reached the door.

Why did his words have such a ring of finality?

The phone machine was beeping when Gabe entered the store the next morning after milking the camels. He set the milk in the refrigerator and went to check. The red light blinked, showing he had messages.

Twenty messages at this time of morning?

Someone had been busy. Gabe clicked on the first one.

Defarge's angry shout echoed around the room. "What do you think you're doing? I'm going to sue you and destroy you and everything you own unless you get the newspaper to retract that false story."

Gabe turned down the volume and then scanned through the rest of the messages. Each one grew increasingly furious and more threatening. He deleted all nineteen from Defarge.

The only other one came from a TV station, asking if he'd appear on the news. Of course not. Gabe pressed delete one more time.

The phone rang repeatedly the rest of the day. Gabe checked the answering machine the first few times. Mostly Defarge. A smattering of news stations wanting interviews. After that, he ignored it.

The store stayed busy all day, mostly from curiosity seekers who'd never heard of camel's milk before the news broke. Quite a few bought a sample bottle to take home.

Several reporters stopped in, and Gabe stumbled through a few interviews. He missed Priscilla. When the door opened later that afternoon and she entered, a deep sense of relief flowed over Gabe.

Her smile brought sunshine to the darkest corners of a room. Her lilting voice lifted his spirits. Her presence brought him peace. She'd become such an important part of this story, his business, and his life.

That realization overwhelmed him and choked back the greeting he'd intended to give. Instead, he swallowed and tried to tamp down his emotions. He only wanted friendship. Nothing more.

He tried to convince himself that was the truth. But he wrestled with his conscience. His feelings for Priscilla had turned into something much more intense.

Acknowledging his true feelings made it difficult for him to look at her. If he gazed into her eyes, he'd be lost.

Lord, please forgive me and cleanse my thoughts. Keep me from dwelling on Priscilla.

Right behind Priscilla, a camera crew muscled its way through the door. A man threaded his way through the crowd and headed straight for Gabe. "You the owner?"

"I am." Gabe shook the hand the man held out.

"I'm Marvin Anderson with"—he rattled off some alphabet letters that meant nothing to Gabe.

At Gabe's blank look, he clarified, "We're a national television news station. We have twenty-four-seven coverage of local and national news."

"I'm sorry. I've never seen it," Gabe said. *Or even heard of it.*

"You've never watched our show?" Marvin gave him an incredulous stare.

"We don't watch any TV," Priscilla explained.

"No TV?" Marvin shook his head and stared at them as if he'd come upon a strange and unknown species of animal.

A woman browsing in the store overheard. She stepped closer and informed him, "The Amish can't watch TV. They don't have electricity."

"Oh, right, right. I did read that in the brief they sent me." His expression revealed he didn't quite believe that was even possible.

"So, we're just going to take a few quick shots and do a brief interview. That work for you?"

Gabe cleared his throat. Marvin hustled through the conversation like a slick salesperson. Would he ignore Gabe's response? Priscilla moved closer. Feeling her support behind him, some of Gabe's nervousness dissipated.

"No," he said a little too forcefully.

Priscilla added, "What Gabe means is that we—the Amish, that is—don't believe in having our pictures taken."

The camerawoman stepped up behind him. "That was in the brief, remember?" She turned to Gabe. "Can I get some shots of the store interior? What about the farm? Close-ups of camels?"

Gabe had answered similar questions for Alyssa. "The farm and camels would be fine. We have a lot of Amish in the store right now, so maybe no shots in here."

Priscilla beamed at him. He'd fielded a difficult

384

question and managed more than a one-word answer. If he could handle the interview on his own, then she'd have no excuse to hang around anymore.

"But you'll let us tape the interview with you, right?"

Priscilla answered, "As long as the camera's not on."

"Okay, okay." Marvin held up his hand. "Audio only. We can show a picture of your camel farm in the background while the taped interview runs." He looked from Gabe to Priscilla and back again. "That work for you?"

Priscilla's *you-can-do-it* smile encouraged Gabe to agree. He took a deep breath before answering. "That's fine." His answer came out steady. Having Priscilla here would help.

Gabe wanted to set one more condition. "I'd like Priscilla to be included in the interview."

"Sure, sure. No problem." Marvin's gaze darted around the store. "Is there a quiet place where we could conduct the interview?"

"My office, I guess. Let me check with my nephew first."

Gabe headed to the counter where Tim was writing receipts for a short line of customers. "Will you be all right alone?"

Tim nodded. "Most people are looking, not buying. And Daed said we can come get him if things get too busy."

"*Gut.* We'll be in the office for a while." Gabe led the way.

"How old is he?" Marvin asked as he trailed behind Gabe. "You're leaving him out here alone to take care of sales?"

"He'll be fine," Gabe assured him. "He works here alone while I'm milking or bottling milk."

Marvin just shook his head.

They all crowded into the small room, and Gabe shut the door. It cut the noise down to a low chatter.

Marvin frowned. "I guess this'll have to do."

Gabe wished he had more chairs. "I can ask Tim for his chair if you want. Or you're welcome to use the boxes." Gabe waved toward the stacks of inventory he and Tim hadn't been able to unpack because the store had been so busy.

When Marvin wrinkled his nose, Gabe pushed the desk chair in his direction. After brushing off the duct-taped seat, Marvin lowered himself gingerly into the chair and fired questions at Gabe.

Taking a deep breath, Gabe answered them one by one. Priscilla's thumbs-up behind Marvin's back assured Gabe he was doing well. He appreciated her support, but she also proved to be a distraction. By the time the interview ended, Gabe was drained. But he'd done it. He'd finished his first solo interview with a stranger.

• • •

Priscilla murmured a prayer of thanksgiving. Although Gabe had stumbled a bit on the first question, after that he'd relaxed—or at least appeared to—and he'd given strong answers to every question.

His success thrilled her, but it also meant he'd have no further need for her support or company. She'd have no excuse for coming here to spend time with Gabe, except for twice-weekly trips to get milk, which she'd find difficult to prolong. Priscilla bit her lip and turned away as Marvin and his crew packed up and left. She didn't want Gabe to see her disappointment. Or to discern her crushed dreams.

"Priscilla?" Gabe said softly after the office door closed behind the reporters. "Is everything all right?"

"You did a great job." She ran her finger over the nearest carton, pretending to read the *Fire Tonic* label and the ingredients. "It's really busy out in the store. I'm sure Tim needs help."

Gabe's boots reverberated on the concrete floor behind her. Good, he's leaving. She'd take a few minutes to compose herself.

Instead, he rounded the desk and came to stand beside her. "What's wrong?"

"Nothing." At least nothing she could admit to him. "You impressed me with how well you did." She attempted to add a cheerful note to her tone, but it fell flat.

"You don't sound happy." He studied her face. "And judging from your expression, I failed."

"*Ach*, no, Gabe. You didn't. It's just that I—" She stopped herself before she revealed the truth.

"It's just that you what?" he prodded when she went silent.

She shook her head. He'd made it clear he had no interest in her. But Priscilla's heart urged her to be honest. "Once you relaxed, you did a terrific job. You won't need me anymore."

"Knowing you were in the room helped. If I'd been alone, I might have frozen up."

"*Neh*, you wouldn't."

"I'm not so sure about that."

Priscilla didn't want to argue the point. Instead, she changed the subject. "I left copies of today's newspaper at the counter. I'd better go."

She opened the office door and threaded her way through the crowd. When she reached the exit, she rushed outside, but she couldn't resist one final glance at Gabe. He stood, staring after her, his eyes bleak.

Had she hurt him with her abrupt departure? She hadn't meant to. But if she'd stayed, she'd have spilled all her secrets. Including the secret she'd been hiding from herself. She'd fallen in love with Gabriel Kauffman.

Chapter Twenty-Seven

Gabe checked both ways before opening the gate to lead his camels across the street the next morning. Then he encouraged the mamas to head to the barn.

A car engine roared. Gabe froze. Speeding vehicles—cars or buggies—sent fear spiraling through him. Louder and louder, closer and closer, it approached the blind curve. The driver could never stop in time.

Gabe shooed as many camels as he could back into the pasture. The car zoomed around the curve, whipped a sharp right, and bounced up the driveway to his store. It rocketed to a halt, shaking from the suddenness of the stop.

Blood rushed to Gabe's ears. He leaned against the fence for a moment. His chest expanded as he sucked in gulps of air.

Despite being out of breath, he rushed across the street to take the loose camels to the barn. He'd thought he'd lost them for sure.

He'd been through this with Matthew only a few weeks ago. He had to contact the government to request a street sign that said, *Slow. Camel Crossing.*

He patted the mamas and babies, speaking as soothingly as he could with a dry mouth and racing pulse. "It's all right. You're safe," he repeated over and over until they calmed and he could breathe normally.

Once he'd secured those few in the barn, he checked for traffic before going back for the others. Before he opened the gate, he made sure the sports car intended to stay in one place. The driver had parked beside the store door.

A sports car? Red convertible. Defarge?

All Gabe's hard-earned serenity fled. What did Defarge want this time? Did he plan to pressure Gabe to sell the business again? Why couldn't the man take no for an answer? Gabe had thought the article exposing Defarge meant he'd never see him again.

While Gabe stood, one hand on the gate, Defarge marched to the store and banged on the door. He pounded several more times and then, shielding his eyes, pressed his face to the glass. After seeing the dark, empty store, he spun around and headed back to his car.

Gabe wasn't about to let any of his camels get flattened by a reckless driver, so he stayed where he was, waiting for Defarge to turn on the engine and zoom away.

Instead, the man leaned against his car and pulled out his cell phone. Although Gabe was too far away to hear any words, Defarge's tight red face, dramatic hand gestures, and flapping lips, which opened wide and snapped shut, made it clear he was yelling into the receiver. Gabe pitied the person on the other end.

Defarge scanned the fields. Gabe wished he could duck, but he refused to cower. He stood up straighter and met Defarge's glance with a direct challenge. The man's mouth halted in mid-scream.

He pocketed his phone and raced down the driveway. With a sigh, Gabe turned his back. He needed to take care of his camels. A group of mamas and babies milled around the fence.

After checking the road, he reopened the gate. Several clomped across the street. At the boots pounding the pavement nearby, several babies grew skittish. Mamas went into protective mode.

"You're not going to get away with this," Defarge shouted. "I'm suing you for defamation of character." He barreled right toward the nearest camel.

"I wouldn't do that if I were you," Gabe warned. He meant startling the camels, but Defarge misunderstood.

"And how do you plan to stop me? You won't go to court."

"You're disturbing—"

Gabe tried to stop Defarge from charging forward, but the man ignored the signals. "This will all be mine soon." Defarge flung his arms out to encompass the fields and barns, almost bopping a camel on the nose.

His shouting and movement agitated the camel. Its head bobbed up and down. Its cheeks bulged.

"Watch out!" Gabe yelled and jumped out of the way.

Shocked, Defarge stared at him.

The camel coughed. Slimy, stinky spit sprayed out. Right in Defarge's face and on his suit.

He bellowed. Then he unleashed a string of swear words. Gabe plugged his ears until the tirade ended.

"What is that?" Defarge wrinkled his nose at the disgusting smell. He wiped his face with his sleeve, smearing the putrid goop around.

"Some people call it camel spit, but it's actually more like vomit. It's undigested stomach contents." Gabe stood close enough to Defarge that the reek made his stomach turn. He could only imagine how much worse Defarge felt. Gabe breathed shallowly to lessen the stench.

"Eww." Defarge looked as if he were about to throw up. "You made the camel do that. I'm going to sue you."

"You already are," Gabe pointed out.

Defarge fired a hateful glare at Gabe. "This is a thousand-dollar suit. You owe me a replacement."

"I tried to warn you, but you didn't listen. Loud noises and aggressive gestures frighten camels."

"You'll be hearing from my lawyers." Defarge stalked off. "By the way," he shouted over his shoulder, "I already have a buyer lined up for this property."

For a moment, Gabe froze. Defarge couldn't take his business away, could he? Not while he was being investigated for illegal activity. Gabe had to trust God. Whatever the Lord had in store for him, he'd accept.

One thing God would have him do right now is be kind. "If you want to clean up a bit before you get in your car," Gabe called after Defarge, "there's a pump for watering horses at the far end of the parking lot."

"My car?" Even from this distance, Defarge's shriek pierced Gabe's eardrums. "If this stinks up my car . . ." He spun around and shook a finger at Gabe. "You'll pay for that too."

Gabe suspected he wouldn't be paying for anything, if the information in the article turned out to be accurate. He prayed the reporters hadn't made a mistake.

Now that Priscilla had acknowledged her true feelings for Gabe, she wanted to avoid him. As a distraction, she threw herself into teaching and worked on lesson plans every evening, grateful she had no reason to go into the store until Saturday.

On Saturday morning, she dallied with her chores until almost time for the milk pickup. As much as she wanted to see Gabe again, she wasn't ready to face him. What if she gave away her real feelings?

Gabe had made it clear he had no romantic interest in her. She couldn't be around him until she could keep her reactions under control. Right now, these emotions were too new and too raw. If Gabe picked up on how she felt about him, it might destroy their friendship.

Priscilla knelt to wash the kitchen floor. She rubbed at the linoleum, wishing she could scrub away her awkward and uncomfortable feelings as easily as she washed away the dirt.

Sarah peeked into the kitchen. "You're not done yet?" She motioned to the bread dough rising on the counter. "I need to bake the loaves before lunch."

Priscilla sat back on her heels. "I'll clean over here until you get them into the oven. But can you ask Mamm if she can pick up Asher's camel's milk when she goes to the bulk food store?"

"You don't want to go?"

Had her interest in Gabe been that obvious? Maybe he'd sensed it too. He had backed away several times. Priscilla bent over and dipped the brush in the bucket, hoping to hide her face from her sister.

"I'm afraid you're going to tear a hole in the linoleum with how hard you're scrubbing." Sarah's eyes filled with concern. "Is something wrong?"

"*Neh.*" When you fell in love, shouldn't everything be right? But it could never be right if the man didn't love you in return. "I'll be fine." *Someday.*

"If you're sure?" Sarah hesitated in the doorway, studying her.

Priscilla scooted around, turning her back to her sister to wash the far corner under the cabinet. "Can you ask Mamm about the milk?" she asked in a strangled voice.

"Be right back," Sarah said. She returned a few minutes later. "Mamm wanted to know why you can't go. I told her you're still washing the floor, so she'll do it. I think she wants you and Gabe to get together."

So do I. Priscilla should have been glad her mother could get the milk, but giving up a chance to see Gabe was hard. How would she deal with not ever seeing him again?

When Gabe opened the store on Saturday morning, two customers were already waiting in the parking lot. The small trickle soon turned into a steady stream. If the store stayed this busy, he'd need to hire some help.

Being so rushed meant Gabe didn't have to think about Priscilla and what had happened the other night. Until her *mamm* showed up. He wondered if Priscilla was avoiding him. Esther, evidently still harboring hopes he and Priscilla

395

might get together, invited him for another meal.

Gabe had a good excuse for declining. "I'm sorry, but I can't manage time off now that business has picked up." He gestured toward the people milling about the store.

Esther looked disappointed, but then rallied. "You could really use Priscilla today. I can send her over when I get home."

He couldn't let her do that. "That's kind, but she works hard all week. Besides, she's been here several times this week already. She needs a rest."

"You're so thoughtful." Esther beamed at him. "I'm sure Priscilla would be happy to come."

Gabe wasn't so sure. Luckily, Saul walked through the door as Gabe struggled to come up with an excuse. "That's my brother. He's here to work." Or he would be as soon as Gabe asked him. "We'll be fine without Priscilla, but *danke* for offering."

Gabe beckoned to Saul, who headed over.

"Looks like business has really picked up." Saul glanced around him at the crowd.

"It has," Gabe said. "Tim and I are glad you're here."

His brother laughed. "You're expecting me to work?"

"That's why you're here." Gabe hoped his brother wouldn't contradict him.

Esther moved closer to Saul. "So you're Gabe's brother?"

"I am."

"I'm Esther Ebersol, Priscilla's mother."

A knowing look crossed Saul's face, and he shook her hand. "I'm Saul Kauffman."

"I'm glad to meet Gabe's family. We really enjoy his company."

"You do?" Saul waggled his eyebrows at Gabe before turning back to her. "I know he enjoys yours."

Esther gave him a dazzling smile. "I'm glad. I'm trying to get him to come to dinner this week, but he says he's too busy."

"I can take care of that," Saul said. "I'd be happy to mind the store any night this week."

"What about Thursday?" Esther glanced from one to the other.

"Thursday's fine with me," Saul told her.

What could Gabe do but agree?

It didn't dawn on him until after Esther left that Priscilla had scheduled the fair for Thursday. He couldn't go for dinner after all.

But he would see Priscilla that day. The thought both excited and worried him. He had to find a way to deal with his attraction before then.

Saul winked at him. "Her *mamm* seems to like you. I hope Priscilla is equally keen."

Gabe gritted his teeth. He had to stop letting his brother's teasing irritate him. Gabe changed the subject. "About Thursday. That's the day of the fair. I'd been thinking about closing the store and putting a sign on the door inviting people to the fair. But if you're willing to work, I could keep the store open."

"Wait a minute. What about dinner with Priscilla's *mamm*? Did you just trick both of us?"

"*Neh*. I forgot about the fair when she suggested Thursday."

"*Um-hmm*. Some reason you don't want to eat with them? Did you and Priscilla have a spat?"

Gabe shook his head. They hadn't argued or even disagreed. "Esther is pushing for something that—"

Several customers interrupted them. By the time they'd been waited on, Gabe hoped his brother had forgotten the conversation.

But Saul eyed him closely. "Pushy *mamm*, huh? That can make courting difficult." He held up a hand when Gabe frowned. "All right, all right. I won't say any more about it." He grinned. "At least not today."

Gabe woke early on Sunday morning and hurried through the milking so he could get ready for church on time. Alyssa's feature would be out today. He wished he could see a copy of the Sunday paper, but he wouldn't buy a copy. His parents had drummed into him as a boy not to spend money on Sunday, so other people wouldn't have to work.

That had been easier when stores stayed closed

on Sunday. Now many *Englischers* seemed not to care about working on the Lord's Day. Still, he wouldn't allow vanity to tempt him to do something that went against his conscience. Even if it meant he missed seeing the feature.

Maybe that was for the best. It prevented him from being prideful.

But after church, Gideon Hartzler beckoned Gabe to sit beside him at the meal. "Daed gets the *Central Pennsylvania Star* delivered every day. Look what's in today's paper." He pulled open the newspaper on his lap and took out one of the sections. "Your farm has a two-page spread with pictures."

Gideon handed the newspaper to Gabe, who stared in shock. He'd been expecting a small article, but Alyssa's feature had five large pictures—camels, the farm, the store interior, the refrigerated room, and a close-up of a bottle of camel's milk—along with two pages of information.

Alyssa had not only talked about the business and described the care and milking of camels, she'd also included quite a few quotes from him and Priscilla about the benefits of camel's milk. She'd even talked to one of the researchers from the study Gabe had mentioned. At the end, she'd included information about Thursday's fair and Hope's therapy farm.

Gideon waited until Gabe had read the whole

article. "That's great advertising. I hope it helps your business."

Saul held out a hand. "Let me see."

Dazed, Gabe passed the paper to his brother. He couldn't believe the publicity Alyssa had given him. Free publicity.

If only he could celebrate this with Priscilla. She'd contributed to the article too. If she hadn't been there for the first interview, he'd never had made it through.

Her encouragement had helped him overcome his fear of interviews. Now he had to face one more hurdle. A speech in front of a crowd. He'd asked Priscilla to give the talk, but she needed to stay with her scholars. He wanted to prove to himself and to her that he could do it.

Even thinking about standing up in front of people chilled him. But with God's help, he was determined to conquer this dread of public speaking. Once and for all. He'd do this. For Priscilla.

Chapter Twenty-Eight

Priscilla read over her checklist the night before the fair. The milk coupons had been printed, and the printing company had dropped them off at Hope's farm yesterday. The church youth group planned to sell pork barbeque, chicken corn soup, and homemade desserts to raise funds for a baby in the hospital.

When Alyssa stopped by the special needs school on Monday to drop off copies of the Sunday paper, she'd told Priscilla she had lined up a newspaper crew to cover the event. According to Alyssa, any event with animals and children always made a big splash in the newspaper. Gabe and Hope should have plenty of publicity. The photographer had been given strict orders to only photograph the Amish from behind. Alyssa also said the TV news intended to mention the fair several times as they covered the ongoing story about Defarge and Moreau's arrest.

Another huge blessing. The newspaper story had prompted an investigation, and a search warrant turned up enough evidence to put Henry, Fleurette, and several of their employees in jail. Priscilla thanked God that Gabe no longer had anything to fear. Their plotting couldn't destroy his business.

Priscilla should have been in bed long ago, but excitement kept her from sleeping. Even more than anticipation about tomorrow, anxiety kept her up. She'd see Gabe for the first time since last week's revelation.

She'd kept up with the news about him and his business. Mamm had told her how busy the store had been on Saturday, and after the Sunday feature, Priscilla imagined the crowds had increased.

Mamm had encouraged her to help Gabe out, but Priscilla claimed she had too much to do with lesson plans and event-planning. She and Ada had been preparing their scholars for the upcoming field trip. They'd learned about camels and role-played many of the expected activities they'd encounter. All the children had many questions. Some used letter boards and other assistive devices to ask theirs.

Priscilla checked the final item off her list— transportation and chaperones for the students. Most of the parents planned to go, so they'd show up after lunch.

As soon as she collapsed into bed, she drifted off into a dreamland where Gabe took her hand and—

Sarah shook her awake. "Are you sick? You've never overslept like this."

Overslept? Priscilla hopped out of bed. "How late is it?"

"You only have half an hour to get to school. I did your chores for you this morning."

"I'll do yours tomorrow," Priscilla promised as she rushed through her morning routine. She'd intended to take her time and look her best. She slipped on her pink dress and pinned on her half apron. Some of the five pins might be crooked, but she'd deal with that later.

She'd promised Ada she'd arrive early to prepare name tags with the school information on them. Hopefully, they had enough parents to keep an eye on everyone, but she and Ada wanted to take extra safety precautions. This field trip would be the first for their scholars.

As she rushed downstairs, Priscilla regretted only having time to whisk her hair into a bob and pin on her *kapp*. She'd wanted to look special for Gabe's big day. Perhaps God wanted her to concentrate on other things besides vanity.

After a hasty breakfast, she and Asher headed for the door. "Asher and I won't be home for dinner tonight," Priscilla reminded Mamm.

"What?" Her mother's voice reached a semi-screech.

"Our school is going to Hope's farm too. Can the rest of us stay at the fair with Priscilla and Asher?" Zeke asked.

Mamm looked from one to the other in dismay. "But—but Gabriel's coming for dinner tonight."

Priscilla froze. *He is? Does he plan to skip the*

fair? Maybe he changed his mind because I didn't help him plan a speech. He did say crowds make him nervous.

"He can't," Zeke said before he banged out the door. "It's his fair. His and Hope's."

Mamm stared after him. "On Saturday, he agreed to come."

And Mamm had kept that secret all week? She must have planned to surprise Priscilla. Instead, the surprise was on Mamm.

"I hope Gabe forgot about the fair when he accepted your invitation," Priscilla said.

Mamm seemed so disappointed Priscilla suggested, "Why don't you and Daed come? The church youth are selling food."

"What about Gabe's dinner invitation?"

"Unless I'm mistaken, he'll be at the fair tonight. Maybe we can reschedule for another time." As much as she'd like to see Gabe, Priscilla hoped he wouldn't accept another invitation. "I need to go or we'll be late."

Realizing she didn't have much time, Zeke had hitched up the horse before taking off on his scooter to school. She thanked God for her siblings today. She loved how they pitched in to help. Priscilla arrived at the schoolhouse five minutes before the scholars.

"Relax," Ada soothed when Priscilla rushed inside. "The scholars may be wild today, so we need to be calming influences."

Priscilla worried she'd be the most restless of all.

"I finished all but two name tags." Ada pointed to the shelf in the cloakroom where she'd lined them up. "If you can print two more, we'll be set. I'll go out to welcome the scholars."

Steadying her hand, Priscilla printed as neatly as she could, but she couldn't control the tossing and turning of her stomach. She took a deep breath and said a series of prayers for the students, the field trip, the fair, the church youth group, Hope, and Gabe.

"Gabe!" Priscilla gasped out his name. She'd forgotten to put his speech on her checklist. She'd spent so much time this week trying not to think about him, she'd pushed the most important part of the event to the back of her mind.

If she'd gone into the store this week, they could have planned it. Did he still want her to speak for him after what happened?

Gabe woke on Thursday morning with a ball of dread in his stomach. He'd stayed up late last night to prepare his speech. He'd look at it one more time after milking and again right before he left. He tried to memorize it because he wanted it to seem natural. Or as natural as it could be when the speaker was petrified.

The whole time he milked the camels and cows, he recited the parts he remembered, working to keep his voice steady. If he could give the speech to animals, he'd do fine. But people were a different matter.

Saul couldn't take off work at midday, so Gabe hung a sign in the window directing customers to Hope's farm. His brother did agree to do the milking that evening while Gabe stayed at the fair. And gave his speech.

He read through it one last time before he left for Hope's farm. He'd arrive almost an hour early, but he wanted to look around and get acclimated before the crowds arrived.

Hope greeted him. "Can you pull your buggy around back? We set up extra hitching posts for today. People can also tie their horses along the split-rail fence back there." She introduced him to Logan, her trainer, and then said, "Logan's handling most of the setup today."

Logan beckoned to Gabe when he returned. "We set up a stage here. Not sure how big the crowd will be, but we erected a temporary stage over here. Come on over and try out the mic."

Stage? Mic? He'd been expecting a casual talk. The weight in his stomach grew to boulder size.

Logan motioned for Gabe to mount the wooden platform. Now he had one more concern. What if, in his nervousness, he tripped going up or got his feet caught in the dangling cords?

"Don't worry. I'll get those wires taped down."

"You have electricity?" Gabe asked.

"I wish." Logan's reply held a sarcastic bite. "No, I brought in battery-powered equipment. Why don't you step up there, and we can check out the sound?"

With growing dread, Gabe mounted the platform. He'd prepared himself for an informal speech. Making it a big deal like this added to his stress. How large did they expect the crowds to be?

Some of the scholars buzzed with excitement. Others grew more and more agitated as the day wore on. Ada and Priscilla relied on Martha's expertise in calming several meltdowns.

After lunch, they began preparing for the trip. Everyone put on fluorescent vests, and Priscilla helped Ada pin tags with the school name to each child's back. They hoped that might be less distracting to some scholars than a piece of paper flapping on the front of their coats. They just had to keep the children from pulling at one another's name tags.

When the first buggy pulled into the parking lot, Ada opened the door, and they ushered the children outside.

Ada turned to Priscilla. "Why don't you go on ahead?" she suggested. "Martha can help me here. That way someone will be at the farm to greet the children and get everything organized."

Hope had suggested Priscilla's scholars come early, so they'd have time to get adjusted before the crowds formed. Hope, Micah, and Gabe planned to do a brief introductory session just for Priscilla's students.

Priscilla and Asher took off before the first buggy. They passed Betty pulling into the parking lot. Her frown probably meant she disapproved of Priscilla leaving school early. No matter what Priscilla did, she managed to get on Betty's wrong side.

It would only get worse when Priscilla spent time around Gabe. Especially if he needed her help with the speech. She braced herself for another lecture.

When Priscilla pulled in, Gabe was the first person she spied. Her heart drew her eyes in his direction. And the pitter-pattering of her pulse warned her she'd better steer clear of him. Otherwise, she'd give away her secret.

Before anyone arrived, though, she could stare at him. She tied Butterscotch next to Gabe's horse, then stood beside her buggy to get a better view. Asher climbed out and headed toward the barn. He had horse therapy with Hope every week, so he knew his way around. Priscilla let him go. Hope would be in the barn, where she spent most of her time.

Until her friend emerged, Priscilla took advantage of being the only one here to indulge in watching Gabe. He stood on a makeshift platform. They had a stage? That must have been Logan's idea. Poor Gabe. He'd be nervous enough without being elevated above the crowd. Logan even had a microphone.

"Testing one-two-three." His voice blasted into the fields around them. "Sounds good. Now you try."

Gabe cleared his throat, startling them all when it broadcast with a loud boom. He stared at the microphone in dismay. "Guess I can't make any sounds up here." Those words also echoed. Gabe held the mic at arm's length.

"Just stand there." Logan pointed to a spot near the microphone stand and waited until Gabe moved into place. "Okay, now try the first few lines of your speech, and I'll make sure everything's adjusted correctly."

Gabe pulled a piece of paper from his pocket and unfolded it. So, he had written his own talk. Would he also deliver it?

Priscilla held her breath as he brought the microphone to his mouth and started speaking. His first few words came out shaky, but then he fixed his gaze on a horse in the paddock and relaxed a little. His sentences reverberated around her, wrapping her in warmth. She closed her eyes and imagined being in his embrace.

"Priscilla?"

She jumped and opened her eyes.

Hope studied her. "Are you all right? Not too stressed about having all the children here?"

As much as Priscilla loved her friend, she wished Hope hadn't disturbed her. "I was listening to Gabe's speech."

"Sorry," Hope said. "At least you'll get to hear it later."

Jah, she would, but she wanted to enjoy it now with nobody around to detect how he affected her. Well, nobody but Hope.

And the questions in Hope's eyes made Priscilla eager to change the subject. Maybe later she could find a private place where she could watch Gabe without prying eyes noticing. Right now, she was here as an assistant teacher, and the children should be her first priority.

"Ada's staying at the schoolhouse until everyone leaves. I came ahead to supervise the others as they arrive."

Hope nodded toward the driveway. "Looks like two of them are here already. I'll tell them where to park. Micah will be coming soon to handle that so Logan and I can work with the children one by one." Hope's features softened when she mentioned Micah's name. Her love for her fiancé oozed into every word and expression.

Until today, Priscilla had never experienced that depth of emotion, that longing to be with someone every minute of the day, to spend the rest of their days together. She blinked back tears. Micah returned Hope's love, but Priscilla's yearning was hopeless.

A gentle touch on her arm brought her back to the farm.

"Do you want me to take the first two children in to work with the horses? Logan will be in as soon as he gets the camel farmer set up." Hope smiled at her. "I'm so glad you came up with this idea."

"Me too." Priscilla kept a surreptitious eye on Gabe as she greeted the two students and their parents. "Hope and Logan will take you to the barn. Asher is already there." She turned to Hope. "Is it all right if he stays there?"

"Of course. He's no trouble. I left him cleaning a saddle. He loves to do that, and he does a wonderful job."

After Hope led the first two children away, Priscilla had a few minutes to watch Gabe. Logan hopped off the stage and entered the barn. Gabe set the microphone back in its stand. Then he stepped down and walked to the paddock. Leaning his arms on the split-rail fence, he stared out at the horse he'd concentrated on earlier. He seemed to be mumbling. Rehearsing his speech, perhaps?

Pride filled Priscilla. Gabe planned to talk despite his fear of public speaking. She admired his bravery. Deep down inside, though, her hopes died. He'd moved on and no longer needed her help.

• • •

Gabe concentrated on the horse he'd spoken to earlier. He'd singled out an animal to focus on while he spoke. Doing that with his camels during milking had eased his nerves, so he ran through the whole presentation one more time using the horse.

But he had another purpose for standing with his back to the parking area. From the minute Priscilla drove in, she'd distracted him. Though he acted as if he hadn't seen her, wherever he went, he remained acutely aware of her.

He missed spending time with her, talking to her, laughing with her, planning for the future— his business future, that is. Though he longed to have the right to consider a different kind of future.

He blocked off that fantasy. He had other obligations and responsibilities that had a claim on his time and life. This talk could help him pay bills and secure that future.

Despite his plan to avoid Priscilla, he couldn't help turning as the buggies drove in. Her beautiful smile as she greeted each child started an ache deep in his chest. If only things had been different . . .

After the sour-faced woman from Priscilla's school dropped off her son, she marched toward him. Gabe's first instinct was to avoid her, but she appeared intent on talking to him.

"You don't know me," she said when she reached him, "but I owe you an apology."

He did know her, though. *Betty somebody. The bishop's wife.* He also was well aware of her disposition. But he kept silent and waited.

"I'm Betty Troyer. My son goes to Priscilla's school."

He held out a hand. "I'm Gabriel Kauffman."

"I know." With only two words, she managed to make him feel foolish. "My daughter, Martha, and my husband insisted we try camel's milk for our son. He's autistic."

Gabe had seen her son's meltdown.

"It didn't help Lukas much. Not the way Priscilla claims it calmed Asher."

"Every child is different, so results may vary. Studies are still ongoing about its benefits, so they can't say for certain it helps everyone." It might also depend where Lukas was on the spectrum.

"He hasn't had a meltdown yet today, so maybe it's doing a little something."

Priscilla strolled toward the barn with Asher and another child. Gabe tried to focus on Betty and their conversation, but his gaze followed Priscilla into the barn.

Betty glanced behind her to check out what had caught his attention. Her lips pursed. "You know she recently got jilted. It's better not to jump into another relationship right away."

She was warning him off Priscilla. Did she discourage all suitors, or only him?

"I'm not in a position to begin a relationship." Not that it was any of Betty's business, but he hoped it might keep her from bothering Priscilla.

"*Gut.*" She stalked off, leaving Gabe melancholy.

He shook off his gloom. Betty's comments shouldn't bother him, because he'd told the truth. He couldn't consider a relationship with Priscilla. Not now, nor anytime in the future.

Chapter Twenty-Nine

One after the other, the children arrived with their parents, and Priscilla had no time to check out Gabe. She made sure each scholar had a chance to work with Hope or Logan. The last two children were finishing up their lessons when Alyssa arrived with Jake.

"Oh, how adorable," Alyssa cooed when she caught sight of Lizzie with her arms around a horse's neck. "Can we get a picture of that? Her face isn't showing."

Priscilla looked at Lizzie's *mamm*, who shyly agreed. Priscilla was glad they'd asked about Lizzie first, because her mother was less strict than Betty, for example.

While she hugged the horse, Lizzie's tics disappeared, but when Alyssa tried to ask her questions, Lizzie flailed her arms and jerked. To Alyssa's credit, she soothed the small girl by talking to her gently about her younger brother. After the spotlight was put on the baby rather than her, Lizzie calmed and answered a few questions.

The scholars needed plenty of special attention and calming when the other schoolchildren and the public started arriving at two. Priscilla and Ada helped Lukas, Will, and Asher into weighted vests to help them deal with the added sensory stress, and Priscilla took them to a quieter spot to watch the activities.

Hope had planned games, and the church youth set up volleyball and baseball games in the back field. They took turns manning the food tables and playing sports.

Gabe and Hope each had a table where people could learn more about their businesses and sign up for the milk co-op or horse therapy. The tables always seemed to be surrounded by people. Micah went from one table to the next, helping wherever he could. Logan conducted group tours of the barn and explained how horse therapy could help with physical, mental, and emotional challenges.

Hope offered discount coupons for a series of lessons, and Gabe handed out coupons for a free pint of camel's milk. People had to go to the store to pick it up. When Gabe first decided to give out the coupons, Priscilla had worried he might bankrupt the business. But Gabe explained that camel's milk didn't go bad as quickly as cow's milk did, so he could use all the bottles he'd filled for Defarge as well as the ones he'd shelved and frozen while the FDA kept the store closed. Giving away free bottles would clear his shelves and introduce people to camel's milk, and many of the customers might return for more. At least they hoped so.

From time to time, Priscilla glanced Gabe's

way, but under Betty's watchful eye, she didn't get many chances. So, when Logan announced Hope and Gabe would be speaking, Priscilla was thrilled. Logan adjusted the microphone for Hope, who did a great job of explaining horse therapy and reinforcing its benefits.

After she answered some questions, Micah brought his twins to the stage to join her, and following a smattering of clapping, he took the microphone. He talked about how hippotherapy had helped the twins. The twins each spoke for a few seconds, Jabin in a low voice, with his head down. Then Chloe stepped forward, basking in the audience attention. She ended by saying, "Hope is the best teacher in the world. And"— Chloe paused for effect—"she's going to be our new *mamm*."

The thunderous applause startled the three boys. Martha helped Priscilla draw them even farther from the crowd.

Ada joined them. "You've been taking care of the children since you arrived, Priscilla. I can do it for a while."

"If it's all right with you, I'd like to get closer to the stage to hear Gabe," Priscilla said.

Ada's knowing look made Hope want to confess that she had no chance with him. But he was already heading for the stage, so she hurried off. She wiggled her way through the crowd until she stood several feet in front of him.

Priscilla prayed Gabe would forget his nervousness and that his presentation would shine. *Please, Lord, be with him and give him Your strength.*

When she opened her eyes, Gabe was staring right at her. Everyone around her had to hear her heart pounding. He'd singled her out, but not for the reason she'd dreamed. She swallowed the lump in her throat. She needed to be there for Gabe. Pushing aside her own disappointment, she sent him a reassuring smile.

No one else had any idea how much courage it had taken for him to get on the stage and speak, but Priscilla did, and her heart swelled at his transformation. As he spoke, her admiration only grew. He'd covered all the important research studies but made them easy to understand. And his words came out smooth and strong.

She joined the applause at the end, clapping so hard her palms stung. He'd conquered his fears and delivered an excellent speech.

Once again, his eyes sought hers, this time with a question in them. One she answered by letting her eyes shine with all her pride and joy.

He'd done it. He'd actually given a speech to a huge crowd. And judging from the response, people had liked it. But Gabe only cared about one person's opinion. He searched her out in the crowd, wanting an honest answer.

What he saw in her eyes took his breath away.

He made his way through the crowd toward her, stopping to answer questions or clarify points, but his total focus stayed on Priscilla. Finally, he reached her.

She looked up at him, starry-eyed. "You did it."

"Thanks to you." He smiled down at her.

She shook her head. "I didn't do anything. You did it all yourself."

"I never would have tried if it weren't for you. And you were beside me through all of the interviews." Today he'd been looking at her while he spoke, saying the words to her, staring into her encouraging eyes . . . all that and more had made his speech a success. "You deserve credit."

Behind them, Hope's *daed* cleared his throat. "Any chance you could bring us a few bottles of the camel's milk? I want to try it for my digestive troubles and high blood sugar." He bit his lip and glanced down at the ground. "You'll have to get the money from my daughter, though."

Priscilla's eyes filled with pity. "I'm sure Hope will pay. Did you want them right now?"

"If you wouldn't mind. I've been in a lot of pain."

"It may take a while for the camel's milk to work," Gabe said. "And I only quoted some studies. I can't promise those results."

"I understand." Isaac shrugged. "I'm willing to try anything that might help."

Priscilla turned to Gabe. "With everything going on, I forgot to pick up Asher's milk yesterday. He has a little left, but if you're headed home, could I stop by to get his order? I also can bring some milk back to Isaac."

Gabe ignored the warning signals from his conscience. "*Jah*, why don't you follow me to the store?"

He should have said no, put it off to another time. A time when he wasn't flying so high and wasn't dreaming of sweeping her into his arms—

Priscilla floated on air as she rounded up children and reunited family groups. Her parents had arrived for a late dinner, and they gathered her siblings.

"Mamm, I'm heading to Gabe's store to get Asher's milk. Isaac needs some too, so I'll come back here to drop it off for him and help Hope clean up."

"Gabe gave a *wunderbar* speech. Remember to ask him for dinner tomorrow night."

"I will," Priscilla agreed before rushing up the hill to the backyard, where Gabe waited.

His smile set her spirits soaring. Was God giving her a chance to be with the man of her dreams?

Gabe waited until Priscilla had hitched up her horse and pulled her buggy behind his before

420

heading down the driveway. At every crossing, he paused until the gap in traffic allowed two buggies to pass safely. Although Priscilla could find her way to the shop if they got separated, he loved having her right behind him.

He wanted to urge his horse into a gallop because he couldn't wait to be alone with her, without a noisy crowd around, without prying eyes. He was eager to hear her thoughts on his speech.

Really, Gabe? That's the only reason you want to be alone?

Gabe ignored the nagging question. After making his first speech, he wanted to celebrate with Priscilla, who'd been such an important part of his victory. Other people had heard only an ordinary talk, but she understood the fears he'd conquered.

It might be straying into danger. But for tonight, he pushed aside his qualms. He longed to celebrate.

You want to do more than celebrate.

Truth be told, he did. Which meant he needed to be very, very careful.

Yet the minute Priscilla pulled into the parking lot beside him and smiled, he forgot every warning.

Together, they entered the store, and Gabe helped her load the milk into her buggy. As they reentered the store together, he removed the sign about the fair from the window. He set it on the counter and turned to face her, not realizing how close she stood until he brushed against her. All caution forgotten, he met her gaze.

The softness in her eyes, her slightly parted lips, filled him with longing. He clutched the counter behind him with both hands to keep from acting on his desire.

"Oh, Gabe."

Her soft sigh and the invitation in her eyes proved his undoing. He could no longer fight the magnetism. Letting go of the counter, he opened his arms to encircle her. As if anticipating his embrace, Priscilla swayed toward him.

No, no, no. This was all wrong. He couldn't, shouldn't let his heart get entangled with another woman.

Gabe placed his hands on her arms to stop her from moving toward him, but her soft skin under his fingers only added to the temptation.

Please, Lord, give me the strength to resist.

He had to tell her the truth. "Priscilla, I can't . . ." At the tender look in his eyes, she sucked in a breath. What was it about Gabe that set her insides spinning like the windmills on Martin's Hill?

The door creaked open behind them, and his face drained of color. "Anna?" He croaked the name as his hands dropped to his sides.

A sick feeling in her stomach, Priscilla turned to face a pretty brunette, her face tight with pain as she planted metal forearm crutches and swung herself forward.

"You're not in a wheelchair." Gabe stared at the woman who'd stopped to catch her breath.

"*Neh*, I promised one day I would walk to you."

"You don't have to do this." Gabe started toward her.

"Don't," she barked. Beads of sweat formed on her forehead as she took another step. She stopped for a moment, closed her eyes, and inhaled deeply.

"Please," Gabe pleaded. "I can come to you."

Anna's eyelashes, damp and spiky, swept upward to reveal brown eyes filled with tears. "Maybe I didn't need to do this after all."

Priscilla had no idea what was going on between them, but she shouldn't be here. "I'll go now. We can talk about the speech some other time."

"Wait, Priscilla. This is Anna, my girlfriend, um, fiancée, from—"

With a strangled "Nice to meet you," Priscilla fled out the door, feeling guilty about her fib. But what else could she have said? *I didn't know Gabe had a girlfriend? No, not a girlfriend. A fiancée. I thought Gabe and I might—*

Might what, Priscilla?

Outside, she leaned against the metal building to draw air into her constricted chest and calm her racing mind. Gabe had lied. Maybe not in words, but in actions. Or had she misinterpreted his friendliness? His caring? His touch? The look in his eyes?

"I'm sorry I interrupted you. I hope I didn't mess anything up." Anna's laugh, hollow and pain-filled, echoed around the cavernous room and ripped Gabe apart.

"No, Anna, you didn't." *I did. I'm the one who's to blame.*

Sweat glistened on her forehead, and her jaw tightened as she took another step in his direction.

"Let me get you a chair." Gabe started for his office. The padded chair was softer than the wooden one.

"Stay there!" The sharpness of Anna's voice stopped him. "I told you I'd give you an answer when I could walk across the room to you."

Jah, she had. And that day had come. Gabe owed her this chance to fulfill her own pledge, no matter how agonizing it was for both of them.

Step after painful step, Anna pulled herself closer. Gabe longed to assist her, but he scrunched his hands into fists and stuffed them in his pockets to keep from reaching out.

She stopped several times to catch her breath. The high neckline of her dress was soaked with perspiration. She was near enough now for Gabe to read the sadness in her eyes. "I wondered after all this time if"—Anna tilted her head toward the door—"you'd found another woman . . ."

Another woman? Priscilla wasn't just another woman. She was—

Gabe tore his thoughts away from Priscilla and concentrated on Anna. "The promise I made still stands."

"We were seventeen, Gabe. Much too young to make life decisions."

He closed his eyes, and all the old memories came rushing over him. They'd both joined the church at sixteen but hadn't started courting until the following year. In fact, they'd only had a few dates before that fateful night.

Gabe winced. His friend John had challenged him to a buggy race late one night. Anna begged to go along. They'd been galloping much too fast.

Wind whipped Gabe's bangs back, flattening his hair to his head, stinging his eyes. The courting buggies drew neck and neck. At Anna's urging, Gabe edged past John.

Anna threw back her head and crowed, "We're going to win."

Young, vibrant, and laughing, that Anna was very different from the woman who stood before him now. Gabe opened his eyes to take in his future bride, and his heart filled with pity. "Please let me get you a chair."

"*Neh.*" Anna's response exploded on a puff of breath. Her pinched face and lips revealed the strain of taking the next step.

If only he hadn't tried to show off when John's buggy nosed ahead. He could have let John and Nancy win. But Anna had begged him to pass them, and pride made him urge the horse faster. They reached the top of the hill and a sharp curve in the road.

Anna's soft hands brushed his as she clutched the reins. But she accidentally pulled in the opposite direction. Had she sensed danger and tried to slow the buggy? The buggy swayed dangerously from side to side.

Then Anna's tugging prevailed. If Gabe had been stronger. If he'd kept control. If he'd slowed before the curve. If, if, if . . .

He'd done none of those things. Confused by conflicting commands, the horse veered off the road and plunged down the grassy knoll toward the nearby woods.

Anna screamed. Dropped the reins. Gabe struggled to regain control of the runaway horse. But the buggy jounced over rocks and ruts, tossing them wildly.

One wheel hit a boulder. The buggy tipped. Anna catapulted over the side. Gabe grabbed for her skirt. Her leg. Her shoe. But his hands closed on empty air. If only he'd been faster. He could have saved her, but he'd missed. Three times.

She crashed against a tree with a sickening thud.

The rest of the night remained a blur. Somehow

he must have stopped the horse. He must have jumped out and run to Anna. Someone called 911.

In his memory, sirens whirred. Had he gone to the hospital with her? He had no idea. He only recalled sitting by her bed for days while other visitors came and went. Hands clasped, head bowed, heart filled with shame, he prayed God would forgive him and heal her.

She lay ghostly pale and unconscious for what seemed like weeks or months. In reality, only three days passed. For the first two weeks, she didn't recognize him. Then, once she did, she turned away. Ordered him to leave.

He refused. He came every day to feed her and help her into a wheelchair to take her for walks. Caring for her had been his responsibility.

It still was.

Priscilla put one foot in front of the other and headed toward her carriage. She brushed her hands across her cheeks. Though moisture welled behind her eyes, no wayward teardrop trickled down to betray her—the way Gabe had.

She flicked the reins and fled down the driveway. All she wanted to do was find a place to hide. Somewhere to be alone with her shattered dreams.

But she had to deliver the milk to Isaac, and she'd promised Hope she'd help clean up. She turned her horse toward Grabers' farm. Though her heart was breaking, she'd do her duty.

She slowed her horse to a walk to give herself time to calm down and process her churning emotions. If she arrived at the farm this agitated, Hope would guess something was wrong.

When she drove up the driveway, Micah was carrying the last table to the shed in the backyard. The teens had loaded the leftover food, tables, and paper goods into the back of a large farm wagon. Laughing and talking, they piled into the bed, sliding things around to make room for everyone to sit.

Priscilla pulled to one side to let them pass. If only she could be that young and innocent again. She'd make very different decisions.

After tying up her horse, she rushed toward Micah with two of the gallon bottles. "Isaac wanted some camel's milk. Hope can pay me later." Priscilla spun around, hoping Micah hadn't noticed her damp eyes.

"Why don't you come in for a bit?" he suggested. "I'm sure Hope would like to see you."

"I—I can't. I have to get home." Priscilla stumbled toward her buggy with blurry eyes.

She hoped Micah didn't think she was rude, but if she went inside to talk to Hope, she'd never maintain her calm facade. Under questioning, the floodgates would open, splashing everyone around her with all the bottled-up pain and hurt. Better to keep it pent up inside until she could figure out how to deal with a second—and much more heart-wrenching—betrayal.

Matthew's betrayal had wounded her pride, but Gabe's had destroyed her completely.

After the doctors told Anna she'd never walk again, Gabe knelt beside her hospital bed and asked her to marry him. She refused, but he persisted.

Finally, she grew so exasperated, she yelled, "I don't care what the doctors say. I'll walk again. And I don't want to see you until I can walk across the room to you. When I do, I'll give you my answer."

Her parents had refused to let him visit her in rehab, so he threw himself into starting the camel farm, determined to make enough money to pay for her hospital and rehab bills. It was the least he could do. That and wait for her answer.

Now she was here. Ready to reply. A reply he was unready to hear.

The guilt churning in his stomach increased to nausea. What had he done? He might have resisted the temptation to embrace or kiss Priscilla, but she'd captured his thoughts and emotions. And his heart.

"I'm sorry. Will you forgive me?"

Anna shook her head.

She wouldn't forgive him? He didn't blame her. What he'd done was unforgivable.

Anna took one last step and stood directly in front of him, her face ashen. "Look at me, Gabe. I want your full attention when I say this."

He raised his guilt-filled eyes. All the pain and suffering he'd inflicted on her for one foolhardy choice. How could an apology ever make up for ruining her life? And for betraying her?

Anna drew in a raspy breath. "My answer to your question is NO." The word rang around the room. "I don't want to marry anyone who would rather be with someone else."

"Anna, that's not—" He'd almost said *true*. But he couldn't lie to her.

"Look me in the eyes and tell me you don't love her."

Gabe lifted his chin, intending to face her, but he couldn't meet her eyes. And he couldn't deny—despite all his attempts to the contrary—he'd fallen in love. But not with the woman he'd agreed to marry.

Chapter Thirty

Her heart scraped raw, Priscilla slipped into the house, praying to make it past the prying eyes of her family.

Mamm caught up with her at the foot of the stairs. "Gabe did a good job with his speech, didn't he?"

Keeping her face averted, Priscilla clutched at the railing. "*J-jah*, he did." An amazing job. So amazing she'd allowed herself to be swirled into a whirlpool of excitement and—

"Did you remember to invite him for dinner tomorrow night?"

"*Neh.*" Priscilla's voice was no more than a strangled whisper.

Mamm laughed. "I worried you might be too busy, although I'm glad you made time to hear his speech. It's all right. I asked him, and he agreed to come."

"He did?" Priscilla could barely choke out the words. They lodged like huge stones blocking her breathing, her swallowing. "He can't come."

"What? Why not?"

"Unexpected company arrived." At least, she assumed his fiancée's arrival had been unexpected. He'd definitely appeared surprised. Or maybe he was only shocked that she'd caught him making eyes at another woman.

431

"Who?" Mamm's sharp tone demanded an answer.

"A friend from his hometown," Priscilla mumbled. After a lifetime of avoiding Mamm's questions and hiding information, Priscilla automatically moved into defensive mode. She regretted it, especially now that Mamm was trying harder not to gossip, but her heart was too raw to deal with any more of her mother's probing.

"That's no problem," Mamm said. "He's welcome to bring his friend along."

No! No, he's not. Priscilla pressed her lips into a tight line to avoid shouting those words. If Mamm knew the truth, she'd never have offered the invitation.

"Be sure to tell Gabe that," Mamm said before scurrying off to get Asher ready for bed.

Priscilla released a long, pent-up breath at her departure. But picturing Gabe at their dinner table seated next to the brunette—the brunette who'd torn Priscilla's world apart—brought the whole terrible scene crashing back, leaving her dizzy and disoriented.

Did Gabe suspect her feelings for him? Did his fiancée? Had she made a fool of herself by dashing away like that?

Anna appeared ready to collapse. "I'll take . . . that chair . . . now." She gulped in a breath.

432

Gabe rushed toward the office, but she stopped him.

"Better yet, why don't you help me out to the carriage?"

She took one shaky step with his support. Then she hissed out a long trembling breath. "I'm not sure I can make it."

"I can carry you." He'd done it many times before, picking her up from her wheelchair and carrying her to her bed in the rehab. Before her parents had stopped him from coming.

"No, no. You don't have to do that. I'll be all right after a rest."

Gabe couldn't ignore the deep lines of exhaustion etched into her face. Disregarding her protest, he scooped her into his arms and waited until she'd transferred her crutches to one hand. She looped her other arm around his neck.

The familiar gesture made him ache inside. It had always made him feel warm and protective. It still did. But it lacked the depth of his feelings for Priscilla.

What Gabe had mistaken for love at seventeen were feelings much like the ones he had for his sisters. Before the accident, Anna had been fun and exciting company. After the accident, Gabe had confused love with pity.

Until he'd met Priscilla, he had no idea of how profound love could be. She'd stirred desires it would take a lifetime to fulfill. She occupied his every waking thought and starred in his dreams each night.

They reached the buggy, and Anna's cousin Emily, who sat in the driver's seat, stared at them with concern. "Is everything all right?"

"I got overtired, and Gabe helped me back." Anna's eyes glistened with tears.

Gabe had hurt two women tonight. "I'm so sorry."

Anna patted his arm. "I know. So am I."

If Priscilla had touched him like that, she'd have set him on fire. Anna's pat reminded him of his mother's.

Just before he shut the door, Anna met his gaze. "I do forgive you, Gabe. I should never have made you wait this long for an answer." She stared down at the floorboard. "Remember I told you no in the hospital? Many times. You should have listened."

Gabe could never have walked away then. How could he leave her when she was hurting and vulnerable? Even when she and her parents forbade him to see her in rehab, he'd assured her his offer of marriage still stood.

"I didn't believe you." He had assumed her denials were because she worried about being a burden.

"I know," she said in a choked voice. "That's why I pushed myself to walk."

All those painful hours in therapy just to

answer him. "*Ach*, Anna, I didn't mean to make you suffer like that."

"I'd never have learned to walk again if it weren't for you."

That still didn't assuage his guilt.

"We should go." Anna turned her head away and sounded close to tears. Without looking at Gabe, she added, "I wish you two the best."

A huge lump in Gabe's throat blocked his response. He stared after the buggy until it disappeared from sight.

Had Anna come to say yes or no? He'd never know. But one thing he knew for sure. She'd matured from a self-centered girl into a generous woman. She could have kept him tied to his promise, but she'd set him free. Free to pursue Priscilla.

That thought should have made him happy, but his unfulfilled vow to Anna lay heavy on his heart. Not only did he bear the guilt for the accident that had destroyed her life forever, he'd also betrayed her. She deserved a faithful husband. A test he'd failed. He'd condemned Matthew for cheating on Priscilla, but hadn't he done the same?

Gabe tossed and turned all night, so sick he couldn't think or pray. He wrestled with his conscience—a battle he couldn't win. Although Anna had offered to free him from his promise, he'd seen the agony in her eyes. Agony he'd caused.

How could he turn his back on her? No matter what it cost him, he had to keep his word. And to do that, he had to erase all thoughts of Priscilla from his mind.

He rose to a sky with clouds as leaden as his spirit. As soon as he'd finished the milking, he cleaned up and headed to Anna's.

Her cousin Emily pulled the door partway open and stopped. "Gabe?" Her tone sounded unwelcoming. Not that he blamed her.

"I'd like to talk to Anna."

"I don't think that's a good idea." Emily started to close the door.

Gabe set a hand on the knob to stop her. "Please?"

"Stay here and I'll check." She left the door open a crack and scurried off. She returned a short while later. "She doesn't want to see you, and she asked that you not come to see her again."

Gabe couldn't accept a secondhand message. He needed to speak to her. To hear those words from her lips. He wanted to assure himself she meant them. And to give her a chance to change her mind.

"I'm not leaving until I talk to her."

"Please just go," Emily pleaded. "Anna's exhausted and not up to having company today." Although Emily didn't say it, the unspoken words *especially not you* hung in the air between them.

Gabe lowered himself to the porch steps. "I'll just sit here until she's ready to talk."

"Suit yourself." Emily went back inside.

An hour later, she headed out the back door with a load of wash and spotted him still sitting there. She shook her head before heading to the side yard to pin the clothes on the line. "It's over, Gabe," she said when she returned with the empty basket. "Just leave her alone."

"I want to tell her one thing."

Emily sighed. "I'll let her know you're still here." She snapped the door shut. A short while later, the door creaked open. "Anna says to come in."

Gabe followed Emily inside to find Anna seated in her wheelchair. The muscles in his gut spasmed as he remembered her struggling across the floor on the crutches leaning against the couch arm. Her eyes, red-rimmed and puffy, made it clear she'd been crying.

"I have only one thing to say," Gabe told her. "I'll honor the promise I made to you, Anna." *No matter how hard it is. No matter how great the sacrifice. No matter if I must live every day with the pain of heartbreak. I'll do what's right.*

"I have some questions for you." Anna's eyes bored into him. "First of all, have you prayed about this? You're sure it's God's will to marry me?"

Gabe hung his head. "*Neh*, I haven't prayed about it." Not before he asked her the first time. And not last night. "I assumed God would want me to take care of you."

"Take care of me? That's why you asked me to marry you?" Anna's voice rose. "I'm perfectly capable of taking care of myself."

"I didn't mean you couldn't. It's just that . . ." He stopped before he said *I felt responsible.* That sounded even more insulting. "I cared about you."

"Care for me. Cared about me." Anna's words hung in the air like judgments. "Did you love me? Or did you pity me?"

How did he answer her? *I thought I loved you.* But what did a teen know of the truer, deeper love he'd experienced for Priscilla? And, *jah*, he did pity her. A lot.

Before he could answer, Anna hurried on, "And I have one more question. If you knew I loved someone else, would you still want to marry me?"

"Of course not." Was she dating another man? Or was she referring to him?

Anna gazed off into the distance, deep sadness in her eyes. "I don't want a man who pities me. A man who sees me as needy. A man who sees marrying me as his duty. And I especially don't want a man who loves someone else."

Anna had scorched him with her reasons. And

438

she'd forgotten to mention the most important one. A man who failed to pray for God's will.

With dread, Priscilla set off for Gabe's shop on Saturday afternoon near closing time. Mamm had been disappointed when Gabe didn't come for dinner on Friday night, and she insisted Priscilla ask him about it when she picked up the milk order. Just before she left, Hope stopped by the house with her payment for Gabe.

"Would you have time to take it to Gabe?" Priscilla asked, praying for a yes. Maybe Hope could also pick up the milk.

"I wish I could help you, but I need to meet Micah in twenty minutes."

If Asher didn't need the milk, Priscilla might have skipped going. She whispered a prayer for strength.

When she arrived, cars and buggies packed the parking lot. Perhaps she could slip in and out without seeing Gabe. Inside, Saul and Tim were busy helping customers, and Gabe's back was to her. Perfect! She ducked into the refrigerated room. Gabe had set her order aside as usual, so she grabbed the bottles and got into Tim's checkout line.

She handed him her money and the envelope from Hope. Now all she had to do was get out without being noticed. Then Gabe's brother glanced her way.

"Hey, Gabe," Saul shouted. "Look who's here."

Most of the chattering around her ceased. Gabe turned to face her, and her mouth went dry. She had no control over her galloping heartbeat, the automatic pull that drew her to him. She couldn't take her eyes off him.

Gabe seemed as mesmerized with her as she was with him. Then he glanced down at the floor. No doubt remembering his fiancée.

Priscilla's chest constricted, and she forced herself to look away. Tim called her name twice before she realized he was holding out her change. Before she could collect it and run out of the store, Gabe zigzagged through the press of people and reached her side.

"Could we talk in my office?" he asked.

"I don't think that's a good idea."

"Please?"

The desperation in his voice made her hesitate. "For a few minutes," she agreed.

He escorted her into the room and shut the door. Priscilla wanted to ask him to leave the door open, but he'd reached for her heavy bag.

"Let me put it here for now." His hand skimmed hers, and electricity zinged through her. She jerked away, almost dropping the bag.

"I'm so sorry." Gabe rescued the bag before it could crash to the floor and placed it on his desk. "Not just for this." He gestured toward the milk. "I owe you an apology."

"*Neh*, you don't." If anyone needed to apologize, it was her.

"I do," Gabe insisted. "I want to explain about Anna." He pushed his office chair in her direction.

"I—I should go." The last thing she wanted to do was hear about his fiancée.

"It won't take long. Please?"

When he said *please* that way, how could she refuse? Priscilla sat in the chair and fixed her gaze on the floor. If she even glanced at him, she'd be lost. Twisting her hands in her lap, she braced herself. How much more agony could she endure?

Gabe struggled to speak. After Thursday's smooth speech, he hadn't expected to be tongue-tied like this again. Yet, here he was, facing the most important apology of his life, at a loss for words. If he didn't say something soon, Priscilla would get up and walk out of the room—and out of his life. Although after he explained, she'd probably do that anyway.

"I should have told you about Anna when we, um, well, we"—he flipped his hand—"you know." What did he call falling in love? "When I got interested in you."

Her startled gaze made him wish he'd phrased that differently. Starting at the beginning might work better.

"When I was seventeen, I was young and foolish. Anna and I had recently begun dating, and one Saturday night, we were together when one of my friends challenged us to a race."

Priscilla had lowered her head when he mentioned Anna's name, but now her gaze flew to his face.

"Anyway, my horse veered off the road."

After all these years, he still wondered if Anna hadn't reached out and grabbed the reins just then, would they have stayed on the road? Most likely, she'd been trying to slow him down, but her sudden action had spurred the horse to run out of control.

Gabe ran his finger in a circle on the desktop. "I had some minor injuries, but Anna ended up badly hurt. They told her she might never walk again."

A sharp indrawn breath made him look up, but before he could meet Priscilla's eyes, he forced his attention back to the desktop.

"While she was still in the hospital, I proposed to her. She refused."

Priscilla's hands stilled in her lap.

"Maybe I should have accepted her answer, but guilt made me ask again. After all, if the accident hadn't happened, we'd probably have married later on."

Gabe tried to imagine that life, but now that Priscilla had entered his world, he couldn't.

"Anna said she'd answer me when she could cross the room to me. Back then, neither of us believed that was possible, but I told her that no matter how long it took, I'd wait for her."

"And she surprised you on Thursday by doing that." Priscilla scooted to the edge of the chair. "Best wishes to the two of you."

"Wait," Gabe begged. "There's more."

She couldn't leave now, not before he reached the most important part—his apology.

"I don't think I need to hear anything else," Priscilla said stiffly as she stood. All she wanted to do was get out of here before tears spilled down her cheeks.

"Hey, Gabe," Saul called from in the store. "It's closing time. Want me to lock up?"

"That'd be good, *danke*."

Priscilla blinked hard to clear the moisture from her eyes. She couldn't go out there now. Gabe's brother would see her distress. She kept her hand on the doorknob and her back to Gabe.

He continued, "*Jah*, Anna walked to me. But she saw us together."

"*Ach*, Gabe, I'm sorry." As much as she wanted a relationship with him, she'd never interfere with his happiness.

"I apologized, but Anna realized something I'd been denying." Gabe dropped his voice to a whisper. "I'm in love with you."

Priscilla was sure she'd misheard. Had Gabe said he was in love with her?

She turned around. "But Anna—?"

"She turned down my proposal."

"You're not marrying her?"

Gabe shook his head. "No, and I owe you an apology too. I never should have spent time around you once I realized I was attracted to you."

Priscilla's eyes widened. "You were attracted to me?"

"You didn't notice? Or realize all the excuses I made to spend time with you?"

"A few times I wondered, but I was afraid it was my own wishful thinking."

Gabe stared at her. "You mean you . . ."

"Several times I almost fell into your arms," she admitted.

Gabe smiled down at her tenderly. "I wondered, but I was afraid it was my own wishful thinking." After echoing her words, he wrapped his arms around her and drew her close.

Priscilla leaned her head against his chest. "This was one of the things I dreamed about. Being in your arms."

"Did you also dream of this?" Gabe murmured as he bent his head.

Umm was all Priscilla could manage before Gabe pressed his lips to hers. She melted against him. The tenderness of his kiss showed how much he loved, honored, and cherished her.

The Lord had worked so many miracles. In the hearts of Alyssa and her friends. In Gabe's business. In Matthew's life. Even in Mamm's. He truly was a wonderful God.

And the most miraculous gift of all stood before her. Gabe, the one she loved with all her heart. God truly had worked everything out for good. He'd selected the perfect man for her.

Epilogue

The early-morning June sun streamed into the barn, striping the floor with shadowed bars interspersed with light streaks. Gabe hummed as he milked the next-to-the-last camel. Only one more day. As soon as he cleaned up, he'd head to Priscilla's house to help set up for tomorrow's wedding.

A rustling near the barn entrance startled him. He turned to find an angel outlined by sunlight— his beautiful Priscilla. His heart overflowed with gratitude that God had given him a helpmeet who loved and understood camels the way he did. And who loved him as much as he loved her.

Now that school was out for the summer, Priscilla spent most of the day helping him at the camel farm, but he hadn't been expecting her today.

"Although I love seeing you this morning," Gabe said, "shouldn't you be at home?"

"I wanted to spend some quiet time with you." She shot him a dazzling smile. "Besides, if it hadn't been for the camels—and God, of course—tomorrow might never have happened."

Talking softly and soothingly, Priscilla moved down the row of camels, calling each one by name, petting mamas and babies. "I already thanked God this morning, but I wanted to thank the camels for the part they played. Without them, you might never have asked me to marry you."

"I would have gotten up the courage eventually."

"Eventually?" she teased, a mischievous smile playing on her lips. "It took long enough to convince you."

"You make it sound like you had to push me into it."

"Why do you think I kept begging you to teach me to milk the camels?"

"Because you're fascinated by camels?"

Priscilla's bell-like laughter filled his heart with joy. "I am, but I'm more fascinated by their owner. And I hoped to make myself indispensable."

"You are." *In every way.* His voice grew husky. "I couldn't live without you."

Eyes sparkling with tears, Priscilla tiptoed around the camel he was milking, stopping to give it a reassuring pat. "I'd like," she said shyly, not looking him in the eye, "you to show me how to milk again."

Priscilla had no need for milking lessons. She'd already become a pro, and surprisingly, all the camels had bonded to her too, so she could work with any of them. She was asking for only one reason. To be close to him. To be in his arms.

They weren't supposed to hug or kiss until they married, but when he wrapped his arms around her to assist her . . . Gabe swallowed hard.

"I'm almost finished here. You can help with the next one." He regretted he had only one camel left to milk. When she first started learning, they'd milked a few together, but even after she'd learned to do it on her own, she often asked him for a refresher.

Once the next camel was in place, he knelt beside her as she sat on the stool, then reached around her to position her hands. She relaxed back against him with a soft sigh. A sigh that set all his pulses thrumming.

He could barely get his next words out. "You know, I've never understood why a girl who milks cows at home needs so much instruction to milk camels."

She nestled closer. "It's hard to concentrate on camels."

"I know." His breath hitched in his throat. He struggled to pay attention to technique with her soft warmth in his arms.

She had no need of his help. Her hands moved smoothly, rhythmically, but he covered her fingers gently with his, enjoying the stolen minutes of closeness.

"Remember when you asked me to marry you?" Priscilla never wavered in her movements.

How could he forget? They'd been milking a

camel together like this. For weeks, he'd prayed about God's timing. Then that day, as his arms slid around her, he knew with certainty the time had come. His heart thumped so hard against his chest he worried she'd feel it, and he could barely get the words out. Waiting the few seconds for her answer had been an eternity. He hoped and prayed she'd say yes.

Once she did, the barn seemed to overflow with a heavenly chorus of angels singing the same song bursting from his heart.

"You know"—Priscilla shifted so she could glance up into his eyes—"if you hadn't asked me that day, I would have asked you."

"You wouldn't have." Even as he said it, a deep knowing filled him. She would have. She wanted to be with him as much as he wanted to be with her.

Priscilla giggled. "And if I hadn't, Mamm definitely would have."

Gabe chuckled, startling the camel. He patted her flank to calm her. He had no doubt Esther would have forced his hand.

Ever since they'd announced their engagement, Priscilla's *mamm* had been thrilled to help plan their wedding. They'd turned many of the details over to her because they were both so busy, and she reveled in handling everything they sent her way.

"Speaking of Mamm . . ." Priscilla sighed and

sat up straight. "I need to get back to the house to help. The wedding wagon will be coming this afternoon, and Alyssa will be arriving in an hour."

"I'll be over soon," Gabe said close to her ear. He wished he could keep holding her like this, but the last camel had been milked, so he had no excuse.

"Only one more day," she whispered, echoing his earlier thoughts.

Right now, a day seemed much too long to wait.

Reluctantly, Priscilla pulled herself from Gabe's arms. If only they could stay like this all day. But Mamm needed help with a long list of chores.

"You'll help unload the wedding wagon?" Priscilla asked as she headed for the barn door.

"Of course. I can't wait. I'll be there well before afternoon." Gabe's smile lit up Priscilla's world.

"I'm so glad." She disliked spending even a short time apart, but she hurried out to her buggy as Gabe finished cleaning the milking equipment. After tomorrow, they'd spend their days and nights together.

Right now, she needed to rush home. Mamm would be frantic that Priscilla had stayed away so long. She'd told her mother that Gabe needed a reminder about helping with the wedding wagon. For once, Mamm didn't ask why Priscilla couldn't call Gabe's business from the neighbor's phone shanty. Now, though, with the length of time she'd stayed at Gabe's farm, Mamm would be brimming with questions.

Instead, when Priscilla walked through the kitchen door, Mamm only said, "Oh, good, you're here. That took longer than I thought."

Priscilla turned toward the basement door to hide her heated cheeks. "I need to go down and finish tying ribbons around the last batch of candles." They'd made candles in small glass jars to put at each place as a favor for the guests.

"Good idea." Mamm had been trying hard to show she trusted Priscilla's judgment, although she clearly struggled to restrain herself from digging for more information. Perhaps in this case, Mamm shouldn't have trusted Priscilla quite so much. At least she and Gabe would be around her family for the rest of the day, so they wouldn't have much time alone.

Before Priscilla finished the ribbons, Mamm called down to her. "You have company."

Gabe had arrived already? She'd only left him a short while ago. Priscilla bounded up the stairs to find Alyssa waiting for her.

"Sorry to get here so early. I'm so excited!" Alyssa chewed on her nail. "My first Amish wedding."

Jake followed her into the house, and Priscilla

451

introduced them to Mamm, who frowned at Jake's camera equipment.

"Don't worry," Priscilla assured her. "He's promised not to take any pictures of people. Alyssa wants to do an article on the wedding wagon."

"I see." Mamm pressed her lips into a thin line.

Because she was upset? Or to avoid asking questions? Priscilla wasn't sure.

"What can we do to help?" Alyssa asked.

Priscilla led them down to the basement to help with the favors. Alyssa tied ribbons, while Jake pasted on labels that said *Gabriel and Priscilla.*

Every time she glanced at the labels, a small shiver ran through Priscilla. Her dream come true.

Gabe arrived, eager to see Priscilla, but her *daed* called to him and asked for help cleaning the barn. By the time the wedding wagon rattled up the driveway, all of them were hot and sweaty, but the barn was ready for guests. Men would gather there tomorrow between meals. And by the time they did, Gabe would be a married man. The thought made him smile.

Everyone—all of Priscilla's sisters, her *mamm*, Alyssa, and Jake—rushed out of the house. The one person Gabe longed to see exited last. Even before she looked at the wagon, she stopped on the porch to search for him, and once she'd found him, her lips lifted in a secretive smile. A smile meant only for him.

Though he'd love to keep staring at her, he turned his attention to the wagon. After they reached it, Jake wove around snapping photos, interspersing shots of the open wagon with interior shots of the crates, the assembled tables, and the benches in the living room and dining room. Alyssa dodged from one spot to the other, unpacking boxes, asking questions, and jotting notes.

Whenever Gabe met Priscilla's eyes, his heart stuttered. He could hardly believe she'd be his bride tomorrow. Once he'd started praying and seeking God's will, the Lord had blessed him with a wonderful wife, one who shared his interests and had a heart for God.

Gabe had also spent many hours on his knees asking the Lord to bring someone special into Anna's life. She deserved happiness too.

Priscilla beckoned to him from the doorway of the small den off the living room. He slipped away from the busy crowd decorating tables, unpacking plates and silverware, or preparing food. He headed into the room and stopped in surprise.

Folding tables had been set up around the room. Gifts covered every available surface, and larger items had been stowed under the tables. "Are all these for us?"

She nodded. "I wanted to show you one that came earlier today."

Gabe deflated a little. He'd hoped she'd called him in here to steal a quick kiss.

Priscilla bent over the table to remove a card attached to a crock filled with cooking utensils. She slid it from an envelope and handed it to him.

Priscilla and Gabe,

I hope these tools help as you start your married life together. I wish you only joy and happiness as you follow God's will for your lives.

Sometimes what appears heartbreaking is only God's way of moving us to a new and better place. God has blessed me in so many ways, and I know He has even more exciting plans for me in the future. I thank Him for bringing the two of you together so He could lead me in a new direction.

With many prayers,
Anna

The words blurred before Gabe's eyes. Anna's note erased the guilt he'd buried deep inside.

"I'm so glad," Priscilla murmured. "I've felt like it's my fault for breaking the two of you up."

"You?" Gabe had no idea Priscilla blamed herself. "The only guilty party here is me." But Anna had absolved him. He could move forward with a lighter heart. "I've been praying for her," he admitted. "I wanted God to bring something special into her life. And it seems as if He has."

"I've been praying too. I understood how she felt. Facing sorrow and loss might seem like the end of the world at the time, but once I met you, I could have written that note to Matthew and Mara. In fact, maybe I will. God has given me the desires of my heart."

Gabe's heart overflowed with love. What a beautiful spirit his beloved had! He reached for her and enfolded her in his arms. "God wants only the best for us, and after the gift of His Son, He's given me the greatest blessing of all. You."

Priscilla snuggled closer and tilted her head. "We're both blessed for sure and certain," she said before he bent to claim her sweet lips.

Books are produced in the United States using U.S.-based materials

Books are printed using a revolutionary new process called THINKtech™ that lowers energy usage by 70% and increases overall quality

Books are durable and flexible because of Smyth-sewing

Paper is sourced using environmentally responsible foresting methods and the paper is acid-free

Center Point Large Print
600 Brooks Road / PO Box 1
Thorndike, ME 04986-0001 USA

(207) 568-3717

US & Canada:
1 800 929-9108
www.centerpointlargeprint.com